GOOD COP BAD COP

SIMON KERNICK

HEADLINE

First published in 2021 by
HEADLINE PUBLISHING GROUP

First published in paperback in 2022 by
HEADLINE PUBLISHING GROUP

1

Cataloguing in Publication Data is available from the British Library

ISBN 978 1 4722 7102 0

Typeset in Sabon by CC Book Production

Printed and bound in Great Britain by Clays Ltd, Elcograf S.p.A.

Headline's policy is to use papers that are natural, renewable and
recyclable products and made from wood grown in well-managed forests
and other controlled sources. The logging and manufacturing processes
are expected to conform to the environmental regulations
of the country of origin.

HEADLINE PUBLISHING GROUP
An Hachette UK Company
Carmelite House
50 Victoria Embankment
London EC4Y 0DZ

www.headline.co.uk
www.hachette.co.uk

For Tom Workman and James Calder,
for helping me walk again.

1

Tonight

Sketty

'So, you're quite the hero, Mr Sketty.'

The man addressing me in a soft Edinburgh accent is Dr Ralph Teller, a short, round individual of about seventy, who reminds me in appearance of Richard Attenborough, the owner of Jurassic Park in the original movie, and the one responsible for all those dinosaurs running loose and misbehaving. Dr Teller has a surprisingly cheerful demeanour considering that he suffers from an advanced and degenerative form of multiple sclerosis, which has left him permanently confined to a wheelchair, and will, in his own words, finish him off for good before too long. Right now, we're sitting opposite each other in the room he calls his snug, although it's at least as big as my living room at home. A log fire burns enthusiastically in the grate, casting shadows across the pitted stone walls, while outside the window, cold December rain lashes down.

'I can promise you, Dr Teller,' I tell him, 'I would have

preferred not to have been a hero. I was just in the wrong place at the wrong time.'

'The bravest men are often the most reluctant to participate in the fray,' he says sagely, taking a sip from his whisky, and I get the feeling that this is a phrase he's just made up, and that he makes up a lot of phrases like this. You see, I'm certain that Dr Teller (the Dr bit comes from his PhD in anthrozoology, whatever the hell that is) is not only a pseudo-intellectual, but also a fraud, the type of guy who's always got a hidden agenda, and the playfully cunning look in his eye as he observes me over the rim of the glass just reinforces my impression.

Teller puts his drink down on the gnarly wooden table next to him, his hand shaking and shivering, and tries to make himself comfortable in the wheelchair before he speaks again. 'I invited you here because I wanted to hear your story. In your own words. And I know what an imposition it is for you to come all this way to see some curious old man, which is why you'll find that the money I promised should already be in your account, if you'd like to check.'

Teller has paid me the princely sum of a thousand pounds to come out to his mansion in the Oxfordshire countryside and talk to him, which is actually less than the going rate. Right now, everyone who's anyone wants to interview me, and I'm a man in demand.

'I'll check later,' I tell him, keen to get this over with. There's a tension in this room and I have a worrying feeling that a trap is being set for me. I need to be careful, but then I knew that before I came here, which is why I'm drinking sparkling water that I've opened myself and not the whisky on offer. I take a drink of the water now and say: 'Where do you want me to start?'

'Where all stories start, Mr Sketty. At the beginning. However,' he adds, his eyes glinting brightly and malevolently in the room's dim light as he leans forward in the wheelchair, 'I want the truth, not your embellished version of events.'

I immediately tense. 'I'm not sure I follow you.'

'I think you do,' he says with a confidence I don't like.

'Look, I came here voluntarily to talk to you about the case. But I'm not prepared to be accused of being a liar.' I put down my drink, thinking that agreeing to talk to this old man was always a bad idea. I don't need the money and I certainly don't need the grief. 'Perhaps it's best if I just leave.'

I start to lift myself out of my armchair. My bad hip has become stiff from me being sat down for the past ten minutes while we did the various small talk. Dr Teller doesn't seem remotely perturbed, however. Instead, he's actually smiling, the sly bastard, and there's something predatory about it. 'Before you go, Mr Sketty, you might want to see this.' He reaches round in his wheelchair, moving slowly, and retrieves a plain cardboard folder from under the table, leaning forward to hand it to me.

I don't much want to take it, but curiosity gets the better of me. It contains a couple of dozen pages of printed A4 paper, complete with photographs, and as soon as I start reading, I can see this is trouble. This man Teller, a doctor of anthrozoology, for Christ's sake, knows everything about my career. And I mean *everything*, including parts that I've kept extremely well hidden. I take a deep breath, retaining my composure. 'How did you get the information in here?'

'My wife died at the Villa Amalfi,' he says, mentioning that terrible night all those years ago that changed both our lives forever. 'She was everything to me. Everything. And I lost her. Just like that.' His face contorts with a savage, almost primeval pain that for a moment makes him look like a man possessed by some evil spirit, then he shakes his head angrily as if banishing it. After a moment, he composes himself. 'I've had fourteen long years to research this case and everyone's part in it, including yours. It's been my focus. My passion. My very existence. And the combination of time, determination and very large sums of money is a particularly effective means of finding things out.'

'If you know so much, what do you need me for?'

'There are still a few gaps, and I believe you're the man who can fill them.'

'And if I don't tell you?'

'Then I'm afraid that everything in that folder gets made public.'

'So you're blackmailing me?'

'I wouldn't put it like that. At the moment, I'm simply giving you an incentive to talk.'

He takes another dainty sip of the whisky while I consider my options. But in truth I don't really have any. The information in this folder is incendiary.

Slowly I lower myself back into the chair and we eye each other warily.

'Take me through it right from the beginning,' he says.

And so that's where I start.

PART ONE

Fifteen Years Ago

2

I can tell you the exact minute it began. 6.42 a.m. on 23 November 2005, when I watched my daughter die in front of me.

After that, it was all over. It just took me a long time to realise it.

But I suppose for the purpose of this story it all started the night we nicked Claud Bradbury. I was in an unmarked surveillance car with my partner and old mate, fellow DC Ty Quelch. A beautiful name for a beautiful man. I loved that guy. We'd worked together on and off for about three years, ever since I'd joined SO11, which at that time was the Met's Organised Crime Branch. He'd already been there a year, and so he'd been the one to show me the ropes. He'd also saved my neck on an op when a suspect had pulled a knife and lunged at me. Ty was like a grand master of tae kwon do, or whatever the equivalent is, and he'd done this amazing move, which he'd tried to teach me and I'd never picked up, and in the space of about three seconds he was sitting on the guy and in the process of cuffing him.

The daft thing was, we weren't even after Bradbury that night. Instead we were on a surveillance job on an estate in one of the less gentrified parts of Balham, keeping an eye on an address where we had intelligence that there was going to be a major delivery of heroin. Surveillance is boring. It's lots of hanging about and talking crap while you wait for something interesting to happen, and this was one of those nights. It had got so bad that Ty and I had resorted to playing I Spy, to which an urban street at night didn't offer a great deal of fodder, and we'd just about exhausted that and were wondering whether the dealer was ever going to show when this giant of a man, clearly on something, came lumbering into view on the other side of the road. His jacket was all askew and half hanging open, and it looked like there was blood on his head.

Ty and I looked at each other, then back at the guy, who must have been about six five, and an absolute minimum of eighteen stone (not a lot of which looked to be fat), and who had a face that could best be described as fierce.

'Who the fuck is that?' said Ty, since no one matching this individual's description was meant to live at the target house, and he definitely wasn't in the state to be doing any kind of delivery.

'I don't know,' I said, 'but he's not stopping at our place.'

And he wasn't. He came lumbering past the target house, banging into a parked car and bouncing off it, and continued up the street in our direction.

Ty and I slid lower in our seats, not wanting to be spotted, although it didn't look like this guy would be doing much spotting, and watched as he stopped on the other side of the street, almost directly opposite our car, fumbled in his pockets for something that he clearly couldn't find, and then commenced banging on the door of one of the houses, yelling for whoever was inside to let him in. This carried on for about a minute, during which time lights came on in the adjoining houses, and at least one person poked their head out from behind the curtain, but then poked it straight back in again, not wanting to get involved.

Finally the door opened, and a harassed-looking woman appeared. I was in the driver's seat and I could clearly see the terrified expression on her face at the sight of him. He didn't wait to be let in, just shoved her aside and stalked past, slamming the door behind him.

Then, a couple of seconds later, I heard a scream – faint but unmistakable – coming from inside.

I turned to Ty. 'Did you hear that?'

'I heard something,' he said.

'It was a scream.' I let the driver's-side window down an inch, and immediately heard the sound of crockery breaking. 'We can't just sit here,' I said.

'Chris, we have to, buddy. We're on surveillance. We can't get involved. Let me call it in.'

Another scream came from inside, and then I was sure I heard a kid crying, and that did it for me. 'We haven't got time, Ty. Someone's getting hurt in there.'

'Shit,' he said, but he didn't try to stop me as I yanked open the driver's door and ran across the street. By that point in my career, a year on from Grace's death, I'd earnt

11

the occasional nickname of Bonkers Sketty for my habit of charging into trouble with no thought for my own personal safety. Like now. Although I was glad that Mr Tae Kwon Do was following close behind, because I wasn't that bonkers and didn't want to have to face a monster like this man – who we later found out was thirty-five-year-old Claud Bradbury, a low-level thug and domestic abuser with a string of convictions long enough to hang your washing on, who was also (unfortunately for us) a part-time cage fighter – on my own.

The door was locked, so I hammered on it hard, yelling that we were police and to open up fast, hoping my tone might encourage him to calm down, and hoping too that they didn't hear me in the target house, a dozen or so doors down.

All I got back was an unintelligible roar from somewhere beyond the door, mixed in with more screaming. The problem was, the only weapons we were carrying were expandable batons, and right then, they didn't feel like much protection.

I looked at Ty. 'You're the one who knows tae kwon do.'

He shot me a look and shook his head angrily before pulling out his baton and telling me to get out of the way.

I didn't need asking twice – like I said, I wasn't that bonkers – and I moved to one side, extending my own baton while he launched a kick at the door, which did nothing except send him stumbling backwards. He then took another couple of steps back, and this time did a flying kick, with exactly the same result, except when he

12

stumbled backwards, he landed on his arse. I would have laughed but I never had time, because a second later the door flew open from the inside and Claud Bradbury came charging out, waving what appeared to be a table leg, and went straight for Ty.

I don't think Bradbury even noticed me, which was a bad move on his part, because the anger and excitement came surging through me then, and without even thinking about it, I whacked him on the arm holding the table leg with the baton. As he turned round, I leapt on him, legs akimbo, like a ballroom dancer, sending him staggering backwards, where he immediately tripped over Ty. The two of us went down hard, but if I thought that was the end of his resistance, I was sadly wrong. I'm not the biggest of guys – five nine and a half, and at the time probably the lighter side of eleven stone – and the bastard literally flipped me over his head and sent me crashing into the neighbour's bins, which thank God were plastic and did a reasonable job of cushioning my landing.

As I clambered to my feet, picking up my fallen baton, Bradbury leapt up and, with alarming speed for a man who only five minutes before had been reeling drunkenly down this very street, grabbed the table leg and squared up to Ty, who went into one of his tae kwon do defensive postures. At the same time, the woman who'd answered the door appeared in the doorway, her shirt ripped and face bloodied. One eye was already swelling over, and she was unsteady on her feet. From inside the house I could hear at least two children – young by the sound of it – crying fearfully, and I remember it was that which gave me the red mist, and almost cost me my career.

Bradbury had his back to me, and as he swung the table leg at Ty, who only just about managed to parry it, I ran up behind him and wrapped the baton round the back of his head. I can't honestly remember whether I meant to hit him there, but it certainly did the trick. He lurched to the side and went down on one knee, which gave me the chance to drive my own knee into his face, and this time he went down properly, collapsing on his back on the pavement while I jumped on top of him, and used both hands to push the baton sideways-on into his face.

I'm certain I would have carried on hurting him, but I never got the chance, because the woman he'd been assaulting jumped on my back, got me in a surprisingly tight headlock and yelled at me to get off him.

By this time, people were poking their heads out of their windows all over the place, several of them filming the melee, which I knew then was probably not going to look good for me, and I was lucky that Ty intervened and dragged her off, kicking and screaming. Which was when Bradbury started struggling again, yelling abuse as he tried to wriggle out from under me and howling all kinds of shit about police brutality.

Reinforcements in the form of a local patrol car arrived to find the four of us out the front of the house wrestling like a dishevelled pair of tag teams, and they managed to help us nick Bradbury and get the woman, who was his common-law wife, back inside the house.

I was once told by a crusty old DS of thirty years' standing to always avoid getting involved in domestic disputes, as they never ended well for you, and I'll tell you this: to my dying day I wish I'd never got involved in that one.

3

I was suspended on full pay for six weeks after the Claud Bradbury incident while those leeches in the IPCC, as it was known then, investigated my conduct to decide whether or not I'd used excessive force during the arrest. My plight wasn't helped by the fact that a) someone had captured me on camera whacking Bradbury round the head with the baton while his back was turned, and then kneeing him in the face while he potentially wasn't in a fit state to fight back, and b) that his common-law wife, the woman we'd been trying to protect by our intervention, had said not only that she wasn't pressing charges against her old man, but that she wanted me prosecuted for assaulting him.

So when I was called in for a meeting by my boss's boss, the joyfully named DCI Perry Stilton, at one of SO11's old operations centres, a two-storey prefab unit on a bleak-looking industrial estate in Feltham – the type of place that wouldn't have looked any worse with a communal urinal directly outside it – I was pretty certain it meant I was going to get fired. At twenty-six, I might have had seven years' largely unblemished service within the Met, but I didn't think that was going to help me now.

And the truth was, when I parked my car outside and walked up to the front door, I really didn't care any more. In my mind, I'd already decided on a career change, although to what I still wasn't quite sure.

But as it happened, I was in for a surprise. Or to be more accurate, a series of surprises.

Firstly, the door was locked and there didn't appear to be anyone in the reception area, and when I pressed the buzzer I had to wait so long that I was beginning to wonder if I'd got the wrong day.

Then a woman I'd never seen before – about thirty, with long, very light auburn hair tied in a ponytail, and wearing a dark trouser suit – opened the door. She was tall and lean with the broad shoulders of a swimmer, and even in her flats she still had a good inch on me.

'Chris Sketty?' she asked, with a half-smile, a raised eyebrow and an accent that spoke of a good education.

I nodded and showed my warrant card. 'That's me.'

'I'm DS Rose Bennett, how do you do?'

'I do not that good at the moment,' I said, shaking her proffered hand. She had a firm, dry grip that expressed confidence and made me think she was probably going places in the Met.

'Come with me,' she said, and led me through the empty reception area, up the stairs to the second floor and along an equally empty corridor to an office at the end.

17

'Where is everybody?' I asked her. The SO11 ops centres, which were effectively just secure bases that could be used by different teams for certain jobs, were usually hives of activity.

'We wanted privacy,' she said over her shoulder, stopping at the office door and knocking.

That was when I got my second surprise, because when she opened the door, there was only one person inside: a small, olive-skinned woman of about forty with very short black hair, who sat behind the room's only desk.

I looked round, puzzled, but couldn't resist a small joke, since I was probably about to be fired anyway. 'No Stilton?'

'No,' said the woman behind the desk, getting to her feet. 'DCI Stilton's not going to be joining us. I'm DCI Marina Reineke of SO15, or as they like to call us now, Counter Terrorism Command. And you've met my colleague Rose.'

I nodded dumbly. Counter Terrorism Command had only been formed a few weeks earlier, an amalgamation of SO13 and SO15 (the Met have always loved their acronyms), and as far as I knew, they had absolutely no interest in internal discipline procedures.

'Please,' said Reineke, pointing at a chair. 'Take a seat.'

My plan had been to stand, so that if I was going to be summarily dismissed, I could simply turn on my heel and walk out without having to listen to anything else, but given this unexpected and somewhat bizarre turn of events, I did as she requested, while Rose Bennett took the other seat, crossing her long legs and taking out a large A4-sized notebook with a flowery cover from a briefcase by her chair, which she placed on her lap.

'Do you mind if I ask what this is all about?' I asked, looking at them both in turn. 'I was under the impression that this was a disciplinary hearing.'

'No, it's not,' said Reineke. 'Your disciplinary hearing's going to be held in two weeks' time, but the results of the IPCC investigation are already in. They're recommending your dismissal.'

'No surprise there,' I said. 'What is a surprise is that it has anything to do with Counter Terrorism Command.'

'We're coming to that,' said Reineke, 'but I'm reliably informed that the disciplinary panel will decide to issue you with a final warning, in light of your otherwise excellent record and, of course, your personal circumstances.'

My personal circumstances. It was a very bland way of describing Grace's death, but I preferred it to any out-pourings of sympathy from people I didn't know. I'd had enough of that over the past year.

'That's good to know,' I said. 'And interesting that you know it.' I decided to be direct. 'So why am I here?'

'We have a job that might interest you.' DCI Reineke leant forward in her seat, elbows on the desk, eyeing me carefully. She might have been small of stature, but there was a steel about her that I strongly suspected made people sit up and listen. 'Now, I don't want to get off on the wrong foot here, but what we want to discuss with you, whether you take the job or not, is not to go outside this room. If it does, you'll face criminal charges.'

Now I was intrigued. Even so, I shrugged, playing it cool. 'Okay.'

She stared at me for several seconds, as if making sure I fully understood the importance of her words. I just sat there waiting.

Seeing that she wasn't getting any further reaction, she commenced her spiel. 'For some time now, ourselves and MI5 have had an individual who goes by the alias Kalian Roman on our radar. We have no idea as to his identity, or even what his true endgame is. However, what we do know is that he's been financing and equipping a variety of extremist groups up and down the country over a long period of time. Five years ago, we broke up a Newcastle-based neo-Nazi cell who were planning a series of shootings of left-wing politicians and ethnic-minority public figures across the north. Their planning was well advanced and, more worryingly, they were well armed, with the kind of firepower that would have been very difficult for them to get hold of on their own. Those firearms came from Kalian Roman, as did twelve thousand pounds in cash to finance their activities. Because we had all four of them on tape talking about exactly what they were planning to do, they all pleaded guilty and cooperated. But the thing is, none of them had ever met Kalian Roman. In fact, they'd never even spoken to him. It seemed he'd approached them online, established a rapport, and the relationship had grown from there.

'Then, three years ago, an almost identical thing happened, except this time with an al-Qaeda-inspired cell of Islamic extremists based out of Birmingham who wanted to carry out an indiscriminate bombing campaign against civilians. Again, we got them at a very late stage in the planning process, and they were already in possession of ten kilos of high-grade C-4 plastic explosives and detonators. None of them cooperated, but we had them on tape mentioning Roman by name as the weapons supplier. There was also the Berkhamsted bomber. Remember him?'

I nodded. 'The radicalised Islamic fundamentalist who blew himself up in Pizza Hut? Yeah, I remember him. Don't tell me Kalian Roman supplied the bomb there too.'

'According to information found in the bomber's flat, Roman supplied him with the explosives and he built the bomb alone. Luckily it didn't detonate properly, otherwise it would have destroyed the bulk of Berkhamsted town centre.'

'How on earth does he get these people to trust him, if they've not even met?' I asked.

'By establishing his credentials. After he'd made contact with the Newcastle cell, he gave them the location of a bag containing two brand-new Glock pistols with a hundred rounds of ammunition that he claimed to have hidden in woodland in Northumberland. Apparently the cell members kept an eye on the area for three days to make sure there was no police presence, then one of them went in and found the weapons exactly where they'd been told they'd be. After that, they assumed he must be kosher, since the police would never have allowed those guns to be in circulation. He did something similar with the Islamic extremists. The point is, when he gets involved, he delivers the firepower, which makes him extremely dangerous, especially as we still have no idea where it's coming from.'

'It's an interesting story,' I said, and then asked the obvious question: 'But what's it got to do with me?'

'We didn't hear any mention of Kalian Roman again after the Berkhamsted bomb, and we hoped he might have stopped his activities, but then three months ago, one of our low-level informants – an ex-soldier with right-wing extremist connections – told his handler that an attempt had been made by one of his former colleagues in the army, a Martin Greene, to recruit him into a cell actively planning terror attacks against government and left-wing targets. Greene told our informant that the cell was being bankrolled and armed by someone with major connections. He didn't say who it was, but when we put a bug in Greene's flat, we heard him mention Kalian Roman by name in one of his phone calls.'

Reineke paused. 'Our informant was frozen out after that, we don't know why. Greene went to ground too and disappeared from his rental flat, and hasn't been seen or heard from since, so it's possible he got spooked. After that, we thought the lead might turn into a dead end. But then, with some help from GCHQ, we managed to ID the individual Greene had been talking to on the phone about Kalian Roman. That individual is a serving police officer, a detective sergeant in the Met, and we have reason to believe he may be involved. The problem is, he's also highly surveillance-aware, making it near enough impossible to bug him, even if we could get the authorisation, which I don't believe we would.' She gave me a wintry smile. 'And that's where you come in, DC Sketty. Would you consider an undercover information-gathering role?'

'I'd consider it, yes,' I said, wanting to hear more before I committed to anything. Out of the corner of my eye I could see Rose Bennett writing something in her flowery notebook. She'd been writing things down in there since the conversation between her boss and me had begun. Or maybe she'd been doodling. It was hard to tell.

'It'll certainly help your career if you do,' said Reineke. 'My understanding is that DCI Stilton is keen to transfer you out of SO11.'

Which was no big surprise. Like too many senior figures in the Met, Stilton was a politician at heart, and clearly saw me as a loose cannon who might cause him trouble if I remained on his watch.

'Well, I guess I'll have to very seriously consider it, then,' I said, feeling in better spirits now that I might actually be in demand by my employers for once. 'Where's the officer in question based?'

'He's part of a team called the Gang Intelligence Unit. They're based out of Hammersmith nick, an offshoot of the CID there.'

'I've heard of them. Is that Devon Andrews' outfit?'

Both women looked interested, as though they hadn't been expecting this. 'You know Devon Andrews?' said Bennett, joining the conversation for the first time.

'No,' I said, turning her way, 'but I've heard about the GIU. Apparently they're doing a good job.' The GIU was one of those units the Met periodically set up to deal with whatever issue was getting the public's and press's attention. At that time, in the early 2000s, youth gang crime had become a major problem across London (which of course it still is), and so a number of GIU units were set up across the various boroughs to combat low- to mid-level organised crime. The most successful, or at least the one that seemed to garner most of the publicity, was GIU West, which was led by DI Devon Andrews, a tough ex-boxer with a busted nose that covered half his face and close to twenty-five years' service, all of them spent on the mean streets of west London. The Met's PR people considered Andrews the perfect choice for the job. Not only was he highly experienced, he was also black, which went a long way to deflecting any claims of racial bias made against the team. It had crossed my mind more than once to put in an application to join them. 'Don't tell me Andrews is your suspect?'

Reineke shook her head, again with that wintry smile. 'No, I don't think he's an extreme right-winger, somehow. Our suspect is his right-hand man, DS Barry Cleaver. He's the one you need to get close to.'

'The Met have upped their budget for the GIU units,' said Rose Bennett, 'and there's currently a vacancy within Devon Andrews' team for a DC. They've insisted on interviewing any prospective candidates, but they haven't talked to anyone yet.'

'We'd like you to apply for the position,' continued Reineke. 'It seems they're quite an aggressive outfit, with very proactive methods of policing, so with your record – both the good and the not-so-good parts – you should make a very decent fit. The idea is for you to join the team, get close to the target and find out what you can from him.

This may mean pretending that you share his extremist views. If the target is indeed part of a terrorist cell, we want him to trust you enough to invite you to become part of it. But the key for us in Counter Terrorism is to find out who Kalian Roman is so that we can stop him before he actually makes one of these plots work.'

'It's not going to be easy,' I said, although I'd already pretty much decided to take the role. 'If the target is as careful as you say he is, he's not going to open up to some newbie on the team. It could take months.'

'We understand that,' said Reineke, 'and obviously we'll be working other angles, so it would be best to consider it as a potentially longer-term role. Your job would be to record Cleaver saying something incriminating enough for us to use against him, so he can be turned. DS Bennett here would be your handler and your first point of contact.'

Rose Bennett closed her notebook and gave me what I'd call a businesslike smile. 'I wouldn't be keeping lots of tabs on you, or demanding weekly progress reports. We'd communicate via secure email and meet when and if you are making real progress so we can discuss the best way to gather evidence against the target in a way that doesn't compromise your safety. You'll also have a dedicated phone number so that if something urgent comes up, you can get hold of me day or night, 24/7.'

I looked at her. She came across as confident and capable, but could I trust her to get me out of a difficult situation? The jury was out on that one. 'Who else would know about my role apart from you two?' I asked.

'Only my direct boss, the head of Counter Terrorism,' said Reineke. 'That's it. As far as DCI Stilton is concerned, you transferred out and joined GIU.'

'And if I say no?'

She shrugged. 'Then you leave here, forget this meeting ever happened and go back to work at SO11 with your final warning hanging over you.' That smile again. 'See how long you last.'

'Are you interested in taking this role, DC Sketty?' asked Rose Bennett coolly.

And so I made the decision that would change my life forever.

4

When I walked into Hammersmith nick the following week for my interview, I was excited. Not because I felt I'd be righting wrongs and preventing terror attacks (I honestly didn't think I was going to have any luck getting the information Reineke and Rose were after). No, I was excited because I desperately needed a role that I could get my teeth into, which would help me forget the mess my life had become by that point.

The rot for me had started one day eighteen months earlier when my wife, Karen, noticed that our five-year-old daughter, Grace, was having difficulty walking. By the time Karen had made an appointment with the doctor, Grace was developing headaches so bad that they'd make her vomit. We were terrified. Up until that point, she'd been perfectly healthy, but within a week she'd been diagnosed with something called diffuse intrinsic pontine glioma, or DIPG for short, a rare, and extremely serious, brain-stem tumour that mainly affects young children. Long-term survival rates are as low as one per cent. And without going into details, Grace didn't survive. She was given a rapid course of radiotherapy, but it did little, if anything, to stem her deterioration, and she died four months after the diagnosis.

The blow was like nothing I've ever felt, either before or since. Our happy family – and I tell you this with hand on heart, we *were* truly happy – was simply destroyed, just like that. At the time of Grace's diagnosis, I'd just been accepted for a job with the New South Wales police, based in Sydney. We were going to emigrate and start a new life in the sunshine, where the plan was for us to try for a second child, something we'd held back on because of finances. Karen and I were still young, having met as childhood sweethearts when we were still at school. We had our whole lives in front of us. So did Grace, even more so. I remember she'd been so excited about the beaches and the kangaroos and the koala bears, and everything kids get excited about.

We had our whole lives in front of us.

And then we didn't.

With Grace's death, mine and Karen's relationship became increasingly strained. We simply couldn't seem to move on. The Australian job fell through when I couldn't persuade her to come with me, and eventually we decided on a trial separation, which became a permanent one when Karen struck up a relationship with the grief counsellor she was seeing, a Kiwi called Bryan, who at the time of my GIU interview she'd just moved in with.

And so, in twelve short months, a happy family of three

had become a fucked-up one-man band.

The interview, which DI Andrews insisted upon because he didn't like people being foisted on him, took place in his office, a cramped room at the back of a larger open-plan office at the rear of the building, from where he ran GIU's operations. Also present was his right-hand man and my target: DS Barry, or Baz, Cleaver. Cleaver was a shaven-headed, well-built gym bunny in his late thirties. He had small hands for a man of his size, and a very round face that would have looked far better on a jolly fat man, but which he compensated for by wearing the kind of fierce, pit-bull-like expression that smacked of some deep-seated insecurity, and I guessed he'd been bullied at school. I already knew that he'd changed his name by deed poll to Barry 'Baz' Cleaver from the significantly less brutish name of Nigel Locock, which was all part of the image he was trying to create of a man not to be trifled with. In fact, I knew quite a lot about Baz Cleaver, courtesy of Rose Bennett, who'd done a good job of filling me in on his background.

I didn't pay him any undue attention, though, just shook his hand, along with Devon Andrews', and took a seat opposite Andrews while Cleaver stood off to one side with a foot perched on a stool, watching me interrogation-style, like he was hunting for any sign that I was hiding something. The bad cop.

And a complete contrast to Andrews, who I liked straight away. He was a big guy with a big grin, revealing a gap between his two front teeth, but there was a depth to him, and a warmth, that I wasn't expecting. 'Look, Chris,' he said, 'before we begin, I wanted to say that I was sorry to hear about your daughter. I'm a dad of two, so I can't imagine what you went through.'

Cleaver mumbled something that sounded like agreement with his boss, although I couldn't really tell.

'Thanks, I appreciate that,' I said, looking at them both in turn.

Andrews pushed back on his chair until it was against the wall, and asked me why I wanted to join the team.

I wasn't nervous. I didn't need to lie. So when I spoke, I told the truth. 'Because I'm tired of reacting to crime. I'm tired of dealing with arseholes after they've already left their trail of destruction. I want to be in a team where the work's proactive. Where I'm getting out there and stopping the crimes before they happen, and where, you know . . .' here I paused for a moment before continuing, 'where you don't necessarily have to hold back the whole time.'

'I see you have a bit of a problem with holding back,' said Andrews, keeping his expression neutral.

'We read about your little fight with the domestic abuser,' said Cleaver, who had a voice that was an octave too high for his overall demeanour, with just a hint of the nasal about it. 'The one who'd been beating up his girlfriend.'

'I don't have a problem,' I told them evenly. 'I was making an arrest. The guy was attacking me and my colleague. I did what I could to stop him causing either of us injury, and I didn't hit him after he was incapacitated.'

Andrews smiled, steepled his fingers under his chin. 'I bet you wanted to, though, didn't you?'

I wondered if this was a trick question. According to Rose, who'd spent more than two hours prepping me for the interview, there were rumours that members of Andrews' team – himself and Cleaver included – had used excessive force and threats of violence. But I figured that if I appeared too eager to tell them how much I'd wanted to hurt the guy that night, they might smell a rat.

In the end, I told them ninety per cent of the truth. 'I was angry, and he was acting like a wild man. And he was a big guy too, with a history of violent offences and assaults against police. So yeah, I reckon he deserved more than what I gave him. And maybe a part of me felt like giving him a sly couple of extra punches, but in the end, I know it wouldn't have done me any good, so I'm glad I didn't. And in that situation again, I'd do the same as I did. Fight back. Incapacitate the suspect. Remove the threat. Nothing more. Nothing less.' The ten per cent I missed out was that I'd had to force myself, through a huge effort of will, to hold back from beating him to an absolute pulp, because in truth, I'd wanted to really hurt him. Believe it or not, even months later, I still did, and when the film of our fight on the pavement was shown back to me at my first disciplinary hearing, watching it actually made me feel excited, something I'm not proud of.

Either way, though, both men must have liked my answer, because two days later I was told I had the job.

I was now a member of Gang Intelligence Unit West and my undercover career had begun.

5

I had two more meetings with Rose Bennett, where we went through all the regulations I had to follow. She also gave me a rundown of how to work my main tool for intelligence-gathering: a state-of-the-art stainless-steel watch containing a miniature audio recorder and camera that you'd only be able to find if you took the whole thing apart. And that was it. I signed a contract and I was on my way.

On my first day on the job, DI Andrews – or the Chief, as he was universally known, and which I'll call him from now on – took me for a ride round some of the neighbourhood gang hotspots in an unmarked BMW X5 the team had just taken possession of, because the local crims had got to know the other cars they drove. Baz Cleaver rode with us too, sitting sprawled across two seats in the back, leaving me to get a bird's-eye view of our territory from the front. Although based out of Hammersmith nick, we also covered adjacent boroughs where they had specific gang-related problems, a wide area that stretched as far west as Ealing and as far north as Kilburn.

As we drove, the Chief gave me his philosophy. 'You know, Chris, some people think this is a war between the police and the bad guys, and in a way it is. But it's not like a normal war where you go out there every day and fight an evil enemy. It's more like a cold war. You try to outwit your foes. You make sure they see you as a serious enough threat that they don't want to take you on. But you also try to educate them, and the people around them, so they realise that what they're doing is pointless in the long run. There are some real bad people out here, don't get me wrong, and we've got to do everything we can to take them down. But most of the criminals round here aren't like that. They're just people who grew up with nothing, and if you present them with an alternative, they'll take it.' He turned and looked at me. 'Where did you grow up?'

'Hemel Hempstead,' I told him, because he probably knew that anyway, and I didn't see much point denying it, even though it made me appear like a middle-class white boy from the suburbs, which clearly I was.

'So, you had it all right. Nothing wrong with that. I bet most of the kids here wish they'd grown up in Hemel Hempstead.'

'I bet they don't,' I said with confidence. 'It was boring as hell.'

The Chief looked over his shoulder. 'Didn't you grow up that way, Baz?'

'No chance,' grunted Cleaver. 'I'm Canvey Island. The Chernobyl of England. Hemel Hempstead's like fucking Barcelona in comparison.'

The Chief laughed, a deep bass sound that filled the car. 'See, there you go, Chris. You had the best start of all three of us. I grew up round here. But you probably knew that, didn't you?'

'I'd heard,' I answered, because there wasn't much about the Chief's past that was secret. Being one of Scotland Yard's poster boys tends to give you a high profile.

'A place called the Finchampstead estate,' he continued. 'Less than half a mile from where we are now. It's gone now, demolished back at the end of the nineties, and I don't think it's ever been sorely missed. You see that apartment block over there?' He pointed to a flashy-looking glass building about six storeys high set between a coffee shop and a Caribbean restaurant, both of which looked busy. 'That land it's built on used to be a piece of waste ground. We'd play footie on it when we were kids. We found a dead body there one summer. An old homeless tramp. We heard later he died of natural causes. He'd been there for days by the time we found him, and the smell was something else.'

The Chief shook his head slowly, a slight smile on his face as if he was reminiscing about a past holiday somewhere mildly exotic, not a rotting corpse. 'They were different days then, you know. Shit ones in a lot of ways. Everyone wanted to escape. Be a footballer, a musician, or whatever. Things have got better. But they've still got to change further. We need to give people hope. I managed to get out. I became an amateur boxer, got trained by a local police sergeant called Vic Hislop. I wasn't good enough to go pro and it was Vic who encouraged me to join the force. My friends all thought I was mad. So did most of my family. But you know what? I've never regretted it, and when it comes to Judgement Day, I think I'll be able to hold my head high and say I did more good in this world than harm.'

'I think we're all hoping that,' I said, 'but right now, my track record on that front's looking pretty skewed. The guy I had a fight with and almost lost my job over looks like he's just going to get community service because his missus won't press charges, and I even heard a rumour that he's planning civil charges against me.'

The Chief fixed me with a look that seemed to go right through me. 'So, in your world the bad guys seem to be winning. Is that the way you see it, Chris?'

I thought of Grace then. Sweet, innocent Grace whose life was stolen from her while scum not fit to clean her shoes wandered the world scot-free. 'Sometimes it feels that way,' I said.

He clapped me on the shoulder. 'Well, you're in the right place to do some good now. Isn't that right, Baz?'

'There's definitely no shortage of bad guys to go after,' said Cleaver from the back, without a hint of irony. 'Especially in this place.'

'Ah yes,' said the Chief, looking over towards a series of buildings appearing on our right. 'The Cliveden Forest estate. We've been concentrating on cleaning up this place for months now, and we're not having the easiest of times. The problem is, the gang who operate here are much better organised than most we have to deal with.'

'How so?'

'Well, for a start, they've got a proper leader. The guy's name's Jayson Jason, believe it or not.'

I laughed. 'Are you serious?'

'Absolutely. Poor kid never stood a chance with parents that lazy.'

It struck me that this was true. I'm no bleeding-heart liberal, but that doesn't mean I don't accept the fact that some people really are doomed from the start, and it's maybe best not to judge them until you get the whole story.

'Anyway, JJ, as we like to call him, runs his outfit with an iron fist. He's twenty-nine now, old for a gangbanger, and he's been in and out of nick all his life. The last time was five years for attempted murder, and since coming out three years back, he's taken over all the crack, heroin and even weed dealing in the whole area. He uses the estate as a hub. The gear gets bought wholesale from outside then brought in here for distribution, so this place is like his own personal fiefdom, and he doesn't like us turning up on it.' As the Chief spoke, we turned off the main street and onto a narrow access road that ran through the estate. The residential blocks – a series of interconnecting mid-rise buildings with open walkways running across the front of the flats – were designed almost like fortifications, and they loomed up on our sides and front, closing us in.

A small communal green containing a rough patch of grass and a playground appeared to our left. There were no kids or parents in the playground, just a group of about a dozen young guys in hoodies, several of them on bikes, loitering next to the swings. They clocked us immediately,

as did a couple of teens, also in hoodies, standing at the
foot of a stairwell, smoking what looked suspiciously like
a joint.

'It'll take about two minutes for JJ to know we're here,'
said the Chief as we drove past, going it seemed deliberately
slowly, barely five miles an hour.

'If that,' said Cleaver from the back. 'That little scrote
by the stairwell's already on the blower.'

'You see, we've got two problems bringing him down,'
continued the Chief as I looked round at the grim concrete
edifice surrounding us, wondering which architect in their
right mind thought this was the kind of place where people
would be happy to live. 'One, he's got so many people on
the payroll that he's got eyes and ears everywhere, so we lose
the element of surprise on any raid. And two, he inspires
total fear in people so it's impossible to get anyone to talk.'

'How are we going to get him, then?' I asked.

'We've got to break down his supply chains, then—'

'Shit!' said Cleaver loudly from the back. 'Isn't that
Sean Bareham over there?' He was pointing to another
kid, whose hood was actually down for once, just inside
the underpass between two of the buildings.

The kid, clearly clocking us like everyone else, immediately pulled up the hood and did a rapid U-turn, walking
fast in the other direction, which was not the best way to
remain inconspicuous.

'It certainly is,' said the Chief, accelerating. 'Right, let's
get him.' He turned to me. 'He's got an ASBO banning him
from this estate, and we're not having him taking the piss.'

Sean Bareham was quick on his feet, and clever enough to bolt away from the road and up a footpath running past the playground towards a gap between two of the buildings, which looked pedestrianised, and where we were never going to catch him in the car.

As the Chief screeched to a halt at the point where Bareham had left the road, the three of us threw open the doors and set off after him at a bolt. I felt a real exhilaration. This was the kind of thing I'd signed up for. Taking the fight to the criminals. And I knew I could catch him too. I was always a fast runner, right from childhood, and at that time I still kept pretty fit, so within seconds I was pulling away from the other two and eating up the ground between me and Bareham. He knew it, could hear my trainers hitting the concrete getting closer, and he took a quick look over his shoulder, saw me closing, then pulled something from the outsize parka coat he was wearing and flung it into a threadbare-looking bush at the side of the footpath.

'I'll get it!' I heard Cleaver shout behind me.

Bareham tripped on an uneven paving slab as he rounded the corner towards the pedestrianised area, stumbled and only just managed to maintain his balance, but he'd lost precious ground and now I was only a couple of yards behind him.

'Stop, or I'm bringing you down!' I shouted. 'And that's going to hurt.'

He seemed to consider it, but only for a second, because I could hear him panting, and then he slowed up and came to a halt, while I reached for my cuffs and grabbed him by the shoulder, pulling him round.

'Okay, I'll take it from here, Chris,' said the Chief, who was close behind me and already had cuffs in his hand. 'Hello, Sean,' he said with a smile to the kid, who was trying to look nonchalant but instead looked scared and resigned. 'Fancy seeing you here. You're under arrest for breaching your ASBO.'

'And possession of an offensive weapon,' added Cleaver, who'd now arrived holding the object that Bareham had thrown away when I'd been chasing him: a large black hunting knife still in its sheath.

The Chief asked Bareham to put his hands behind his back, his tone relatively gentle, as if he didn't want to have to be doing this, which he probably didn't, and the kid complied without complaint as he was cuffed and read his rights.

But as we turned back towards the car, making a phalanx around our prisoner, I could see that this wasn't going to be the ultra-smooth first arrest I'd been expecting.

'Uh-oh,' I said. 'Looks like we've got company.'

The group of youths hanging out by the swings had peeled away from them and were now moving towards us as one, hoods down, some with scarves round their faces to prevent identification, cutting off our path to the car. They were brimming with aggression and righteous anger – you could see it – and they were playing to an audience too, because there were people appearing on the balconies to watch what was going on.

'Don't worry, it's just a show. They'll back off,' said the Chief, granite-calm, his stance reminding me of something my old boss, DCI Stilton, who tended to be a font of wisdom, had told me early on in the job: 'People will do and believe anything you say as long as you sound confident saying it.' It seemed we were now about to put his homily to the test.

'Don't give an inch,' said Cleaver, who I now realised was behind me, the tightness in his voice suggesting that he was more scared than he was letting on.

The group were ten yards away from us now and instinctively they slowed down, coming to a halt and blocking the path.

The Chief didn't break pace. He just kept coming, facing them down, the confidence total, a powerful, physically imposing figure who wasn't going to stop of his own accord. They knew it too, you could see it in their faces, uncertainty mixing with the bravado, wondering who amongst them was actually going to take the Chief on. And I'll be honest, it was in that moment, aged twenty-six, that I learnt how inspirational real leadership was. His stance made me feel brave, almost invincible, and I kept on coming too, the group moving out of the way as we marched through them.

But it wasn't over yet. They followed us back to the car, staying only feet behind, keeping up an invective about this being a wrongful arrest, that we'd planted the knife, that it was police brutality ... all the usual flack we have to deal with. But the Chief was right. It was a show designed to intimidate us, to make things difficult, and maybe with a couple of PCSOs it might have worked, but with us it didn't. They reminded me of hyenas. When one of them came too close, we'd snap at them to get back, acting with calculated aggression so they'd know not to take it too far.

This is how so many violent incidents begin. You've got to remember that when two opposing individuals or groups square up, the whole thing's like an intricate dance. Everyone wants to posture, to show what a man they are, but no one really wants to get hurt. The problems start if one of you pushes things just that little bit too far, so that the others have to react or lose face. Then it can turn into something very nasty, with blood and injuries and occasionally worse, and right then, being outnumbered at least four to one, I knew I had to play my part just right. We might have been cops, but being plain clothes, we had no stab-proof vests and were only armed with a can of pepper spray each, while our prisoner, Sean Bareham, had already given us a demonstration of what these boys might be carrying.

As we neared the car, another group of six or seven approached us from the underpass where we'd first seen Bareham, and I saw the Chief look up towards where a man in a very loud red tracksuit, and equally loud matching bandana, was leaning on the fourth-floor balcony railings staring down at us.

'There he is, the man himself,' said the Chief, turning to me. 'JJ. He's their real audience.'

In truth, he didn't look that impressive. Or that bothered by what was going on.

'He doesn't go for camouflage, then?' I said, studiously

ignoring the insults being levelled at me from the harrying pack.

The Chief grinned. 'No, you'd never accuse him of blending seamlessly in, would you?'

As we got to the car, we were quickly surrounded by the group, now bolstered in numbers to at least twenty strong. They inched forward menacingly, still giving us crap over the arrest, their voices growing louder now, the nearest of them only a couple of feet away, and easily close enough for a rapid knife thrust.

'Get him in the back,' said the Chief, and I opened the rear passenger door, having to back towards the crowd as I did so, while Cleaver manoeuvred Bareham, who was looking a lot more confident now, towards it.

'Let him go!' yelled a big guy of about twenty, right in Cleaver's ear.

Cleaver swung round fast, still holding on to our suspect. 'Back off!' he roared, but something about him just didn't look quite menacing enough and, although the guy did actually move back a foot or so, he still stayed very close by, and as Cleaver pushed past the open door and I grabbed hold of Bareham's arm, I saw that he was looking far too flustered.

I shoved Bareham into the car, careful to push his head down so he didn't bang it on the frame and give some more ammunition to the mob, who were still keeping us hemmed in. Someone pushed up against my back, and I elbowed whoever it was in the stomach and pushed back harder, swinging round to face them, my hand on the pepper spray, beginning to lose my patience and worried that at any moment Bonkers Sketty might make an appearance.

The guy I'd elbowed – sixteen, seventeen tops – was holding his stomach and looking angry, and also surprised. His friends glared at me like angry bulls, willing each other on, but none prepared to make the first move now that we were face to face.

'All right, that's enough,' said the Chief, marching over so he stood between Cleaver and me, his voice loud and authoritative as he addressed the crowd. 'He's coming with us, whether you like it or not. Now you can cause a scene like this, in which case we'll call for reinforcements and then you can all come down the station. Or you can calm down, let us do our job and get him processed, and then who knows? He might even make bail.'

'Bullshit,' said someone from the back, but no one else spoke.

The Chief turned to us. 'Let's go.'

I didn't need asking twice. Neither did Cleaver. I jumped in the back with Bareham, watching as the Chief walked round the front of the car, shoulders back, head held high, while the crowd peeled away, giving him space.

As soon as he was in the driver's seat, though, they came forward again so they had the car surrounded, blocking our exit.

'You know,' said the Chief with a loud sigh, 'sometimes you've just got to wield the stick.' And with that, he shoved the car into reverse and started backing up, knocking several of the mob out of the way as he picked up speed before stopping and doing a three-point turn in the middle of the road. The crowd ran towards us, remonstrating and posturing, and someone was just about to launch a kick at the car when the Chief shoved open the door and stared hard at him.

'Touch the car, Raul Jackson, and I'll nick you right here, right now. You want that?'

The guy stopped dead, his foot actually in mid-air, then slowly lowered it.

'I thought not,' growled the Chief, and with that, he shut the door and we pulled away.

And as I sat back in my seat, stifling a sigh of relief, I had a feeling that I was really going to enjoy myself here.

But already something was bugging me. It was Baz Cleaver's expression as we drove out of the estate. He was looking at the Chief, and there was definitely an element of hero worship going on there. And that struck me as odd. Because Cleaver was meant to be a right-wing extremist, and yet here he was looking up to a black man almost like he was some kind of god. It didn't sit right.

But it would be many years, and a lot more dead bodies, before I finally worked out what was really going on.

6

It's fair to say my first three months in my new assignment were my happiest time since the days when Grace, Karen and I had still been a normal family.

There were eight of us in the team – seven men and a lone female, DC Arietta Bailey, known to everyone as Nix for a reason I never got to the bottom of, who took no crap from anyone, colleague or criminal. I won't introduce the rest of them, because they're not relevant to this story. Anyway, to use that old cliché, we worked hard and played hard, and there was a real camaraderie that you only get from being part of a tight-knit unit. They welcomed me in too. When it became clear to the Chief that I was going to be on my own on Christmas Day for the first time in years, he invited me to spend it with him and his extended family. I still remember it vividly – a house full of noise and laughter and good food and company. I ended up getting utterly pissed, falling asleep in the Chief's armchair and leaving the house, dazed, hung-over but eternally grateful, after an extended breakfast the next morning.

In the end, it was Baz Cleaver, my target, who was probably the most distant of the team, and I wondered if it was because I'd seen him all flustered that day in the Cliveden Forest estate and he didn't like it. Either way, I got the feeling that he wasn't going to let his guard down with me until he was absolutely ready. It didn't matter. I wasn't going to push things with him, nor was I expected to. Rose got in touch via email every couple of weeks, just to see where I was with everything, and we had one phone conversation, just after Christmas, where she reminded me to make use of the James Bond-style watch I'd been provided with to record any information I could, however inane. 'You never know what you might pick up,' she said, 'and it would be good to have at least something to go to Reineke with, so she knows that nailing Cleaver's still your top priority.'

But Rose was sensible and long-sighted enough to accept my lack of progress without complaint. Which was exactly how I liked it. We were busy in the extreme. Not only were we still trying to build up a case to bring down JJ's burgeoning drugs empire, but we were also dealing with the myriad low-level gang wars going on across the boroughs we covered, some of which were directly or indirectly fuelled by JJ's operations. I liked the proactive way the team dealt with matters. Sure, they could be a bit rough with suspects. I once saw Baz Cleaver smash a suspected mugger's face into his bedroom wall during a raid, and then drive a knee into the small of his back, but then the suspect had been violently resisting, so what the hell did he expect? I didn't bother mentioning it in my report, even when I overheard Cleaver telling the boss that the suspect was talking about making an official complaint, and the boss replied that they'd pick him up for a word to make sure he kept his mouth shut. It was easier, both for my conscience and the op itself, just to turn a blind eye, and the suspect never did make that complaint.

I think they liked the way I worked too. I didn't hold back when making arrests either. If someone resisted, I made them stop. I was rough but fair. Occasionally Cleaver or the Chief would make a passing comment along the lines of 'I bet you wished you'd given him a couple of slaps', and I'd give them the stock reply that I'd done it before and look where it had got me.

And then one cold February evening, everything changed. A twelve-year-old girl called Leonie Foley went missing in Hammersmith while walking the half-mile home from her friend's house. She'd left the friend's at 7 p.m. and the alarm was raised by her mother two hours later. Because of her age, and the fact that she had no history of running away or turning up at home at crazy hours, a major incident was declared. By the next morning, and still with no sign of her, the story had made the news, and the GIU team joined more than a hundred officers on the streets, making inquiries and checking CCTV. Eventually we found a witness who remembered seeing a white van with blacked-out windows driving very slowly up and down her street several times about the time that Leonie would have been walking past. She hadn't seen the driver but managed to write down the last two letters of the plate. Then another witness on the same street came forward and said he'd heard what sounded like a child screaming outside his window. By the time he'd opened the curtains and looked outside, all he saw was a white van, which matched the approximate description given by the other witness, accelerating away.

And that was all we had. The street had no council CCTV cameras – it wasn't considered a high-crime area – and there were no working private cameras facing the road either. But the boss was adamant that the abductor would be a local man who knew the area, and thanks to the partial plate number, it didn't take long to identify white-van-owning convicted paedophile Roger Munroe, who lived barely a mile from Leonie, as our prime suspect. What was more, thirty-nine-year-old Munroe had been jailed for seven years in 2000 for attempting to abduct and sexually assault a seven-year-old girl (he served four), and his van had been caught on camera on the nearby Goldhawk Road at 7.17 p.m., only a few minutes after the second witness reported hearing the screams.

In situations like this one, time is of the essence. We all knew Leonie might still be alive, but there wasn't enough evidence for a warrant to search either Munroe's van or his flat. The head of the investigation was DCI James Calder of Hammersmith CID, and I can't say for sure exactly what happened, but my guess is that he was feeling the pressure so much that he secretly reached out to the Chief and asked him to lean on Munroe to get him to give up Leonie's whereabouts. I've got no proof of that but either way, on the afternoon after she disappeared, the Chief took Cleaver and me aside and told the two of us to pay our suspect a visit.

Cleaver didn't look impressed. 'Shouldn't you and me be the ones going on something like this, boss? No offence, Chris.'

'None taken, Baz,' I said.

'I can't go,' the Chief told him. 'I need to be here to help coordinate things and make sure we hold back on putting any surveillance on him until you're done. It's time Chris got chucked in the deep end.' He turned to me. 'You've been a dad. You know what it must be like for the family. And you'll do the right thing, won't you?'

I looked him straight in the eye and told him I would.

'Then that's settled.' He clapped me on the shoulder. 'Now get moving, both of you, and don't let Leonie's family down.'

7

Roger Munroe lived on the third floor of a well-kept tower block in East Acton reached via an outside walkway.

Cleaver peered in through a window. 'He's in there,' he said, moving away so he couldn't be seen. 'In the kitchen. He hasn't spotted me. Looks like the fat bastard's making food.' He turned to me, his eyes narrow and hard, searching me for any sign of weakness on my part. 'If he doesn't want to talk voluntarily, he's got to be made to talk. You know that, right?'

'I was a father to a five-year-old girl,' I told him. 'I know it better than anyone.' It struck me then that the Chief was taking a big risk sending a man with my background to get information from a potential child abductor (and possibly killer), but if I came through, he'd know that my loyalty to the team, and to him, couldn't be questioned.

Which should have set alarm bells ringing, but didn't, because I didn't want to hear them.

Cleaver gave a cursory nod and hammered on the door, before leaning down and shouting through the letter box.

'Mr Munroe, this is the police. We know you're in there. Open the door, please. We need to ask you some questions.' He stood up. 'There's no way out the back, so he's going to have to talk to us.'

'What's it about?' Munroe called from behind the door, his voice high-pitched and whiny, and I felt a growing anger in my gut.

'It's about a missing girl,' said Cleaver. 'We just need to know your movements yesterday.'

Munroe opened the door. He was exactly what I expected a paedophile to look like: unkempt and out of shape, scruffily dressed in pyjama bottoms and a food-stained sweatshirt that rode up over his ample gut; pallid, unhealthy skin, and greasy dark hair in a side parting that hadn't been in fashion since sometime before I was born. But it was the sunken piggy eyes skulking behind the rolling flesh of his cheeks that I can still remember to this day, because they glittered with a malevolence that he couldn't quite hide. Behind him, Abba was playing somewhere in the flat. I remember the song was 'Dancing Queen', which I hate.

'Are you sure you're police?' he said, leaning forward to inspect our warrant cards.

We didn't look much like police, it has to be said. GIU tended to dress in civvies, and the shaven-headed Cleaver in his bomber jacket, black boots and well-honed fierce expression looked like a thug straight out of central casting. I looked nicer, but not that much.

'Yes, sir, we're police,' said Cleaver with a predatory smile. 'Do you mind if we come in?'

'It's not a good time right now.'

'Thanks,' he said, driving a hand into Munroe's chest, knocking him backwards, and striding inside with me following.

Munroe started demanding to know what the hell we thought we were doing, but he didn't get very far because Cleaver punched him hard right in his expansive belly while I closed the door behind us. Munroe made this noise like an injured duck and collapsed to the floor looking like he was going to vomit.

'Right, grab his other arm,' said Cleaver, yanking him to his feet. 'Let's get him out of view.'

There was no point arguing, so I did as I was told and we dragged him through the flat, past the kitchen with its stink of decaying fried food and into a bedroom with an unmade bed and lots of clothes scattered about, where we dumped him on the floor. Cleaver then pulled off Munroe's sweatshirt so he was naked from the waist up and told me to watch over him for a moment. The guy looked scared and sick and I felt the first flush of doubt as I realised that we weren't just bending a few rules here, we were committing full-scale assault. I didn't mind running head-first into danger, but it was different when you were taking out someone who wasn't fighting back.

Cleaver reappeared with a rickety wooden chair and we put Munroe in it. He then produced two pairs of non-issue handcuffs from inside his bomber jacket and used them to secure our prisoner.

'Look, what's going on here?' whined Munroe, his voice shaking now.

Cleaver leant down so that their faces were only a few inches apart. 'What's going on is you're going to tell us where Leonie Foley is. Or we're going to hurt you very badly.' He shrugged. 'So why not save yourself a lot of pain and tell us now?'

'You can't do this,' said Munroe.

'Well your problem right now is that we *are* doing it,' said Cleaver with a smile, and backhanded him across the face so hard his head snapped sideways. Baz turned to me, looking like he was enjoying this, although perhaps that was because Roger Munroe was a far easier target than the kids from the Cliveden Forest estate. 'Turn up the music, then see if you can find a newspaper anywhere in this shithole.'

I didn't need asking twice. I was feeling a little sick. Mainly with worry. If we got caught for this, I was finished. We both were. And yet Cleaver was acting as if getting answers like this was the most natural thing in the world.

Abba were singing 'Fernando' now, which had been one of Karen's favourites and reminded me of far better times, so it was through gritted teeth that I cranked up the volume and then looked round amidst the various detritus for a newspaper, wondering what the hell Cleaver wanted one for.

I found a raggedy old copy of the *Sport* underneath a smelly cat litter tray in the kitchen, brushed it off and went back into the bedroom, where Cleaver had now taped Munroe's mouth shut with duct tape, which I could only assume he'd brought with him especially for the purpose.

'Ah, just what I needed,' he said, taking the paper from me.

As I watched, he rolled it as tightly as he could on the bed before folding it in half. While he worked, he gave us both a brief explanation of what he was doing. 'What I'm making here is something called a Millwall brick. It's an improvised weapon used by resourceful football hooligans back in the seventies for when they were searched at the stadium gates by the police. No one was ever going to stop them from carrying a newspaper, right? So they were able to bring them right into the ground. And that turned out to be a bad move. Because these things hurt like hell.' Cleaver tapped the rolled-up paper, which was now about a foot in length and four inches wide, against the palm of his hand with an audible thwack. 'And what makes them perfect for our purpose is they don't leave a single mark.' He smiled down at a terrified Munroe before whacking him with it on the right nipple.

Munroe howled behind the gag, his eyes wide in pain, and struggled in the chair.

'See what I mean?' said Cleaver, before hitting him again, this time on the left nipple.

Sure enough, neither blow left a mark on Munroe's chest. Cleaver kept hitting him, while I watched, varying the blows so they took in the belly, the side, the arms and once the face.

Munroe was crying and wailing, the sounds drowned out by 'Money, Money, Money', followed by 'I Have a Dream'. Twice he fell over in the chair as he tried to avoid the blows. Twice we picked him back up, pushed the chair against

54

the wall and Cleaver continued the assault. He worked unhurriedly and methodically, not speaking to either me or Munroe. And it was clear he was enjoying himself. I wasn't. But every time I began to weaken and considered stepping in, I forced myself to think of this bastard torturing Leonie Foley. If, of course, it was him, because we had no concrete evidence, which is why we couldn't arrest him and were having to resort to this.

It occurred to me to use my watch to record what was going on, which I could easily have done, and which would have given Rose and Reineke exactly the kind of leverage against Cleaver they needed, but there were two major problems with that. One, I was involved and any recording would automatically incriminate me. And two, and more important, a twelve-year-old girl's life was at stake. So instead, I waited and watched, hoping we weren't making a major mistake.

Finally, with a satisfied sigh, Cleaver stepped back and looked down at Munroe, who was in terrible pain. He turned to me. 'See what I mean about the lack of marks?'

'It's impressive,' I agreed.

'It's very impressive. So, are you ready to talk yet, you fat fuck?'

Munroe nodded frantically and Cleaver ripped the duct tape off.

'Go on. Where is she?'

'I don't know, I swear it,' panted Munroe. 'I had nothing to do with her disappearance. I wouldn't lie to you.' He looked frantically at me, as if hoping I might be able to help.

I had doubts. Jesus, I had doubts. But I glared straight back at him, not prepared to offer any hope.

Cleaver turned to me. 'You think he's lying?' His own expression told me that he thought Munroe was.

Knowing what I did about Munroe, I was ninety-eight per cent certain he was guilty, which might not have been enough to convict him in a court of law but at that moment was good enough for me, although God only knows what our next move was going to be.

'Yeah,' I said. 'I think the bastard's lying.'

'I'm not. I swear on my own life—'

'Shut the fuck up!' snapped Cleaver, giving him another whack on the nipple.

Munroe squealed.

Cleaver ignored him, turning back to me. 'Put the kettle on.'

I didn't ask him why. There was going to be a reason for it and it wasn't likely to be to make us all a cup of tea. So I went next door and once again did what I was told, wondering what on earth Karen would think if she knew what I was doing. She still cared for me, I knew that, and she'd be angry that I was risking my job and my freedom. That I was effectively aiding and abetting in the torture of a suspect, something that would shock a nice middle-class girl like her to the core. But Karen had also been a mother. She loved kids. It was why she'd been a primary-school teacher. And like me, she'd suffered the loss of a beloved daughter. If she thought Leonie was alive somewhere – scared and alone – and that the man we were torturing had genuinely abducted her, then I was pretty certain she'd have some sympathy for our actions.

When I returned with the freshly boiled kettle, I saw that Cleaver had blindfolded Munroe with a pair of boxer shorts and stuffed a sock into his mouth, which he was holding in place with his hand.

I went to hand him the kettle, but he shook his head, pulling off the blindfold so Munroe could see what was going on.

'This is where you prove yourself, fella,' he told me. 'I'm going to take the sock out and hold this bastard's nose. Then, when he opens his mouth, you pour about half a cup's worth in, just to give him a taster of what to expect.'

I was shocked at what he was asking me to do, although I'm not quite sure why, since it was obvious he was going to want to involve me at some point. I now had two very unpalatable choices. Tell him no and risk ruining this whole assignment. Or pour boiling water down a man's throat.

Cleaver gave me a hard look. 'You ready?'

I pictured a crying Leonie Foley and kept her image right there in the forefront of my mind, then nodded once, stepping forward so I was right in front of Munroe. 'Let's do it.'

Cleaver yanked the sock out in one rapid movement and threw it on the floor before grabbing Munroe by the throat with one hand and squeezing his nose so that he was forced to open his mouth.

I crouched right down, so close to him now that I could see the tiny droplets of sweat seeping from his pores, hoping like hell I wasn't going to have to follow through with this.

Munroe kept his mouth shut tight as a razor clam, holding his breath and looking like he might have a coronary at any moment.

'Get ready,' hissed Cleaver, his voice barely audible, but simmering with a mixture of rage and enjoyment. 'As soon as this cunt opens his mouth, stick the kettle in and make sure you hold it there, otherwise he'll spit the water out all over us.'

I nodded tightly. Waiting. Somehow keeping the hand that was clutching the kettle from shaking.

It didn't look like Munroe could hold his breath much longer, and if he didn't talk now, it meant he was almost certainly innocent. It also meant I was about to commit GBH on a suspect for no good reason. And what the hell happened if he died on us? Which right then was looking like a distinct possibility, judging by the colour he was going.

Be strong, I told myself. Be strong.

But I was weakening. I didn't want to go through with this.

Munroe's mouth finally opened in a gaping wave of fetid breath. The spout of the kettle was two inches away, the steam already burning his face.

'Now!' hissed Cleaver.

'She's alive!' howled Munroe, just as I moved the kettle to his lips. 'At a flat in Plaistow.'

'Whose flat?' demanded Cleaver.

'Someone I know from online.'

'Address?'

Munroe hesitated as the fear began to subside.

Which was a mistake on his part, because now that I knew the bastard was guilty, there was suddenly no reason to hold back, and Bonkers Sketty suddenly appeared. 'Tell us, you fuck!' I snarled, and pushed the kettle spout against his lips, burning him.

He yelped in pain but couldn't move because Cleaver had him held firm. As his mouth opened, I went to pour the boiling water in, but he immediately blurted out the address.

I stepped back and put the kettle down on the floor, feeling tense but vindicated, and wrote it down in my notebook.

'How many people are there with her?' demanded Cleaver.

'Just the man whose flat it is.'

'Name?'

'Alan Pugh.'

Cleaver stood back up, taking out his phone. 'Gag him and watch him. I'm going to call this in. And by Christ, she'd better still be alive, Munroe.'

It turned out she was. Ten minutes after Cleaver's call, local police forced entry into the flat and found a traumatised and naked Leonie Foley tied up and gagged in a cupboard. Munroe and Pugh had raped her repeatedly, and she was in a bad way, but after a stay in hospital, and months of therapy (partly financed by a whip-round organised by the GIU team that raised close to a grand), she went on to make a decent recovery. Munroe, of course, claimed that we'd tortured a confession out of him and made a formal complaint about our behaviour, but apart from a pair of blisters on his lips where I'd burned him with the kettle, he had no visible injuries, and we already had our story ready. Both Cleaver and I claimed that he'd voluntarily let us in, but while talking to us had become agitated by our questioning and had tried to make a run for it. There'd been a struggle, and as he was being cuffed and told he was being arrested on suspicion of Leonie's murder, he'd admitted that she was alive and given us her location, saying there'd never been any plan to kill her, even though a brand-new bone saw had been recovered from Pugh's flat, along with heavy-duty bin bags and all kinds of unopened cleaning products, the majority of which had been purchased three days previously.

Our story might not exactly have been foolproof, but it held together well enough, and anyway, to most people we were heroes who'd saved a young girl's life. The press feted us. Members of the public wrote in to congratulate us. The complaint was thrown out as erroneous. And even the brass couldn't make a fuss, not with all the good PR they were getting as a result of our actions. So it was good news all round, and got me closer to the man who was meant to be my target.

Only Rose Bennett showed any real concern. She called a meeting, which we held on neutral ground in Richmond Park a couple of days later, and asked me straight out if I'd told the truth about how we'd got the confession.

I knew there was no point playing the innocent on this. 'We leant on him a bit,' I said, 'but nothing for anyone to get upset about.'

Rose raised an eyebrow, which clearly signified scepticism. 'I understand he's made a complaint.'

'That's his lawyer talking. He's making up some cock-and-bull story that we tied Munroe to a chair and tortured him, but it's all bullshit. Nothing will come of it, I promise you.'

'If it does, that's between you and him, and nothing to do with us.' Her words were delivered in an even tone, but there was no mistaking the warning in them. If things went tits up, I wasn't going to be getting any support from CTC. But I knew that. 'Did you record Cleaver assaulting Munroe?' she asked.

'No. And he didn't assault him. Not really anyway.'

'You don't sound very sure, Chris. Look, we're pleased that you're getting close to Cleaver, but what we need is some leverage on him. And to do that you're going to have to either record him making compromising statements, or behaving in a compromising manner. Have you made any recordings so far?'

I knew where this was going. 'I haven't, but that's only because the right situation hasn't presented itself.'

'I'm willing to bet the right situation presented itself at Munroe's flat, but for some reason you chose not to record it.'

'I was more concerned with a missing girl at the time.'

Rose slowed down and looked at me properly. 'And I understand that, but don't lose sight of the job you're meant to be doing here. That watch has the capacity to record forty-eight hours of audio and four hours of video before

61

the microtape needs changing. So start recording – any-thing – and see what you pick up. Okay?'

'Okay,' I said, and that was that.

But what most pleased me about the whole thing was when Karen called the following morning to congratulate me on helping to free Leonie Foley, and to ask if she could come round for a drink one evening. Maybe I was just being naïve, but I genuinely thought there might be some sort of rapprochement, and that she'd decided to give that unethical bastard Bryan, who'd only ever been a rebound relationship anyway, the shove.

Alas, however, when she came round that evening, it became very clear very fast that the news wasn't good. Which was a pity, because I'd gone to a lot of trouble, getting home an hour early so I could shower and change into something decent – in this case a navy blazer she'd bought me for my twenty-fourth birthday, with a nice dress shirt beneath and freshly ironed jeans. I'd also whipped up a Thai curried seafood stir fry with fresh crabmeat and tiger prawns, which had just finished simmering on the hob and which had always been one of her favourites, hoping I could tempt her to stay for some dinner too.

But the look on her face when I opened the door told me I'd completely misread the reason for our meeting. She gave me a tight, anxious smile as I invited her in.

'Everything okay?' I asked her.

She nodded, but it was clear it wasn't. I offered her a drink, and she said she'd have a glass of white wine, fol-lowing me into the kitchen and waiting while I poured it.

She looked at the curried seafood on the hob, then back at me, the anguish almost etched into her expression.

'I thought you might want some,' I said, pouring myself a Peroni, knowing that whatever Karen had come here to tell me wasn't going to be good. She'd always been a sensitive soul, and it was clear she was dreading saying it.

'No, it's okay,' she said quietly.

I turned to face her. 'What is it, Karen?'

Our eyes met. I still yearned for her as much as when we'd first started going out, and I wondered then if she felt anything for me.

She opened her mouth, but it took a good three seconds for the words to come out. 'I don't know how else to tell you this, but Bryan and I are getting married.'

That word, 'married', was like a punch, and I felt myself physically reel. Trying to retain my composure, I put my beer glass down on the kitchen top and took a deep breath. 'Don't you think that's a bit hasty? It's the first relationship you've had since me. You need time to think . . .' My words were coming out in a jumble as I tried to think of anything I could to dissuade her from going down this route.

'I don't need any more time to think, Chris. I've thought about it for a long time now, and I've made my decision.'

I looked at her and saw the relief now that she'd told me, and I knew there was no way back from this. I felt sick. 'Okay,' I said, because I wasn't sure what else I could say.

'And we're moving to New Zealand.'

It was like another physical blow. 'What do you mean?

You didn't want to go to Australia with me, but you'll go to New Zealand with him.'

'Please don't make this hard, Chris. I still really care about you, but our relationship's over, and there's nothing keeping me here.'

'Well, your parents for one.'

'They've given me their blessing. They think a new start will be good for me after everything that's happened.'

'What about Grace? You won't be able to visit her memorial stone.'

'We'll be coming back. And obviously I've got her ashes. So I thought perhaps if I took half of them, I could get the other half put in a special urn for you to keep.'

After Grace's passing, we'd kept her ashes rather than scatter them somewhere. This was more Karen's doing than mine. She told me that having the ashes at home made her feel closer to Grace, and when she'd left, we'd decided that she could take them with her.

'It's okay,' I said wearily. 'You keep them. I'll stick with the memories. I prefer it that way.'

She nodded. 'All right. Thank you. I'll look after them for us.' She took a self-conscious sip of her wine and remained standing. She still had her coat on, but I had the feeling she wasn't going to get round to taking it off.

'When are you planning to leave?'

'At the end of term, the beginning of April.'

'That's quick.'

'There didn't seem much point in delaying it.'

I swallowed, felt tears sting my eyes. 'Please don't go,' I said, my voice cracking.

There were tears in Karen's eyes now too. 'I've got to, Chris. I can't stay here. Not with the memories.'

'Couldn't we just try to make it work one last time? Please. I love you.'

'I'm sorry,' she said. 'I really am. But this is best for me. And I know it's hard to hear, but I do love Bryan.'

I managed to steady my emotions and stop the tears from coming. I've never been a man afraid of showing my sensitive side, but somehow I didn't feel it would help now. Instead, I simply stood there dumbly, not wanting her to go but at a loss as to what I could possibly say more than I'd already said.

Karen knew me well enough to see my pain. She put down her glass and came over, wrapping her arms round me. 'You'll be okay, Chris,' she said softly. 'You're strong. And you're a hero. You helped save that little girl's life. Don't lose sight of that.'

God, I wanted to kiss her then. To hold her tight and never let go. But I knew there was no point. 'Please stay in touch.'

'I will,' she said. 'And I'll come and see you before I go.' She let go of me. 'Take care, Chris. Okay? Promise me.'

I nodded slowly and watched her leave, wondering how many more huge blows life was going to land on me.

But you know the answer to that. They were only just beginning.

8

The Munroe incident cemented my place within the team. Even Cleaver started being nice to me. During the celebration drinks at the White Horse, the pub we always used, on the night after we'd brought Munroe in, he'd collared me at the bar, already drunk, slung an arm round my shoulders and whispered in my ear: 'Good job, Chrissy boy.' And then, with just a hint of malice: 'Would you have poured that boiling water down his throat?' To which I gave the honest answer: 'Yes.' Which seemed to please him, because he then bought us both a double Jameson, paying with a fifty-pound note, and told me that him and me were going to get along just fine.

That was when the two of us began hitting the pub after work a couple of nights a week.

The thing that struck me most about Cleaver was that he was a lonely guy. Divorced, childless and, at forty-three, banging on the door of middle age, he seemed to spend his spare time either in the gym, drinking with whichever teammates were around, or online dating, where he didn't appear to have a great success rate. However, this didn't stop him advising me what I needed to be doing now that I was officially (albeit involuntarily) single.

'You've got to put yourself out there, Chrissy boy,' he told me while we were hanging on the bar of the White Horse one night. 'And there's no better way of finding the talent than all these new internet dating sites. It's like being a kid in a massive sweetshop. I've been doing it a year, and, mate, I am truly loving it.'

'But you're still single, Baz,' I told him. 'You're not exactly a ringing endorsement.'

He turned and gave me a drunken leer. 'But I'm getting laid, Chris. Never forget that. I'm getting laid.'

Although from what I could gather, the women at the business end of Cleaver's affections weren't exactly sprinting back for more. Nix once even referred to him behind his back as 'One-Date Wonderboy'. And that was another thing with Cleaver. He was one of those guys who wanted everyone to know that he was hard as nails, a ladies' man extraordinaire, and that he thought emotions were for wimps. But underneath it all, it was clear that he was hopelessly insecure, and just trying to cover it up with aggression and bluster. On those very rare occasions that he let the mask drop, he did reveal a more sensitive side. I was driving with him once when he saw a scraggy-looking dog with a bad limp and no collar, which in the old days we'd have called a mongrel, wandering up and down the Goldhawk Road looking frightened and hungry. Cleaver insisted we stop and help it. I wasn't quite sure what he had in mind, but after chasing it round like an idiot and finally cornering it in a halal butcher's doorway, he scooped it up and, ignoring its struggles and the bemused gazes of passers-by, brought it back to the car.

'Now I know how your dates feel,' I told him as he got back in, keeping the poor thing clutched tight to his chest.

But it was clear he had the dog's best interests at heart. He cooed over it, gently stroking its head and whispering words of comfort like a mum to her injured kid, before insisting we detour to a vet's, where he paid out of his own pocket for it to be treated.

'I've always loved dogs,' he told me by way of explanation as we left the vet's. 'I grew up with them and they really are man's best friend. Did you have a dog when you were growing up, Chris?'

'We had a cat,' I told him. 'His name was Lionel.'

Cleaver stopped dead, his face darkening, and fixed me with one of his fierce looks. 'I fucking hate cats,' he said. And left it at that.

I don't know if he felt he had to act the hard man to prove that he wasn't a dog-loving softie, but either way there was definitely a deep vein of rage running through him that I could see he struggled to hide. He was a very violent man, but the reason he'd lasted as long as he had in the Met was because he was always disciplined. He knew when not to overreact. One time we did a major early-morning raid on a suspected crack house of JJ's in Acton, as part of our campaign to disrupt his business. We were accompanied by a camera crew from BBC London. Even though the raid took place at 5 a.m., the three males and two females (one of whom was only fourteen years old) in the place were all still awake, and when we smashed through the reinforced front door – a task that took Cleaver and his enforcer no fewer than seven whacks – we got more resistance than we'd bargained for. The guy who ran the crack house on JJ's behalf, Leon Warman, decided to slug it out rather than surrender or run, and went straight for Cleaver, trying to hit him with a roundhouse right. Luckily, he was so bolloxed he completely missed, and Cleaver quickly wrestled him to the floor as the camera crew looked on. The problem was, Warman wasn't giving up, and he was also seriously angry. As Cleaver tried to pin him down, and the rest of us piled in to help, Warman spat full in his face.

There was a split second when we all thought Cleaver would lash out. The rage in his eyes was truly intense.

But he didn't. He knew the cameras were there. He knew any reaction now would get him in trouble. So he made a noise of disgust, wiped his face and helped turn Warman over so we could cuff him. But I could tell he'd banked the transgression. It would get paid back at some point.

And, of course, it did. Even though Warman had assaulted a police officer, was suspected of sleeping with the fourteen-year-old girl, a foster-home runaway called Lara Phoenix, and had been present in a house where a hundred and fifty rocks of crack had been recovered from the premises, along with a pound of skunk and some wraps of heroin, he still somehow managed to make bail, which tells you everything you need to know about the British justice system.

On the plus side, though, the fact that he made bail meant he was present two weeks later when we carried out a raid on another of JJ's crack houses. This one was in Shepherd's Bush, although the word 'house' was something of an exaggeration, as it was basically a burnt-out derelict building awaiting demolition that had been turned into a walk-through drugs supermarket staffed by JJ's dealers.

The place was often deserted, and we'd got permission from the developers to put a camera inside to record what was going on. Then, early one afternoon when they were just opening for business, we staged a raid. The whole eight-man team was involved, backed up by about a dozen uniforms, and we hit both ends of the building at the same time. There were two dealers in residence, along with Leon Warman as security, and a handful of users sprawled in a couple of empty rooms.

This time Warman did actually make a bolt for it, and there was an unspoken agreement within the team that Cleaver would be the one to take him down. Because he and I were new best buddies by this point, it was the two of us who ended up chasing him down a corridor towards a fire exit we hadn't been aware of.

Cleaver jumped on Warman's back just short of the fire exit door, sending them both crashing through it and into an alleyway outside. Warman hit the wall opposite shoulder-first, and as Cleaver swung him round so they were facing each other, he delivered an elbow strike to Warman's face.

An elbow strike – especially one delivered at very close range by someone who lifts a lot of weights – is easily enough to stop any attacker, but as Warman's head smacked back against the wall, Cleaver delivered two more in rapid succession before flinging him to the ground on his front.

Even though Warman was a big guy, he was in no position to resist further, but Cleaver wasn't finished yet. After taking the briefest of glances up and down the alley to check it was empty of witnesses, he drove a knee into Warman's back, and then used both hands to slam his face into the litter-strewn tarmac, ripping hair from his head at the same time. Warman cried out in pain. 'Stop, please,' he said breathlessly.

Everything had happened so fast – four or five seconds at most – that it's unlikely I'd have had time to intervene even if I'd wanted to, and the truth was, I was never going to break my cover for a lowlife like Leon Warman, who had a string of convictions as long as an orang-utan's arm, mainly for violence.

'That'll teach you to gob on me, you filthy fuck!' Cleaver hissed in his ear, and the two of us cuffed his wrists behind his back and dragged him to his feet.

Warman turned to me, his face covered in dirt and blood, his nose looking squashed and one eye was already beginning to swell. He appeared indignant, as if he couldn't believe he'd just been on the wrong end of violence, which is something I've often noticed with criminals. They don't mind dishing out but get very peeved if the favour's returned. 'You saw that. He fucking assaulted me.'

'I didn't see shit,' I told him, 'except you tripping over and hitting that snout of yours. You should get that looked at.'

'You people think you're fucking untouchable,' he hissed. 'But we can get to you and your family easily enough.'

Saying that to me was always going to be a red rag to a bull. Without warning, I hit him hard in the stomach, and as he bent over, grunting in pain, I grabbed his balls beneath his jeans and yanked them so hard that if they'd had eyes they would have been staring at his arsehole.

The fire door had closed behind us, but I could hear shouts and movement coming from the other side. I ignored them for a moment, enjoying this sudden feeling of power. 'You ever mention my family again and I will kill you,' I told Warman blankly, still gripping his gonads, while Cleaver held the rest of him in place.

'I'm sorry, I'm sorry,' he wailed. 'Let go, please, you're killing me . . .'

I gave them a final squeeze goodbye and looked at Cleaver, who was smiling at me. 'I didn't see a thing,' he said.

A second later, we pulled Warman out of the way of the door as it was thrown open from the inside and the Chief and Nix came running out, accompanied by two uniforms.

'Ouch,' said Nix, seeing Warman's battered chops.

The Chief looked at me and Cleaver in turn.

'These bastards assaulted me,' said Warman.

'He fell,' we both said at the same time.

The Chief didn't say anything, just motioned for us to bring him through.

When we were back at the station, though, he took me

to one side and asked me if I was sure that Warman had 'indeed' fallen. I wasn't sure what answer he wanted from me, so I told him once again that that was exactly what had happened. 'He was going at a fair old pace when he went crashing out that door. It was no surprise he hurt himself.'

The Chief nodded slowly, eyeing me carefully. 'Fair enough, but be careful, Chris. Especially with your record. We don't want too many complaints about manhandling suspects. That'll just bring us the kind of scrutiny we could do without, and interfere with the good work we're doing here.'

'I know,' I said, 'but we did nothing wrong today, I promise. And it was good work, eh, Chief? Closing another crack house and nicking Warman.'

'Yeah, but at the moment, Warman's going to walk. He wasn't holding any gear when he got nicked and no one's going to speak up against him.'

So much for the good work we were meant to be doing.

'Listen,' he said, seeing my look of disgust, 'these things take time. We're disrupting JJ's business, that's the main thing.'

'Yeah, but we're just getting the small fry, not the big boys. JJ's probably replaced those dealers already.'

The Chief shrugged. 'Well, what would you do to alleviate the situation?'

'I don't know,' I said, because I didn't.

He smiled. 'You've got to think laterally, Chris. There's more than one way to skin a cat. Come on, let's pay Warman a visit. He's in the cells.'

A uniform let the two of us in to see him, even though it wasn't strictly legit. By rights, we should have waited until he was in the interview room with his lawyer, but back in those days, you could still get away with bending the rules.

Warman was sitting on the cell's single bunk looking angry when we walked in. He'd been bandaged beneath the eye where Cleaver had elbowed him. 'What the fuck do you want?' he demanded. 'And what's *he* doing here?' He motioned with his head towards me. 'He assaulted me, along with that bald fuck. I want him out.'

'We're going to give you a chance to walk free,' said the Chief, leaning against the wall while I stood next to him.

'What are you talking about? I'm going to walk free anyway,' scoffed Warman, all full of bravado. 'You ain't got nothing on me.'

'Well, that's not quite true,' replied the Chief. 'That fourteen-year-old girl you've been sleeping with—'

'I ain't been sleeping with no fourteen-year-old.'

'Lara Phoenix, the runaway we recovered from your crack house. Remember her? Well, we've got you on camera banging her in that crap hole where we just nicked you.'

This thing with Lara Phoenix was all news to me. I hadn't heard any mention of it from the Chief before, but then I hadn't seen the footage from the camera that we'd planted at the crack house either. And it was obvious from the look on his face that Warman had been having sex with her there. But he wasn't giving in yet. 'This is all bullshit,' he said with a dismissive wave of his arm. 'I want my brief.'

'He's on his way,' said the Chief. Then to me: 'Remind me. What's the charge for having sex with an underage girl, Chris?'

'Statutory rape, Chief,' I said.

'That's right,' he said, nodding. 'Statutory rape. You've been done for rape before, haven't you, Leon? I wonder how lenient the judge'll be this time round.'

Warman sat on the edge of the bunk, staring at the floor, his shoeless feet drumming relentlessly on the linoleum. He was a big guy, full of pent-up aggression, and I was glad the Chief was in here, because I wouldn't have fancied my chances if he'd gone for me. 'What do you want?' he asked eventually, without looking up.

'You help us bring down JJ, and the footage we've got disappears and the charges go away. All you need to do is tell us where his next shipment of gear's coming from, and when, and we'll do the rest.'

This time he did look up, but there was defiance in his expression. 'No way. JJ's my homeboy, and I ain't no snitch. Charge me with that other bullshit stuff if you want, but it won't stick. You're just blowing smoke.'

The Chief, though, was as unfazed as ever. 'Sure,' he said with an exaggerated shrug. 'Your choice. You'll be charged with statutory rape, but I'll tell you what. We won't even oppose bail.' He smiled. 'What we will do is start spreading the message on the street that the reason you keep getting bail is because you're a snitch, that you were the one who told us about the two crack dens we raided. That you're in our pockets.'

'JJ would never believe it,' said Warman, shaking his head, but he looked worried.

'Sure, you might be able to deflect things for a little while. But we'll keep feeding the streets the word that you're on our side. Every bust we make on JJ's business, we'll credit to you. Eventually the doubts will set in, and then how long do you think you'll last?' The Chief walked over to the bunk, crouching down in front of Warman. 'But it doesn't have to be that way, Leon. We could lose the footage of you having sex with a fourteen-year-old girl, and then you walk out of here a free man, no charges hanging over your head, and once again you'd be a hero with your homeboys for putting one over on us. And all you have to do is give us the details of the next shipment. We'll take down JJ, and who knows? You might even take over. Then you can be king of the estate.'

'You can't do that,' said Warman. 'I've got rights.'

'Watch us,' said the Chief. 'You've got one hour to decide.'

When we were back outside in the corridor and out of earshot of anyone else, I asked the Chief if he thought Warman would cooperate.

He shrugged. 'I don't know. Everyone's terrified of JJ, but Warman's probably one of the least terrified. They've known each other since they were kids. He might call our bluff. But the key is to get him to believe we'll carry through our threat, and I think he thinks we will.'

'Do we have footage of him having sex with the girl?'

'Yeah. It's not good quality, though, so I don't know if it would stand up in court, particularly if she doesn't cooperate, and she's infatuated with him, so there's no reason to think she will.'

'And if *he* doesn't cooperate, are you going to go through with your threat and spread those rumours about him?'

He looked at me carefully. 'What would you do?'

Again, I wasn't sure if this was a trick question or not. I gave the honest answer. 'Yeah, I would. We've got to make him fear us, because right now he doesn't.'

'Absolutely. I said to you before, Chris. A lot of these kids don't have any choice but to get into gangs. Most of them have good hearts, although sometimes they hide them well. But a few of them are just devils. And Warman's one of those. I'm happy to drive a wedge between him and JJ, but I'm hoping it doesn't come to that. Because the only way we're going to get to JJ is by getting someone close to him to talk.'

Half an hour later, we got the news that Warman had agreed to help us.

The Chief had shown me how it was done, and now I realised that I was going to have to do the same with Cleaver.

77

9

Two nights later, I finally got my chance.

I was out having a couple of after-work drinks in the White Horse, and Cleaver asked me if I fancied grabbing a takeaway curry and heading back to his place for a few more beers. It occurred to me that he might actually be coming on to me – not that there was any intelligence that he was either gay or bisexual – and I remember feeling hesitant. Not just because of that, but also because I really didn't want this assignment to end. We were doing a good job out there, actually making improvements. This was in spite of the fact that at every turn, it seemed those in control, whether it be the brass eager to cover their arses and not be accused of heavy-handedness, or the judges who constantly let scum like Leon Warman back on the streets, were constantly undermining us.

However, I couldn't pass up the opportunity to be alone with Cleaver on his home turf, so I took up the invite.

I left my car at the pub, switched on the watch's audio recorder, and we took a taxi to Cleaver's place, via an Indian takeaway he knew where we'd pre-ordered something of a feast. No one could say he wasn't security-conscious. He didn't let me see the code that he punched in to open the front door to the building where he lived, and he'd triple-locked the front door of his flat using top-of-the-range deadbolt locks that would have been a nightmare to get through.

'You can never be too careful,' he told me as we stepped into a remarkably clean and tidy living room, with minimal yet expensive furnishings (two comfortable-looking reclining leather chairs, a low glass coffee table that literally gleamed in the reflection of the ceiling lights, and a wall-mounted plasma TV). He was clearly a neat freak. I had no clue how he got the time to keep the place clean. He worked long hours and Rose had told me he didn't have a cleaner, or anyone they knew who had a spare key. It was why he was so hard to get to.

But that wasn't the half of it. After getting me to remove my shoes and leading me through to an equally neat, though slightly cramped, kitchen with a table and chairs taking up much of the space, he asked me to unpack the food at the table while he took a handheld bug finder from one of the drawers and gave it a walk round the confines of the flat, looking for any signs that someone had planted a listening device.

I wasn't bothered. I knew the best bug finder in the world wouldn't pick up the audio recorder in the watch, because it wasn't emitting a radio signal, making it impossible to find without physically taking the watch apart piece by piece, and I was pretty certain even Cleaver wouldn't attempt that.

'You know, Baz, I think you *can* be too careful,' I said when he returned a couple of minutes later. 'Who do you think's listening in on you? Leon Warman?'

'I don't want any nasty surprises, that's all,' he said, taking a couple of bottles of Peroni from the fridge and popping the lids, before handing me one and taking a seat.

'Well, no one's going to catch *you* out, that's for sure,' I told him, my interest now piqued, because the intelligence on Cleaver, though thin, clearly had substance. This guy was obsessed with not being spied on, which meant Rose was right: he was definitely hiding something, and by the price of the bug finder – which, like the locks, was top-of-the-range – it was something big. As I've already said, though, it was hard to imagine him as a right-wing extremist when you'd seen as I had how much he looked up to the Chief. You could tell from the dynamic between them that Cleaver would do pretty much anything for him. So much so that it was almost touching. But as I was finding out, there was a lot more to Baz Cleaver than met the eye.

Apart from the odd snippet of small talk, we ate largely in silence, both tearing into the food. As with all take-away curries, I'd hopelessly over-ordered, and I couldn't finish my king prawn madras, or the sag aloo, but Cleaver kept going, machine-like, until he'd scoffed every scrap, including what was left of mine. After he'd removed the food cartons, cleaned up, and then sprayed air freshener in the kitchen, which I thought was a little OCD, we retired to the comfortable chairs in the living room with a second bottle of Peroni each. I was almost afraid to drink it in case I spilt any on the upholstery, which I had a feeling would probably end our friendship there and then, but Cleaver seemed more relaxed now.

That was another thing with Cleaver. He was a particularly manic individual, and his periods of relaxation never lasted long. Within a matter of seconds, he was shaking his head and frowning while staring into space as another unwelcome thought planted itself in his mind. He then snapped to attention in his chair and fixed me with an intense stare. 'Can you believe that that fuck Warman's free again?'

'Well, at least he's working for us now.'

'Yeah, we'll see about that. I don't trust the bastard. And I'll tell you something else. He should be behind bars permanently. Do you know he's got twenty-six convictions? Twenty-fucking-six.'

I did know. It was common knowledge within the team, but I let Cleaver vent.

He leant forward, his round face dark with anger. 'Do you know when he was seventeen, him and three other of his little bastard mates raped a sixteen-year-old girl with special needs. They took her to a flat, plied her with drugs and took turns on her.' He shook his head in disgust, as if trying to force the image of it from his mind. 'She tried to struggle, but they put a knife to her throat and smacked her around. And then when they'd finished, when they'd had enough and this little sixteen-year-old girl was lying there on some

81

shitty crack-house floor, do you know what they did? They emptied a bottle of drain cleaner on her to try to get rid of the DNA evidence. She almost died.' Cleaver looked truly anguished as he told the story. 'That's who Leon Warman is, an animal. He got eight years for that attack, and served less than four. What kind of justice system allows that?'

I knew the details and, like Cleaver, it made me angry. 'There is no justice,' I said, with a venom I genuinely felt, taking a sip from the Peroni. 'Not while scum like him walk the streets with total impunity. I mean, what the hell does he have to do to get a proper sentence? Eat one of the prime minister's kids?'

Cleaver made a kind of grunting noise in agreement and took a hard pull on his beer, finishing it. I'd noticed he was a big drinker, but he tended to hold it well and I'd never seen him drunk before, although it did tend to loosen his tongue, which was useful. 'Do you want another one?' he asked, getting to his feet.

I told him I was fine, and relaxed back in the chair and looked round the room while he went off to resupply himself. There were no pictures on the wall or anything personal in there. It was like a show home. I wondered whether his bedroom was the same, and thought that if it was, then Cleaver lived an odd, and somewhat depressing, life.

Not that I could talk, of course.

'What would you do with Warman if you had the chance?' he said, sitting back down with his third Peroni.

I decided to eschew subtlety in favour of just going for it. 'I'd kill him,' I said, looking down at my beer bottle.

An unpleasant smile spread across his chops. 'Are you serious?'

I appeared to think about it for a couple of seconds, then nodded. 'Yeah,' I said. 'I'd do it. He's an animal. He shouldn't be walking this earth while my five-year-old girl, who never did anyone any harm in her life, isn't.' I felt bad even mentioning Grace in that conversation, but the truth was, a part of me really did believe what I was saying, and I could see that Cleaver believed me too. He had one of those very expressive faces that would be terrible for poker, and it was obvious he wanted to tell me more.

'How would you like to do something about it?' he asked.

I frowned. 'What? Kill Warman? Isn't that a little bit risky?'

'No. I mean, do something about it *all*.' He swung his arm in an expansive gesture. 'The whole thing.'

'What do you mean?'

'Listen, Chris. If you want to do something to change the world for the better, to get rid of some of the shit that drags us down, to make the fucking politicians sit up and listen, you tell me now, and I'll tell you how.'

I paused, watching him, knowing I was tantalisingly close. 'Are you serious?'

'How much do you really care? Enough to fight? Enough to kill rather than just talk about it?'

We stared at each other. I made it look like I was weighing my options. Something in his expression told me he was already worrying that he might have said too much.

'I care enough,' I told him. Pause. 'Yeah, I care enough.'

'Then we'll talk again, because there are people out there who are willing to take the law into their own hands and really do something to change things.'

'And who exactly are these people?' I asked.

At first he wouldn't tell me, and rather than push it, I let him move the conversation on to other things. We kept drinking, with me going at approximately half the rate he was, and I was just about to call it a night after my fourth Peroni when he seemed to suddenly come to a decision and turned to face me, wearing an expression of such intense determination it looked like he was holding in a huge fart.

'We're an organisation of like-minded men,' he said without warning. 'Fighters. Men who aren't prepared to accept the shit any more. We don't have a name, and we only allow a select few into our ranks, but if we let you join, you'll be part of a crew who'd die for each other. And you'll get paid as well.'

This was interesting, and explained the expensive furnishings and why Cleaver was always flush with cash. 'Who by?'

'All in good time, Chris,' he said with a knowing nod. 'All in good time.'

'I want in, Baz.'

'You can't just talk the talk, Chris. You've got to be prepared to walk the walk, and get your hands dirty.'

'I'm not afraid of that.'

He nodded. 'Good. I need to talk to some people. Then I'll get back to you.'

And I knew then that I was in.

10

I'll be honest, I hadn't been expecting Cleaver to open up to me like that. In fact, I was genuinely surprised that he *was* actually some kind of extremist. I'd hoped right up until the minute he came out with it that it was all some mistake, because now, for the first time, I could see an end to this assignment. I was angry with him as well. Why couldn't he just stick to being a cop putting criminals behind bars? Why complicate everything?

Sadly, I had no choice but to tell Rose Bennett of this latest development, so I called her the next day, and emailed her the downloaded recording of mine and Cleaver's conversation. We arranged to talk again at 8 p.m. that night when I was home from work. Rose seemed pleased, and told me I'd done a good job. 'But we need more, Chris. He could just claim the drink was talking. We need something we can use to lean on him.'

That 'something' arrived on a Friday just over a week later. I was in a pool car with Cleaver on the way to White City to meet with one of his informants. Three days earlier we'd had the first murder in the borough since I'd joined the GIU team – a sixteen-year-old called Marlon Venn stabbed to death in broad daylight by a group of four or five kids in hoodies who'd chased him on mountain bikes. We were certain plenty of people had seen it happen, but no one was coming forward, and Cleaver was hoping the promise of money might elicit some info from his informant, who lived nearby.

It was the first time he and I had been alone together since that night in his flat. The audio recorder on my watch was running and Cleaver was venting about the murder and the apparent lack of witnesses. 'These people fucking amaze me,' he said, shaking his head angrily. 'No one wants to help us and yet they're constantly complaining that their estates are being taken over by gangs, and that we're not doing anything about it. In this job, we're damned if we do, damned if we don't.'

'Maybe they're scared,' I said. 'I would be. The killers are probably their neighbours. If they speak out, that's their lives there finished.'

Cleaver was unconvinced. 'No way,' he snarled. 'They need to grow some balls. Stop acting like sheep the whole time. You know, that's the problem with this country. The people really are fucking sheep. They let the criminals, the politicians, all the scum trample all over them, and they do nothing. Nothing!' He literally spat that last word out, flecks of saliva spraying the windscreen, winding himself up into a rage.

'I know what you mean,' I said, sensing an opportunity.

'I know you do,' he said, his voice suddenly calming. 'That's why I got you this.' He pulled a mobile phone from his pocket and chucked it into my lap. 'Bought in cash and totally untraceable.'

I looked at it. Then at him. 'What do I need this for?'

'If you want to be a part of the organisation, the first rule is that when you communicate, you use burner phones supplied by us.'

'That's all well and good, Baz,' I said, 'but you still haven't told me exactly who "us" actually is. I'm not interested in joining an organisation that I know absolutely nothing about. Why the hell would I?'

'Fair enough, but you've got to understand, Chris, that what we're involved in is dangerous and could end up with us going down for a long time, so we need to trust you.'

I stared at him. It was time to lay my cards on the table. 'You either trust me or you don't, Baz. Make your choice. Because I'm not going any further with this until you do.'

Which was when he obviously made his choice and finally opened up. 'We're an army, Chris. And we're planning insurrection. The way we're doing it is targeting enemies of the people and taking them out.'

'Killing them?'

He took a deep breath and his jaw tightened. 'That's right.'

I almost felt sad then. I had him bang to rights, and it meant the end for him. 'So who are these enemies of the people you're looking to take out?'

'Left-wing public figures; Islamic hate preachers; released

paedophiles like that animal Munroe. The kind of targets who ordinary people hate. And that's how we're going to build our support. They'll see our successes, and they'll realise they can actually fight the power. We'll be the catalyst, Chris, the ones who get the revolution moving; but it'll be the people themselves who make the changes and put in a government that actually defends its citizens, deports Muslim terrorists and their supporters, puts criminals like Leon Warman behind bars for decades – or better still, strings him up like a dog – and finally makes the streets a safe place for our kids.'

Cleaver delivered this diatribe with real passion, his voice filling the confines of the car, unworried by the fact that what he was proposing was utter fantasy, but then I guess that's the thing about extremists. They're dreamers. They're interested in the glory, not the practicalities, and they don't worry about any of the contradictions, because it's the emotion that drives them.

'That's what I want as well,' I told him. 'Real justice. I don't know if I could actually kill someone, though. Have you ever, er . . .?'

He shook his head emphatically. 'No. But that's not our job. We operate in cells with very little communication between them. That way we're protected. But we have soldiers who carry out the attacks – and that's actual soldiers, not pretend ones. And then we've got those like us – police officers – who are there to provide intelligence and reconnaissance. And high-level business people who provide the finance.'

'It sounds well organised.'

'It is. We're very selective and we only use people with a good track record.'

'And who runs it?' I asked, probing deeper now that he seemed to be on a roll.

'We've got someone at the top who oversees it all.'

'Does he have a name?'

'No.' Cleaver's look was ice as he turned my way. 'He doesn't. And it doesn't pay to ask too many questions either. Not before you've proved yourself.'

I wanted to ask if there was an op currently in the offing, but I held back, knowing I'd already gone too far. 'I want in,' I said. 'Tell me how I prove myself.'

He pulled the car over next to a kids' playground where we were meeting the CI. 'Keep that phone on you the whole time. Only two people know its number. I'm one of them. You'll get a call in the next couple of days. Follow the instructions you're given.'

This was potentially moving into dangerous territory. 'At least give me some idea of what I'm going to be expected to do.'

'Just a proof of loyalty.'

I wasn't sure I liked the sound of that. 'You mentioned something about payment, Baz. I'm not exactly flush with money these days.' Which was true. Having to buy out Karen and pay the mortgage on my own had left me pretty brassic. And now that he was admitting everything to me, I wanted to get him on tape offering me money.

'All in good time, Chris,' he said, opening the car door. 'You've got to earn it first.'

And that was when I made one of the biggest mistakes of my life.

11

Tonight

Teller

'And that was when I made one of the biggest mistakes of my life,' says Chris Sketty, pausing in his story to look at me.

I nod slowly, taking it all in.

Sketty's an interesting character, and a good storyteller. If you look at photos of him from his old SO11 days, as I have done on many occasions, you will see an undeniably good-looking man with dark curly hair, cut a little long for a police officer, and a boyish face that looks like it's easily given to smiling. There's a photo in my possession taken around the February or March of his undercover days. He's leaning against the bar of the White Horse pub, grinning at the camera, clearly a little inebriated but looking in genuine good spirits. You can just make out DS Cleaver at the edge of the shot, ordering a drink from a female bartender, his bald head appearing to shine in the light. But the point is that Chris Sketty looks like a nice guy. The sort of man you would trust with your daughter. Someone who would do the right thing.

It's his secret weapon.

The last fourteen years haven't treated him that kindly. He's thinner, his face more lined, the hair now grey and beginning to recede at pace, and I suspect very strongly that the smiles don't come much any more.

But it's his own fault. Chris Sketty is the architect of his own demise.

He's sitting there now, still looking at me and wondering if I'm going to ask him what this so-called 'biggest mistake' was. It's not mentioned in the dossier. I made sure that not everything is in there. That's because I want to lay a few traps for him, see if he walks into them or not. He's good. There's no question about it. A real smooth operator. When he tells his story, I almost want to believe it happened just as he says it did.

But always I have to tell myself that the man sitting in front of me is a manipulative killer.

'And what was that mistake?' I ask him, breaking the silence.

'You want to know the truth?' He gives an empty laugh. 'Of course you do. Well, I'll tell you. My mistake was that I didn't report that conversation to DS Bennett.'

I was aware of this, of course. And I wasn't sure if he would admit it or not. I'm impressed. 'Why didn't you report it?' I ask. 'Surely if you'd given her the recording of Cleaver's admission of his involvement, that could have ended everything there and then?' Because it would have done, and then my beautiful Victoria, the woman I worshipped with every breath in my body, would still be alive and here with me now, making my last years on earth a pleasure rather than the bleak, lonely trudge to the end that they are now. I take a long breath and my words when I say them are quiet in the room but simmer with a deep anger. 'It could have saved my wife's life.'

He sighs. 'I know that now. And I'm sorry, I really am. But at the time, it was complicated. I didn't want Rose and Marina Reineke to use that recording to lean on Cleaver, and there are two reasons why. One: I didn't think it would be enough to turn him. I thought he'd probably front it out. After all, he hadn't given me any money, and he was still vague. And it would ruin the whole op and mean I'd have to leave the GIU team there and then, and under a cloud too. And two: I thought that if I did whatever act of loyalty Cleaver had in mind, that would give me the extra leverage we needed.' He sighs a second time, looking away towards the fire. 'I suppose I just thought I knew best. I was young. I was probably naïve. And I didn't want to lose what I had with that team.'

A plausible answer, I'll admit. And he's right, he was young, and by his own admission, somewhat gung-ho. But put yourself in Sketty's position. You're an undercover police officer hoping to stop a potential terrorist attack, under pressure from your bosses to get a result. You'd report every important conversation you had with your target, wouldn't you? That way you'd always be able to cover yourself.

But he didn't.

I take a sip from my whisky and our eyes meet once

again. There's pain in his, and he really wants me to believe him. Do I? I have to admit I believe much of what he's told me so far. The chronology fits, and he's admitted to some minor infringements that aren't on the public record. But now we're getting to what I would describe as the murkier parts of the story, and when you hear more, I think you'll find that you'll be just as sceptical as me.

12

The problem for me was that everything happened so fast. Like I said, it was on the Friday that Cleaver had given me the burner phone and told me that I needed to prove my loyalty. That same night it was the team's end-of-week drinks in the White Horse. All afternoon I'd been debating whether or not to tell Rose Bennett about the new development, but when the eight of us were sat round our usual corner table, exhausted after a week of twelve-hour days, and with the drinks and the conversation finally flowing, I convinced myself to mull on the best way forward over the weekend. After all, I still had the recording. And I was pretty certain, given Baz Cleaver's surprisingly cheery demeanour that night, that no major attack was imminent.

As per Cleaver's instructions, I kept the burner phone on me all weekend, and it was when I was heading up to bed on Sunday night that it finally started ringing.

I looked at my watch: 11.10. I'd cooked a big meal that night – ribeye steak, portobello mushrooms and sautéed paprika potatoes – and I'd been in the pub at lunchtime with my old mate Ty Quelch for something of a session, so I was knackered and I almost didn't answer. I often wonder what would have happened if I hadn't. Maybe it would have made no difference. I was in with Cleaver at that point and potentially already on the road to disaster, but it's also possible things could have been completely different. That I might have somehow avoided what was going to happen.

But you can think about something in the past all you like, it's still the past, and the fact is, for better or for worse (and for me it was definitely worse), I did answer that call.

'Who's this?' I asked, without identifying myself.

'Your good buddy,' answered Cleaver. 'I've got a job for you. It's urgent. Tonight. Get a pen. You need to write this down.'

I looked round, found one on top of the chest of drawers. 'Go on.'

'Drive to the junction of Chiswick High Road and Marlborough Road. There's a photographer's next to it on the right if you're heading west. Get there for midnight.'

'Tonight?'

'I told you it was urgent,' said Cleaver

'Jesus, why are you foisting this on me now? I'm in my pyjamas, and that's a good forty-five minutes away.'

'It's thirty-eight from your place. I've just checked on the map. If you leave in the next ten minutes, you'll be there on time. Do a good job and there'll be a bonus for you.'

I made a grunting noise down the phone to show him I was irritated (not that he would have cared), but really, I was also a little excited at the prospect of getting further inside Cleaver's organisation. 'What am I doing when I get there?'

'You're picking up one of our people. He'll be wearing a black hoodie with the hood pulled up, and when he opens the car door, he'll identify himself by saying "Hi, Winston." You need to help him break into a vacant flat. I remember you said they taught you lock picking in SO11. He'll plant something there, then you just take him back to wherever he wants to be dropped off.'

'I need to know what he's planting, Baz.'

'No you don't, Chris. That's the beauty of it. You're just providing a little bit of help for our man, and if you have any problems, like being stopped by the police, you show them your warrant card and then you're on your way.'

Rose had informed me more than once of all the rules and regulations I was supposed to follow while I was undercover. But the thing about undercover ops, especially fourteen years ago, was that the rules were pretty fluid. I was allowed to commit minor crimes in order to prove my loyalty to the criminal organisation I was infiltrating, but there was no set definition of what a minor crime was, and in truth, with no idea what it was the operative was planting in this vacant flat, it was hard to know whether I was putting my career in jeopardy by taking part. It was also clear from the short notice I'd been given that Cleaver still wasn't entirely sure he could trust me. He wanted to keep me off guard until I'd proved myself, which was another example of how careful he was.

So, you can appreciate the difficult position I'd been put in. But it was also a time for quick decisions, and I made mine.

'I'm on my way.'

13

I was out the door in nine minutes, and took my time on the drive. I didn't want to get there early and have to hang around. The recorder in my watch was on, but I didn't call Rose. I was certain I was in no danger, and there was no time to set up a sting to catch Cleaver's man in the act of breaking in.

On the drive to the rendezvous, though, my excitement gave way to gloom that this was what my life had come to. Working on a cold, damp March evening while the rest of the world were relaxing indoors with their loved ones, making the most of the weekend's last gasp. Sundays had always been a special time for Karen, me and Grace. We'd always do something in the day – drinks with friends, a walk – followed by an early-evening roast, then, when Grace was tucked up in bed and I'd read her a story, Karen and I would settle down on the sofa, entwined in each other's arms in front of the TV with a decent bottle of wine and an easy detective show like *Midsomer Murders* or *Poirot*, where even the criminals had class, and the murders were done with some decorum. Fun times. Not like this.

It was 11.58 according to the car's clock when I pulled up outside the photographer's. Chiswick High Road's usually a hive of activity in the evenings, but it was raining hard and the street was quiet. A young couple walked past, laughing underneath a shared umbrella, and I was just thinking that that was what Karen and I had been like only a few short years earlier when a figure with his hoodie pulled up appeared out of nowhere, walked right in front of the couple as if they weren't even there, forcing them to stop, then pulled open the passenger door and slipped silently inside.

Sometimes you know immediately when you're in the presence of someone dangerous. Your body reacts instinctively, releasing adrenaline, and you feel every muscle tighten, as if preparing for fight or, more likely, flight. The man sitting next to me was tall and lean, with very long arms and legs, almost like a spider's, and large, gloved hands. His face, pale as ice and full of sharp angles, radiated a simmering evil beneath the hood, reminding me of a snake that could strike out at you at any time. But it was the smell that came off him – musty, almost decaying – that made his presence in the car next to me so oppressive. Without looking my way, he placed the rucksack he was carrying on the floor between his legs and stared straight ahead through the rain-splattered windscreen. After a pause that made me wonder if he was actually the man I was meant to be picking up, he finally spoke, his voice a deep, throaty whisper.

'Hi, Winston.'

And that was my introduction to Aaron Clarn.

At that time obviously I didn't know his name, and knew there was no point asking it. Instead I asked him where he wanted to go.

That was when he finally turned my way. I'd half expected him to look like some sort of gargoyle, but he wasn't bad-looking if you liked the rugged, craggy type. He had a long, narrow face ending in a jaw that jutted out a little too far, and there was a thin scar on his lower cheek. His eyes were narrow and cold, though, as he observed me like I was some kind of specimen under a microscope. This was not the sort of man who was looking to win friends and influence people. I made a mental note of his features, knowing that I might have to ID him from police mugshots later.

'You know Sherman Road in Fulham? Head for there.'

I nodded. This was in the days before smartphones, but luckily I knew west London well.

We drove in complete silence. He had this way of staying completely still and staring straight ahead. It was disconcerting, but I had a feeling it was a deliberate act on his part, a clear power play, so I did my best to ignore it, cursing Cleaver for not being here in my place. This wasn't how I'd expected the undercover job to go. I suppose I'd always figured I'd be introduced to Cleaver's fellow conspirators and that there'd be some kind of shared camaraderie and they'd just tell me all their plans while I recorded them. But clearly that was a dramatic underestimation of the situation, because right now it was me who was being led by the tail. All I had going for me was that I'd switched the watch to video on the way here, so at least I'd hopefully capture an image of him.

It wasn't until we got to Sherman Road that he spoke again, giving me directions in barked orders, usually without looking at me, until five minutes later, he told me to stop.

We were now on a plush, tree-lined residential road of large detached and semi-detached houses.

'That's the place,' he said, motioning with his head towards a three-storey Edwardian property set back from the road behind a low wall, with half a dozen cars parked in the driveway. There was a light on in one of the second-floor windows, and an outside lamp illuminating the front door.

'I was told it would be vacant,' I said. 'It doesn't look very vacant to me.'

'It's flats. We need to get into the ground-floor one. It's empty.'

I decided to try my luck. 'What are we planting in there?'

He fixed me with a stony stare. 'You should have been told not to ask questions. So don't. Just get me inside the building, and inside the flat. Then come back and keep watch. Understand all that?'

I wanted to answer back, to tell him he could get in there himself if he was going to be like that, but I didn't. Because I had no idea how he'd react. There was something unhinged about him, and it scared me. 'Okay,' I said calmly, silently cursing Cleaver once again.

Like Clarn, I was wearing gloves and a hoodie, and I pulled the hood over my head as I got out of the car and followed him across the road and through the open double gate into the driveway.

The gravel crunched noisily beneath my feet, forcing me to almost tiptoe over to the front door. Clarn, on the other hand, seemed to glide across it, making virtually no sound at all. When we reached the door, he stepped aside while I produced a set of picks from my pocket.

Every surveillance officer worth his or her salt knows how to break into a property. It surprises most people when they find out that we're taught how to do it, but then you have to remember that part of our job is planting bugs in suspects' houses without them realising we've been there. I was a good lock picker. I enjoyed the challenge.

There wasn't much challenge with this lock, though. It was a standard Chubb at least ten years old, providing only the most basic of deterrents. Even more conveniently, the outside lamp provided all the light I needed, and I quickly went to work, using the torque and picks. I didn't like having Clarn there standing over me watching – his was the kind of looming, silent presence that would put anyone off their game – but I ignored it, and thirty seconds later, the door clicked open.

I followed him inside. The hallway was dark, with a button on the wall that activated the light. I didn't turn it on, not wanting to attract attention.

He motioned towards the door to my right, and I slipped on my head torch and checked the lock – a new Yale dead-lock, which was a bit more of a challenge than the other one, but nothing insurmountable. Three minutes later, I felt a sense of relief as it clicked open, pleased that my part in this was over.

He didn't acknowledge what I'd done, simply gave me a dismissive look and mouthed the words 'wait for me', then slipped inside, the pack containing God knows what on his back, silently closing the door beside him.

I didn't hang about, heading straight back to my car, already wondering if I'd made a big mistake. Because this was the problem. I wasn't an undercover officer by training. In fact, I'd had no training at all bar a couple of lectures on the dos and don'ts of the job. I was twenty-six years old, experienced as a police officer but not that experienced, and still grieving for my daughter and my marriage. What I'm trying to say is that my judgement wasn't what it should have been, and that's always the problem when you're on your own and out on a limb.

I sat there in the car with the engine and lights off, slumped down in my seat out of sight so I wouldn't be spotted by anyone walking past. I felt exposed out here. And cold too, without the engine running.

Across the street, a light came on in the ground-floor flat that we'd broken into. I looked at my watch. He'd been in there for five minutes now. What the hell was he doing? Surely it couldn't take that long just to plant something incriminating. I might not have been a burglar, but I still knew that the first rule of burglary was to be in and out fast.

Another minute passed and a second light came on inside. I took a deep breath, told myself to stay calm. It crossed my mind that the flat might have been occupied, and the occupant had ambushed Clarn and was now in the process of calling the police. But I dismissed that notion quickly enough. Someone like Aaron Clarn wouldn't have been taken out without a serious fight, and one that would probably have woken up the whole building, as well as alerting me.

Then what was the hold-up?

Headlights appeared in my rear-view mirror, and I slid right down in my seat as a car came past, driving slowly. Thankfully it was just a taxi. It spooked me, though. I didn't like being here in my own car. I didn't like being here full stop. The second light had gone off inside now, but the other one was still on. Clarn had been in there almost nine minutes now by my estimation.

I knew I couldn't leave him there, but I couldn't sit here any longer either, not without knowing what the hell was going on, because this wasn't just about planting evidence. It couldn't be. He'd have been out of there ages ago.

When the time hit ten minutes, I got out of the car and went back over the road, but instead of heading for the front door, where I'd have to pick the lock again, I walked slowly round the outside of the building. The windows were double-glazed and the curtains pulled so I couldn't see or hear anything coming from inside, even when I put my ear right up to the glass.

It was when I was coming to the end of the building that I heard it. A noise from the other side. I stopped, took a tentative step forward and craned my neck round the corner.

And saw a silhouetted figure climbing out of the nearest window.

Straight away I could see it was Clarn. He was only ten feet away, crouching like a monkey on the ledge, the pack still on his back. He must have sensed my presence, because his head suddenly snapped round my way, his expression murderous beneath the hood, and in the next second he'd landed on the gravel in a crouching position, a huge black-bladed hunting knife appearing in his gloved hand like a lethal appendage.

'It's me,' I hissed loudly, stepping out into the open and raising my hands in an instinctively passive gesture.

But it was too late. Clarn was on me before I fully knew what was happening, effortlessly driving his hand through mine to grab my throat while the knife blade shot towards me, stopping only a bare inch from my eye.

Which was when I realised there was blood on the blade.

Clarn's eyes were ice and his grip on my throat was far too tight. 'What the fuck are you doing?' he snarled. 'You're meant to be in the car.'

Anger overcame my fear then. 'Let go of my throat,' I hissed at him. 'You were so long I thought something was wrong.'

His grip loosened and he lowered the knife, thrusting it into a sheath hanging from a shoulder holster beneath his coat, but he was still giving me the death stare. 'Don't ever creep up on me again,' he said. 'You're lucky I didn't kill you.'

And I knew I was. He'd been half a second away from it,

and there's very little that's more frightening than knowing you've been half a second away from death. I stepped backwards, rubbing my neck, wanting to ask him why the hell he'd come out of the window with blood on a knife I hadn't even known he had, but concluded it was a lot easier to just stay quiet.

Turning his back on me, Clarn crept quickly back over to the open window and, while I watched, slammed his elbow into it three times in quick succession until the glass broke, the noise loud in the silence of the night. He then pushed the window shut and stalked past me, pulling his hood down over his face with a hissed 'Move!'

I was still shocked by the way he'd turned on me, and how vulnerable I'd been, but self-preservation was also kicking in and I knew we had to get out of there fast. I followed him across the driveway, watching for any lights coming on in the building, because the last thing I needed was someone clocking my car leaving, but none did, and the street was still empty as we crossed back to the car. The rain was coming down harder now and I was grateful for the way it muffled the noise as I started the engine and pulled away, knowing in my heart that this time I'd really messed up.

14

I dropped Aaron Clarn off twenty minutes later at the end of a narrow street of terraced housing in White City. The journey there had been made in silence, although I could see from his body language that he was agitated, and the musty smell he gave off was more pronounced. All he said on parting was 'Remember to keep your mouth shut.'

And then he was gone, a long shadow stalking away into the darkness.

It was far too risky to follow him, and in truth, I wanted to put as much distance between that bastard and me as possible, so I took a quick note of the street name, waited a few more seconds and then pulled away, by which time he'd already disappeared from view.

But I was way too wired to sleep, and I needed some answers.

Only one person could provide me with them, and I drove straight to Cleaver's flat with the window down to get the stench of Aaron Clarn out, and called him from the street outside on the burner phone he'd given me.

The phone rang for a long time and I was contemplating just going up to the front door of his block and holding my finger down on the buzzer when he finally answered with an irritated and confused 'Hello?'

'It's me,' I said. 'We've got a serious problem.'

'What kind of problem?' He seemed more awake now.

'We need to talk about it in person.'

'Can't it wait until tomorrow?'

'If it could wait until tomorrow, I wouldn't be calling.'

He sighed. 'Where are you?'

'Sitting in my car just down the road from your flat.'

'Okay, give me a minute and come up. I'll buzz you in.'

Five minutes later, I was standing outside his front door while he unlocked it from the inside. He opened it a few inches on a chain, looking worryingly alert for the time of night, and having presumably satisfied himself that it really was me, and I'd come alone, he let me in, closing the door behind me and bolting it. He was dressed in a T-shirt and tracksuit bottoms and he didn't look pleased to see me. But then I wasn't pleased to see him either.

He picked up his bug finder and ran it up and down my body, before patting me down.

'What the hell is this?' I demanded. 'I thought you were meant to trust me.'

He grunted derisively. 'I don't trust anyone a hundred per cent.' He paused the bug finder over the watch, which was already recording. It didn't bleep, but he still took an unhealthy interest in it. 'Take the watch off,' he said.

'What for? It's my watch, for Christ's sake.'

'You want to talk to me, you take it off and put it on the table.'

I did as he demanded while he pulled out the two phones I was carrying, flipped them both open to check the screens, then put them on the table next to the watch, covering everything with a cushion, before beckoning me into the kitchen. 'Right,' he said, leaning against his worktop. 'What's the problem?'

'I think you know.'

He rubbed his eyes. 'Don't piss me about, Chris. It's one thirty in the morning. Just say what you have to say.'

'You set me up. That animal I picked up tonight didn't just plant something in that flat I helped him get into. He stabbed someone. I saw the knife. I saw the blood. And I want to know who it was and why the hell he did it.'

Cleaver cursed and looked away, running a hand over his bare head. What worried me most was that he looked surprised too. 'I honestly don't know anything about that,' he said, looking back at me.

'Are you serious?' I demanded, trying hard not to raise my voice. The last thing we needed was the neighbours listening in. 'What kind of organisation is this where one hand doesn't have a clue what the other one's doing?'

'The type that's successful.'

'And who the hell was that psycho you had me pick up tonight? He belongs behind bars, not on the streets.'

'You don't want to know.'

'I do. Trust me.'

'He's an operative of ours. One of the soldiers. That's all you need to know.'

I shook my head with genuine anger. 'Why did you get me involved, Baz? I thought you were meant to be my friend.'

'I got you involved, Chris, because you said you were prepared to fight for our cause. And to kill.'

'Not like this, though. I told you that if I had to kill, I would, but I'm always going to want to know who the hell I'm meant to be killing, and why. Do you even know who lives at that flat?'

'No, I don't. I was told what I told you.'

'I don't believe you, Baz. And do you know what? I think I might go and talk to the Chief about this, or maybe my old colleagues at SO11.'

'And tell them what, Chris? Just assume someone *was* stabbed in there tonight—'

'I'm not assuming it. It happened.'

'Either way, remember you helped Clarn break into the place. You're an accessory to the crime. How's that going to look?'

And that, thankfully, was Cleaver's first mistake. Mentioning the man I'd picked up tonight by name. I immediately memorised it before answering him. 'So, you're blackmailing me?'

He shook his head. He appeared genuinely concerned, as if he really didn't want to have to be doing this to me. 'It's not like that, Chris.'

'It is from where I'm standing.'

'We have to be certain we can trust you. I'm sorry

about what happened tonight, and you getting lobbed right in at the deep end. But I can tell you this, hand on heart: whoever the person was in that flat – assuming it *was* a person, not an animal – it will be someone who's an enemy of justice.'

I needed to take advantage of the guilt I could see he felt and make him open up a bit more, so I said: 'That's not good enough.'

'It's going to have to be good enough. Don't do anything to rock the boat, Chris. I'm warning you. You'll be playing with fire.'

'Now you're threatening me.'

He shook his head. 'No, mate, I'm not. I'm just telling you. You're in deep now, you're a part of us. You'll be paid well, you'll be protected, and if you do as you're told, you'll prosper. But you can't leave now. It's too late.' As he spoke, he stared at me imploringly, as if he had my best interests at heart. Unusually for him, there was no threat in his posture, but unfortunately there was a certainty in the way he delivered his words, and I knew without a doubt that he'd been in my position once. Caught up in something out of his control.

'Is that how you got involved? One day you found yourself in too deep like me, and you had no choice but to go along with things?'

Straight away, I could see I'd hit a nerve. He nodded. 'Yeah. It is.'

'What did you do to give them the hold over you?'

'I don't want to talk about that.'

But I kept probing. 'How many more of us are there in the same boat?'

'I don't know exactly, but there are more of us than anyone thinks. We succeed because we're careful.'

'And who pulls the strings? Who is it we're all working for?'

Cleaver was silent a few moments, evidently deciding how much to tell me. 'The man at the top is called Kalian Roman,' he said at last. 'He's the one who controls everything. I've never met him and I've got no idea who he is. But I do know that if you cross him, you're dead. It doesn't matter who you are. He's like some sort of Keyser Söze figure, but he has tentacles everywhere, and a lot of important people in his pocket. That's why I don't want you to do anything foolish.'

'What did you recruit me for? You must have known how it was going to pan out.'

Cleaver sighed. 'It's my job to find like-minded people. And you're like-minded.'

And that was my problem. I'd proved to be too good at my job, and now I was caught in a trap. I could go to Rose and tell her what had happened. As I said, I was allowed to commit certain minor crimes to prove my loyalty, and breaking and entering could potentially be included on that list. But what if I had indeed been complicit in murder? Because if that was the case, I had no doubt CTC would cut me loose in an instant, and I'd be on my own.

Cleaver gave me a sympathetic look. 'Do you want a drink, now that I'm awake?' he asked. 'I've got Jameson.'

I did want a drink – Jesus, I did – but I was exhausted too, and didn't much fancy spending any more time with Cleaver that night. 'No, I'd better be going. We're on duty in seven hours.'

'Sure,' he said, and at that moment, the phone in his track-suit bottom pocket bleeped. He took it out and read whatever message he'd received, which was when I noticed that the phone was a Nokia, like the burner one he'd given me, not the Sony Ericsson he used for work. He put it back in his pocket, trying to act casual. 'I'll see you in the morning, right?'

'Will do,' I said, and, after retrieving my phones and watch from under the cushion on the hall table, walked out of there, wondering who it was who'd texted him.

My car was parked a hundred yards up from his building, and when I got back to it, I sat in the driver's seat for a few minutes with the engine off. Not sure what I was waiting for. Just a hunch, I suppose, that the text Cleaver had received was important. And that something might happen as a result of it.

And it did, because while I was sitting there, I saw him come striding purposefully out of the front of the flats. He'd got dressed and was wearing jeans and a bomber jacket. He stopped and looked up and down the road, and I slid down in my seat because I knew he was checking to see if I was still there, although my car was well hidden amongst all the others parked on the street. Then, apparently satisfied that he was safe, he walked away from me to his own car – a black Ford Escort with dark windows – gave it a quick once-over with the bug finder, then got in and drove away.

There was no point trying to follow him at this time of night. He'd clock me in a minute. But his actions told me everything I needed to know. He was far more involved in what had happened that night than he was letting on.

The question was: what was I going to do about it?

15

It was still the question bugging me as Monday dawned and, to my eternal regret, I decided to hold back until I found out whose blood it had been on Clarn's knife.

Monday passed, with the team still busy on the Marlon Venn murder. You remember, the one a few days earlier where the sixteen-year-old kid was stabbed by thugs on mountain bikes. I kept my ear out round the station and scanned the news and the papers for word of anyone attacked in their home in the Fulham area, but there was nothing. It was the same on Tuesday, and I began to feel irrationally optimistic that maybe it *had* been a guard dog Clarn had stabbed, and that for whatever reason the owner had decided not to report it.

Then, when I walked into the station on Wednesday morning, fifteen minutes early for the 8 a.m. shift, my optimism died an immediate death. The Chief was the only one in our team office and he was in the process of putting his coat on. 'We've just got a report of a dead body at a flat in Fulham,' he told me. 'No one from CID's here at the moment, so you and me need to help secure the scene.'

All the way over there I was praying the report was wrong.

But of course it wasn't.

When we pulled up outside the block, only a few cars down from where I'd been sitting three nights earlier, there were already two squad cars double-parked opposite the entrance. We put on plastic gloves and strode over to where four uniforms were talking to a group of half a dozen civilians, who looked like the other residents, on the driveway.

One of the uniforms peeled away as we approached, and we produced our warrant cards as the Chief introduced us, asking the uniform – an older guy in his forties – what we had.

'It's pretty gruesome,' he said, pulling a face. 'Young woman. Looks like she's been stabbed.'

'Who called it in?' asked the Chief.

The uniform motioned towards a tall, striking-looking woman in her early twenties with a thick head of curly black hair, who was being comforted by a female uniform. 'Her friend there. She hadn't heard from the victim for a few days. She came round. There was no answer, and when she walked round the side of the building, she saw that the kitchen window had been broken. She called us, and we forced entry. And don't worry, we haven't touched anything.'

'The victim got a name?'

'Kerry Masters.'

I felt a wave of nausea. A name personalises everything.

The Chief immediately took charge. 'Keep everyone outside and well away from the front door,' he told the uniform, 'and put someone on the main entrance to stop anyone else coming through. And don't let the friend go anywhere. We'll need to speak to her. Which flat is it?'

'The ground floor, on the right.'

The Chief thanked him and motioned me to follow as he strode purposefully up the steps and into the building.

'Shouldn't we wait for SOCO?' I asked, desperate not to have to look inside. Strictly speaking, now that the death of this young woman (I couldn't bring myself to say her name) had been confirmed, the scene was off limits to us until we were fully geared up from head to toe in protective coveralls, but like I've said before, things were a little more flexible in those days.

'I want to see what we're dealing with here,' he said. 'It's not that I don't trust the uniforms, but, you know . . .' He let the words drift off.

The door to the flat – the one I'd picked while that animal had stood behind me waiting – was now half open, where the uniforms had forced it.

The Chief turned to me. 'You ready? You don't have to come in, you know. You can talk to the victim's friend.'

He'd given me an out, and I wanted to take it, but something forced me to say no. I don't know what it was. Bravado? A desire to prove myself to him? Or punishment, for what I'd been a part of? Probably a mix of all three.

But either way, I felt a sickness in my gut as I followed him inside.

The flat was cold, but it didn't disguise the smell of decay. I swallowed, following the Chief through into a surprisingly spacious living room with a sofa and two armchairs arranged round a modern TV. It was relatively tidy, if lived in, with a used mug and an empty wine glass on a side table, and there were no signs of a struggle.

The kitchen – narrow and long – was off to one side through an open door, and from where we both stood we could see right through it to the broken window at the end. There was only one other door, and it was slightly ajar. The Chief walked over, and as soon as he opened it further, the smell grew stronger.

'Shit,' I heard him say, my view of what he was looking at temporarily blocked by his bulk.

Then he took a step into the bedroom and moved to one side.

The bloated corpse of a blonde-haired woman dressed in pale silk pyjamas lay face upwards on a double bed with crumpled sheets, one arm hanging over the side, legs splayed apart as if they'd been pulled open. There was blood pooled on her pyjama top from the neck to the belly with a separate pool round her groin; and more was splattered on the sheets around her. This woman had died violently, horribly, and even from a distance I could see that she'd fought for her life.

I turned away, unable to look, the atmosphere suddenly stifling.

The Chief looked at me. 'Are you all right?'

'Yeah, I'm fine,' I managed to answer, even though it was pretty obvious I wasn't. I'd seen and smelt dead bodies before, of course – you can hardly avoid it when you're a cop – but not ones whose deaths I was indirectly responsible for. I told him I'd see him outside because I didn't want to contaminate the crime scene.

'Grab the friend, find out who she is and anything she knows about the girl. I'll meet you out there.'

I almost stumbled out of the flat, my legs unsteady, my mind racing as I tried to work out what to do now. The first thing was to find out why Cleaver's organisation had wanted her dead. And then at the very least I could avenge her death and expunge the guilt for my part in it.

The friend was sitting on the ground, cross-legged and with her head in her hands, as the uniform who'd spoken to us stood above her with the WPC, looking concerned.

I took a couple of deep breaths, savouring what passed for fresh air in central London, and walked over to them. 'Is everything okay?'

'Miss Brown's just had a bit of a turn,' said the WPC. 'We're giving her a minute.'

The friend – Miss Brown – was breathing rapidly as if she was about to hyperventilate.

I crouched down beside her. 'It's going to be all right.' I looked up at the WPC and mouthed: 'What's her first name?'

'Anna,' she mouthed back.

'Take your time, Anna,' I said gently. 'My name's DC Sketty. We just need to ask you a few questions.'

'How did she die?' asked Anna Brown without looking at me, or taking her hands from her mouth.

'We don't know yet,' I said honestly. 'The doctor should be able to give us a good idea.'

'Was she murdered?'

I tensed. It wasn't an obvious question. Most people don't expect a friend or loved one's death to be murder, because in almost all instances it isn't. 'Why do you ask that?'

'Because of the broken window,' she answered, which showed that in those days I probably wasn't the best detective.

'It looks from first glance like it could be murder,' I admitted, knowing that it was going to be reported as such very soon anyway.

'Oh God,' she said, her sobbing and rapid breathing getting louder and quicker. 'What am I going to tell her sister?'

Before I could ask her anything else (and given that I knew who'd killed her friend, I wasn't sure what I *could* actually ask), one of the station pool cars pulled up on the pavement and the head of Hammersmith CID, DCI James Calder, got out, along with two other CID guys.

I went to meet them. 'It's murder,' I said quietly, not wanting Anna to hear. 'A young woman.'

'Christ,' said DCI Calder, 'that's all we need. The second one in just over a week.'

I heard a crunch of footsteps on the gravel behind me and the Chief appeared at my side. 'It looks like a break-in gone wrong,' he told the DCI. 'The killer came in through the kitchen window, entered the bedroom and stabbed the poor girl to death. Some of the drawers were pulled out as if he was looking for valuables.'

'Any sign of sexual assault?'

The Chief shook his head. 'Not obvious. She was still wearing her pyjamas, although it looks like he stabbed her in the groin, so maybe that's how he gets his kicks. I've called SOCO. They're on their way.'

The DCI took a deep breath, looking like a man who was forever disappointed in the kind of savagery he had to see. He was a decent man. I could tell it hurt him. 'All right, Devon,' he said, 'we'll take over from here. You get your team to concentrate on the door-to-door for Marlon Venn.'

The Chief told him we were on it, then clapped me on the back. 'Come on, Chris. Let's get moving.'

When we got back to the car, he gave me a concerned look. 'Are you all right? You looked pretty cut up in there.'

'Yeah, I know,' I said, speaking slowly and wishing there was a way I could confide in him. The Chief had the kind of solid, calm presence that meant he'd know what to do, whatever the problem. But there was no way I could tell him about this. 'I don't like seeing an innocent young woman in the prime of her life torn apart like that.'

'None of us do,' he said. 'I was once the first on the scene where a whole family were dead. Mum and two sons stabbed to death in their beds, and the dad hanging in the bathroom. It gets to you having to be the one that sees it, I know. But that's who we are, Chris. The ones who clear up the mess. And we'll get this bastard. I promise you that.'

'I hope so,' I said, and I actually meant it too. But it also left me with a huge dilemma. Come clean and tell Rose, and risk losing everything, including my liberty, if they decided not to support me. Or try to sort it myself.

And to my eternal regret, I chose the latter.

16

Cleaver was already over in White City doing house-to-house inquiries, and he was just finishing talking to a woman on her doorstep when I pulled up on the other side of the road.

'Where have you been?' he asked, coming over to meet me.

The street was quiet and the woman had gone back inside her house, but I had no desire to air our dirty linen out here. 'I need to talk to you. Urgently. Let's do it in my car.'

He looked me up and down. 'I'm parked over here, we'll do it in mine. What is it?'

I wanted to punch him, I was so furious. 'You know exactly what it is.'

He glanced up and down the street, then motioned me to follow him. 'Come on.'

His car was parked in a deserted alleyway between two large blocks of flats that led down to an electricity sub-station.

'I went to see our murder victim in Fulham today,' I said,

once we'd got in. The audio on my watch was going but I wasn't sure how the hell I was going to be able to use any information I got without incriminating myself.

'What murder victim?' he said, frowning.

'The flat your friend Clarn went to in Fulham, and from which he emerged carrying a bloodied knife, contained the body of a young woman in her twenties, murdered in her bed. We got a call this morning at the station. Me and the Chief were the first detectives at the scene.' I looked at him with disgust. 'An enemy of the people, that's what you called her, Baz. She was just a girl.'

Cleaver looked poleaxed. If he was acting, he was damned good. 'Look, Chris, I had no idea of her ID.'

'But you knew I was being sent to a murder, right?'

'I just knew it was an op. That's all. I didn't realise it meant someone was going to be killed. And I don't like it either. But it was the boss's call.'

'Who? Kalian Roman?'

'Listen,' he hissed, 'stop mentioning his name. And don't ask questions. It's done now, and there'll be a good reason for it, I promise you.'

'How the fuck do you even know that? You didn't see her body. You didn't see what that animal did to her. He cut her to pieces with that knife. That doesn't bother you?'

He took a couple of deep breaths and gripped the steering wheel until his knuckles turned white. When he looked at me, he seemed genuinely torn up by what I was telling him. 'It wasn't meant to happen like that. It was meant to look like suicide. He fucked up.'

'So you *did* know it was a murder? And telling me he fucked up is meant to make me feel better, is it? What the hell is wrong with you?'

'Listen, we've just got to forget about it and move on.'

I shook my head furiously, the anger building. 'It doesn't work like that, Baz. I'm not being a part of this shit. Not any more.'

He turned to me, his expression cold. 'I don't think you understand, Chrissy boy. You're too far in to pull out now. That's how it works. It's like quicksand. Once you're in, you can't get back out.'

'Not for me. I'm out.'

'No,' he said firmly. 'You're not. You're party to that murder as well. You drove the killer there, broke into the victim's flat, then drove him away afterwards.'

'I didn't know what he was going to do. If I'd had half a clue, I'd have run a mile.'

'No one's going to believe that,' he said, and the problem was, I knew he was probably right. I was trapped.

But I didn't show it. 'No way,' I said. 'I'm an innocent in all this.'

'You're not an innocent in *this*, though, are you?' He leant over me to open the glove compartment and pulled out a digital camera. He pressed a couple of buttons on it until an image filled the screen, then thrust the camera under my nose.

As I watched, he pressed another button and a video started playing. It was of a darkened room, and because the quality wasn't brilliant, I had to squint to get a better view, which was when I saw the figure of Roger Munroe tied to a chair in his bedroom, blindfolded and gagged. As I watched, Cleaver came into view, walking over to Munroe and keeping his back to the camera.

A few seconds later, I entered the room with the kettle. There was no sound and I could see that Cleaver was still deliberately keeping his back to the camera, not that it would have done him much good in a court of law, as everyone knew he'd been there. The problem was, I was easily identifiable as I approached Munroe with the kettle, and then bent down to his mouth with it.

I looked away from the screen and glared at Cleaver. 'You bastard. You filmed me?' I couldn't believe he'd done it. Strangely, it felt like an even bigger betrayal than setting me up with the murder.

'I did it when you went into the kitchen,' he said, holding my gaze, looking almost proud of himself. 'I even blind-folded Munroe so he wouldn't see me. It's always good to have some leverage.'

It was that look that made me snap. With an angry yell, I grabbed him by the throat and threw a punch.

But Cleaver was fast. He thrust his head backwards, deflecting the blow with one hand while using the other to yank my arm away from his throat, then slammed a palm into my face as I kept coming.

I felt a sharp pain in my nose that made my eyes water, and now it was Cleaver's turn to grab my throat, his grip vice-like as he brought his face close to mine. 'Don't do anything stupid, Chris. If it's any consolation, I don't want to be in this position either. I like you. I always have. But I've got no choice. And now neither do you. Think about the money you're going to make, and the bigger picture. You said you were prepared to kill for the cause. You just have. Now leave it.'

He let go of my throat and I sat there shell-shocked, realising I'd been outmanoeuvred at every turn.

'Come on,' he said at last. 'We've got more statements to take.'

He got out of the car, and I had no real option but to follow.

17

No more was said about it, believe it or not, for the rest of the day. Cleaver and I did our door-to-door inquiries, both of us silent and brooding, before returning in separate cars to the station.

I was trapped, and the longer I left it without going to Rose, the harder it was going to be for me to come clean. The nightmare scenario was that the investigating officers would find a witness who'd seen me at the scene, although this, thankfully, was unlikely. Three days had passed before the girl's murder had been reported which meant it would be hard for the coroner to determine an exact time of death. The best he'd probably manage was a twenty-four-hour time period. But that still didn't mean I hadn't been spotted by someone, and my presence there wasn't something that could be explained away.

An outside team had been brought in to lead the investigation, bolstered by members of the station's CID, and they'd set up an interview room on the third floor. Later that afternoon, I collared one of the DCs I knew, Charlie Turner, and asked her in as casual a manner as possible whether they'd picked up any leads. I knew that, like us, CID had been doing house-to-house inquiries that day, and I was relieved when she told me that so far, also like us, they'd drawn a blank. 'No one ever sees anything in London, do they?' she said with a weary shake of the head. 'They're always too busy looking the other way.'

'Don't I know it?' I said, telling her about our own lack of success pounding the streets.

'Without the cameras and the forensics, we wouldn't solve a single case,' she said, and I smiled tightly, while my insides did a somersault as I wondered if any cameras had picked me up on Sunday night.

'Have you managed to get any footage of the street outside the victim's flat?' I asked.

She shook her head. 'Would you believe it, the street's not covered by council CCTV. If we get this guy, it'll be forensics.'

I could have kissed her, such was my relief. Instead, I headed back to the GIU office, where most of the team were in residence, and where a mountain of paperwork – the bane of police life – was waiting on my desk. I forced all thoughts of the killing out of my mind, deciding that for now I would continue to play everything by ear, and sat there quietly just getting on with things.

I was still sitting there at 5 p.m., and thinking about going home, when the Chief strode into the office followed by Cleaver and announced that we had a major breakthrough, not only in the Marlon Venn murder, but also in our ongoing quest to bring down our chief nemesis, JJ.

18

'We've had a double result with Leon Warman,' the Chief told us. 'He tells me that JJ is the one who ordered Marlon Venn's murder. Apparently the kid had been dealing in JJ's territory. Warman's also agreed to wear a wire for a meeting with JJ to discuss a drug shipment coming in to the Cliveden Forest estate.'

The office door was shut and we were all sat round in a semicircle while the Chief stood by the whiteboard, with Cleaver on a chair close by, ever the faithful lapdog. I could hardly bear to look at him.

There was a murmur of excitement from the team at this news. I tried to share it, but it wasn't easy.

'Nothing I'm about to say goes outside this room,' continued the Chief, surveying us in turn as he spoke. 'Understand?'

Everyone nodded.

'Good. This is a big one for us. Warman's meeting with JJ over at his flat tomorrow night at ten p.m. We're hoping he can get JJ to admit his part in the Marlon Venn killing then. Obviously Warman wants protection in case anything goes wrong, so we'll have spotters inside the estate and the rest of the team plus armed backup close by.'

'How are we meant to get spotters inside?' asked Nix. 'JJ's got the whole estate sewn up. No one gets in or out without him knowing.'

'A tenant's agreed to let us use her flat for surveillance,' answered the Chief. 'Chris and Baz: you're our two spotters. We'll be doing a major drugs sweep of the estate tonight at eleven p.m., going in with lights, dog units, TSG backup, and as we clear the area, you slip inside the tenant's flat on my signal. Simple as that.'

Cleaver and I looked at each other warily. The last place either of us wanted to be right now was in each other's company.

'What's the problem?' demanded the Chief, sensing the mood. 'You two had a lovers' tiff or something?'

'All good here,' said Baz.

Seeing as I didn't have much choice, I nodded as well. 'And with me, Chief.'

'Good. That's how I like it. Once you're in there, you set up the camera feed and then it's just a matter of waiting until tomorrow night, so bring your toothbrushes. The tenant, Mrs Abanks, will be in residence. She says she'll cook for you, you lucky boys.' He grinned. 'Treat it as a mini-break.'

I stared at him, aghast. 'In the Cliveden Forest estate?'

The Chief shrugged his huge shoulders. 'At least it's not self-catering. Anyway, you two are first responders in case anything goes wrong, although the rest of us will only be two minutes away, and we're not expecting any trouble. Warman's a trusted member of the crew and JJ's beginning to get cocky.'

'Are we going to be armed, Chief?' asked Cleaver.

'Telescopic batons and pepper spray only,' said the Chief. 'No guns. Warman says JJ has only very limited access to firearms, and we can't afford the team to be involved in an unauthorised police shooting. We'll have an SO19 gunship in reserve, but that's it.'

That, to me, was always the problem with the British brand of policing. The under-protection of the front-line officers. Whether it was facing a baying, petrol-bomb-throwing mob with nothing more than riot shields and batons, running into an unknown situation where you could be facing a gun without one of your own, or potentially worst of all, knowing that any action you took in the heat of the moment might one day lead to you being fired, or even thrown behind bars, you were always on your own. It's a situation that hasn't changed.

People used to ask me back in those days why I'd joined the force, given that I often vocalised these sort of complaints in conversation, and the truth, I told them, was that I really wasn't sure, other than it was more fun than working in an office and at least provided a decent pension (which it doesn't any more). But those weren't really the reasons at all.

There was only one reason I'd joined. And that was to prove myself.

When I was a boy of about ten or eleven, I was walking with my kid brother, Tom, who was eight, and these two much bigger boys were coming towards us the other way. Some animal instinct told me what was going to happen before it did: it was the grinning, predatory look they both gave us. As we stepped off the pavement to get out of their way, they stepped off too, blocking our path, and without warning one of them punched me in the face while the other punched my brother. Then they carried on walking. Just like that. As if it was the most natural thing in the world to punch a kid.

And we carried on walking too. My brother was trying hard not to cry. He couldn't manage it. I wanted to comfort him, but I didn't. I felt so helpless. My cheek was smarting from the punch, but it wasn't the pain that got me, it was the shame. I'd been punched and I hadn't punched back. The heroes in the books I read and the films I watched would never have allowed themselves to be humiliated like that. To the rational mind, I did what any kid would have done in the same circumstances, but that's not how you look at it when you're young. My humiliation was reinforced when my dad got back that night from work and, after Tom had blurted out what had happened, sat me down and demanded to know why I hadn't protected my brother. He even called me a coward, and told me to get even with the two kids, who both went to a nearby school.

But I didn't. I was scared, and this seemingly trivial little incident affected me deeply. Tom forgot about it as far as I know, but I didn't. And even though my dad, who was not an especially happy man, died of a heart attack when I was seventeen, I still felt deep down that I had to prove to him that I wasn't a coward.

This was why I was happy enough to head into the lions' den of the Cliveden Forest estate that night with just a baton and some spray for protection. The thought scared me, I won't try to deny that, and for all his faults (and by God there were many), I was glad I was going in with Cleaver rather than alone. But it would give me another chance to prove myself to those whose judgement mattered: the Chief and the rest of the team; my ex-wife and her new man, the grief counsellor. My beautiful daughter. My dead father. Even the brother I'd lost touch with a long time before.

But always, ultimately, to myself.

19

Considering the short notice, the raid on the Cliveden Forest estate was big, with all the trimmings: two dog units complete with barking German shepherds; two vanloads of officers from the Territorial Support Group, or TSG, in full riot gear; the whole of our team; and a dozen further uniforms from the station.

It was a miserable night and raining steadily, and those individuals stupid or desperate enough still to be out in it quickly made themselves scarce. In truth, very little dealing was done on the estate itself. Most outside buyers were too scared to enter it, especially at night, so most of the trade was done on the surrounding streets, and sometimes a lot further afield, which was where issues occasionally arose with rival gangs, and individuals like Marlon Venn.

As our raiding force fanned out across the centre of the estate, Cleaver and I and a couple of uniforms followed the Chief up onto the third floor of Jasmine House, the block that faced across the playground to Orchard House, where JJ had his base. As we moved along the walkway in front of the flats, the Chief told anyone poking their heads out to get back inside, his deep, authoritative voice and larger-than-life presence quickly ensuring compliance. He was well known on the estate, and respected by a lot of those who lived there as a man who had their best interests at heart, and it made me think that if we had a few more like him, the streets would be a lot safer.

The plan was simple. When the Chief passed the front door of the flat where Cleaver and I were staying, if he decided the coast was clear and there was no one watching, he'd knock once and keep going. The occupant had been primed to be waiting. She'd open the door, and we'd slip inside.

And that was exactly what happened. One moment we were out in the cold and wet of the estate, the next we were inside a small, comfortable sitting room with the TV on and an electric fire going.

As Cleaver put his backpack containing the camera equipment on the floor, our host, a tiny but formidable-looking white-haired lady of at least seventy-five, wearing a dressing gown and furry slippers, closed the door behind us.

'I'm Cecilia Abanks,' she said. 'You must be hungry. I've made you some dinner.'

'You needn't have,' I said as Cleaver and I took turns to shake her hand. But in truth I was glad she had, because whatever it was smelt good, and I was starving, having managed only a meat pie of questionable origin and a side order of some soggy, luminous lumps that were supposed to be carrots from the station canteen. If you are indeed what you eat, then the occupants of Hammersmith nick were fucked.

'It's the least I could do for the Chief,' she said. 'Now give me your coats and sit down at the table, and I'll bring it in.'

She motioned to a tiny table in the corner of the room with three rickety-looking chairs crowded round it. I removed my coat and took a seat while Cleaver set up the camera.

The meal Mrs Abanks had cooked was fish curry, and it was delicious, if murderously spicy. Cleaver, who liked to boast that he could eat vindaloo for breakfast, tried hard to appear like he was enjoying it, but he was sweating like a dyslexic on *Countdown*, and he had to cry off having managed barely a third of his plateful, claiming that he'd eaten earlier, even though I knew he hadn't. Mrs Abanks herself was chatty and open, and I helped her clear and wash up, then stayed talking with her at the table while Cleaver messed around with the laptop, trying to get the feed from the camera up and running. She was actually eighty-one years old, which I told her truthfully I'd never have guessed, and she'd lived on the estate for twenty years. She'd been widowed two years previously, after fifty-six years of happy marriage, and had three children, six grand-children, and her first great-grandchild on the way.

'I bet they keep you busy, Mrs Abanks,' I said.

'They keep me *alive*,' she answered, a real joy in her voice. 'Do you have children, Mr Sketty?'

'I did,' I said. 'A daughter. Grace.'

'Oh my,' she said, putting her tiny hand on mine. 'I'm so sorry, I didn't mean to cause you pain.'

'It's fine,' I told her with a reassuring smile, keen not to make her feel bad. 'You didn't. She brought a huge amount of joy to my wife and I while she was here, and that's good enough for me.'

It wasn't, of course. It never could be. But I didn't want to weaken. Not in front of her. Or, God forbid, Cleaver.

She gave me a smile that seemed to come right up from her heart. 'You're a good man, Mr Sketty,' she said.

'I try,' I said, gently extricating myself from her hand and getting to my feet. 'I do try.'

But I could picture the body of the blonde-haired woman, now officially identified as twenty-year-old Kerry Masters, bloated and bloodied on her bed, and I knew that I could never try hard enough.

20

Surveillance jobs are not only boring, but they can also be intensely claustrophobic. And when you're stuck doing one with someone you really don't like, and have nothing to say to, it's almost physically painful.

Cleaver and I took turns to sleep on the sofa. Whichever one of us was awake monitored the laptop showing the camera feed. The camera itself was hidden in a specially created fake vase that Cleaver had brought in his backpack, and which could be put on the windowsill without attracting attention. Not surprisingly, there wasn't much to report, although in the early hours of the morning, after the rain had cleared, I could make out a couple of kids hanging round the stairwell in front of Jasmine House, shooting the breeze and sharing a joint. But that was it.

The next morning, Mrs Abanks was up early and cooked us both a hearty breakfast of eggs, bacon and home-made fritters, saying how nice it was to have guests, and I made a mental note to leave her some money to help pay for all the food.

While we ate, she put on the local news, and one of the lead stories was the Kerry Masters murder.

'Poor girl,' said Mrs Abanks, shaking her head. 'Taken in the prime of her life.'

I glared at Cleaver, who at least had the decency to look away from my stare, and said something along the lines of how awful it was. But I couldn't bring myself to look at the screen. I still didn't know exactly what she looked like, having done everything I could to avoid the story, and it made it easier to handle if I couldn't put a face to the name.

'The streets just aren't safe these days,' continued Mrs Abanks. 'And this estate is terrible. There are a few bad apples who make life hard for everyone else and corrupt the young with promises of money for nothing.'

'That's why we're here, Mrs Abanks,' said Cleaver. 'To make the estate safer.'

'And I sincerely hope you do,' she said, but when she looked at him, I could see she wasn't entirely convinced that he was the kind of man she'd want doing it. Which was always Cleaver's problem. He'd been too successful in creating an image of himself as a hard man, and sometimes he came across as as much of a thug as the people he was chasing.

After cleaning the flat, Mrs Abanks went out to meet friends at the community centre, leaving Cleaver and me sitting there mentally prowling round each other.

'We can't carry on like this,' he said eventually, breaking the silence. 'We've got to work together.'

And the thing was, I knew it was true. For the moment,

I had no choice but to appear to cooperate with him while I tried to work out how I was ever going to dig myself out of this quagmire. But I also couldn't let what had happened go too easily either. 'You expect me just to forgive and forget?' I snapped. 'She was twenty years old.'

'You didn't kill her, Chris,' he said, pacing the tiny room. 'Remember that. You're just a soldier fighting for a cause, and sometimes people die for reasons you don't understand.'

'I don't even know what our cause is meant to be, Baz. And if it's killing young women, I don't want any part of it.'

'It's not,' he said firmly.

'Then why did she die? I need to know.' And I really did, because if I had the motive for her murder, then I might actually have some kind of leverage.

'I don't know,' he said, exhaling loudly. 'I'm trying to find out what I can. And when I do, I'll let you know. But that's all I'm willing to say right now. Okay?'

'Well, no, Baz. It isn't okay.'

'It's just going to have to be,' he said. 'Maybe this'll make you feel better.' He retrieved something from one of the pockets of his backpack and threw it into my lap.

It was a stack of twenty-pound notes bound by a couple of elastic bands and sealed in a plastic evidence bag.

'Five grand in sterling, totally untraceable. It's a bonus for your troubles, and to keep you onside. You might want to start thinking about setting up an offshore account for the cash. There'll be more coming. I could point you in the direction of someone who could help.'

It occurred to me that although Cleaver might have

believed in some kind of nutty right-wing cause, in reality this whole thing was about money more than anything else. He was being paid by Kalian Roman or one of his subordinates to do his bidding, and that bidding clearly included the murder of a young woman.

I stared at the money for a few moments, then got up and put it in the inside zip-up pocket of my jacket. I had no choice but to take it. If I appeared cooperative, then he might confide further in me, because I was certain he knew a lot more than he was letting on. 'I don't want to be involved in anything like that girl again, understand that?'

'You won't. You've got my word. Only the bad guys now.'

But I was right not to believe him.

21

After a long and tedious day, in which we just hung around drinking coffee and waiting, we finally got the call on the radio from the Chief at 9.50 p.m. to let us know that Warman – who was now referred to as Alpha – was in a taxi just about to enter the estate.

'He's fully wired up and ready,' continued the Chief, 'and all units are in position.'

It was a strange situation. There were me and Cleaver, wearing semi-covert earpieces and mics as we sat together bent over the laptop showing the camera feed like a couple of schoolboys, while Mrs Abanks sat in her chair a few feet away with a cup of cocoa watching an old episode of *Miss Marple* ('A Caribbean Mystery', one of her favourites and mine).

Cleaver used the laptop keys to move the camera around so we were able to pick up the taxi as it pulled up outside Jasmine House. Warman got out, wearing a very bright puffer jacket, and started walking to the main stairwell at the end of the building, head held high, arms swinging by his sides, looking like a man without a care in the world. You had to hand it to him, he had balls.

As Cleaver provided a running commentary of Warman's movements to the rest of the team, I got up and peeked round the curtain to get a better view of the scene.

The playground was empty tonight, bar a couple of young lovebirds sitting on the roundabout chatting, and Warman stood out like a lighthouse beacon in his jacket as he passed the communal bins.

There was a kid of about fifteen up on the third-floor walkway opposite, hood pulled down over his face, watching Warman. He leant over the balustrade and called out to him, and Warman responded with a languid wave, like he was a member of the royal family, which I suppose he as good as was round here, as one of King JJ's most trusted lieutenants.

As he entered the main stairwell at the end of Jasmine House, almost directly opposite us, and began climbing the steps, the kid who'd signalled to him from the third floor made his way towards the stairwell as well. On each floor there was a small alcove that was located between the walkways and the stairs. This was where the lifts were situated, and it was obscured from our view. Each alcove was lit by a single overhead light, and as I watched, the kid picked up a baseball bat that had been propped up against a wall out of view and, standing on tiptoes, used it to hit the light, plunging the alcove into near-total darkness.

'Shit, Baz, did you see that?' I said, turning round to where he was hunched over the laptop.

He nodded rapidly. 'Yeah, I did. OP1 to all units. We might have a problem. It's possible Alpha could be walking into an ambush.'

I grabbed the binoculars from the coffee table and peered round the curtain again, focusing them. I could see movement inside the alcove, figures silhouetted in the gloom. I moved the binoculars to the stairwell. Warman was on the flight between the second and third floors, probably ten or fifteen yards distant from them.

'This is OP1,' I said into my mic. 'There are figures next to the lifts on the third floor and they've cut the light. I'm certain it's an ambush. Request that you call Alpha and abort. He's only ten seconds away from them.'

'OP1, are you absolutely sure?' said the Chief into my earpiece.

'Ninety per cent,' I answered, because I couldn't be a hundred.

'I'll call him now.'

The problem was, we couldn't communicate with Warman directly, because for security reasons he was only wearing a hidden mic recorder, not an earpiece.

I could see through the binoculars that the Chief was calling him, because Warman looked down towards his pocket and pulled out his phone. He was still moving, though, and a second later he'd stepped out of sight behind a concrete pillar as he reached the door that would take him straight through into the alcove, where there were at least four shadowy figures waiting for him. But there was absolutely nothing I or anyone else could do except watch, as a couple of seconds later, a sudden violent commotion broke out in the darkness.

Even as Cleaver was frantically relaying this information over the radio, Warman came tumbling into view on the walkway, with two hooded attackers clinging to his coat and two more coming at him from the sides, both armed with knives. He was struggling like a wild man as he tried to throw off the two holding him, stumbling forward onto the railings lining the walkway. Trapped and with nowhere to go, he wasn't able to stop the two knifemen, who moved in close from either side and began stabbing him again and again through the puffer jacket. As Warman went down on one knee, all four of them fell on him like a pack of hyenas, thrusting their knives into him.

The whole thing happened in the space of five or six seconds, during which time Cleaver and I were just helpless spectators. But I wasn't going to stand there and watch Warman die. I flung down the binoculars and raced for the door, Cleaver following me, still firing out the running commentary into his mic. We were out of there fast, but Cleaver managed to shut the door quietly so as not to let on where we'd come from, and we sprinted along the balcony in the direction of the attack.

As I ran, I extended my expandable baton. The attackers, still some fifty yards distant, hadn't noticed us yet and continued their onslaught on Warman, who was now down on both knees, hanging onto the railings with one hand.

One of them finally spotted us just at the moment I yelled: 'Stop, police!', my voice echoing round the buildings, and they all bolted at the same time, charging into the stairwell from which Warman had just emerged and racing down the steps.

At the same time, the Chief and the rest of the team, backed up by three squad cars, came roaring up the access road, skidding to a halt outside Jasmine House just as the four attackers came spilling out of the ground-floor stairwell in front of them. Two of them immediately took off across the kids' playground, while the other two turned round and ran back up the steps the way they'd come.

I don't know whether these latter two thought they might be able to hide in someone's flat and wait for everything to calm down – in truth, I don't think they had time to think about it at all – but now Cleaver and I, who by this point were no more than twenty-five yards away, had a real chance of cutting them off.

A pedestrian walkway three floors up connected our building to Jasmine House and led directly into the stairwell, and I ran across it, seeing the two fleeing attackers running up the steps, only a few yards in front of me now. They must have heard my trainers clattering on the concrete, because they both looked over their shoulders, spotted me, and raced through a fire door ahead, only a matter of feet away from where they'd carried out their attack.

I took a quick look over my own shoulder, saw Cleaver maybe ten yards behind me, running with his baton extended, then looked down and saw the Chief, Nix and several uniforms racing into the stairwell from the ground floor.

I kept going, flat out on adrenaline, flinging open the fire door and running right in, teeth clenched against the impact of any assault, baton raised in front of me, knowing I was going to be the first to make contact with the attackers. But that was the thing about me in those days. I always rushed in, the fury and the excitement, and maybe even some kind of latent death wish, crowding out any fear that I might have had, and that might have helped protect me.

As I came into the darkened alcove, my shoes crunching on the glass from the broken light, I saw the two of them in the gloom running down the corridor that led to the walkway at the rear of the building.

One of them was lagging behind now, though, running awkwardly and bent forward. He was a big guy, but overweight, and I remembered him as being one of the two who'd come at Warman from the sides before knifing him repeatedly. What he'd done wasn't manslaughter, it was murder, and I wanted him badly.

In seconds, I was right behind him.

He heard me coming and looked back over his shoulder. He looked terrified, and he was young too. Fifteen, sixteen tops.

I yelled at him to stop, only a couple of yards separating us now, and he slowed up, turned round and threw up his hands. I couldn't tell in the darkness whether he was still holding his knife, so I instinctively lashed out with the baton, striking him across both forearms, before grabbing him round the back of his collar and slamming him against the wall, spitting out the words: 'You're under arrest!'

149

Cleaver arrived at that point, yelling into the mic that we had a suspect on the third floor by the lifts, before pulling handcuffs from his belt as the two of us forced the kid's wrists behind his back.

The second suspect had disappeared round the corner now, still running, but I'd already had a sniff of glory and wanted more, and as the Chief's voice came back into my earpiece saying he'd be with us in thirty seconds, I told Cleaver to hang onto the suspect, then took up the chase again, the adrenaline still going crazy.

But as I rounded the corner, hoping to see the suspect running along the rear balcony in a futile attempt at escape, I experienced the heart-in-mouth terror that all those who run headlong into an ambush must get, because instead of the suspect, who seemed to have disappeared entirely, all I saw were half a dozen men with bandanas covering their faces charging towards me, wielding all manner of weapons. But there was only one weapon that was grabbing my attention, and that was the machete in the gloved hand of the man leading the charge – a huge guy whose wife-beater vest looked like it might rip under the pressure of all the rippling muscles beneath.

These guys were ten yards from me and closing in fast.

I just had time to skid to a halt and hold up the baton two-handed as a makeshift shield while at the same time screaming 'Help!' before they were on me, the machete seeming to sail in slow motion through the air at my head. I managed to use the baton to stave off the blow, the force of it travelling right up my arms, and then I was being thrown backwards into the wall by the weight of the whole group, my head slamming against the concrete with an angry crack.

An intense, eye-watering pain ripped through my skull, but I hardly had time to think about that, because I suddenly found myself being thrust back against the balcony railings so I was half hanging over it. I don't know how many of them were attacking me. There were at least three, but all my concentration was on the man with the machete, who had one of his hands on my throat and the other pushing the machete down against the baton, forcing it ever closer to my face. Another attacker was twisting my wrist in an effort to get me to release the baton, while the third was trying to lift me up by my legs.

I was flailing like a fish on a line, trying simultaneously to keep my feet on the ground, the machete away from my face, and somehow find an escape route, and all the time the image of Leon Warman being stabbed to death was right there at the front of my mind, along with the fact that I was very likely to be next.

In that moment, I was so scared I would have pissed my pants if I hadn't been too busy trying to get these men off me. I felt one hand being parted from the baton, and then the baton itself hit the bridge of my nose with a painful whack, the machete landing on top of it, only an inch separating me from the blade.

Machete Man now leant back and raised his weapon above his head, preparing to strike another blow while simultaneously holding me in place by the throat.

Which was when I remembered a move I'd once been

told about by an informant, which he'd claimed was a guaranteed way of getting someone to let go of you if they had you by the throat. The move is simple. Grab one of their fingers and break it. It doesn't matter how strong your assailant is, and how weak you are, because in the end a hand's always going to have more strength than a finger. That's the theory anyway, and I had no choice but to try it out. So, with my newly free hand, I managed to grab hold of one of the gloved fingers round my throat, and immediately bent it backwards with everything I had until it snapped.

Machete Man yelled in pain and let go, momentarily lowering his weapon, but if I'd thought that was going to save me, I was wrong, because the next second, my baton was pulled free from my other hand by another attacker, and rather than nurse his wound, Machete Man instead raised the weapon once again.

And then I heard it.

A howled battle cry that somehow I knew belonged to Cleaver even before I saw him rush into view, baton flailing like something out of a kung fu film as he set about my three attackers. As they turned to ward him off, I grabbed for my own baton, but my vision blurred and my legs went from under me.

Machete Man bumped into me as he was knocked backwards by something or someone, and his weapon clattered to the ground. Then all three attackers were scrambling out of the way, with Cleaver wrestling one of them.

I fell to my knees, clutching at the railings like I'd seen

Warman do only minutes earlier, my vision cleared enough to make out a melee by the lifts, with figures everywhere. Then the Chief came running down the corridor towards us, followed by a couple of uniforms, and did this amazing flying kick on Machete Man, sending him bouncing off the railings and crashing to the ground, before jumping on his chest and punching him hard in the face.

The attackers still on their feet were all running now, and I tried to get up, but the pain in my head was like nothing I'd ever felt, and instead I leant over and vomited.

I felt a hand on my shoulder and heard a gentle voice in my ear. It was the Chief. 'Chris, are you okay?'

'Yeah,' I said with a croak. 'I'm fine.'

Then I blacked out.

22

They kept me in hospital overnight for observation, with suspected concussion, but by the following morning, all I had was a very nasty headache and an underlying feeling of nausea. I was sitting up in bed, drinking a cup of bad coffee, when a nurse popped her head round the door and said I had visitors.

It was the Chief and Cleaver. They both looked really pleased to see that I was up and about. They'd brought gifts too. The Chief a bottle of Jameson; Cleaver a selection of sweets, a cup of decent takeaway Americano from the stand outside, and a box of headache tablets, which he seemed to think was uproariously funny.

In truth, I was touched. Maybe I'm easily pleased, but it was nice to know that these guys cared enough to come and make sure I was all right.

After the handshakes, they took seats either side of the bed. It was me who spoke first. 'Before either of you say anything, I just want to thank you both for saving my neck. Literally. If you gents hadn't been there, I think I'd be in the morgue now rather than here.' I meant what I was saying too. Cleaver especially might have caused me no end of problems, but that still didn't detract from the fact that I quite possibly owed my life to him and the Chief.

'You'd have done the same for us,' Cleaver said. 'And it's what friends are for.' He gave me a pointed look.

'Baz is right,' said the Chief, trying to get comfortable in the plastic chair, which groaned under his bulk. 'We're a team. That's how we operate.' He asked me how I was feeling.

'Just a headache. I'll be fine to come back to work.'

'Take a few days off, Chris,' he said. 'You always want to watch head injuries, and you've been through an ordeal. You were right. You were very lucky not to end up like Warman.'

'I'm guessing he didn't survive.'

The Chief shook his head. 'He died at the scene. Multiple stab wounds. Thanks to you and Baz, we've got one suspect in custody. So far, he's not talking, but he'll break if he thinks he's the only one taking the rap for the murder. And right now, he is.'

'Did we manage to nick any of the ones who attacked me?'

'Just the one who tried to split your head in two. Roberto Ailman.'

I recognised the name. He was a senior member of JJ's crew. 'Is he talking?'

'Not yet,' said the Chief. 'And realistically we may only be able to get him on assault and possession of an offensive weapon.'

'He didn't hurt you enough, Chris,' said Cleaver with a half-smile. 'And he also says you broke his finger.'

'I did. That's because it was wrapped round my neck at the time.' I took a sip of the good coffee he'd brought with him, savouring the taste, and looked at them both. 'So what do we reckon happened? Why did they go for Warman like that? It looked like a deliberate hit.'

'We think JJ must have suspected he was working for us,' said the Chief.

That surprised me. 'How would he know?'

'It might just be enough that he guessed. JJ's a ruthless operator. That's why he's done so well. He's seen that Warman keeps getting bail, and he probably asked himself why and didn't like the answer he came up with.'

'It's a pretty big move to kill him.'

'Sends a message, though, doesn't it?' said Cleaver. 'That anyone he thinks might have crossed him pays with their life, and that no one's safe. Even his right-hand man.'

'It may also be counterproductive,' said the Chief. 'It shows that he's paranoid, and that might lead to the break-up of his crew. But it's definitely JJ behind it. No one would do that on this estate without his say-so and you can see from the way his people tried to stop us nicking the attackers that it was all planned. Although proving it'll be another matter.'

'But at least Warman's out of the picture. Permanently,' said Cleaver, who couldn't resist a smile at the prospect.

'Well, that's something, eh?' I said aloud, but inside something didn't feel right about the whole thing, although I wasn't going to shed too many tears for an arsehole like Warman.

At that moment, the Chief's mobile rang. He excused himself and got to his feet, heading out the door with the phone to his ear.

The moment he was gone, Cleaver leant forward and whispered: 'You still managed to keep hold of that money I gave you, didn't you?'

'Yeah, I've got it,' I told him. It was still in my jacket pocket, burning a hole.

He looked pleased. 'Good. You did well last night, you know. You had some real balls on you.'

'I was an idiot,' I said. 'I almost got myself killed.' But secretly I remember being proud of myself too. I wondered what my old man would have thought of what I'd done. Probably picked holes in it. Well, fuck him. He was dead.

'Better to live one day as a lion than a hundred years as a sheep,' said Cleaver sagely, doubtless quoting someone who'd never had the wrong end of a machete an inch from their face.

'Even better to live eighty or so as a fully functioning human being,' I said, and I meant it.

Cleaver shrugged as the Chief came back into the room. He was smiling. 'Good news, gentlemen. It seems the boy you nicked last night for Warman's murder is willing to cooperate. We need to get back and talk to him, Baz. Enjoy the rest, Chris.'

'Let me know how you get on.'

He leant over and squeezed my shoulder, giving me a

look that was almost paternal. ''Course we will. I'm proud of you, Chris. We all are.' Then just as he and Cleaver were halfway out the door, he turned back round. 'Oh yeah, I almost forgot to tell you. When we were searching Warman's flat this morning, we found a bloodstained knife under his bed. So he's obviously been involved in a recent stabbing. We need to check if he's a possible for Marlon Venn. That'd be good for the team's clear-up rate.'

'And save a trial at the taxpayer's expense,' added Cleaver helpfully.

I tried to sound enthusiastic as I said my goodbyes, but inside I was reeling, because I would have bet anything that it wasn't the Marlon Venn knife under Warman's bed; it was the one used to kill Kerry Masters.

23

Two days later, while I was sitting at home, bored and finishing off my recuperation, I got the confirmation that I was right. The Chief called my mobile and told me that blood on the blade of the knife they'd found under Leon Warman's bed matched that of Kerry Masters.

'It's cut and dried, Chris,' he told me. 'Forensics also found one of Warman's hairs in Kerry's bedroom. That and the blood means there's no mistake. The bastard killed her.'

I swallowed, my heart thumping, remembering how I'd broken into her flat while the real murderer stood waiting beside me. But I kept my voice calm. 'That's brilliant news, Chief. Do we have any idea of his motive?'

'It could have been robbery. Apparently some stuff was missing. Or sexual. She was an attractive woman, and he had form for both crimes.'

But it also presented me with a huge dilemma. I knew Warman had been set up. I wasn't sure how Cleaver had managed it, but it wouldn't have been impossible. He'd had ample opportunity during Warman's second arrest to have got hold of one of his hairs (I'd seen him rip hair from his head), which he could easily enough have given to Clarn to leave at Kerry's flat. At the same time, Clarn could have given Cleaver the murder weapon to plant at Warman's place. I'd watched Cleaver leave home in a hurry that same night. It stood to reason that he was collecting the knife from Clarn. And, I had to admit, it had worked out perfectly, because Warman was no longer around to protest his innocence. One of our most wanted thugs, who Cleaver had told me he'd love to see dead, was now exactly that, and with a murder pinned on him that now would never be pinned on the real culprits: Cleaver's organisation and the mysterious Kalian Roman.

Which meant I had to ask myself: was Leon Warman's murder a set-up too? JJ's people might have carried it out – I'd witnessed that myself – but had JJ been told by someone that Warman was a grass? It wouldn't have been hard for Cleaver to have planted the seeds of suspicion, and he could have done it anonymously through one of his informants. JJ had then acted accordingly, probably having no idea that the GIU team would be witnesses to the whole thing.

Cleaver wouldn't have been able to arrange it on his own, I was certain of that. But then he would have had plenty of help. He'd said himself that the organisation he belonged to had particularly long tentacles. If Kalian Roman was the Machiavelli that Cleaver and indeed CTC thought he was, then yes, it was eminently possible.

And worst of all, I was now a part of it. One of Kalian Roman's pawns who'd been lured into exactly the kind of trap I'd been meant to set for Cleaver. And the truly terrifying thing was, this Warman thing suited me too. No one was going to investigate Kerry Masters' murder any further. It had been solved. They had their killer – a convicted robber, rapist and all-round lowlife who'd clearly broken in one night, tried to rape her, and when she'd resisted, had stabbed her to death. No one was going to waste a huge amount of time trying to pick holes in that narrative, particularly with Warman dead.

And I knew then that I wasn't going to say a word to anyone about what had really happened that night, and who'd killed Kerry.

I know you'll be quick to judge, but you have to remember, I was scared. I genuinely didn't want to cover anything up; I wanted the man who'd done it brought to justice, as well as the others involved. But I also knew that if I came clean, there was no way I'd survive the fallout unscathed. Especially if Cleaver made good on his threat to publicly share the footage of me using the kettle on Roger Munroe as he sat tied to a chair in his bedroom. At best I'd lose my job. More likely, I'd end up in jail, and not just for a few months either. Perverting the course of justice; GBH; potentially even murder. We'd be talking years.

And you know what? I wasn't prepared to go to jail. I didn't think I deserved it. I felt awful for Kerry Masters, I really did. But I told myself that I'd avenge her eventually by continuing my undercover role and looking for the moment that Cleaver made a mistake that gave me an in. Because he would. I was sure of that.

And of course, he did.

The problem was that when it happened, he took us all down with him.

24

I was signed off work for two weeks because of the injury. I'd have gone back a lot sooner, but I had a temporary blackout three days after my release from hospital. One minute I was in the kitchen making a cup of coffee, the next I was lying on the floor, pieces of the cup and hot coffee all round me, and a searing pain in my head. I think I was only out for a couple of minutes at most, but it meant going back to the hospital, having some more tests, and a delay in being signed off as fit to return to duty.

During that time, things were relatively busy on the work front. The suspect I'd nicked that night on the Cliveden Forest estate named the other three men involved in Leon Warman's killing, as well as the man who'd paid them to carry out the hit, one of JJ's lieutenants, who in turn implicated JJ himself. So in the end, JJ was one of a total of six people who were charged in connection with Warman's murder. As for Machete Man, as Cleaver had predicted, he got away with just charges for assault and possession, but because he was already on bail for other offences, he ended up in custody too.

So, results all round, and a big plus for the residents of Cliveden Forest, who for a while at least enjoyed some temporary peace before the arrival of the next Mr Big, and for Mrs Abanks (to whom I sent fifty pounds in cash and a box of chocolates as a thank-you). But most of all for the GIU team, and for me personally, being the man who'd got the collar that had led to the other arrests. I even managed to get out for the celebration drinks at the White Horse when JJ was charged, although I stayed off the booze because I was still paranoid about my blackout, and I only stayed for an hour, which was long enough to be toasted by the whole team, and worth it just because of that.

Rose got in touch too, to check that I was okay. I told her I didn't have anything new to report, that things between Cleaver and me hadn't progressed with everything else going on, and she bought that because, ultimately, what else was she going to do? But now, having lied to her, I was really on my own, although for the moment at least I could breathe a bit easier.

On the domestic front, things were more painful. Karen and Bryan the grief counsellor finally left to start their new life in Christchurch, New Zealand, which I worked out from the map was literally the furthest city in the world from London. We had a final conversation on the phone and she offered to come round for what she termed a goodbye cup of tea, but I couldn't face it. I know I would have broken down and made a spectacle of myself, as my grandma used to say, and I didn't want to show Karen that she still had that kind of power over me.

The morning in early April their flight left was my last official day of sick leave, and I knew I couldn't spend it hanging around the house wallowing in the memories of when we were a happy family, with our own plans for a new life on the other side of the world. Instead, I went for a long walk along the Thames Path as far as Hampton Court, before doubling back on myself. It was a route Karen and I had done many times, both before and after Grace was born. There was a pub near the river in East Molesey where we'd stop for lunch in summer, have a couple of drinks, and then meander back. It was called the Barley Mow, but when I went past this time, it was gone and a bland-looking block of flats, with beige brickwork and glass balconies, had been flung up in its place. As I stared at the block's upmarket ugliness, I thought about the fact that someone had pocketed a load of money to turn something pretty and useful into something horrible, and it made me wonder why people were always willing to destroy so much in pursuit of money. It just seemed so utterly pointless.

And yet the sun was shining that day, and standing there made me realise that I couldn't stay stuck in the past, re-fighting battles in my head that had already been lost. That I had to move on, find a new relationship and look to the future and maybe a new family. After all, I was still young. I remember I was actually feeling pretty good about things as I headed back home. I'd survived my undercover role so far; I'd survived grief, divorce, an attack with a machete. I wasn't exactly feeling invincible – the guilt over my part in what had happened to Kerry Masters was still there – but I'll tell you this, I was feeling a lot better.

At least I was until I was ten yards from my front door and saw Cleaver's unmistakable black Ford Escort with the privacy windows parked directly outside.

I wondered what the hell he wanted that couldn't have been dealt with by a phone call, but there was no avoiding walking past it, so I decided I might as well find out.

As I slowed down alongside, the passenger window opened and Cleaver leant over from the driver's seat. 'I was just about to call you,' he said, with a smile that somehow didn't promise good things. 'You're looking better.'

'I'm getting there,' I answered. 'And I'm back in tomorrow.'

'No need to hurry,' he continued. 'We're just about surviving without you.' He patted the front passenger seat. 'Jump in. We need a chat.'

The last thing I needed was a chat with Cleaver, but I figured I had little choice, so I climbed inside.

Which was when I realised that there was someone in the back seat directly behind me.

Before I could turn round to see who it was, the locks on the doors clicked shut and a plastic bag was thrust over my head and pulled tight.

At the same time, as the car pulled away from the kerb and I realised I couldn't breathe, Cleaver said the words I'd thought I'd never hear on this assignment, because I'd been so careful.

'We've heard you're an informant, Chrissy boy.'

166

25

I clawed at the plastic bag, trying to pierce it, but the material was too thick and my fingers couldn't make a hole, and all the time I couldn't breathe and I was panicking like crazy, thinking this can't be happening, not on the street that I've called home for the past seven years, and right in the middle of the afternoon.

I began to feel myself passing out, but I couldn't die like this – I wouldn't – and with one last desperate effort, I punched my two thumbs together into the material covering my half-open mouth, and this time it created enough of a hole for me to gasp some air through. Immediately I yanked my thumbs apart, ripping the bag further, conscious of Cleaver stopping the car at the end of the road, then indicating as he turned right, making no effort to hurry.

Suddenly the bag was yanked back off my head and I took a series of deep breaths, already turning round in my seat to take on my assailant, only to find myself looking straight at the barrel of a gun.

I stopped dead and saw that the man holding it was

Clarn. The one who'd stabbed to death a twenty-year-old woman in her bed, and who appeared very much to have got away with it.

He stared at me with cold, narrow eyes that were a strange reddy-brown colour, making them look like knife wounds carved into the pale skin of his bony, hollowed-out face.

I knew that not only would he not hesitate to kill me, but that he'd almost certainly enjoy it too. He had the air of a sadist. Someone who relished wielding power and inflicting pain.

But I couldn't let myself panic, or worse, admit the truth. To do so would sentence me to death, and however brave I thought I was, however little I sometimes felt I had to live for, I didn't want to die. Not here. Not like this.

'What the fuck are you talking about?' I demanded, aiming my question at Cleaver, who I knew was my only hope. 'I'm not an informant. Where did you hear that from?'

Cleaver looked conflicted as he stared straight ahead out the window. I could tell he didn't want to be doing this, but as I was beginning to find out, he wasn't the one calling the shots.

'You fucked us up, boy,' said Clarn from the back seat, his voice a low, mocking growl. 'Now you've got to pay the price.'

'If you tell us the truth, Chris,' said Cleaver, still staring straight ahead, 'about who you're working for and what you've told them, then as long as you resign with immediate effect, tell your bosses you've made a mistake and disappear, you can get out of this car and you'll never see us again.'

I'll tell you one thing now. I was tempted to come clean. It was the psychology behind the offer. You want to believe it because it gives you an out. In my heart, of course, I knew that it was bullshit. As soon as I told them a thing, I'd be a dead man. But the alternative, if they chose not to believe me, was death anyway.

Even so, I had to stay strong. And fight back. That was the essential thing. 'You bastard, Cleaver!' I snarled. 'All I've ever done is prove myself to you, even though you and your buddies have fucked me up the whole way. I've never been undercover. I'm not a snitch. I want to know who you heard it from, because I'll kill them.'

'Mr Roman's got sources everywhere,' said Clarn from the back seat. 'Including CTC.'

I instinctively stiffened at the mention of CTC, and my heart did a somersault, but I didn't show it. 'I'm sure he has,' I said, turning to meet Clarn's accusatory gaze and doing my best to avoid the sight of the gun, 'but if one of them's told you something about me, then he's wrong. End of. I've got nothing to hide.'

But even as I spoke the words, the doubts were mounting. Could it be I'd been betrayed? Only three people were meant to know about my role. Rose; her boss, DCI Marina Reineke; and the head of CTC itself. Surely it couldn't be one of them? Why would they do it now? And yet it was possible that someone had let slip something to someone else, and that Roman, the man of many sources, had got hold of it. And that's the problem in a life-or-death situation like this. You just don't know. And you're not thinking straight either. Because the fear infects everything.

'Your choice, Chris,' said Cleaver. And I thought I could detect a hint of regret in his voice. 'But you're going to tell us one way or another.'

As he spoke, he pulled up at a junction on the Richmond Road, and took a right towards the river. It was bizarre. Outside in the spring sunshine, everything looked so normal. People sat at pavement cafés, couples walked hand in hand, gangs of kids in school uniform hung about the street corners. And yet in this tiny enclosed space my fate was being decided for me, and potentially my life expectancy could be measured in minutes.

'Where are we going?' I asked Cleaver.

'Somewhere quiet,' he said ominously. 'Where we can talk privately and get some answers,' he added, just in case I was in any doubt about what was in store for me.

Again the doubt hit me and I had the sudden urge to blurt out everything. I pictured Kerry Masters dead in her bed, torn apart by Clarn. I couldn't die like that. Jesus, I couldn't.

It took a superhuman effort, but once again I managed to force down the panic. 'Let me save you the trouble,' I said, glaring at them both in turn. 'I'm not working for anyone except the GIU unit, and now you people. You can torture me all you like, but what I tell you isn't going to change, for the simple reason that it's the truth.'

The car fell silent. No one said anything. Clarn stared

back at me, his expression utterly inscrutable. Cleaver made another turn, onto a quiet residential road I didn't recognise.

I sat there breathing heavily, knowing there was no point trying to escape. I didn't think Clarn would shoot me in Cleaver's car. He certainly wouldn't want to. It was way too risky. But I wasn't prepared to bet against it either, and with the Escort's central locking button on the other side of Cleaver, I was effectively trapped. 'You're making a big mistake, Baz,' I told him.

He still didn't say anything. It was clear he was terrified of Clarn and wasn't going to intervene to help me. If Clarn wanted me dead, then dead I was going to be.

We drove in silence. I could hear my heart pumping. I don't how long we went on like that for. Probably no more than a few minutes, but it felt like hours. And all the time, it was taking every ounce of energy I had to remain strong.

Cleaver made a couple of turnings and then pulled into a narrow lane just off the river, with what looked like a deserted boathouse at the end, shielded by trees from the neighbouring buildings. There was no one about as we stopped directly outside.

'Last chance to tell the truth, Chris,' he said, leaving the engine running as he turned to me properly for the first time since I'd got in the car.

I took a deep breath. Hesitated.

Then said it.

'I'm not undercover. I'm exactly who I've always said I was.' I turned to Clarn then, and I'm forever proud of what I said to him. 'And if you don't believe it, then pull the trigger and have done with it.'

I looked directly into his cold, dead eyes, holding his gaze. The gun didn't move. The end of the barrel was still barely two feet from my face, where it had been for the whole journey.

And then just like that, he smiled – not the smile of a killer, but the smile of a normal man – and lowered the gun.

'You've passed the test,' he said. And out of the corner of my eye, I saw Cleaver heave out a sigh of relief.

He wasn't anything like as relieved as me, though. But I didn't show it. Instead, I acted furious. 'What the hell is this? Is it all a fucking game for you two?'

'It's all right, Chris,' said Cleaver, putting out a conciliatory hand, which I immediately batted away. 'We had to know for sure you were one of us.'

'You know that already, Baz. For Christ's sake! What else do I need to do to prove myself? You pair of arseholes. I've had my fill of this. Let me out.'

'It doesn't work like that,' said Clarn, who'd suddenly lost the smile. 'You don't just get to walk. You work for Mr Roman now.'

'Well, Mr Roman needs some lessons in employee relations, because this isn't the way to treat volunteers.'

'Mr Roman doesn't need lessons in anything,' said Clarn, 'and you'd better learn some respect, boy.'

'All right, gents, let's keep this amicable,' said Cleaver. 'I'm sorry about that, Chris, but every one of us has to take that test before we're fully accepted. Now you're one of us, so you don't have to worry about anything again. There'll be no more surprises.'

'Tell him about the job,' said Clarn.

Cleaver nodded like the subordinate he so clearly was. 'We've got something for you. A bigger role. And another five grand. Except this time we'll set up an offshore bank account for you through a shell company, way out of reach of the taxman. You'll be able to put the rest of your cash in there too. You've still got it, right?'

I nodded.

'Invest it well, you could make a lot of money, isn't that right, Aaron?'

'You can make some good money if you follow the rules,' said the man I now knew as Aaron Clarn.

It was hard to come to terms with the fact that I was now receiving financial advice from the men who literally only three minutes earlier had been assaulting and threatening to murder me at gunpoint. They took the carrot-and-stick approach to a whole new level. Yet I could imagine it working. Do what you're told and the money really flows in. With this new payment, that would be ten grand I'd received in the space of less than three weeks, which was close to half my annual police salary after tax. And the stick? What better motivation was there to stay loyal than to have a lunatic like Clarn point a gun at your head?

I took a deep breath and sat back in my seat. I was sweating profusely, and the car felt stuffy and airless, not helped by the musty, stale odour that emanated from Clarn, who looked like he was still wearing the same clothes he'd worn the night of the murder, more than three weeks back now.

'Can you open the window?' I asked Cleaver. 'I need some air in here, and I need a cigarette.'

'I didn't think you smoked,' said Cleaver.

'I started again,' I told him. 'It's being round you.'

'You can't smoke in here,' said Clarn.

'Then I'll smoke outside. Let me out. I won't go anywhere.'

I pulled a pack of Marlboro and a lighter out of my jacket pocket to show them I wasn't bullshitting.

Clarn nodded his assent and Cleaver pressed the central locking button.

I got out of the car, shutting the door behind me, and took a deep breath before lighting up. It was true. I'd started smoking again in January, having successfully quit three years earlier. I'd started with the odd one here and there, but was now up to a pack every other day, and had been seriously considering quitting again. However, I don't think I've ever needed a cigarette so much in my life as I did at that moment, though that wasn't the only reason I was out here, because as I went to light it, with my back to the car, I clicked the recorder button on my watch in one casual movement. If nothing else, I was leaving here with an image of Aaron Clarn to give to Rose.

I finished the cigarette and got back in the car. 'So, what's the job?'

'It's a gun buy,' answered Cleaver. 'Mr Roman's brokered it with a group of Ukrainian businessmen, who've got some very high-quality firearms and explosives already in the country that they're prepared to sell us.'

I gave a casual nod, but inside I was excited, knowing this could be my chance to end this thing.

'We need you to drive me and two of my associates to the buy,' said Clarn, 'so you can provide cover if we get stopped by the police.'

'I'll be driving a different car and recceing the place to make sure it's safe,' said Cleaver. 'But Mr Roman has vouched for these guys, which means they're legit, so this'll just be a standard security job for me and you. Another five grand for one night's work, a couple of hours tops. You're not going to get better money than that anywhere, Chrissy boy.'

He was right there, and I was genuinely disappointed that I was never going to receive this last payment, or keep the rest of it, because this gun deal was going to be the end of the gravy train. My only hope was that I could still somehow stay on with GIU, maybe even move up the ranks now it looked like there might be a Cleaver-shaped vacancy.

'When's it going down?'

'The time and location are being arranged now,' he said, 'but it'll be in the next few days. We don't want you back in work until after it's done. We can't have you being held up at the station on a case and having to pull out. At least one of us has got to be there.'

'I told you. I'm meant to be back in tomorrow.'

'Just say you've had another relapse. And you need a few more days. That's all it'll be. Are you in? Because we need you on this. Getting guns is going to make a big difference to the cause.'

Out of the corner of my eye, I could see Clarn staring at me intently. The gun was in his lap now, but I had strong feeling it would be back pointing at my head if I turned the job down.

Although of course there was no way I was going to turn it down. This was my out.

I nodded. 'As long as there are no more surprises.'

'There won't be,' Cleaver said solemnly.

I've been told a lot of lies in my life, but that one was by some distance the biggest.

26

They drove me straight back home after that. Before I got out the car, Cleaver handed me a new burner phone and told me to get rid of the other one, and as I put it in my jeans pocket, I turned in my seat so that I was facing Clarn, trying to angle the watch as surreptitiously as possible so the camera could capture his image.

Then I was out of there, and I don't think I breathed again until I was inside the house with the door double-locked behind me. I was shaking as the shock of what had happened finally began to set in, and I had to sit down. You'd think you'd get used to dealing with dangerous situations, but in my experience, rather than diminishing in severity, the shock and anxiety can actually get worse with each recurring event. And that afternoon's incident, where I was utterly helpless and trapped, had hit me far harder than the fight with Machete Man in the Cliveden Forest estate, where at least I could fight back, and where there were people nearby who could help me.

I sat on the sofa for a good half an hour before I felt

ready to think about my next move, and when I finally got to my feet and went upstairs to fetch my laptop so I could download the watch camera footage, I suddenly felt intensely paranoid. Throughout this whole four-month op I'd always assumed that I was the one doing the watching, but the people I was up against were far more sophisticated than I'd ever truly given them credit for, and though I might have been careful with my security, it was possible that they'd also been watching me the whole time.

Either way, though, it was time to end this whole thing for the sake of my sanity, and now I'd been given a unique opportunity to take out Cleaver and Clarn. They wouldn't go down for the Kerry Masters murder, of course, but as I've already pointed out, that suited me just as well. Hopefully I wouldn't even need to give evidence. It would be a done deal. We'd all get nicked together and I'd be let go. It might mean I became a target for Kalian Roman, but I'd have to cross that bridge when I came to it. Being the driver would be risky. If Clarn and his crew were armed and decided to shoot it out, I could be caught in the crossfire. But I figured the risk was worth it, and it beat being dragged any deeper into this morass.

I dug out my CTC emergency phone from the hidden compartment in the wardrobe where I kept my passport and the five grand I'd been given by Cleaver while we'd been at Mrs Abanks' place, and then, just to be on the safe side, I went out into the back garden to make the call to Rose, noticing that the grass already badly needed cutting. I didn't come out here much these days. It reminded me too much of Grace. We used to play out here the whole time when she was a toddler on sunny afternoons like this one, and I felt an immediate lump in my throat at the thought that all that laughter had been replaced by an unending silence.

After making sure none of my neighbours were out in their gardens, I crouched down in the shade of the yew tree by the back fence and called Rose's emergency number.

She answered quickly with a simple 'Yes.' It sounded like she was outside somewhere.

'We need a meeting, urgently,' I whispered. 'I have information that needs acting on, and it's possible I've been compromised. I need to be very careful.'

'Keep this phone on,' she said. 'Press the panic button if you need it. We'll be tracking you. Let's meet at seven thirty, Reserve Spot 1.'

Reserve Spot 1 was the Kew Retail Park in Richmond, about half an hour's drive away at that time of the evening.

I put the phone away and went back inside, and by the time I'd had a long shower, got changed and grabbed a bite to eat, it was almost seven and I was running late. The shock of Clarn's assault on me hadn't faded. If anything it had got worse, and I felt like I was on the edge of a major panic attack. I tried to ignore it. For the moment, I needed to stay calm and focused.

But as I pulled on my coat and opened the front door, my heart did another leap and I almost jumped backwards, because there, standing on the doorstep, was Cleaver, a surprised look on his face.

'Where are you heading in such a hurry, Chris?' he asked.

27

One of the things Rose tried to drill into me when we were prepping for the undercover op was that when you were put on the spot, you always needed to react aggressively, because it tended to throw the people questioning you off balance.

'Jesus Christ!' I snapped at Cleaver. 'What the hell are you doing? You scared me.' He was on his own and appeared unarmed, so I was guessing he didn't mean me any harm.

'Sorry,' he said, taking a step back and putting up his hands in a semi-passive gesture. 'I didn't mean to.'

'I was just off for a walk,' I said, knowing I was meant to be on standby for this driving job. 'I haven't been able to settle after what happened today. What do you want?'

'Can I come in for a moment?'

Cleaver had never been in my house before, and I wasn't keen on him coming in now.

'I just want to talk,' he said, clearly sensing my reluctance. 'And apologise.'

I nodded, figuring I didn't have much choice. 'Okay. Come on in.'

I led him through to the lounge and turned to face him, without offering him a seat.

'I'm really sorry about what happened today, mate,' he said, a pained expression on his face. 'It's not what I wanted.'

'It's not I wanted either, Baz. That lunatic was threatening to kill me. And now I'm meant to be his chauffeur. I can't go on like this.'

He stood there with his hands on his hips, nodding his head and not quite managing to meet my eyes. He looked genuinely distressed by everything that was going on, but then he often did. The problem was, he still kept landing me in it.

'Look, Chris,' he said. 'You're in now. Clarn's an animal, but he's right. Like it or not, you work for Kalian Roman, and he's the one who makes the rules.'

Not for much longer if all goes well, I thought. I was conscious that I was going to be late for the meeting, but I couldn't pass up the chance to pump Cleaver for some more information.

'Does anyone have any idea who Kalian Roman really is?' I asked him.

'I don't know of anyone who does,' he said.

'And yet we do his bidding under fear of death.'

He sighed loudly, almost visibly deflating. This was a big, strong man brought low by circumstances. I felt sorry for him.

'I suppose when you put it like that, yeah, we do,' he said.

'But you report to someone, right? That arsehole Clarn?'

'No, not him. He's just a soldier.'

Although he was a soldier who scared the living crap out of Cleaver. I looked him in the eye. 'Why did you recruit me specifically, Baz? Were you told to do it by someone, or did I just look like a suitable victim?'

'It wasn't like that, Chris. I didn't look at you like a victim. I was told to always be on the lookout for people who fit the bill. You're angry, anti-establishment. You're prepared to break the rules, and to kill, if necessary. And, you know, with due respect, you haven't got much to lose.'

He had me there, except for the bit about killing. At the time, I didn't want to kill anyone. Except maybe that monster Aaron Clarn, and even then, when push came to shove, I wasn't sure I'd have the balls to do it.

'Did you have to go through what I just went through? Facing down a gun and being told you were going to die?'

He looked away, then back at me. 'I went through worse,' he said, and by the expression on his face, I believed him.

I asked him what had happened.

He hesitated, and something dark crossed his face. 'It was bad,' he said. 'I was made to do something terrible to someone while that bastard Clarn and another man, the one who recruited me, watched.' He sighed, staring up at the ceiling for a long moment before looking back at me, and I thought there might be tears in his eyes. 'So yeah, I do what I'm told, Chris. And I justify it when I can because I know it's for the greater good. And the fact that the bloke I was hurting was a fucking lowlife. It's amazing how you can keep going and push what you did to the back of your mind.'

I thought of Kerry Masters then and I believed him.

'Jesus Christ,' I said quietly. 'Where does it end?'

'I don't know,' he answered, shaking his head like he was trying to shake out the memories, 'but there's not normally anything like as much happening as this. I got recruited four years ago, and I've only been involved in three or four support ops, and none of them involving violence.'

'Have you got any more news on when this new op's going ahead?'

He shook his head again. 'No. But like I said, it's going to be soon. Then I'm told things are going to calm right down and we can go back to proper police work, getting rid of the scum off the streets, eh?'

He looked at me in a way that was almost pleading for forgiveness, and I knew without a doubt that he would dearly love to be out of all this. That he was a victim too. I'll be honest, I felt sorry for him, and I even contemplated confessing that I was undercover and that there was a way out for him if he chose to cooperate with CTC, but I held back. One wrong word from me and it could ruin everything.

'Anyway,' he continued, 'I've said what I came here to say. I won't keep you from your walk. And don't forget to keep that burner phone on you, and think about the extra five grand and the holiday you're going to have afterwards.'

'That's what's keeping me going,' I said, showing him to

183

the door and watching as he walked down the path through our tiny, unkempt front garden and back out onto the road, wondering if I'd ever work with him again, and how I'd feel when he finally went down.

28

It was 7.44 and getting dark when I finally pulled in to Kew Retail Park, a large, ugly block of chain stores of the kind you get in most British cities, but which had the advantage of always being busy, and having a huge parking area out the front. The agreement was that Rose would try to park opposite the front entrance to Marks & Spencer, and as far away from it as possible.

That night, the car park was almost full. I drove round it once, just to make doubly sure I hadn't been tailed, clocking Rose's navy-blue Golf in the shade of one of the few trees in the vicinity, and next to some litter bins. I found a spot about fifty yards away, waited for one minute to see if I'd missed something, then got out and walked casually over, stopping to throw something in the bin before climbing into the Golf's passenger seat.

Which was when I got my second big shock of the day. Rose was in the driver's seat, but there was also someone in the back, just like earlier, and I'll be honest, I actually leapt out of the seat, hitting the roof and letting out a yelp so high-pitched that an octave higher and only dogs would have heard it.

'Jesus Christ!' I snapped when I'd landed back in my seat, seeing for the first time that the passenger in the back was DCI Marina Reineke, CTC's second in command and a woman I hadn't seen since that winter's day at the industrial estate in Feltham, four and a half months and a thousand years ago. 'You scared the shit out of me.'

Rose immediately asked me if I was okay.

'Yeah, I'm fine, I'm fine,' I answered with a sigh.

'You might have been undercover too long,' said Reineke from the back, not sounding remotely sympathetic.

'If you knew what had happened to me, you might not be quite so blasé,' I told her.

'Remember who you're speaking to, DC Sketty,' she said icily.

'I'm sorry, ma'am,' I said, through at least partially gritted teeth. 'I got accused of being undercover today by Cleaver and a friend of his I'd never met before and never want to see again. They said they had a contact in CTC.'

Reineke shook her head firmly. 'There's no leak. Only one person outside of this car knows about your role, and he's known all along. If any of us were working for the other side, we would have leaked details of your operation before it began.'

I looked at Rose.

'This op's airtight,' she told me. 'But you've obviously been through an ordeal. What happened?'

'I got picked up outside my house by Cleaver this

afternoon and there was a guy in the back seat with a gun pointing at me. Hence my reaction just now. They drove me to an isolated spot and told me that they knew I was undercover, and if I didn't admit it, they'd kill me there and then.'

'My God,' said Rose. 'Were you hurt?' Which at least was an acknowledgement of my plight. In the back, Reineke didn't say anything.

'It goes with the territory,' I said, realising I was trying to impress Rose. I had no idea of her personal life. She'd never told me a thing about it, but she didn't wear a ring, and she was attractive and intelligent. 'Anyway,' I continued, getting back to the task in hand, 'I managed to convince them that I was kosher, and it seems they believed me, because they want me for another job.'

Rose frowned. 'Another job?'

'My understanding is that you'd only recently been brought into Cleaver's confidence,' said Reineke.

Straight away, I realised my mistake, which is what happens when you're not concentrating properly. But I was getting to be an accomplished liar by now and I didn't miss a beat. 'Sorry, I meant a proper job. It's getting very confusing with all the stuff going on within the GIU team. Anyway, the man with the gun was definitely the one in charge. I think his name's Aaron Clarn, and I managed to get some footage of him, and audio of the two of them discussing a big gun buy they're going to do. It's on here.' I took off the watch and handed it to Rose and waited while she hooked it up to her laptop.

'I've got no idea of the quality,' I said as the video of my watch-eye view of the interior of Cleaver's car kicked into life, and DCI Reineke leant forward so she too could see.

We watched in silence as Cleaver discussed the gun deal with the Ukrainians that they were planning, and my proposed part in it. Although most of the footage was of the Escort's footwell, the audio was clear, and I got enough shots of him to make it clear who was talking.

'This is exactly what we need,' said Reineke. 'Cleaver incriminating himself like this.'

'Move the footage along,' I said, 'and you should get a view of Clarn.'

While Reineke poked her head through the gap in the seats to take a look, Rose moved the video forward until we came to the part where Cleaver stopped the car outside my house. As I got out, the camera on my wrist moved so that it was looking into the back of the Escort, capturing Aaron Clarn's face and upper body in all its glory.

Rose paused the image and focused in, editing the screen's brightness and tint so we could get a better look at him.

Seeing him then – hollow-faced and narrow-eyed, utterly merciless – brought back memories of how close I'd come to death that afternoon, but there was a sense of pleasure too, because now the bastard was caught on camera.

It was Reineke who spoke first. 'I recognise him. I thought the name rang a bell. Give me a moment, I need to look something up.' She took a laptop out of the briefcase next to her, inserted a dongle into it and started typing away.

'Are you sure you're all right, Chris?' asked Rose, concern

in her voice. 'If you don't mind me saying, you look like crap.'

Even after everything that had happened that day, I was still vain enough to check the mirror to see whether she was right.

She was. I'd lost a lot of weight round my face and had the haunted look of a fugitive who hasn't slept in several days. That was the problem with living alone and working long hours. You tended not to check the mirror.

'It's been a hectic assignment, Rose,' I told her. 'But when this is all over, I'd like to stay on as part of the GIU team, and if there's a way we can nick Cleaver and his buddies without implicating me, it would be a great help.'

'We'll see what we can do,' she said, but I could tell from her expression that she was doubtful. Fair enough. I knew it was a highly optimistic scenario too.

'Is this the same man who threatened you today?' said DCI Reineke, leaning forward with her laptop so that I could see a mugshot of a younger but just as grim-looking Aaron Clarn.

'Yeah, that's him,' I said, deliberately leaving off the 'ma'am' in one of my rather pointless acts of rebellion.

'What have we got on him, ma'am?' asked Rose.

'Quite a bit,' replied Reineke, putting down the laptop. 'His real name is Vincent Berken. Born in 1972, and convicted of the violent abduction and rape of a thirteen-year-old girl when he was just fifteen. He strangled her unconscious and left her for dead in woodland near his home, but somehow she survived. He served four years in youth detention before disappearing while out on licence. He then turned up in Croatia in 1991 and joined a local militia during the war of independence with the Serbs, which is where he got some military and firearms training. He saw action a number of times in both Croatia and Bosnia between '91 and '93, and was identified by MI5 as having been involved in atrocities against Muslim and Serb civilians, including rape and murder.

'But then in 1993, Berken was reported killed in action in eastern Bosnia. We believe he faked his death in order to avoid being charged with absconding from the UK while on licence, or for any war crimes he might have committed over there. He somehow slipped back into the country undiscovered, and then created at least two fake identities using the old *Day of the Jackal* method of stealing the names of dead children born about the same time as him. One of those was Aaron Clarn. Eventually his ruse got found out when he was arrested in 1996 for being part of a notorious gang of armed robbers targeting security vans. The interesting thing about this gang was that they were made up of violent right-wing extremists, with links to football hooligan firms, which provides a potential link to Kalian Roman. This time Berken got a fourteen-year sentence, served seven, and when he was released on licence in May 2003, he disappeared again and hasn't been seen or heard from since. Until now.'

'Well, I can tell you he's a real charmer,' I said, unsurprised by these revelations. I'd seen him in action. He was an animal, and it struck me as ironic that the criminal justice system that Cleaver professed to hate so much had been responsible for leaving Clarn to roam the streets freely.

'And today was the first time you've met him?' asked Reineke.

'That's right, ma'am,' I said without hesitation.

'They're putting a lot of trust in you given that you only expressed an interest to Cleaver in private about getting involved in their activities.'

There was just a hint of suspicion in her voice, but her expression remained inscrutable.

I had no choice but to go along with it. 'I guess I must have been convincing.'

'It might also be a trap.'

'I don't think so. I've got to know Cleaver well over these past months. That was their test of my loyalty back there in the car. This is definitely a kosher gun deal.'

'That may be so,' said Reineke. 'But we can't risk you taking part in it.'

'If I don't drive that car, they'll know for a fact I'm undercover and they'll probably postpone the buy. And that'll be the end of the whole op, without anyone nicked, and me completely compromised. I know you don't want that.' I didn't want it either. I wanted to be there being nicked with them, because that way they'd be far less likely to suspect me.

'It's not a question of what I want. It's a question of our duty of care to you. It's too dangerous.'

'Are you serious, ma'am?' I said, exasperated. 'Two weeks ago, I had a man with a machete holding me over a third-floor balcony trying to slice my face off, and no one seemed too worried about that. I'm willing to take the risk.'

'And that's commendable. But this is different. It would be knowingly – and that's the key word here – sending you directly into extreme danger when there is possibly another way.'

'But that's the problem,' I said. 'There is no other way.'

There was a silence. We'd reached an impasse.

It was DCI Reineke who broke it. 'Actually, I think there might be.'

29

I'll be honest. When I heard Reineke's plan, I didn't think it would work. And technically it didn't. Although not in the way any of us expected.

I understood the brass's reluctance to let me drive Clarn and his mysterious associates to the gun deal. Even if it wasn't a trap, the whole thing had the potential to go tits up if Clarn and his buddies decided to shoot it out. And the brass definitely didn't want the embarrassment of one of their undercover officers being shot on the job, let alone the potential lawsuits.

But you know my problem. I needed this gun deal to go ahead, which was why I sat there and argued against the plan. However, it was all to no avail. It was the boss's brainchild and she liked it, and so I returned home that night frustrated and worried, and consequently slept badly again.

The next morning I called the Chief and told him I'd had another blackout and needed to go for some further hospital scans so probably wouldn't be in for the next couple of days.

He told me to get straight down the hospital, and even offered to drive me there himself, which was a measure of the guy and why I liked him so much. But I said it was okay, that I had a taxi coming, and he reiterated that I should only return to work when I was fully fit. 'You'll be back stronger than ever, Chris,' he said. 'I've got faith in you.'

That was another real stress for me at the time. Knowing that the Chief would feel his faith in me had been misplaced if he ever found out my role in his second in command's downfall. But that, at least, was the advantage of DCI Reineke's plan. If it worked, he'd never know.

It was a Tuesday, and I waited round all day for a call from Cleaver to tell me that the deal was on. But no call came, and I got increasingly angsty as afternoon turned into evening. Reineke's plan relied on me having at least a few hours' notice of when I'd be needed. If Cleaver or Clarn, or whoever, simply turned up at my door and told me it was on, which was the way they seemed to like to do things, then I was in trouble.

CTC already had an armed surveillance team from my old outfit at SO11 on standby, as well as three SO19 gunships, so they'd be ready to go the minute they got the word. The whizz-kids in the CTC tech department had also turned my regular phone into a microphone on which they could listen in, so they would know the minute I was contacted and could act accordingly.

Even so, I felt alone and paranoid, and it was with a sense of real relief when it got to midnight that I finally hit the sack.

The next morning I called Cleaver on the burner phone with CTC listening in. 'How long have I got to be waiting round like this?' I demanded. 'I'm like a caged animal, and what's worse, it's interfering with my sleep and giving me headaches again. And I really don't need that, not after everything I've been through.'

'It looks like tonight, all right? I'll keep you posted, but you need to be ready to leave your place by eight.'

'Am I meant to be driving my own car?'

'Yeah. We'll be meeting up beforehand. I'll text you the rendezvous as soon as I've got it.' He rang off without adding anything further.

A minute later, my regular phone rang. It was DCI Reineke. She told me it was time to put the new plan into action. 'In three hours' time, just before one p.m., you phone Cleaver. You say you've had another blackout. That you're not feeling good, and you need to get to hospital. If he wants to take you to make sure you're not making it up, let him. The hospital you go to is Kingston. We'll contact them and explain the situation. If Cleaver is there with you, we'll get the doctor to let him know that your situation is serious, and that they've got to operate. He'll fall for it if you play your part well enough.'

'Then what? We'll lose our chance.'

'If the gun deal's real, it'll still go ahead. If it isn't real, then we've just saved your life.'

'But, ma'am, you know how surveillance-aware Cleaver is. If you put a team on him, he'll spot it straight away.'

'We won't need to. We've got a location for Aaron Clarn. We'll put one on him instead.'

'How did you manage that so fast?'

'Cleaver's made three calls in the last three days to the same unregistered mobile number from his new burner phone. We don't know the content of the calls, but we triangulated the number to an address in East Acton. The ANPR camera system also showed that Cleaver's car was in the vicinity of that address after he and Clarn dropped you off on Monday afternoon. The tenant registered at the address is a man called Brian Willis, which is another of Clarn's aliases. According to the team we've got down there, he's in residence at the moment.'

'That's useful to know,' I said, as I tried to work out whether this was a good thing for me or not.

And then I made a fateful request. 'I want to be in on the op at the gun deal. I'll be able to positively ID Clarn and Cleaver to the surveillance team. I think I deserve that.'

'That's a good idea,' she said. 'As long as you stay well back from the action. I'll authorise it.'

I wish she hadn't.

30

At 12.50 p.m., impatient with waiting, I called Cleaver's burner phone.

'What is it?' he demanded, sounding testy.

'I'm not good,' I told him, putting on my best sick-note voice. 'I've had another blackout.' I was breathing rapidly, like I was about to hyperventilate. 'Where are you?'

'Over in Hanwell. I'm meant to be meeting a bunch of community leaders.' Cleaver didn't have much time for community leaders, and he spat out the words as if he was referring to paedophiles or defence lawyers. Come to think of it, he didn't have much time for the communities they led either.

He was a good twenty-five minutes away, but I decided to go for it anyway. 'Can you take me to the hospital?'

'How bad are you?'

'I'm bad, mate. I wouldn't ask otherwise. I was out for a while, and I think I must have hit my head when I fell, because it's killing me.'

'Shit,' he said. 'This isn't good.' And I wasn't sure if he

was referring to my ailment or the fact that I'd potentially messed up his plans. 'I'll knock this community leader thing on the head and come over. Are you sure you're up to waiting for me?'

'Yeah, I'll wait,' I said. 'I think I'll be okay. It's probably quicker than calling an ambulance, and it might be nothing, you know.'

'It doesn't sound like nothing. Stay where you are, get yourself a drink of water and I'll be with you asap.'

There was genuine sympathy in his voice. I knew then that he believed my story, and I felt the first pangs of guilt as my other phone rang and Reineke told me I'd done well.

Cleaver picked me up exactly twenty-two minutes later, looking as concerned as he'd sounded on the phone, and we went straight to Kingston Hospital. The whole way I sat listlessly in the front seat – the same one in which I'd been talking for my life less than forty-eight hours previously – leaning against the passenger window, playing the role of a sick man to the hilt. At one point, I shut my eyes and slumped my head to one side, and Cleaver almost crashed the Escort as he reached across and shook me vigorously, telling me to wake up, something close to panic in his voice.

I opened my eyes again, tried to sit up, acted like I couldn't quite make it, and gave him a weak smile.

'I'm here for you, Chrissy boy, just stay awake for me, okay?' The tension was etched all over his face as he looked from me to the road and back again, and it struck me that right then he was one of the few people in the world who actually cared for me. Everyone else was gone.

But he was still here.

And my actions were about to wreck his whole life.

It wasn't a pleasant thought, but self-preservation was always going to win. 'Thanks, mate,' I said quietly. 'I really appreciate it.'

As soon as we found a space in the hospital car park, I shoved open the passenger door, and half staggered, half climbed out, banging into the car next to me and placing both hands on the roof to steady myself.

Cleaver immediately ran round, put an arm round my waist and manoeuvred me towards the hospital entrance, so wrapped up in the situation that he forgot to lock the car.

The rest of it panned out as planned. The two of us stumbled through to Casualty, which at that time of the afternoon was reasonably quiet, and I was quickly seen by a doctor. Cleaver was allowed to come into the treatment area with me, and was what you might call an active presence, bombarding the doctor with questions, and words of encouragement along the lines of getting this man sorted out fast or else . . .

The senior consultant on duty – a tall, cadaverous bald man who Cleaver immediately treated with respect – decided I needed an urgent MRI brain scan to check for signs of an aneurysm, and Cleaver was told to wait in Casualty, or to go home and call back later.

Our final goodbye was rushed. As I was helped into a wheelchair, he squeezed my arm, looked me in the eye and told me that it would it all be fine and that he'd be back as soon as he could. Then he was gone, much to the relief of the medical staff.

Instead of a porter wheeling me to the radiology centre, it was the senior consultant himself, and we'd barely got round the corner when he told me I could get out of the chair now.

'I gather this is all some sort of charade,' he said as I stood up and brushed myself down.

'That's right,' I said. 'Thanks for your help.'

He looked at me. 'All I can say is you're in the wrong profession, and the West End's missing a star.'

31

Eight p.m., just under six hours later. Darkness had fallen, and I was sitting in the back of a black four-door Alfa Romeo thirty yards down the road from Aaron Clarn's flat in East Acton.

By one of those quirks of fate, it was my old team from SO11 doing the mobile surveillance, and my mate Ty Quelch was in the front, along with DC Sheila Flanagan. Sheila was a recent addition who'd only joined the team after I'd left, but who Ty talked highly of, and who I knew he'd been seeing too, which was typical of him. Ty, who was quite literally tall, dark and handsome, had always been something of a Lothario.

On the way here, he'd been bombarding me with questions about what exactly I was doing on what was clearly an anti-terrorism op, when to all intents and purpose I'd gone off to join a unit dealing with low-level gang crime.

I stuck to my cover story that I'd discovered by chance that my new colleague was involved with right-wing extremists and that I'd seen him meet Clarn, who I was there to ID.

Ty had laughed, a bizarre duck-like honk that always attracted stares. 'Christ, Chris, you've had a time of it. Rescuing abducted kids, catching killers, dodging machetes. All in less than six months. I think I want to join. Have they got any vacancies?'

'They may have one after tonight,' I said.

I remember thinking how cool it would be to have my old mate working at GIU with me. That this would be the perfect outcome from this whole debacle. I even thought that if all went well that night, it might actually happen.

Anyway, Ty bought my cover story and nothing more was said about it. Like everyone else involved in the op that night – and there were a lot of us – he'd been briefed that Clarn was a violent extremist, possibly armed, who along with some colleagues – including a serving police officer – was planning to buy a selection of unspecified high-quality firearms from Ukrainian organised-crime contacts, to use in a terrorist atrocity. Information, as you know, was scarce. We didn't know the identities of the Ukrainian contacts or where the buy was going to take place. But Reineke had told us in the briefing that it looked like it was going ahead that night, and that Cleaver would be one of the people accompanying Clarn. Apparently, after he'd left me, there'd been a flurry of phone calls between his and Clarn's burner phones, the last of which had only been an hour ago, and another surveillance team who were watching Cleaver's place reported that he'd left home about half an hour earlier. Because he was surveillance-aware, they'd held back from following. Instead, the op's controllers, led by

Reineke as Gold Commander, were tracking his progress using the burner phone. According to the regular updates we were getting over the radio, he was now only minutes away from Clarn's place.

I couldn't help feeling gutted at the knowledge that Cleaver was driving to his doom. You'd probably say he deserved it, and you'd be right. But when you've worked with someone as closely as I had with him, it's still hard. I was conscious too that even though my original motives might have been pure, I was betraying someone I'd befriended. So as I sat there that night, I was not feeling good about myself, and I was thankful that because all three of us in the car were mic'd up and connected to the control room, the conversation in the Romeo was minimal.

'Control to all cars,' said Reineke into our earpieces. 'Target 2 now turning north into Bradshaw Road, approaching Target 1 address.'

Poor old Cleaver, I thought. He wasn't even Target 1.

'This is Alpha 3,' answered Sheila Flanagan in the front, checking her wing mirror. 'We have the eyeball.'

I turned round in my seat and squeezed into the far corner so I could just about see up the street, using binoculars. There was Cleaver's Escort coming slowly towards us. I focused in on it, immediately recognising him, even though he was wearing a black beanie cap pulled down low.

Then a man who was unmistakably Aaron Clarn came striding out of the target address, wearing dark clothing, a hood pulled up high, a backpack hanging from one shoulder. In the dusk, and from a distance, I couldn't actually see his face, but I recognised that bouncing gait, and the unfeasibly long arms. 'Target 1 has just come out of number 21,' I said into the mic.

'Is it definitely him, Alpha 3?' asked Reineke.

In the end, it was down to me if I got it wrong, and no one wanted another case of mistaken identity, like Jean Charles de Menezes, which had only happened a couple of years before. But I knew I hadn't, although I waited until he'd stopped by the car and looked up the street straight into the gaze of my binoculars before I said: 'It's him, Control. One hundred per cent. And it's definitely Target 2 driving.'

Now that Cleaver had shown up and collected that bastard Aaron Clarn, I felt less guilt about what was going to happen to him. As I watched the two of them converse in the front seat, I have to admit there was a part of me hoping that when they were confronted by firearms officers, they'd choose to shoot it out, because that way no one would ever know about my involvement, and I'd be able to continue my role with GIU, my secrets safe.

As the Escort came towards us, I ducked down in my seat, as did Ty and Sheila, but it was fading light and there were parked cars lining both sides of the street, so even a surveillance-aware operator like Cleaver didn't clock us.

'This is Control,' said Reineke. 'They've turned their burner phones off. We need to follow, but keep well back.'

And that was it. We were on the move.

These were the days before drones, so with a target as slippery as Cleaver, we had to do things the old-fashioned way. And it's not like in the movies either, where you just pull out and follow at a safe distance. Luckily my old surveillance team was ten strong, and operating from four cars and two motorbikes, so we could take it in turns taking the 'eyeball', and not arouse Cleaver's suspicions. Because if at any point he clocked us, then everything was off, and all those months of investigation would go up in smoke. Worse than that, suspicion would probably fall back on me as being the one who'd set them up, and that would be a real problem.

I remember the exact path of the journey that night. I've even walked chunks of it since to remind me of what my last taste of normal life was like.

Cleaver made several classic anti-surveillance plays. He drove back on himself; made last-minute turns, including a completely illegal uey on the Uxbridge Road, but my old team excelled themselves, and kept him in sight.

Things got more complicated when he took a dead-end turning in Shepherd's Bush that led to a row of lock-up garages. Anyone following him down there would have stood out a mile, so the surveillance team had no choice but to hang back.

When after five minutes there was still no sign of them, Reineke began to get angsty that the gun deal was going on inside one of the lock-ups, and she was just in the process of authorising a member of the team to have a recce on foot when Cleaver drove back out of the alley, except this time he was behind the wheel of a black Land Rover Discovery with blacked-out windows. I think we all did a double-take, because he was also wearing a pair of glasses and what looked suspiciously like a false beard, while Clarn, who was sitting beside him, had a scarf pulled up over the lower half of his face so only his eyes were showing. It also looked like there were a couple more people in the back, but it was hard to tell as the Discovery hung a rapid left turn and took off up the road, moving fast.

As Ty fired off the Discovery's reg number into his mic, and the surveillance car parked further up the road took up the eyeball, I began to get my first misgivings. It seemed odd to wear disguises, particularly conspicuous ones, for a gun deal where you weren't expecting to be disturbed.

I was even more troubled when Control came back in the earpiece, informing us that the Discovery's plates were fake. Because that didn't make sense. The whole point of using a police officer to drive you to a gun deal in a police-issue pool car was to avert suspicion. That was the beauty of it. No other cops were going to stop you.

But I didn't say anything. Whatever they had planned, we had more than enough firepower to deal with it. Because it was meant to be a gun buy, the whole surveillance team were armed as a precaution (including me, even though technically I was only there as an observer), and there were a dozen specialist firearms officers from SO19 following us from a distance in unmarked cars, who'd be the ones making the arrests when the time came.

In those last minutes, I genuinely had no idea how it was all going to end up. Instead, I watched from the back of the surveillance car as the Discovery made its way out of Shepherd's Bush and into the more crowded streets of

Kensington, through Sloane Square and up towards Hyde Park. Cleaver no longer tried any counter-surveillance moves. It was as if he'd decided he was safe, now that he was driving a car not registered to him.

It was a chilly night, but clear, and the traffic was much busier now, the streets thronged with people. As we turned onto Pont Street in Knightsbridge, heading into the heart of the bustling West End, it was our turn to take the eyeball again, three cars back from the Discovery. I remember looking at the clock on the dashboard, seeing that it was 21.05, and wondering how far away the rendezvous was.

Then it all happened very fast.

Up ahead, Cleaver braked suddenly, causing the cars behind him to brake hard too, and almost causing us to go straight into the back of one of them. He then took an immediate left onto a side street with a plush-looking Italian restaurant on the corner. We were far enough behind him that we could make the turn without causing suspicion, so Ty followed, while Sheila Flanagan gave a rapid-fire update of his movements into the mic.

That was when I saw that Cleaver had stopped the car in the middle of the road about twenty yards down and put on his hazards. Now we were right up his arse, and instinctively I crouched low in the back seat while Ty indicated and went round him, cursing under his breath.

Remembering that my windows were also blacked out, I turned and stared at the Discovery once we were safely past, which was when I saw Clarn and two other men get out of it. Clarn still had the scarf pulled up over his face, and he was now wearing tinted glasses, along with a long black coat rather than the hoodie he'd been wearing when he left the flat, and a baseball cap. The other two were dressed identically. Long, loose-fitting coats; dark glasses; scarves pulled up. These men were trying to disguise themselves. Not only that, it looked like they were all concealing bulky items beneath their coats, and you didn't have to be Sherlock Holmes to know that something was really wrong here.

'The targets are double-parked outside Warrens dry-cleaner's,' continued Sheila into the mic as we kept driving. 'Three men, including Target 1, now getting out and walking up Gulliver Crescent towards Pont Street. Target 2 remaining in car.'

Ty pulled into a free parking spot on the other side of the road twenty yards or so further down, while I used my binoculars to focus in on Clarn and the other two, who were now marching purposefully into the restaurant in single file, with Clarn at the head. 'Control,' I said, 'they're going into the Villa Amalfi restaurant. This does not look like a gun deal.'

'What do you want us to do?' asked Sheila.

'Stay put. Keep the eyeball,' replied Reineke. 'Everyone else remain nearby but out of sight. I'm now handing over control to Silver Commander on the ground,' she continued, referring to the lead SO19 firearms officer.

As the radio chatter continued, I stared back through the binoculars at Cleaver, who waited in the car thirty yards up the road, still double-parked and now wearing a surgical mask over his false beard – the kind we see all the time these days, but didn't back then. Even from this distance, I could see the tension in his eyes as he sat there like a statue with his engine running, partially blocking the traffic and making no attempt to move. I still had no idea what the hell was happening, and it seemed from the radio chatter that neither did anybody else. It was clear they weren't buying guns in there, but they weren't exactly dressed for dinner either, and in that moment it struck me that this could be one of the hits that Cleaver had told me about that he and his people were planning – some metropolitan left-wing progressive politician, exactly the type who might be eating in a plush Italian restaurant. I was just about to say something . . .

And then *bang*. It happened. My question was answered as the unmistakable sound of gunfire erupted from the direction of the restaurant. And it was coming from at least two different weapons.

I remember freezing in shock as I caught sight of the muzzle flashes through the restaurant's open glass frontage, and saw a young couple on the pavement turn round in its direction, then, realising what was happening, immediately start running down the street, past the Discovery, where Cleaver still sat motionless behind the wheel.

But when you're a police officer, especially a younger, hungrier one like I was then, you don't freeze for long, because your instincts are always to run towards danger, so as Sheila and Ty both simultaneously yelled into their mics for urgent assistance, I yanked the Glock 17 from my shoulder holster and exited the passenger door on the pavement side, stumbling in the process and going down painfully on one knee, the adrenaline pumping. But I was up quickly, shoving on my black police cap so everyone would know I was one of the good guys, thankful that the gun hadn't gone off by accident, and knowing that whatever happened now, my cover was well and truly blown.

At the same moment, I saw a body come crashing through the restaurant's plate-glass window and land motionless on the pavement outside, and heard Ty yell a shocked 'What the fuck?' as he and Sheila jumped out of the car too, guns drawn and caps on. Because the worrying thing was, there were still shots being fired inside the restaurant, including bursts of automatic fire, which meant that this wasn't a hit on some specified target either, and could only mean one thing. My intelligence was wrong. Cleaver had fed me a lie. This wasn't the gun buy needed for some kind of terrorist atrocity. This *was* the terrorist atrocity. And now, as I ran onto the street, I could just make out terrified diners behind the shattered glass as they crawled round manically on all fours trying to find some kind of cover in an enclosed space, like goldfish being hunted in a bowl.

That was when Cleaver saw us. I don't know if he recognised me or not – with everything that was going on, I suspect he probably didn't – but it was clear he now knew he had no choice but to try to escape, and he immediately pulled away, accelerating in our direction, keeping his head down to avoid being ID'd.

Sheila was the one nearest to him, and she ran across the

road to cut him off, gun held in front of her two-handed, screaming at him to stop, but he just kept coming. Ty and me were running across too, following her, but everything was happening too fast. At the last second, Sheila must have realised that there was no way Cleaver was going to stop, and she fired two rounds at the Discovery's windscreen, but it was too late. The vehicle hit her head on, sending her hurtling over the bonnet like a rag doll. She hit the windscreen and bounced off, ending up on the tarmac under the front wheels.

Cleaver was right beside us at this point, and still not looking our way. He'd instinctively slowed the car to a crawl as he presumably realised that he had two choices. Stop the car and surrender, or drive straight over the police officer he'd just hit, and add another decade to the sentence he was already going to get for his part in what had happened. Ty raced towards the driver's-side window, screaming at him to put his hands up. I was literally just behind Ty as he grabbed the door handle with one hand while pointing his Glock inside with the other, which was the moment Cleaver made his choice and accelerated over Sheila Flanagan, crushing out any life that was left in her.

But Ty didn't let go of the handle, and was forced to break into a run as the Discovery picked up speed.

By now, I was facing the Discovery's rear window. I thought about taking a shot at Cleaver, because even though I couldn't see him through the tinted glass, I knew where he'd be sat, but I also knew that if I took a shot at an unarmed man and hit him (which probably wouldn't happen anyway), it could be the end of my career, because that's the way it works for us. You try to do your job and protect people, but the moment you're perceived to have made a mistake, even in the heat of the moment where a wrong decision can cost you your life, you're hung out to dry. By your bosses; by the media; by the lawyers and the pressure groups; and even by the public. And do you know what? I didn't want to kill him either, because I knew him. He'd saved my life. It was all too personal.

Behind me, I could still hear shots and the sound of cars screeching to a halt, but I didn't turn round. Instead, I continued to point my gun at the Discovery, finger tensed on the trigger, knowing that my window of opportunity, which you could count in micro-seconds, was already disappearing. Ty was still holding onto the door and screaming at Cleaver to stop, but any second now he was going to have to let go, because otherwise he'd fall and get dragged along.

And then a single shot rang out.

Ty stumbled back into one of the parked cars, bouncing off it in the process, and for a second I thought it was him who'd been hit, but then the Discovery gradually came to a halt a few yards further on, and when the horn started going as if someone was leaning on it, I realised it was Ty who'd fired the shot, and at that range he could hardly miss. Which meant that Baz Cleaver, the man I'd got to know so well over these past few months, was probably dead.

Ty straightened up, holstered his gun and without even glancing at me, ran over to where DC Sheila Flanagan lay motionless on the ground.

So far, the whole thing, from the first shots being fired to where we were now, had taken no more than ten seconds, and as I turned back in the direction of the restaurant, I saw one of the surveillance cars pull up directly outside it, and two men I used to work with – Joe McCallister and Mehmet Tekin – jump out with their guns drawn. At the same time, one of the gunmen appeared in the restaurant doorway, scarf pulled up over his face and holding what looked like a machine pistol, which he pointed straight at them.

People sometimes say dramatic events happen in slow motion. Let me put that myth to bed. They don't. When violence breaks out, the protagonists operate almost entirely by instinct, which means that they react far faster than they would if they had time to think about it, and at that point it seemed like all three of them opened fire at once. I was running towards the restaurant now, still twenty yards away, too far to get a decent shot in with a pistol, but close enough to see the muzzle flashes. Mehmet took a full burst of fire and went down, while Joe disappeared from view behind the car and I couldn't see whether he'd been hit or was just taking cover. The gunman was still on his feet but staggering round aimlessly, like he was drunk, his grip on the gun a lot looser. At the same time, further shots erupted from inside the restaurant, shattering more of the plate-glass window and sending another member of the team, who'd just arrived on his scooter and who I didn't recognise because he was wearing a helmet, tumbling off it before he'd even had time to stop. Everything had gone crazy. It was surreal. Like some insane, drug-induced dream. And I was right in the middle of it. I knew I had to do something, so I kept running towards the gunman, Glock outstretched in both hands, yelling at him to drop his weapon.

He staggered round to face me, still clutching the machine pistol, and out of the corner of my eye, I could see Joe, my old colleague who'd disappeared behind the car, getting back up and pointing his own weapon towards him.

By now, the gunman and I were less than ten yards apart. He wasn't dropping his weapon, and I had to make a decision – and the thing was, I'd already made it, and I was automatically slowing up so that I could get more accuracy, and then I was pulling the trigger. Two shots. A double tap, aimed at his torso.

They hit their mark too, and he staggered backwards. But he was still upright and holding the gun, so I cracked off two more, my arms jolting from the Glock's kick, and this time he went straight down without pulling the trigger, landing on his back amongst the shattered glass from the restaurant window that was scattered all across the pavement.

Almost immediately, another of the gunmen appeared from behind the restaurant door. He saw me, I saw him, and I was already turning my gun his way, trying to use a parked van as cover, only a few yards between us, but then he'd darted back inside the restaurant. I had no idea if it was Clarn or not – he'd already disappeared from view.

I came out behind the car, and I don't know what made me do it – adrenaline probably, and the old Bonkers Sketty mentality – but I ran towards the restaurant entrance, gun still outstretched, and that was when I caught sight through the glass door of the two surviving gunmen running towards the back of the restaurant.

There was no way I should have been pursuing them in a confined space. It broke all the rules. We needed to wait for the SO19 gunships, and Silver Commander, to make sure the scene was safe to enter, and that there weren't more gunmen or booby traps waiting inside, because otherwise it raised all kinds of legal issues. But I knew for a fact there were only two gunmen, and they were running, and for some reason SO19 weren't there yet, even though I could hear the sirens, and I could see already that innocent people were injured. There was a woman lying in a foetal position clutching her stomach next to an overturned table, her face a mask of agony. She looked maybe fifty, and she was wearing a spangly top and black trousers. Her partner was lying down, trying to cover her from any more shots, his face frozen in shock as he stared at the shattered window. If we waited around, she could die. And these two bastards – including Clarn – could escape. And right then, I just wasn't ready to accept that.

I computed all these things in the space of maybe two seconds, then I threw open the front door and ran in there, ignoring Joe's shout telling me not to go in, that we could get them round the back, which might have been true, but it might not have been too, and anyway, the rational part of my brain wasn't really working right then.

As I ran through the foyer and into the main part of the restaurant, which suddenly seemed deathly silent, although it could have been the ringing in my ears from the gunshots, I saw one of the gunmen turning into a corridor that looked like it led down to the toilets. I had a split second to glance at the scene around me. The restaurant appeared empty, because everyone was lying on the floor. People stared up at me with terrified faces. Others lay motionless or injured, blood already pooling around them.

I had no time to stop and help. Instead, I took off down the corridor after the gunmen, ripping out my earpiece so I didn't have to listen to the manic chatter coming through it as everything went to shit.

I was sprinting, almost slipping on the shiny floor, and as I rounded a corner that led to the fire exit, I just had time to see the fire door slam shut behind them. I was pretty certain they didn't know I was coming, but if they did, then the chances were they'd be waiting on the other side of it to take me out as I came through, and that would be it, I'd be a dead man. But I didn't stop, didn't even hesitate, because it was like I was operating on some kind of kamikaze autopilot. I kicked the fire door, and as it swung open, I saw the two gunmen stopped dead at most five yards away, both with their backs to me, both pointing their weapons towards something to our right.

They swung round fast as they heard me coming. The one nearest to me was a big guy – much bigger than Clarn – which made him an easy target. He was holding a short-barrelled shotgun – a Remington or similar – and getting ready to fire.

'Armed police!' I yelled, but I was already pulling the

Glock's trigger, and this time I kept pulling it, hitting the man in front of me repeatedly. Shots were coming back the other way too, although it must have been Clarn firing, because the guy I'd hit had already dropped his shotgun and was lurching all over the place like he was being hit from the back as well as the front, and I jumped back inside the building, flattening myself against the wall as the heavy fire door swung closed again, bullets splintering it and ricocheting madly through the corridor.

The shooting stopped as quickly as it had begun, and I counted to three in my head, then kicked the door open a second time, though staying well to the side in case Clarn was waiting to take a potshot at me. But this time no shots came back, and I couldn't believe he was that cool a character that he'd stand there and wait for me to show my face, especially given the fact that I could now hear sirens coming from all directions, so I ran back out and saw the man I'd shot lying motionless on the ground, and Clarn scrambling cat-like over a high but dilapidated wooden fence that looked like it led into an alley.

I knew by this point I was taking unnecessary risks, but I felt like I was on fire, and more than anything right now, I just wanted to take down this bastard. So I took off towards the back fence, jumping over the other gunman's prone body.

That was when I saw a young woman crouched down behind a row of recycling bins, staring over at me. She had the tense, hunted look of an animal, and her eyes were wide with fear.

I motioned for her to stay down and mouthed the words 'you're safe now' while I continued my insane one-man pursuit, leaping up onto the fence and popping my head over the top like a jack-in-the-box. The fence did indeed border an alley, and Clarn was already climbing the eight-foot-high gate that led out onto the main street. He didn't look back, just disappeared over the top.

But I was moving fast too. You've got to remember that in those days, I was an angry, hot-headed guy who only really felt alive when I was taking big risks. I sprinted to the end of the alley and jumped up at the gate, grabbing the top with my hands and hauling myself upwards.

Clarn was in the middle of the road now, pointing his weapon – it looked like an MP5 with a retractable stock – directly at the driver of an oncoming car. The car wasn't going fast – there was too much traffic for that. The driver did an emergency stop and I could see that she was a scared-looking woman in her thirties. I was still hanging by both hands from the gate, with only my head and shoulders showing, so there was nothing I could do to intervene as Clarn pulled her out of the driver's seat.

I heard the shouts of armed police from further down the street telling him to drop his gun. Instead, he grabbed the woman and held her in front of him, using her as a human shield as he opened fire on them with controlled three-round bursts.

Then he was jumping into the car – a two-seater Saab convertible – and I was scrambling over the gate and down the other side, yanking out the Glock, trying to remember how many rounds I'd fired, no longer caring about how exposed I was, determined to get the bastard.

But as I hit the pavement and rolled over, all I could see was the Saab hurtling up the road between the two lines of traffic, leaving the woman lying terrified but unharmed on the pavement. 'Police! Stay down!' I called to her as I ran past into the street, dodging the traffic, thinking about taking a shot at the Saab's tyres, but it was already too far away, and anyway it was far too dangerous with all the other cars about.

An unmarked surveillance car with the blue light flashing on the dashboard was hurtling towards me from the direction of the restaurant, and I stood in the road, gun in hand, the black police cap still on my head, incredibly, and flagged it down.

That was when I realised it was Ty in the driver's seat, a look of manic concentration on his face. He slowed up immediately and I jumped inside.

'One gunman in that Saab ahead,' I said breathlessly, and he fed the information calmly into the mic while accelerating away, forging an extremely tight path through the traffic, most of which had come to a halt as the drama unfolded all around.

The Saab was maybe fifty yards ahead. Coming towards it from further up the road were several more unmarked cars with blue lights flashing, which I guessed must have been the SO19 gunships, although God knows where they'd been for the last few minutes.

The Saab was trapped, and its brake lights came on as

Clarn slowed down and took a sudden sharp left turn into the stationary traffic. He found a gap between two cars and literally forced his way through it, hitting both of them in the process, before taking off up a side street.

The SO19 cars were still a hundred yards distant, and Ty clearly didn't want to risk losing the Saab, so he slowed up too and followed Clarn through the gap he'd made, all the time giving a tense running commentary of the pursuit into the mic.

The adrenaline was still pumping through me. I was leaning forward, resting my gun on the dashboard, and it was only then that I realised I hadn't put my seat belt on. It didn't matter. I wanted to be able to move fast.

Ty had always been a good driver, and he accelerated fast into the turning, mounting the pavement to dodge an illegally parked van with its hazards on. We were now on a narrow residential street lined with whitewashed town houses that probably cost a couple of million apiece. Barely twenty yards now separated us from the Saab, and we could both read the plate on it. Ty was still in the process of reciting it into the mic when Clarn suddenly made an emergency stop in a ferocious screech of tyres.

'Get out the car!' I yelled as Ty slammed on the anchors. I was already ducking down in my seat and throwing open the door, gun still in hand, as the car came to a halt and the interior resounded with the sound of automatic gunfire, bullets peppering the windscreen in a wild pattern of holes.

I literally dived out of the open passenger door, using it as cover, and hit the tarmac hard, rolling over and catching a split-second glimpse of my old mate Ty slumped sideways in his seat, belt still on, clearly hit. But it was self-preservation time now, and I crawled like crazy towards the back of the car, trying to get out of the way as another burst of gunfire tore it up and I felt a rain of broken glass land on the back of my legs.

I flipped round onto my back, raising the gun to fire in case Clarn was coming round the side of the car, but he wasn't. Instead, through the ringing in my ears, I heard a door slam, and then the Saab was pulling away at speed, and even amidst the carnage and the fear, I couldn't help feeling just a tiny touch of admiration for the way this guy simply wouldn't give up. But at the same time, I wanted more than anything to kill him, and I started to scramble to my feet, ready to take up a firing position behind the bullet-ridden car door – which was when my right leg literally went from under me and I fell backwards onto the road, and I realised that I'd been hit too.

32

Tonight

Teller

Sketty finishes speaking. He's told this part of the story in a manner that's fast and furious, and I can tell that he's genuinely reliving the events of that night. No one – *no one* – is that good an actor.

He takes a deep breath, sits – no, almost slumps – back in his chair as if the recollection has taken it out of him, and stares at me with a pain in his eyes that looks so real, it demands that you believe him. It's what's so disarming about this man. He looks as he sounds. Like one of the good guys.

'And that's how it happened,' he says at last. 'My best friend, Ty Quelch, died of his injuries, as I'm sure you know. He was wearing a ballistic vest, but he took a bullet in the eye. One of ten innocent people killed that night. And many injured.'

'Including yourself,' I say, giving him a sympathetic look.

'Yes,' he answers. 'Including myself. I was hit by a single

round in the hip, which caused a major fracture and eventually resulted in traumatic osteoarthritis and a shortening of the left leg. I've walked with a limp ever since. And do you know what? I don't know about you' – he nods towards my wheelchair – 'but whenever I dream, I'm always able to walk normally, or even run. It's like none of this ever happened.'

That's another thing about Sketty. He draws you in like the best salesman. Finds shared experiences for you to talk about. Feigns interest.

'I'm the same,' I say with a rueful smile, pretending it's working. 'It's as if a part of our brain refuses to accept what's happened to us. But it makes it painful to wake up and have to accept reality once again.' I sigh. 'Thank you for sharing your recollection of that night with me. I know it must be hard to recount it.'

'I relive it in my head all the time. Always wondering why I did what I did. I was mad running into that restaurant, and keeping up the chase like that. I should have just left it. There's not a day that goes by when I don't regret it.'

'I can understand that,' I say, and an image of dear, beautiful Victoria comes into my head. 'There's not a day that goes by when I don't think about that night either. I lost the love of my life in Villa Amalfi.'

Sketty nods. 'I know. I remember you telling me in the email.'

'The Villa Amalfi was one of the worst terrorist atrocities in British history. It was also a terrible intelligence failure.'

'I did what I could,' he tells me, his expression hardening.

'Yes. But there have always been so many questions unanswered. That's why I've spent the fourteen years since searching for the truth.'

'And I've been as truthful as I can. I've even told you about my part in the killing of Kerry Masters. No one else in the whole world knows about that.'

Which isn't entirely true. I already knew. But I didn't put the details in the dossier. I knew better than to do that. I kept it out as a trap to see if Sketty would admit his part voluntarily. And I was surprised that he did. But that doesn't make him innocent of the charges I'm building against him. Far from it. I'm convinced he is a monster. An ice man.

But perhaps you're wondering why I am so suspicious. What do I know that you don't?

'Plenty' is the answer to that question. And as I'm sure you've guessed, there's more to come in this story, but reflect on this: his account of events so far is almost entirely uncorroborated. The people who could contradict him are all dead. He walked around for the full five and a half months of that undercover operation with a recording device on his wrist, and yet he only ever made two short recordings. And think on this too. If you'd been a witness to a murder like that of Kerry Masters, would you not say something to your bosses? Even if you'd had some (unwitting) involvement in it? The fact that he was an undercover police officer doing a dangerous job would surely have been taken into account. But he kept quiet. Allowed himself to be pulled in deeper.

You might not share my suspicions yet, but you will. I have set a new trap for Sketty now, one I feel certain he'll step into as this story continues. Then the truth will finally come out.

The fire is beginning to die, and I manoeuvre my wheelchair over and use the tongs to add another couple of logs to the embers, watching as they catch, thinking that tonight has been the culmination of so much work, and I wish to savour it.

'What more do you want from me?' asks Sketty as I reverse back to my position by the drinks table, facing him across the room.

'Only the truth,' I say. 'Would you be good enough to continue your story, about how you finally broke open the Villa Amalfi case?'

He sighs, looks mildly irritated, but of course he knows he has no choice. After all, I have the dossier on him. 'Where do you want me to take it up from?'

'From when Tania Wild made contact with you.'

And when I say that, I see him visibly tense, even though he must have known this was coming.

PART TWO

Six Weeks Ago

33

When I was a young boy, my mum used to tell me to enjoy my childhood, because being an adult was hard, harder than a kid could ever imagine. She was a very unhappy, very stressed woman who felt that she'd been let down by life, and that her job was to prepare my brother and me to be let down too, so that somehow it wouldn't affect us as badly as it had clearly affected her.

That's my theory anyway. And her influence worked. Because deep down I've always been fearful of happiness, knowing that it could be ripped away from me at any time. And in those few settled periods of my life when I have been happy, that's exactly what's happened. It's been ripped away by outside events.

As a consequence, I tend to spend a lot of time looking back on those good times with a profound but comforting melancholy, resigned to the fact that whatever happens, I'll never experience that kind of happiness again. I also like to fantasise about what might have been had things just turned out a little bit differently – the life I could have led;

the loved ones I could have spent more time with; the places we could have travelled to – and I was in the process of creating one of those fantasies, while staring at a framed photo of Karen and Grace that still sits on my living-room mantelpiece, in the same house where I've now lived for almost eighteen years, when my phone rang.

I didn't want to answer it. I was imagining the three of us on a beach somewhere in New South Wales, north of Sydney, where we'd planned to settle, young again, carefree. I could still hear Grace's high-pitched giggle as she played in the sand, even after all these years. I wanted to keep that sound in my head forever.

I was conscious of a single tear running slowly down my cheek. I cry a lot these days, fourteen years on from the night that destroyed my life, and left me alone and lame, living in my past.

But then, with a sigh, I broke off from the fantasy, knowing I was just torturing myself, which was something I had plenty of time to do later, and reached over to pick up the phone from the coffee table.

I didn't recognise the number, and when that happens, I tend to leave it to go to voicemail, but this time for some reason I just answered, giving the caller a curt hello that suggested I wasn't in the mood for small talk or a sales pitch.

A woman's voice. 'Mr Sketty? Chris? My name's Tania Wild, I'm an investigative journalist researching the Villa Amalfi massacre. I was hoping you'd spare the time for me to interview you as the man who shot dead two of the terrorists.'

I tensed immediately. 'How did you know about that? The information's not in the public domain.'

'As I said, I'm an investigative journalist. And I—'

'Well I don't want to talk about it,' I said, cutting her off, 'nor do I want anything about me put out in public. I've been trying to forget what happened for the past fourteen years.'

And making a very bad job of it too. But I wasn't going to tell her that.

'Do you believe the official version of events? That it was a terrorist attack? Because I've got information that suggests it wasn't.'

Again I tensed, a finger of curiosity scratching away somewhere inside me. 'No one in the last fourteen years has called it anything other than a terrorist attack,' I said, making no attempt to lighten my tone as I reached over and opened my laptop. 'Can you spell your name for me?'

'T-a-n-i-a W-i-l-d. I've got a good track record, Mr Sketty, and do you mind if I call you Chris?'

'Yeah, I do,' I said, googling her name. An attractive woman with short dark hair and a confident look, somewhere in her forties, appeared on the screen. She had her own website, and it appeared she'd written for some of the nationals and had won several press awards. She wasn't big-time but she did indeed have a good track record. If it was actually her, of course. I'd learnt to be sceptical of everything I was told until the evidence showed otherwise. 'So what was it, then, if it wasn't a terror attack?' I asked her.

'I'll tell you everything I know – and I can promise you, it's good – and I'll even show you the evidence I have to back my theory up, but only if you're prepared to talk to me in detail about your own take on the case.'

'My take's the same as everyone else's. It was a terror attack. And I don't want to talk about it. Not to you. Not to anyone. It's the past. And if you write anything that identifies my role in public, I'll sue you.'

'I won't,' she said calmly, 'but I think you'll be interested in what I have to say. Please. I'll even come to you. I'd buy you a drink somewhere, but I really don't want to discuss this in public.'

I'd been on the verge of ending the call, but curiosity was getting the better of me. In the months after it happened, I'd had numerous calls from journalists wanting to talk to me about the Villa Amalfi massacre, but those calls had dried up many years ago now. I considered her offer. It was a grey Tuesday afternoon in November. I was technically unemployed. I clearly didn't have anything better to do. 'Okay,' I said, somewhat reluctantly. 'But I'll come to you if you don't mind. I could do with getting out of the house.'

'No problem,' she said, and gave me an address in Highgate. 'When can you do it?'

I looked at my watch. It had just turned 1.30. 'How about three o'clock?'

'Three o'clock it is.'

34

The Villa Amalfi massacre scarred the country. Like so many terrorist attacks, it was brutal and pointless. Eight civilians died inside the restaurant. Thirteen others were wounded. Two police officers – Ty Quelch and Sheila Flanagan – also died of their injuries, and four others, myself included, were wounded. The two gunmen I shot were Martin Greene, the ex-soldier whose original phone call to Cleaver had started the whole undercover operation going, and Tomas Luzanyc, a Croatian associate of Clarn's from his days in the Yugoslav civil war. Neither survived. Nor did their get-away driver, Baz Cleaver, who'd been killed instantly by the single round that Ty had fired at him.

As for the third gunman, Aaron Clarn, the man who'd shot me and killed Ty, he escaped that night, abandoning the Saab he'd fled in close to the row of lock-up garages where he and Cleaver had collected their accomplices earlier that evening. Within an hour of the attack, armed police had surrounded the lock-ups. But when they finally identified and raided the one they believed the gunmen had rented, there was no sign of Clarn. What they did find, however, was a large patch of blood in the far corner, which DNA tests later matched as being his. One theory was that he was executed inside the garage and his body taken away by his killer or killers. In truth, it had never sounded a particularly likely story, and left far more questions than answers, but in the fourteen years since the massacre, all attempts to locate him had drawn a blank, and he was still officially listed as missing, presumed dead.

As for whoever had organised the attack (and those in charge of the police inquiry had always suggested there were others involved), no one was ever tried, or even charged, for their part in the events, and the CTC inquiry, which had started off involving literally hundreds of officers, had now been wound down to almost nothing. The last I'd heard, they still had two token DCs working on it, but with so many other terrorist attacks and plots to deal with in the intervening years, CTC had their hands full, and it felt as though they'd let Villa Amalfi pass into the history books, which some might argue was convenient for them, since in many ways they were culpable for it happening.

Not that it had harmed the careers of the two officers most involved in the run-up to the attack – Rose Bennett, and DCI Marina Reineke, as she was then. Now she was Commander Reineke, the head of CTC and the country's most senior anti-terrorist officer, while Rose had risen to the rank of DI.

Even so, I wasn't entirely surprised that an investigative journalist like Tania Wild had started looking into the case. Ten innocent people had died that night, and there were still some huge unanswered questions about the whole thing, not least the motive, as well as Aaron Clarn's complete disappearance in the face of one of the biggest police manhunts in UK history. In many ways, I was surprised other journalists hadn't asked probing questions about the attack before. There'd been plenty written about it over the years (two of the injured survivors even wrote books about their experience) and no shortage of madcap conspiracy theories, but because one of the gunmen had allegedly shouted 'Allahu Akbar!' before opening fire, the general consensus of opinion was that the massacre was probably carried out by a group of violent home-grown losers trying to shoot their way into legend and pin their crimes on Islamic extremists.

And my opinion? Well, I just wanted to try to forget the whole thing. I'd always had my doubts that Clarn was dead, and for a long time I bore huge anger towards him for everything he'd done and the way he'd ruined my life. In some of my darker moments, I'd played out fantasies in my head where he was tied to a chair and I beat, stabbed and burned him. Tortured him in numerous gruesome and imaginative ways, while all the time he begged and bleated for mercy. But I never showed him any, and when the fantasy had finally finished playing out and Clarn lay slumped dead and broken in the chair, hardly recognisable as a human being, I'd be sweating and exhausted, my rapid heartbeat loud in my chest, as if I'd actually carried out the attack rather than simply imagined it. In the end, I'd sought psychiatric help, and after more than a year of sessions with a psychologist who specialised in treating PTSD sufferers, I learnt not to waste my time and my energy on Clarn, and instead consigned him to my past, where, like the Villa Amalfi attack itself, he was now meant to reside peacefully but never quite did.

Which was probably why I was intrigued by what Tania Wild had to say, even though I still wasn't sure how much I was prepared to share with her.

It was bang on three when I arrived at the address she'd given me, a modern detached house at the end of a leafy cul-de-sac that backed onto Highgate Cemetery. I'm no estate agent, but it was probably worth two million at the very least and definitely not the kind of place you'd buy with an income from journalism. A six-foot-high stone wall surrounded the front of the property, and access was gained through a security gate with a buzzer but no camera that I could see, which was currently open.

My hip was hurting and my limp more pronounced as I climbed the steps to the front door using my walking stick for support. I'd come by Tube and walked the half-mile or so from Archway station, and I was paying the price for it now. I've always found it hard to come to terms with my injury. Walking used to represent freedom for me. I would go on long hikes alone, often way out of London, to get rid of life's stresses, and the fact that I no longer can has actually grown harder to bear with time. It's why I still take every opportunity I can to put one foot in front of the other, even though it often hurts.

Tania was already opening the door as I reached it. She was dressed casually in a loose-fitting sweater, yoga pants and moccasin slippers, and looked younger and somehow fresher in the flesh.

'Your work's obviously paid you well,' I told her with the vestiges of a smile.

She smiled back, and I thought that even her gleaming white teeth looked fresh. 'Hardly. I'm house-sitting for the people who live here while they're in Barbados for the next two months.'

'How the other half lives, eh?' I said as she led me through a large entrance hall dominated by a staircase wide enough to drive a car up, and into a kitchen with a long, curving island running down the middle that faced out onto a small but pretty garden with a kid's swing hanging from the branch of an oak tree at the end. It was the type of garden I would have loved if I'd still had a family, and just the sight of the swing made my stomach turn a somersault. They say time eases suffering. In my experience, close to sixteen years now since the death of my daughter, it doesn't.

'Absolutely,' she said, 'but at least these people aren't arseholes. That would have really stuck in the throat. Can I get you a drink?'

'Coffee, please,' I said, noticing a Nespresso machine. 'Black, no sugar.'

While she located a capsule, I asked her why she had started investigating the case.

'Because it intrigued me,' she answered as the machine hissed and bubbled. 'Here we have a full-on terror attack committed by right-wing extremists, and yet what was the point of it? They attacked a restaurant patronised almost exclusively by white people, and made no attempt to deliberately kill any of the people of colour in there. In fact, there were no people of colour amongst the dead.'

'I thought the working theory was that they were trying to make it look like Muslim extremists. Didn't one of them shout "Allahu Akbar"?'

'And do *you* think that was the motive?'

'I honestly don't know,' I said, taking the proffered coffee. 'I do think that the gunmen saw the Villa Amalfi as a symbol of the liberal establishment, and it's the establishment itself that they wanted to bring down. They had a getaway driver, so they obviously planned an exit after they'd shot up the place, and it wouldn't have hurt their cause to make it look like an Islamic attack. Extremists tend to be violent fantasists. The act of killing is as important to them as the final goal, which is often something vague and far in the future. In other words, they're not exactly rational actors.'

Tania shrugged. 'Perhaps, but that wasn't the case here. I believe they wanted to make it look like a terrorist attack, but that wasn't their *actual* motive that night.'

She sounded very certain, and that intrigued me. 'Then what was their motive?'

'Let me show you something,' she said, climbing onto a stool next to an open laptop on the island. I climbed (more slowly) onto a stool next to her while she tapped a key and brought up an image.

I leant in closer and saw that it was paused film from

inside the Villa Amalfi, clearly taken from one of its own CCTV cameras, and from the date stamp in the bottom left-hand corner, I could see that it was from that night. The time said 20:56, which I knew was just before the attack started. The quality of the image was good. The restaurant was full, and I could make out the individual diners as they ate, drank and chatted without a care in the world, having no idea that within a matter of seconds, all their lives were going to change irrevocably, and in some cases come to an abrupt and terrifying end. A young couple sat at one of the tables. The girl had lustrous, brightly dyed red hair, but her face wasn't visible because her back was to the camera, while her boyfriend was holding a glass of red wine to his mouth and smiling. I tried to remember if they were amongst the casualties, and then stopped myself. I really didn't want to know.

'Are you okay watching this?' Tania asked me, with what looked to be genuine concern on her face.

'Am I going to learn something?'

She nodded. 'I believe you will.'

'Then go ahead and press play,' I told her, trying to keep the tension I was experiencing out of my expression. I could feel my anxiety levels growing as I looked at the screen. PTSD does that to you. Certain situations – they could be innocuous, or they could be more serious, like experiencing violence once again – will trigger something in the brain that takes the person right back to the traumatic event. I'd spent a long time being treated in an effort to minimise the effects of my PTSD, but it was never going to go away entirely, and watching real-life footage of what had happened was probably the worst thing I could have done. But at the same time I couldn't take my eyes off the screen as she started the film running at half-speed.

'I really don't like watching this either,' she said, 'but shockingly, I'm getting more used to it.'

I didn't reply as on the screen the three gunmen moved rapidly into shot in single file, shoving the female maître d' to one side. They were already drawing their weapons, scarves pulled high up over their faces, making identification next to impossible. I knew who they were, though, from their guns, and it was Clarn, the leader, who was at the front.

The three gunmen fanned out into the restaurant as if they knew exactly what they were doing and had already rehearsed this move several times. Martin Greene, the gunman I'd shot out the front of the restaurant, was pointing his gun at a separate section to the right of the front door, while Clarn and the other gunman, Tomas Luzanyc, covered the fifty or so diners in the main dining area.

'Watch Clarn,' said Tania, slowing the film right down. 'Do you see the way he's scanning the room like he's looking for someone? There's no sound, but this is the time that, according to two witnesses, he shouts "Allahu Akbar, nobody move!"'

I concentrated on his movements, surprised now the film was running that I didn't actually feel that anxious any more. Now I just felt anger as I watched him, tall and spider-like, revelling in his power. But I wasn't sure what Tania meant by Clarn looking for someone. Yes, as he stood there holding the MP5 machine pistol with the retractable stock that he'd used to shoot Ty and me, he was definitely surveying the room, but that would be a natural thing to do if you wanted to make sure that you had everyone under control.

'I don't see how you can tell he's looking for someone,' I said.

'He is. His head moves from side to side, then settles in the middle of the room. At this point, he looks agitated. And I believe that's because he has two targets he's been told to kill, who were meant to be sitting together. Except one's there and the other isn't. So for a couple of seconds he doesn't know what to do. Do you see him looking round again?'

'Yes, he looks agitated, but then he would be. The adrenaline would have been pounding through all of them in there.'

She paused the film. 'But the thing is, he's wasting time. They all are. They're just standing there. Not firing, not doing anything, for a full nine seconds after Clarn appears to shout "Allahu Akbar". And then suddenly this.' She started the film again. 'Look. Clarn sees something off camera to his left.'

As I watched, it did indeed look as though something had caught his eye, making him turn round very fast, already raising the MP5, holding it two-handed, with the retractable stock pushed into his shoulder, military-style.

Tania slowed the film right down. 'And that something is the second target he's been looking for,' she continued.

'The one he couldn't see at the table. She's on her way back from the toilets, seemingly blissfully unaware of what's going on, when Clarn sees her, and immediately, without any hesitation, he opens fire.'

She stopped the footage as flame shot from the MP5, then minimised the image on the laptop screen. 'Now let's see what he was shooting at,' she said, bringing up a different image, which came from another of the Villa Amalfi's CCTV cameras. This one covered the side of the restaurant to the right of the front door, and showed a blonde woman in her twenties, a phone to her ear, rounding the corner from the corridor that I remembered led down to the toilets and the rear of the building. The woman's face was already registering shock as she saw what was happening. In the corner of the screen, with his back to her as he covered the other diners, was Martin Greene, the third gunman.

Tania started the filming running again at half-speed and I watched as the blonde woman turned on her heel, stumbled and, keeping low, literally dived out of the way, sending her phone flying, before scrambling up the corridor out of sight. It was clear from the way other people in the vicinity were also diving for cover that the gunfire from the MP5 was coming their way.

'Clarn was deliberately trying to hit that woman,' said Tania, 'and it's only after she's gone that he and Luzanyc turn and direct their fire into the other diners. And look at Greene, the third gunman. He seems to be as much caught by surprise as the diners, which leads me to think he wasn't privy to the plan to open fire indiscriminately, and may have thought it was some kind of individual hit rather than a massacre.' She sat back and looked at me. 'Now, are you prepared to watch what happens next, Chris? I've got to be honest, it's pretty grim.'

At that point, I still wasn't sure if Tania was actually on to anything, but I figured that as I'd come this far I might as well continue. 'Keep going,' I told her. 'I was there, remember?'

She nodded and brought back up the paused footage from the main camera, frozen on Aaron Clarn firing the MP5 at his off-screen target, then placed it alongside the footage from the other camera so we could watch them simultaneously.

She started both films rolling, this time at quarter-speed, and I took a deep breath and watched as dispassionately as I could as Clarn temporarily stopped shooting at the blonde woman, then turned back towards the assembled diners, who were already scrambling for cover, and opened fire on them, moving his gun in a tight arc, appearing to aim indiscriminately but always careful not to cross fire with Luzanyc, who had also started shooting into the diners, keeping his weapon – a Remington automatic shotgun – steady the whole time, as if he was just engaging in a bit of target practice as he fired from the shoulder. I'd read later that Luzanyc – a huge man, six feet three and eighteen stone, and a former member of the same extremist militia as Clarn – had been suspected of war crimes, including rape and mass murder, in Bosnia during the early nineties but had never been charged, before coming to the UK, where he'd resided up until the night he'd died.

So, like Clarn, he was used to killing, and probably enjoyed it.

In the footage, he shot an elegant-looking woman in her forties who was sitting on her own several tables away from him, just as she was in the process of scrambling out of her seat.

'That woman Luzanyc has just shot is one of the targets,' said Tania, without any doubt in her voice. 'Look at him now.'

I watched as Luzanyc walked between the tables, moving the shotgun in a tight arc as he fired again, hitting a middle-aged man who appeared to be making a run for it, sending him flying into the restaurant's plate-glass window. I suddenly remembered vividly seeing that same man from the street as he crashed through the window and landed on the pavement. But I wasn't thinking about that now. I was concentrating on Luzanyc as he slowed up, turned his gun on another male diner, who was crouched down on his hands and knees by his table, and shot him in the head as the poor guy put out a desperate, imploring arm. The quality of the footage was good enough to see the blood and matter spraying from the exit wound, and I took a sharp intake of breath as the guy rolled over onto his side, probably already dead.

Luzanyc then turned to his left and took two steps over to where the woman Tania had identified as a target lay injured and unmoving on the floor. With his back to the cameras, he appeared to fire another shell into her.

'It's a headshot,' Tania informed me. 'Apparently it killed her instantly.'

On the screen, Luzanyc then clearly saw the surveillance officers from my old team arriving just outside and he fired another shot through the shattered window at them before retreating and reloading. Clarn stopped shooting too and loaded a new magazine from under his jacket into his MP5.

At this point, barely ten seconds into their attack, according to the clock at the bottom of the screen, the two men seemed to call it a day, and I watched as Luzanyc headed straight for the restaurant's front door, which Martin Greene had just exited seconds earlier. I'd read afterwards that Greene hadn't actually fired his weapon inside the restaurant, which the investigating officers had theorised was because he hadn't realised that the other two were planning a massacre, as Tania had just suggested, although I'd never been sure of that myself. I'd always figured he just panicked under pressure and then tried to shoot his way out because that was better than prison.

Tania pointed to the screen and told me to watch Clarn, who in the footage didn't immediately make for the front door but instead ran over to the corridor leading to the toilets and fired a burst of rounds down it. 'It's impossible to see who he's firing at,' she said, 'because that part of the building wasn't covered by the cameras, but my guess is his target's the blonde woman he fired at a few seconds earlier.'

I didn't say anything, watching as Clarn now went to join Luzanyc at the front door, where he was firing into the street at the arriving police officers. Then both men, now seemingly realising that they weren't going to escape that way, retreated rapidly down the corridor towards the toilets and the back of the building, temporarily disappearing from view.

Strangely, watching the actual massacre was somehow less harrowing than it was looking at the faces of the diners before the violence erupted. And even when the footage showed me entering the restaurant seconds later, holding my Glock two-handed, the police cap askew on my head, I still didn't feel any emotion. It was as if I'd detached myself from the whole thing. But I turned away from the screen anyway, because I didn't want to see myself as the man I used to be – someone who was able to sprint across a road without thinking about it. These days I can't even break into a slow jog without stumbling.

Tania stopped the footage and pushed the laptop away. 'Sorry to put you through that. I know it must be hard.' She tried not to sound patronising, but it didn't work, and I had no desire to tell her about how much I missed being a normal, fit, healthy human being, so instead I said: 'Where did you get this footage from?'

'I'm a journalist, it's my job to dig out information.'

'But you'd have to have incredibly good sources to get this. People very senior in the original CTC investigation.'

'And I do,' she said, meeting my gaze. 'Someone who also wasn't convinced this was just a standard terror attack. And before you ask, I'm not going to betray my sources. Not to anyone.'

'Fair enough,' I said with a shrug, taking a sip of the coffee, conscious that my hand was shaking ever so slightly. Maybe I was more affected by the footage than I cared to admit. 'But I still don't see any evidence that anyone was deliberately targeted.'

'I've just shown you the woman Tomas Luzanyc shot, the one he deliberately went over to finish off.'

'He also shot at least two other people.'

'That was to deflect attention.'

I was unconvinced. 'Who's the woman you think was targeted?'

'Her name was Cathy de Roth, and she ran a fashion agency.'

'Why was she singled out?'

'I've got some ideas, but I don't know for sure yet. I do know she had some very powerful friends.'

'And powerful enemies, if what you say is true. But what makes you so certain that this was a targeted attack? You could be reading things into it.'

'The blonde woman Aaron Clarn first shot at. She was sitting having dinner with Cathy de Roth earlier in the footage. She went to the toilet two minutes before the gunmen burst into the restaurant. When she wasn't there, it confused them. You can see it in the body language of Clarn and Luzanyc. They were meant to go in there and start shooting straight away, knowing their targets were in that restaurant. They may even have known what table they were at. Their plan was to make it look like some random Islamic terror attack, then get the hell out. But their second target wasn't there, so they hesitated, not sure what to do. Then the second target suddenly appears, not knowing what's going on because she's on the phone, and

Clarn immediately shoots at her, then runs back after her once he's fired into the other diners. He and Luzanyc then leave the restaurant through the rear exit, as you obviously know, and that's where they actually spot her again. There's a security camera covering the rear of the building that captures the moment. The woman's hiding behind some bins – it looks like she climbed out of the toilet window – and you can see that Clarn sees her as he runs past and is actually in the process of turning his gun her way when you intervene.'

'I know there was a security camera covering the back of the restaurant,' I say. 'It was used to exonerate me in Luzanyc's shooting. So you've got that footage as well?'

She nodded. 'I do. Do you want to see it?'

I shook my head. I've never wanted to see that footage. 'No thanks.'

'But do you remember the woman? The camera shows you looking her way as you run past after Clarn.'

'I remember her very vaguely,' I said. 'But I haven't thought about her in years. It was all happening so fast that night, and I think I would have forgotten seeing her entirely if it hadn't been for the fact that she came to visit me in hospital.'

'Really?' Tania looked very interested now. 'What did she say?'

I sighed, thinking back. 'I was in there for two weeks in all, and I think she came on the second or third day after my first operation. I remember her name was Sophie. She said she wanted to thank me for saving her life. At the time,

I wasn't in a good place. I knew I wasn't going to be able to walk properly again, and so I was very down, as well as being in a lot of pain. She told me I was a hero, but I didn't really feel like one. I felt like half a man.' I didn't add that I still felt that way. 'Anyway, she didn't stay long, just said what she'd come to say, and left me a pack of giant chocolate buttons and a bottle of wine. I remember her saying that buttons always cheered her up. I said it was very kind of her, and that was it. She was on her way. I haven't seen or heard from her since.'

'And that's the problem,' said Tania. 'No one has. She disappeared shortly after the massacre, and that's the last anyone's seen of her. No one even knows her full name. In fact, for all we know, you might have been the last person to see her alive.'

'Did no one try to find her?'

'Not as far as I'm aware. They certainly didn't at the time. No one thought she was the target.'

'Except, of course, the person who supplied you with this footage.'

She gave a nod, conceding the point. 'That's true. But finding her was never a priority for the official inquiry. As far as CTC were concerned, she was just one of the witnesses who slipped through the cracks. They obviously put out a number of witness appeals in the weeks and months afterwards, but there's no record of her giving a statement.'

'Have *you* tried to find her?'

'I have. She looks pretty enough to be a model, but I trawled through de Roth's catalogue of models and she wasn't one of them. And without a name, I don't know where else to look. She didn't give you a last name, then?'

'Not that I remember, and I was never interested in finding out. Back then, I just wanted to be left alone.' I finished my coffee and put the cup down on the island. 'I'm sorry I can't be of more help.'

'I think you can be of plenty of help, Chris. I mean, let's face it, you're right in the centre of this case. You were there when it happened. You killed two of the men involved. And my understanding is that you were seconded to CTC on the night as a spotter to ID the gunmen. They were meant to be buying guns, isn't that right? And they were going to be arrested when they made the buy?'

It didn't surprise me that she knew this. If she'd been talking to someone high up in the case – and she must have been to get this footage – she would have known about my role on the night. 'That's right. We were acting on intelligence.'

'I know,' she said. 'But what really interests me is that the intelligence came from you.'

Now my hackles were up, because this was something she *really* wasn't meant to know, and that was because it could put me in danger. I felt like telling her that I didn't know what she was talking about, but there was no point. I could tell she wasn't fishing. She knew.

'I don't want to comment on that,' I said tightly.

'Look, Chris. I'm not here to do a hatchet job on you. I just want to find out what happened that night, and why.'

She gave me a soft look that said: 'Trust me.' But that was

the problem. I didn't. She was too tough, too ambitious. I could see it in her eyes. And she'd sink me like a stone if it gave her a better story. 'I told you I'd sue if any of this gets out into the public domain.'

'I know,' she said. 'And I guarantee that it won't. But you have information that could really help this case.' She leant forward and put a hand on my arm, keeping that look on her face, and I realised that I hadn't been this close to a woman for at least a year, probably longer. And it felt good.

But I also knew she was just softening me up, and it wasn't working. 'I'm sorry,' I said, moving my arm. 'I don't think I can help.'

'Don't you want to know why it happened, Chris? I'm getting somewhere with this, and you can help me. I know you were undercover in the GIU team, going after Barry Cleaver, and that you infiltrated that extremist group. That you knew them.'

'It didn't happen like that,' I said.

'Then how did it happen?'

'It's the past. I don't want to dredge it up.'

'Sometimes we've just got to dredge things up. There's been a huge injustice done and it needs to be rectified.'

'Well, I'm afraid you're going to have to rectify it without me,' I said, climbing off the stool and grabbing hold of my stick. And then I told her the absolute truth. 'I just want to be left alone.'

'Please,' she said, following me as I limped through that grand house. 'I'll sign a contract that says your name will never get out there. But help me on this so that I can find out why those two women in the Villa Amalfi were targeted.'

'Thanks for the coffee,' I said over my shoulder as I reached the front door. 'I appreciate it.'

'Do you think Aaron Clarn is really dead?'

That stopped me momentarily, because it was something I'd turned over in my mind a lot over the years until the PTSD therapy finally allowed me to move on. 'I hope so. But if he's not, then I'm sure he's a long way away from here and won't be showing his face again.'

'You don't care that he might be out there somewhere walking free after what he did to those people, and to you?'

I turned round to face her, leaning on my stick. 'You know, I don't think about it any more. I've moved on.'

She stared at me, hands on hips, disappointment and frustration tightening her features.

But her reaction left me cold. I was through with this. I didn't know why I'd come.

And then she said something that made my whole body go cold. 'What about Kalian Roman? Don't you want to find out who he is? Because he's the one who organised the whole thing, isn't he?'

I held her gaze, trying to keep the tension out of my own features. I wanted to tell her that it would be very much in her interests never to mention that name again, because that was a rabbit hole no one wanted to get trapped down.

'Kalian Roman doesn't exist,' I told her, and limped out of there.

252

35

The Present

Sketty

'No,' says Teller.

I look at him. 'No what?'

'That's not what Tania Wild said to you. I know what her parting words to you were. It was me who hired her, Mr Sketty. I spoke to her that day.'

The room falls silent. He's got me here. We both know it. And this is bad, because I can't believe he knows this much. I realise he's got huge resources, but even so, this was one secret that I was sure had been kept.

'So are you going to tell me what Tania really said to you at the door?'

I make a decision. It's time to tell the truth.

We continue to stare at each other across the room, increasingly looking like two verbal combatants. The rain outside is getting harder again, lashing the window pane.

I take a deep breath. 'She said: "Don't you want to talk about Kerry Masters?"'

36

When Tania mentioned Kerry Masters' name to me at the front door, I was utterly shaken, because as far as I knew, only three people definitely knew of my involvement in her death. I was one of them; Baz Cleaver was another; and finally there was Clarn. In other words, the only people who could have told her were either dead or had been missing for years.

The only other person who could possibly have known was the individual who'd ordered the killing, Kalian Roman, and even if he did exist, what did he have to gain by imparting the information to an investigative reporter?

I turned to Tania, put on my best puzzled expression and told her I didn't know who she was talking about, and then, before she could say any more, I stalked out of there, slamming the door behind me.

All the way back home, I was worried. In truth, I'd tried for years not to think about Kerry Masters. Or say her name, even to myself. It hadn't been hard.

With the revelation that Leon Warman, a brutal thug

with a history of violence, had been her killer, the story had faded from the news very quickly. It was just a sad little home-invasion murder, devoid of any mystery, the kind that scares the middle classes but that no one wants to dwell on too much. And with Warman's own death (something the tabloids had celebrated as being poetic justice), there hadn't even been a trial to rekindle interest. Kerry Masters had become the past.

I'd long since convinced myself that her death hadn't been my fault. I'd been trying to do the right thing in my undercover role, and had inadvertently been dragged into it. I justified my silence with the thought that nothing I could have said would have led investigators to Aaron Clarn any sooner, and with Warman dead, even the miscarriage of justice was minimal. Better to let sleeping dogs lie.

And yet now it seemed they'd woken up.

It was only after I'd got home and made a strong coffee that I began to calm down. I'd been too hasty charging out of there like that. Tania Wild hadn't elaborated on what she knew about Kerry Masters, and it might be she knew nothing of any substance. Even if she was aware of my involvement, the information gave her no leverage over me, because she had no evidence to back it up. Kerry's murder had been solved fourteen years ago. There would be no appetite within the Met to reopen it, not on the say-so of a freelance journalist. I just had to front it out.

The meeting with Tania had left me restless, and not just because of the mention of Kerry Masters, but also all these new revelations about that night.

It's hard when you've spent years trying to forget something and then it's thrust right back in your face, and in a manner that tells you that there's no way you can continue to ignore it. I couldn't say for sure if Tania's theory of a targeted hit was right, but the more I turned it over in my mind, the more it seemed likely. The attack on the Villa Amalfi, which had never made total sense to me, made a lot more when you looked at it like that. And the disappearance of the young woman called Sophie got to me.

I didn't have many hospital visits after the shooting. No one from the GIU team came. I was told that word had got out that I'd been undercover the whole time, investigating Baz Cleaver's links to extremists, so none of them wanted to know me, including the Chief, and the team was disbanded soon after that.

Family members came to see me, of course. My mum and my brother. But just once each. We weren't especially close. A few old colleagues from SO11 made the journey, but not as many as I'd hoped, and obviously the investigating officers from CTC turned up on several occasions to interview me, but the point was, at the time I didn't feel like the most popular man in the world, and so I recalled perfectly when Sophie came to see me with chocolate and wine. I was touched. I guess it made me feel valued. But as I'd said to Tania, I was also depressed. I'd just been told that I was going to have to learn to walk again, and that months, potentially years, of physiotherapy lay ahead, so I hadn't been the best of company, and she hadn't stayed long.

But to find out that she hadn't been seen in fourteen

years, and that no one even knew her full name, piqued both my sympathy and my interest.

Life for me had become pretty dull. I'd finally retired from the force on health grounds, on a pretty decent pension, five years back, having spent the intervening period on desk duties, and in truth I hadn't done a lot since. My last relationship broke up more than a year ago, and my evenings were lonely affairs, usually spent sitting on the sofa with my cat, Trevor, watching box sets, or listening to jazz music and thinking about a past that was long, long gone. I'd thought about going off and seeing the world, but in truth I hadn't wanted to leave Trevor behind. It was sad to say, but he was probably my best friend, and at ten years old he still had a good few years in him yet.

I knew that living like this hadn't been doing me any good. I was becoming agoraphobic. Lost too much in my own head. A part of me wanted to help Tania uncover the true motive for the Villa Amalfi attack, and also find out exactly what she knew about me, and where she'd got the information from. But another part of me said it would be a lot safer to do nothing.

The problem was, doing nothing hadn't helped me these past years, and maybe it was time to get the truth out there.

I sat and considered my options for a long time. While I was doing that, I googled Cathy de Roth on my laptop and found a handful of images of a thin, bird-like woman of about fifty with sharp, angular features and big hair, who'd had more work done on her face than was beneficial. She didn't look particularly pleasant, I have to admit, and in the photos where she was smiling, it looked forced. In most of them she was at fashion awards or black-tie dos, mingling with people who looked like they came from money. There were also a few news articles about her, but they all related to her death at the Villa Amalfi. From what I could gather, she'd been a successful businesswoman with a flourishing modelling agency, and was divorced with no children. Nothing at all to suggest she'd been a deliberate target of well-organised and well-armed killers. And that intrigued me more, because Tania Wild was adamant she'd been exactly that.

In the end, it was curiosity that finally made my decision for me, and before I could change my mind, I made the call.

Tania picked up on the second or third ring. 'I'll be honest, I wasn't expecting to hear from you again,' she said, and it was hard to tell from her tone whether she was pleased or not.

'Maybe I was too hasty earlier,' I told her. 'I'm sorry. I'm happy to talk as long as we've got some guarantees in place that it won't put me in any danger.'

'Why the change of heart?'

Because it might actually give me a reason to get up in the morning.

'It just struck me that if there is more to this than the official version, then I want to know. And I'd like to know what happened to Sophie.'

'Do you want to talk on the phone?'

'No, let's do it at your place, if that's okay.'

'Sure,' she said, as if she was actually quite pleased with the idea of my company. 'Come on over.'

It was 8 p.m., and I decided it would be a lot quicker to drive this time. I took a bottle of red wine from my paltry collection as a peace offering (not that I intended to drink any myself), spruced myself up so I was looking as presentable as I was ever going to manage, told myself that this wasn't a date as I put on aftershave, and headed out the door.

I didn't expect anything to happen between us, of course. She'd given no sign that she was interested and what would she see in a lame recluse like me anyway? But I was still feeling uncharacteristically nervous as I rang her doorbell for the second time that day.

There was no answer.

I waited, leaning on my stick, not too bothered. You learn to be patient when you've been a cop, especially when you've spent a lot of time on surveillance.

I gave it a good thirty seconds, then rang again. We'd only spoken half an hour earlier, and all the lights were on, so I was pretty certain she was in there. I pushed my face up against the frosted glass on the front door. I couldn't see anything, but I could hear the faint sound of music coming from somewhere inside.

Frowning, I put down the wine and opened the letter box, but the brush in the gap blocked my view of anything.

That was when I heard it.

A whimper. Coming from somewhere in the hallway, only a few yards away.

It stopped almost as soon as it had begun. As if I'd just imagined it. Except I hadn't. I've always had excellent hearing. And now I could make out something else, barely audible, but making my skin crawl.

Breathing.

But not normal breathing. These were the short, very tight breaths of someone under stress.

'Tania, are you in there?' I called out, feeling slightly foolish.

No response. Even the breathing seemed to stop.

It crossed my mind that I was imagining things. The problem is, when you've been a cop as long as I had, and seen some of the things I had, you become paranoid. It then crossed my mind that she might be having sex with someone and hoping I'd go away. Maybe a boyfriend had popped round, and they were indulging in a quickie before I arrived, thinking that I wouldn't get here so fast.

I released the letter-box flap and straightened up, feeling a combination of nervousness and embarrassment. I walked back down the steps, being careful not to slip, and looked back towards the house. I'd parked my car on the road outside, and I considered returning to it and waiting for Tania to finish whatever she was doing.

Except my instincts were telling me that something wasn't right. And that Tania, an investigative journalist involved in a very controversial case, was in trouble.

I stood there for a few seconds, the wind cold against my face, while I debated what to do next. I could hardly call the police. But I couldn't just ignore it either.

The truth was, I was scared. While once I'd been prepared

to throw myself into the kinds of terrifying situations where your life really is on the line, the adrenaline and bravado that had driven me in those times had long since faded away, along with my fitness and my health. If she really was in trouble, what could a man like me actually do to help?

Still no sound came from the house.

I took a deep breath and, ignoring the pit of dread in my stomach, made the decision to see if she was all right. Before I could give myself time to have second thoughts, I'd started off round the side of the house, keeping close to the shadows, my grip tight on my stick, a sturdy thing made of oak and a useful weapon in case someone attacked me.

A high wooden fence with a gate set in it blocked off access to the back. There was no way I was getting over the fence, but surprisingly, the gate was unlocked. I was conscious that I might be about to cause myself huge embarrassment here, but I went through anyway, trusting my instincts.

The lights were on in the kitchen, but it was empty. An ashtray with half a dozen cigarette ends in it was perched on top of a birdbath next to the bifold doors. One of them was still smoking, which meant Tania had been out here recently.

I tried the door and it opened, the music growing louder. It was some kind of relaxed chill-out stuff, the kind you get at yoga classes.

But there was no other sound.

This time something stopped me calling out as I stepped quietly inside, closing the door behind me to keep out the noise of the wind.

I took a step forward, then another, feeling like a burglar.

But the thick oppressiveness of the silence told me that something was definitely wrong.

And then, through the open kitchen door, I saw her. Lying on her front next to the staircase, wearing the same clothes as earlier, her feet bare. She'd suffered a major head injury that even from here I could see was the result of being battered with a blunt instrument. Her hair was sticky and matted with blood. More blood – almost black in colour – had formed a large halo-like pool round her head as it soaked into the carpet.

For a second, I stood rooted to the spot by the shock of what I was witnessing. It had been fourteen years since I'd seen violent death. I'd thought I'd left all that far, far behind me. My heart was thumping, fear threatening to overwhelm me, because less than five minutes ago, I'd heard breathing when I'd opened the letter box. Had it been Tania's breathing or someone else's?

From my position inside the kitchen, I could only see about the middle third of the hallway. Neither the front door nor the stretch leading to the back of the house was visible. I hadn't heard anyone leave either.

My grip tightened on the walking stick and I reached inside my jacket for my phone, preparing to retreat. I'd call the police from outside.

And then Tania's hand moved very slightly, and she let out a faint gurgling sound.

Jesus, she was still alive.

I didn't move. In that moment, I was too scared. In case the killer was still there waiting for me.

The music had stopped now and the silence in the house was deafening.

Tania moaned. A small, animal sound. Her head moved as she tried to lift it.

I took a step back and pulled out the phone.

A shadow appeared in the kitchen doorway, and in the same second a figure dressed all in black and wearing a balaclava suddenly burst out from behind the door and charged straight at me. I just had time to register that he was holding a bloodstained brass poker above his head, and then I dropped the phone and raised my stick in both hands in a desperate defensive motion, already stumbling backwards as I lost my balance.

I bounced off the kitchen island and landed on my back as, with an animal roar, my attacker brought the poker down. The stick blocked the blow, but the force of it made my hands reverberate with the shock.

He was standing above me now, and I could see the bright savagery in his eyes. This was a man who truly enjoyed violence. I've only met a handful of them in my life, but it's a look I'd recognise anywhere.

He brought the poker down a second time, and again I used the stick to block the blow, but let go of it long enough to grab the end of the poker with my left hand and try to wrestle it from his grip, while simultaneously lashing out with my feet to force him to let go.

But he was bigger, stronger and in a far more advantageous position than me, and he yanked the poker free and took a step backwards, while I slid round on the floor on my back, moving in a circle and using my feet to keep him away from me, ignoring the pain in my hip from all the twisting and turning.

He brought the poker down again, this time aiming at my legs, and I cried out in pain as he landed a blow on the shin of my bad one. But when you're fighting for your life, you don't stop, and I kicked out like a donkey with my good leg, connecting with his knee this time and sending him stumbling backwards.

He lashed out one more time, hitting me on the foot, but it was more a parting shot than any real attempt to do harm, and then he threw the poker at my head. I deflected it with the stick and could only watch as he ran over and pulled open the bifold door.

It was the way he seemed to lope as he moved, covering the ground rapidly and in silence, long arms down by his sides, that made me realise who he was.

At the door, he paused for a moment to stare back at me, and there was the glint of triumph in his eyes. Because he knew that I knew.

It might have been fourteen years, but I knew without a doubt that I was looking at Aaron Clarn.

And then he turned away and disappeared off into the night.

I tried to get to my feet, slipped and fell backwards again. My shin was in agony, but the adrenaline that surged through me made it temporarily manageable. Rolling round on the floor, I found my phone, then, using the stick as a support, I stood up, still reeling from the shock of the sudden violence, and the identity of the man who'd inflicted it. I was shaking so much that I had to lean against the island, and the realisation that I was terrified filled me with a sense of shame. I felt useless. Clarn had bested me yet again, swatting me aside like a fly, showing me who was boss before leaving, knowing that I was in no position to follow. It made me want to cry.

But first I had to help Tania. Taking a deep breath, I staggered into the hallway and over to where she lay.

Up close, her injuries were catastrophic. The blows to her head – and there'd been several of them – had exposed the bone, and blood was still seeping out of the deep holes created.

As gently as I could, I turned her over. Her eyelids flickered, and she made another small noise.

'It's going to be okay, Tania,' I whispered, dialling 999 and putting the phone to my ear. 'Stay awake for me. Try to focus, okay?'

When the operator answered at the other end, I immediately identified myself as a former police officer and told her that we needed an ambulance urgently. I had to look up Tania's address to give it to her. 'Please hurry. This woman's injuries are life-threatening. She's barely conscious.'

But as I spoke to the operator, a small sound like a sigh escaped Tania's mouth, and her whole body slumped. Her eyes closed and her head went limp in my hands, and it was as if I could see her life leaving her, and even though I pleaded with her to hang on in there, telling her that help was coming, it didn't work.

And then, just like that, she was gone.

37

'And then, just like that, she was gone.'

I fidgeted in the hard-backed chair, trying to make myself comfortable while I regarded the two detectives – a woman and a man – who were facing me across the desk in the interview room at Hampstead nick. The lead detective was a hard-looking woman about my age with bleached blonde hair who'd introduced herself as DI Franka. Her colleague, a studious guy in a decent suit, about ten years younger, was called DS Singh.

It was 11 p.m., just over two hours since I'd arrived at Tania Wild's house, and according to DI Franka, the attack on her had now officially turned into a murder inquiry. Although I hadn't been arrested, something in their overall demeanour told me that I wasn't exactly being treated as a regular witness either.

'This man who attacked Ms Wild, can you describe him?' asked Franka.

'I can do better than that,' I told her. 'I can name him.'

'You said he was wearing a balaclava,' said Singh, consulting the notes he was making on an HP laptop.

'He was, but I saw enough of him to be certain it was Aaron Clarn.' I knew how this made me sound – Jesus, it sounded insane enough to me – but I could hardly keep quiet about it.

Even now, fourteen years on, Aaron Clarn's name still clearly rang a bell with these two. They looked at each other, and neither of their expressions came close to suggesting they believed me.

It was Singh who spoke. 'Aaron Clarn? Not the gunman from the Villa Amalfi attack in 2007?'

'The man who's been missing presumed dead for the last fourteen years?' added Franka, raising both eyebrows.

'Look, I know how it sounds.' I didn't want to have to tell them too much, but I could see from the way they were looking at me that I was going to have to. 'You know I'm a retired police officer. I was one of the firearms officers at Villa Amalfi. I killed two of the gunmen, and was wounded by the third, Aaron Clarn. It should be on my record. I also met Clarn when I was on an undercover job. That part might be redacted from my record, but Commander Marina Reineke, the head of Counter Terrorism Command, will vouch for me.'

'We didn't know that,' said Franka, expressing no obvious reaction, although Singh, at least, had the good grace to look mildly impressed as he continued tapping away on the laptop. 'And what was your relationship to Ms Wild?' she continued.

This was where I knew I had problems. 'There wasn't much of one, if I'm honest,' I answered. 'I only met her for the first time this afternoon. She was an investigative journalist and she contacted me about the Villa Amalfi massacre. She said she was researching it and thought there might be a case for it to be reopened. Look, I wasn't wrong about Clarn. If you don't believe me, run DNA checks in the house. You'll find evidence he was there. And check the area's CCTV.'

'Thank you, Mr Sketty. We know how to do our job.'

'Sure,' I said, not wanting to irritate her further.

At the same time, Singh angled the laptop's screen so she could see it. I knew they were checking my record and hoped this might actually get them on my side.

She nodded at him, then turned back to me, her expression inscrutable. 'What aspects of the case did Ms Wild want to talk to you about?'

I didn't want to give too much away. You didn't need to be Sherlock Holmes to work out that Tania's attempt to dig up the case was almost certainly the motive for her murder, which made it a very sensitive subject. But if I didn't come clean, it was going to make me look guilty, and right then, I wanted that even less. 'She had a theory that it might have been a targeted attack rather than just an attempt to kill as many people as possible. We met at her house this afternoon, and she showed me some CCTV footage from inside the restaurant that she thought backed up her theory. She was very well informed, because she knew about my undercover role, and that's supposedly always been a very closely guarded secret.'

'And where did she get that information from?' asked Singh.

'An anonymous source. She wouldn't say who.'

'If you'd already discussed the case once, what brought you back to the house a second time, only a few hours later?' asked Franka.

'I was probably a bit dismissive of her theory first time round, but when I gave it some more thought, I felt it was worth investigating further.'

They exchanged glances again, and I had the feeling they didn't entirely believe me, which was disconcerting, especially considering I was a lot more used to being on the other side of the desk in interrogations.

Franka leant forward, resting on her elbows on the desktop, her face breaking into something akin to a smile. 'I notice you've got aftershave on. Did you put it on for your second visit to Ms Wild's home? And was it your wine we found on the doorstep? Rioja Reserva, 2008. Very nice.'

I shrugged, trying to appear nonchalant. 'I thought it would be polite.'

'It's a terrible coincidence, though, isn't it? You only meeting her this afternoon, and then a few hours later she's murdered and you're the one who finds the body.'

I didn't like the way this was going. 'I think her murder might be linked to her work on the Villa Amalfi case,' I said, meeting Franka's gaze. 'Did you find her laptop at the crime scene? Because she had all her information on that, as well as the CCTV footage she showed me. It's a rose-coloured MacBook. It was on her kitchen worktop this afternoon.'

'We'll check,' said Franka, her expression suggesting I was some kind of deluded fantasist. 'But you can see our problem, can't you, Mr Sketty? You were the last person to see Tania Wild alive and there's no sign of forced entry to the property. You blame it on a man who's officially dead. Someone who, by your own admission, you haven't seen yourself for fourteen years and only met briefly. And who was wearing a balaclava. You have the victim's blood on your clothes, and I suspect we're going to find your prints and your DNA on the murder weapon.'

When she put it like that, even I had trouble believing me, but I ploughed on nonetheless. 'I told you why I had blood on my clothes,' I said, trying not to raise my voice. 'She died in my arms. And as for any prints or DNA you might find on the poker, they'll have come from when I was defending myself. You won't find anything on the handle because I never touched it. And anyway, what motive would I have to kill a woman I hardly knew?'

For a long few seconds, they both simply stared at me without speaking, and I was just about to tell them that if they insisted on treating me like I was a suspect, then I was leaving, when DI Franka finally spoke.

'Christopher John Sketty, I'm arresting you for the murder of Tania Kay Wild.'

38

That was when I called an end to the interview and demanded to see my lawyer.

I do actually have a lawyer too, not that I've ever had to use him much. His name's Thomas (not Tom) Workman, and he first got in contact with me five years ago when he heard the Met were trying to force me into early retirement on only half a pension. The reason they wanted me out was a result of an incident that had happened one afternoon while I was off duty and out for a walk not far from my house. I'd taken a shortcut down an alleyway, and as I'd emerged, a gang of teenagers – fifteen-, sixteen-year-olds, six of them in all – were blocking my path. I asked them to move, and reluctantly they inched out of the way, forcing me to squeeze through. They were laughing at me as I went. One of them said: 'Keep moving, hopalong!' It wasn't much, just kids bantering, but I found it intensely humiliating, because it drove home how far I'd fallen. I heard a couple of them whispering behind my back, chuckling. I just wanted to get home, put my head under a pillow and escape from the outside world. And then, as I passed by the last one, I slipped slightly, bumping into him, and he shoved me, hard enough to make me stumble.

That was when I lost it. Righting myself, I swung round and lashed out with my stick, hitting him across the jaw. The blow was hard, knocking him into one of the others and causing him to yell out in pain. I was bellowing with rage, the red mist fully descended, and I would have lashed out again, but I lost my balance and fell over on my side.

The kid I'd hit was down on his knees, clutching his face, and his friends were yelling and swearing at me, but making no move to attack. Instead they were talking about having me done for assault. A couple of them were filming me as I lay there.

Finally I got to my feet and walked away. They continued to jeer and follow me until someone opened a window in one of the houses and yelled at them to leave me alone.

That was when they split, but a few hours later, I got a knock on the door from the police. The kid I'd hit had gone home and told his parents about it. My blow had left a painful red welt and bruising round his jaw, and they wanted to press charges. I was arrested, and even though his parents were informed of my background, they didn't back down.

So there I was, having been charged with ABH and bailed, and with an embarrassed brass trying to usher me out the door on the cheap, when a knight in shining armour in the shape of Thomas Workman intervened. He was a flamboyant figure with thirty years' experience, mainly as a defence lawyer, and one of his bugbears was police malpractice. A friend of his had been in the Villa Amalfi restaurant on the night of the attack, and Workman didn't like the fact that a man who'd risked his life to end it was being hung out to dry.

Within a month, he'd worked his magic, managing to get the parents to drop the charges on the proviso that I meet the kid and apologise, which I did (although I don't think the surly little bastard appreciated it), and even getting the Met to allow me to retire on a full pension. I didn't want to leave. My job was the only thing keeping me sane, even if it was just desk duties, but Workman told me there was no choice. They wanted me out and they weren't backing down, so I took the money and limped.

Workman, who liked to refer to himself as Mr 24/7, had said he'd always be there for me, and incredibly, when I phoned him that night at 11.45, he lived up to the name and answered straight away, saying he'd be with me imminently.

He turned up forty minutes later, immaculately dressed in a pinstriped three-piece suit of navy blue and a loud paisley tie. He was small in stature but big in confidence, and as soon as we were back in the interview room, he was on DI Franka like a flash, demanding to know why I was being held. 'This man is a hero, a decorated police officer wounded and disabled in the line of duty, who witnessed a murder and immediately dialled 999, and yet you've arrested him. Why?'

I had to admire Franka. Workman might have been small but he was an imposing presence, and he had right on his side, but she didn't take any shit from him, giving him the kind of withering look she'd given me earlier, before explaining firmly the reasons for my arrest and finishing with: 'Your client has a history of violence dating back to 2006.'

Workman wasn't having that. 'How can you say that?' he demanded. 'As a police officer, my client struck out once in self-defence while he was trying to subdue an extremely violent suspect, and once again ten years later when he was being harangued and assaulted by a gang of young thugs. That is not a history. It's two incidents, neither of which resulted in a conviction, and to equate them with the brutal murder of a young woman is truly clutching at straws.'

'He also shot dead two men, and has had extensive psychotherapy for PTSD. My point is, he's not unused to violence.'

'So now you're using his heroism against him? He stands up to protect the innocent and you throw it back in his face?'

'Let's just go through everything again, shall we?' said Franka wearily.

And that's what we did. It wasn't one of those classic 'no comment' interviews. I had nothing to hide and I wanted the truth to be known, but I kept my answers succinct, and when Workman thought I was talking too much, he'd put a hand on my arm to stop me. At the same time, he parried Franka's and Singh's questions, refusing to give them any ground, and generally making a nuisance of himself. Like most police officers, I'd always taken a dim view of defence lawyers, assuming that they were all greedy sociopaths whose sole purpose seemed to be ensuring that justice wasn't done. But it's different when you're on the other side of the table and you know you're innocent. Now I wanted Workman to pull out every stop so he could make this whole thing go away.

The arrest had really shaken me, and I couldn't understand why Franka thought I was behind the murder. I had no motive for wanting Tania dead. During the interview, the DI hinted that it was because I'd fancied her and therefore it could have been sexual, but when they tried to push this, Workman quickly nipped it in the bud. Tania had been found fully clothed. I knew they wouldn't find any signs of sexual assault. It also wouldn't take them long to work out that I'd arrived at the house only minutes before she died. I'd driven there in my own car, so all they'd need to do was check the ANPR cameras. Hardly enough time for Tania to reject my advances and then for me to fly into a rage, find a poker and brutally beat her to death while leaning on my walking stick.

In the end, Workman managed to get them to release me on bail, after his attempts to get them to de-arrest me ran up against a brick wall, and we finally left Hampstead nick at just after three in the morning. He gave me a lift back in his flashy new Tesla to get my car, which was still parked on the road outside the house where Tania had died.

On the way over, I asked him whether he thought they believed me.

'I think Singh did,' he answered, his voice filling the car. 'I'm less sure of Franka. I suspect she operates to the maxim that the most obvious suspect is likely the guilty one, and you're definitely the obvious one. But they need to tell a plausible story to the jury to secure a conviction, and at the moment, you as killer isn't plausible.' He turned and gave me a stern look. 'They're not going to find anything else out, are they?'

I frowned. 'Like what?'

'Like that you had more of a relationship with the victim than you're letting on.'

'I didn't,' I said firmly, realising that even he didn't entirely believe my story. 'Everything I've told them, and everything I've told you, is the absolute truth. They need to be looking for the real killer, and for the real motive.'

'That's your main problem, Chris. Your claim that Aaron Clarn is the real killer doesn't sound plausible either. Too much time has passed for you to be absolutely sure, especially given that he was in disguise.'

'I know,' I said, conceding the point, 'but even if I'm wrong, they still need to be looking for a man in dark clothing who fled that house.'

'How long did Tania Wild say she'd been working on the story about the Villa Amalfi attack?'

'She didn't, but she'd obviously been on it for some time. She'd collated a fair amount of evidence.'

'So if anyone wanted her dead because of her work on this story, they probably could have killed her before. And yet they do it just as you turn up at her house, only five hours after you'd met her for the first time. That looks an awful lot like a big coincidence. And as you well know, Chris, no police officer likes one of those.'

39

It took me until dawn to get to sleep. I tossed and turned; I kept picturing Tania lying there on the hall floor, dying in front of me, her head a bloody pulp. Terrors of the past and present tore through my mind, one after the other, and when I finally managed to drift off, the nightmares came at me, leaving my sleep restless and fitful.

I finally rose from my bed at eleven, feeling sick with exhaustion, but with a cold fear lurking close to the surface. I'd seen Aaron Clarn the previous night, I was sure of it, and the thought that he was potentially back in my life terrified me, even after all these years. He knew where I lived. I hadn't moved after Villa Amalfi. I'd stubbornly stayed in the place where Karen and I had brought up our daughter together, and even now I was sitting only twenty yards from where Clarn had thrust a bag over my head in Cleaver's car and come close to killing me, all those years ago.

Clarn wasn't my only worry either. The police investigation wasn't just going to suddenly go away. Franka had the bit between her teeth. I might have been bailed, but I was a long way from being in the clear.

The day was sunny, so I went for the longest walk I could tolerate without causing too much pain in my hip, which turned out to be about an hour and a half, albeit moving slowly and with several stops. Walking, although limited in its duration these days, is still my only salvation. It allows me to breathe the fresh air and to dream, to forget what my life has become, but it didn't calm me that day and I didn't feel fully safe again until I was home and had double-locked the front door behind me.

It reminded me of how I felt when I'd been allowed back home after the Villa Amalfi attack. Back then, I was convinced that I'd become a target for right-wing extremists. After all, I'd helped break up a terror cell and killed two of its members in the midst of an attack, and the man who'd allegedly been financing and arming them – the mysterious Kalian Roman – was still, presumably, out there somewhere. For several months, I'd had police protection, but it was finally removed when it was deemed unnecessary by the brass, who claimed that there was no intelligence that anyone was gunning for me. Not surprisingly, I was less convinced of this, and so I decided to take matters into my own hands.

I've never admitted this to anyone before, but I tried to buy a gun. I used an old informant of mine from my days in SO11 to point me in the direction of an underground gun dealer. After a couple of clandestine meetings where I was simultaneously terrified of being arrested or violently ripped off, I was finally told by the dealer that the best he could sell me was a Taser that also doubled as a torch, and which delivered a shock that at close range could stop even the most determined of assailants. I paid five hundred pounds for it, and considered it a worthwhile investment.

For a long time, I slept with it under my pillow, before finally it dawned on me that a) I clearly wasn't a target; b) Kalian Roman, whose name had never been mentioned on the news, probably didn't even exist; and c) at some point, my new girlfriend at the time was likely to find it under the pillow, and how the hell would I explain my way out of that one? So I'd placed it in a hidden drawer under the shoe rack in my wardrobe and largely forgotten about it.

But that afternoon I dug it out and gave it a complete clean before putting it on the sofa next to me in the living room while I sat there rigid and restless, drinking strong coffee and slowly coming to the realisation that I couldn't carry on like this. Tania Wild had given me information that could potentially turn the whole Villa Amalfi case on its head. Someone somewhere felt that information was worth killing her for, and they might well come after me next. I could sit there cowering behind double-locked doors while I waited for them, or I could actually do something productive for once, and take up where Tania had left off. When you've been living alone for as long as I have, it can be very hard to motivate yourself. But something was stirring in me that afternoon. Anger. I was angry with whoever had killed Tania; not only the perpetrator, Clarn, but also whoever had ordered it. Because someone had. And that person was responsible for the fact that I couldn't walk properly. Worst of all, they were getting away with it.

But I could change that.

I was a detective for a long time. Not an especially good one, but I like to think that was because I was never given the chance to do any real detective work. Most criminals are idiots. They tend to get themselves caught. But the person or people behind this were clever and cunning, and now I was going to have to show the same traits in order to find them.

The first thing I had to do was find out who it was within the Villa Amalfi inquiry team who'd leaked the footage from the restaurant and told Tania Wild that the official theory of a terrorist attack was wrong. The CTC inquiry had been huge, as you'd expect, and although many of those working on it would have had access to the footage, my gut feeling was that the leaker was someone high up. Most of the detectives would have been given very specific tasks – chasing up leads, checking suspects' backgrounds and phone records, that sort of thing – and wouldn't have been looking at the big picture. And only those right at the top would have known about my undercover role.

I only had two, very out-of-date, contacts at CTC, but both knew the details of my undercover role. One was Commander Marina Reineke, who'd risen right to the top of CTC, even though she'd been Gold Commander on the night of Villa Amalfi and therefore should have carried the can for the failure of the police to stop the massacre happening. However, it seemed Reineke was one of those lucky few who are able to position themselves well away from the firing line, and I'd watched her progress with some bitterness, given that I'd never heard another word from her after my injury. Occasionally she'd appear on TV, usually after a terrorist atrocity, to talk about all the work CTC were doing, and I'd read a magazine article about her once in which she'd been featured with her new husband, a wealthy and apparently famous architect with the somewhat ridiculous name of Klevin (not Kevin) Waintree.

Straight away, I discounted Reineke as the leaker (as the head of CTC, she wouldn't need to leak, she could just change the shape of the inquiry herself). I also doubted she'd give me any help, since she'd done such a good job of ignoring me these past fourteen years.

My second contact, of course, was Rose Bennett, who I wasn't even sure still worked at CTC. I doubted Rose had been the leaker either, but she was more likely to be able to point me in the right direction. She, at least, had had the good grace to phone a couple of times after Amalfi to see how I was, although her calls had dried up pretty fast.

I still had the number she'd used back in the day, and I dug it out now, and before I could question whether it was a good idea or not to get in touch, I made the call.

It went straight to voicemail, and I left a slightly rambling message asking if she could call me urgently over a work-related matter. 'Nothing to worry about, just something you could really help me with,' I finished by saying.

It was close to an hour before she called back, and I was just in the process of making a cup of tea. The London news was on in the background, and Tania Wild's murder was the main story, although she hadn't yet been officially identified. The reporter mentioned that a man had been arrested in connection with it and bailed pending further inquiries, but thankfully I wasn't identified either, which meant that Rose wouldn't know anything about my involvement.

It sounded like she was outside somewhere, and there was traffic noise in the background.

'Hey, Rose, long time no speak,' I said with fake cheeriness. 'How have you been?'

'Busy,' she said, with a brusqueness she didn't try hard to hide. 'I've got a husband and two young kids now. You?'

'I'm retired. Living alone. Not up to very much, to be honest.'

'You said it was urgent we speak.'

'It is. Are you still at CTC?'

'I am,' she said carefully. 'Why?'

'Because I need to talk to someone about the Villa Amalfi case. I've got new information.' I told her the details of my first meeting with Tania Wild the previous day. 'She knew all about my undercover role and I have no idea where that information came from.'

'It didn't come from me,' she said firmly.

'I didn't think so. Look, I just need to be pointed in the right direction, because whatever Tania Wild knew, it was enough to get her murdered.'

Rose gave an audible gasp down the phone. 'Murdered?'

'That's right. Last night. Only a few hours after I met her.' For obvious reasons, I didn't mention that I'd been arrested in connection with it.

She was silent for a couple of seconds and I could tell from her reaction that she knew, or at least knew of, Tania Wild.

'I don't want to talk over the phone,' she said. 'Meet me at the Albert Memorial, Hyde Park, ten a.m. tomorrow. The Albert Hall side. And make sure you're not followed.'

She cut the connection, leaving me staring at the phone, and I knew then that I was on to something serious.

40

I was ten minutes early for our clandestine meeting the next day.

The Albert Memorial, an ornate Gothic pavilion with a gold-coloured statue of Prince Albert in the middle, sits at the southern edge of Hyde Park, directly opposite the Royal Albert Hall. The area tends to get busy with tourists, and there were plenty of them sitting on the steps at the foot of the memorial when I got there, even though it was a typically grey November day, with a sky that was threatening rain.

I couldn't see Rose Bennett amongst them, but I walked the length of the memorial anyway, moving slowly, and as I got to the end, she broke into step beside me.

'Keep walking,' she instructed, taking my arm and steering me so we turned back into the park itself.

'This is just like the old days,' I said, looking at her as she led me down one of the paths. She was still striking in appearance, with the same lean, willowy build, pale skin, and long light auburn hair straight out of one of those shampoo adverts, and it seemed that, unlike me, she'd grown into her forties pretty seamlessly, with nothing to show for it bar a few extra lines around the eyes.

But there was a clear tension in her features that day, and she asked me whether I was sure I hadn't been followed.

'Absolutely not,' I said. 'I've done this before, remember?'

'A long time ago,' she said.

'It's like riding a bike. You never forget. And I've got good reason to be careful.'

'I know you have,' she said, giving me a sideways look. 'I almost didn't come today. I checked the details of the Tania Wild case. You didn't tell me you were arrested for her murder.'

'I know I didn't, and I'm sorry about that. I didn't think you'd turn up if I told you the truth. I'm being set up for this murder by whoever killed her, and I think the killer was Aaron Clarn.'

'Chris, there hasn't been a sniff of a sighting of Aaron Clarn in fourteen years, and there was one of the biggest manhunts in British history to find him. The consensus at CTC is that he was murdered after the attack to keep him quiet. There was the matter of his blood all over the floor inside the gang's rendezvous, remember?'

'Murdered by whom?'

'It's no secret that we've always thought there were more people involved in the attack. But we've never been able to identify anyone.'

'What about Kalian Roman?'

Rose shook her head. 'There hasn't been any sign of him

in fourteen years either. I think senior management have concluded he doesn't actually exist.'

It struck me that if this was the case, then my whole assignment had been an utter waste of time. 'And what's your opinion?' I asked her.

'I honestly don't know,' she said, with a small shrug of her shoulders. 'I've always felt uneasy about the official motive for the Villa Amalfi attack. It felt like we were missing something. But that's a personal opinion. I wasn't even put on the case because of my previous involvement in your op.'

'But you knew Tania Wild, didn't you?'

She stopped, which I was glad for, given that her pace had been getting a bit too fast for me and my stick. 'I can't afford for this to go any further, Chris. You're not recording this conversation, are you?'

I pulled a face, surprised she'd asked the question.' Of course not. Who would I record it for? I'm the one in trouble, not you.'

'Tania Wild approached me about a month ago,' she said as we started walking again. 'I'd heard she'd been sniffing round CTC trying to get people to give their opinion on Villa Amalfi. Anyway, I agreed to talk to her.'

'You said you weren't on the inquiry team.'

'I wasn't a part of the original one, but I was brought onto it four years ago, around the tenth anniversary. Senior management wanted some fresh eyes on the case to show they hadn't forgotten about it, which I think they largely had, and I spent the next two and a half years reviewing everything we'd collated. Tania wanted my take on what I'd found. Hence our meeting.'

'Did she come to you with the theory that the real target was Cathy de Roth?'

She looked at me sharply. 'How do you know about that?'

'Because she told me and showed me the footage.'

'I'm surprised.'

That caught me. 'Why are you surprised?'

Rose gave me a strange look then. 'She asked a lot of questions about you, Chris. She already knew all about your undercover role and she knew I'd been your handler. And before you ask, I don't know where she got that information from. But I got the feeling she didn't trust you.'

'On what grounds?' I demanded. 'She didn't even know me.'

'What worried her about you is what's always worried me. That you've got a real knack for being in the wrong place at the wrong time. When things go awry, you always seem to be at the forefront of it. Like Villa Amalfi. According to you, that was meant to be a gun buy. Except it wasn't. They already had the guns. It was a massacre. '

'That wasn't my fault,' I said defensively. Because it hadn't been.

She stopped again, and I could see anger in her eyes. 'It was a failure of intelligence, Chris. And the intelligence you provided was always sketchy. The whole thing almost cost me my job.'

'It cost me a lot more than that,' I told her, my own

anger flaring now. 'Look at me, I'm a cripple. That's because of the job I did for you people. I may not have been that good at it, but if we hadn't been following the terrorists that night, and if I hadn't intervened, it would have been a hell of a lot worse.'

'And that's the only reason I'm here, because you did risk your life that night. So I'm fairly certain I can trust you.'

'I don't even know what you're actually accusing me of. Incompetence? Being in cahoots with the men who shot me?'

She took a deep breath, held her hands up. 'Okay, I'm sorry. I'm not accusing you of anything. I guess maybe you are just very unlucky.'

'Yes, I am,' I said, looking her squarely in the eye. 'But being unlucky's not a crime.' I sighed. 'Look, can we sit down over there?' I motioned to a park bench set beneath an oak tree a few yards back from the path and out of the way of the joggers and cyclists periodically coming past.

When we were seated, I asked Rose once again who'd come up with the theory that Cathy de Roth and the un-identified blonde-haired woman with her had been the real targets.

'It was me,' she answered with a sigh. 'But it wasn't brilliant detective work on my part that did it. I looked at the footage plenty of times, but I didn't really put two and two together until I got a call out of the blue from a retired Met detective called Keith Bowen, who worked out of Wandsworth. This was sometime in 2018, when I'd been on the inquiry about a year, and right after the Me Too movement had hit the news. Bowen told me he'd arrested de Roth not long before the Villa Amalfi massacre after one of her models made a complaint about her.'

'What was the nature of the complaint?'

'That de Roth was some kind of high-class madam, effectively pimping her girls out to very wealthy society clients by encouraging them to sleep with them. The complainant, a woman called Anna, claimed that she was raped by a client when she refused to play ball, and when she told this to de Roth, de Roth called her a liar and said that if she ever mentioned a word of it to anyone, she'd never work again. Anna obviously felt strongly enough to go to the police, and that was when de Roth was arrested and brought in for questioning. She denied absolutely everything, as did the man accused of the rape, and although Anna claimed she knew of another woman who'd been raped by the same man and was prepared to come forward, this woman never materialised, and then Anna retracted her statement, saying she'd made the whole thing up. So the case was dropped and de Roth's very high-powered lawyer made sure that his client was de-arrested and the whole thing expunged from her record.'

I frowned. 'It's hardly a good reason for Bowen to call CTC about it ten years later, surely? So, she was a high-class madam. No one's going to put two and two together and think that was the reason that she was murdered along with nine other people, especially ten years later. And it might have been that de Roth was telling the truth.'

Rose shrugged. 'That's what I thought too, but Bowen was plausible. He'd risen to DI level before retiring, and done a full thirty years in the Met, and he said the case had bugged him for years, and it was only the advent of the Me Too movement that made him confident enough to speak out. So I met him, and what he told me convinced me to look closer at the footage, which is where I finally got my suspicions that it might have been a targeted hit.'

'And what did he tell you?'

'That he visited the original complainant at home after she'd retracted her statement. He said she looked exhausted and terrified and as good as slammed the door in his face, making him convinced that someone had threatened her, or worse. Because she wouldn't cooperate, there was nothing he could do, but he started digging into the affairs of de Roth's modelling agency and almost immediately saw that there'd been a very recent murder case involving a victim who was also a model.'

I felt my jaw tighten as suddenly I was transported back to the night of that first fateful meeting with Aaron Clarn, and I had to work hard to keep my expression neutral as Rose continued.

'Bowen spoke to the SIO in charge of the murder case, and it turned out that the victim . . .'

Don't let it be her, for Christ's sake.

'. . . was a young woman called Kerry Masters, who'd been on the books of Cathy de Roth's agency but had recently left. Bowen told me he suspected Kerry was the other rape victim Anna had referred to, and that it was her murder that had spooked Anna into retracting her statement.'

I felt sick. Truly sick. Knowing my part in all this.

'But then it turned out she'd been murdered by someone else, and so once again there was nothing he could do. But he said it always bugged him, and I can see why.'

Rose looked at me. I hadn't said anything for a few minutes as my mind whirred and spun. I had no doubt that Rose had given all this information to Tania and then Tania had also met Roger Bowen. From there it wouldn't have been hard to establish a connection between Kerry Masters, me and the GIU team, including Baz Cleaver.

'You remember that case, don't you?' said Rose, interrupting my thoughts. Although it was couched as a question, it sounded more like a statement.

I wasn't sure how much – if anything – Tania had told her about my links to the case, but there was no point in lying.

'Yeah, I remember it,' I said. 'Too well. I was the first detective on the scene, along with the Chief. Sorry, Devon Andrews.' Even after all this time, I still automatically referred to him by his old nickname. 'It was CID's case, not ours, but the man who killed her was one of the GIU team's targets, Leon Warman. He was murdered in an unrelated incident.'

'During a GIU op, I understand.'

I could hardly deny it. 'That's right. I suppose in hindsight Baz Cleaver could have set him up for the killing. Which would establish a connection with the Villa Amalfi massacre. So you were on the right track.' I needed to steer this conversation away from me. 'What did you do with the information that Bowen gave you?'

'I went upstairs with it, of course, and managed to get a meeting with our old friend Marina Reineke, who at that time had just taken over as head of CTC. I told her everything, showed her the footage, but she concluded there wasn't enough evidence to go any further with it.'

'What about the alleged rapist? Who was he?'

'A High Court judge, who by the time Bowen came to us had been promoted to the Supreme Court. So with no evidence of any kind against him whatsoever, no one was going to touch it, least of all CTC, who don't even deal with that kind of thing. I tried to locate the blonde-haired girl who was with de Roth at the time, but without a name, I drew a blank. After that, there really wasn't much more I could do, so I let it lie. But when Tania came calling, I decided to talk to her.'

'Well, whatever Tania knew, it was enough to get her killed.' I looked at her. 'What do we do now?'

She met my gaze. 'We don't do anything, Chris. Or at least I don't. I told the SIO on Tania's murder team that she'd been in touch with me about the Villa Amalfi case, and that we'd talked briefly, but I didn't give any more details, because frankly, I don't want to be involved.'

'You *are* involved, Rose.'

She shook her head emphatically. 'No, Chris. *You* are involved. Not me. I don't know if it's Kalian Roman behind all this, but whoever it is, they have a long reach. I'm a mother of two young children, and I really don't want anything happening to my family.' She stood up, signalling that this was the end of our meeting. 'I've probably told you too much, and I'm relying on you to keep it confidential, but I'm out of this now. And if I were you, I'd stay out of it too, and don't do anything to attract DI Franka's attention. I hear she's something of a Rottweiler. It's a good thing you've got a top-notch lawyer. Thomas Workman, the police baiter, no less.'

'I take help where I can get it,' I said, getting up as well, using the arm of the bench for support.

Rose stuffed her hands in her coat pockets and looked at me with, I like to think, a hint of sadness in her eyes. 'Take care, Chris,' she said. 'I'm truly sorry about what happened to you. But please don't contact me again.'

And with that, she turned and left me there, standing in the drizzle like a pariah.

41

I returned home in a state of shock.

I'd guessed that Kerry Masters' murder had had some-thing to do with the attack thanks to Tania Wild's unwelcome mention of her name, but the full extent of the criminal enterprise at work here – the corruption, the cover-ups, the framing of innocent men – was almost mind-boggling.

I was now certain that Cathy de Roth was indeed the gunmen's target that night at the Villa Amalfi. My theory, which I'd formulated on the journey home, was this. De Roth had clearly been pimping out her models to high-end establishment clients, in cahoots with the mysterious Kalian Roman, who was then able to gain influence with these clients, potentially by blackmail. When you considered that de Roth's client list included a High Court (now Supreme Court) judge, who'd allegedly raped two of the girls, this could give a potential blackmailer a huge amount of power, and he wouldn't want anyone or anything upsetting the apple cart. So when one of the models had started making complaints, he'd acted decisively and ruthlessly, using his enforcer Clarn to murder Kerry, whose testimony would have added serious weight to Anna's accusations, and by doing so, scaring off Anna too.

This, though, was where my theory ground to a halt. I suspected that at some point shortly afterwards, Kalian Roman had decided that de Roth knew too much and was a liability, and then had her murdered too, but the problem was that killing ten people in a restaurant just to get to one woman seemed way too much like overkill. Kalian Roman had clearly demonstrated that he had the resources to set up murders and frame innocent people for them. It would have been far easier just to have killed Cathy de Roth off quietly, when there was little to no chance that her murder would be linked to Kerry's.

It was possible, of course, that Roman was killing two birds with one stone. Getting rid of an errant employee while at the same time continuing his extremist agenda of encouraging terrorist attacks. And this simply raised its own nagging question: What type of individual was Kalian Roman? Neo-Nazi? Islamic extremist? Crime lord? Corrupt businessman?

He could have been all of these things. Or none of them.

Either way, I knew I was missing something. Something that was just on the edge of my peripheral vision.

I made myself a coffee when I got home, and sat there for a long time thinking about it, letting my mind wonder.

Clarn and his fellow gunmen had also been after the blonde-haired woman, Sophie, who'd been with Cathy de Roth that night, and they'd known when and where the two of them were going to meet. It was obvious that the whole gun deal Cleaver had told me about was a ruse. In reality, he and Clarn had been planning to use me as the driver for the Villa Amalfi attack, and had probably even intended to dispose of me afterwards (although I still like to think Cleaver wouldn't have done that to me). But the point was, the attack had been planned well in advance, and Roman was prepared to make big sacrifices to make sure it succeeded, which in turn made me wonder what it was Sophie and de Roth had been meeting about. According to Tania Wild, Sophie wasn't one of the models on de Roth's books, but she was clearly someone who Kalian Roman wanted eliminated.

So who was she?

Something struck me then. A comment Anna had made in the driveway of Kerry Masters' apartment block while I'd been trying to comfort her. And that led me to do something I'd spent the last fourteen years avoiding. I googled the name Kerry Masters on my laptop, and tapped on the first image of her.

I'd never looked at Kerry's picture before. It had flashed in front of me on the news in those few fleeting days when she'd found posthumous fame, but I'd always turned away quickly. Now I forced myself to stare at the smiling young woman – God, so young – who filled the screen. She was very pretty, but in a natural, girl-next-door kind of way, with big hazel eyes, great cheekbones and a cute button nose. I could imagine her advertising summer clothes in one of those fashion catalogues where everyone's young, healthy-looking and harmless, and the sky's always a perfect blue.

Then I remembered her lying dead on her bed – as vivid as if it had been yesterday – cut to pieces by the same man who'd murdered Tania Wild, and who continued to evade justice.

I shut my eyes and tried to picture Sophie again from the footage on Tania's laptop.

What am I going to tell her sister? That's what Anna had said outside Kerry's flat.

Could it be possible that Sophie was Kerry Masters' sister? I couldn't say for sure without comparing photos, and I didn't think Rose would appreciate it if I asked her to supply an image of Sophie from the Villa Amalfi footage. Certainly there weren't striking similarities. If there had been, I suspect Tania Wild would have noticed.

But there were other ways to find out. So I went back into the news reports of Kerry's murder from 2007, forcing myself to read through them. It took me a while – the best part of an hour – but then I found a clip from the *Daily Mail* in which Kerry's sister described her as 'a beautiful person who everyone loved' as she tearfully appealed for any witnesses to come forward.

And her name was Sophie.

There was no photo of her accompanying the picture, but it didn't matter. I knew she was the one I was looking for. I just had to hope she was still out there somewhere.

Luckily, I knew where to start looking.

42

Time wasn't exactly on my side, so I didn't hang around, and it was later the same afternoon that I parked my car down the road from a terrace of about a dozen cottages overlooking a field at the edge of a village at the northern end of the Chilterns that had probably been pretty once but was now sprawling in all directions as bits had been added to it over the years.

Geoff Masters, father of Kerry and Sophie, hadn't been that hard to find. His name had also come up in one of the news stories about his daughter's murder, as he asked for witnesses to come forward, but again with no photo of him attached. I'd googled him, and having trawled through all the posts relating to the veteran Aussie golfer of the same name, had come across a headline from 2012 entitled 'Theft Shame of Tragic Dad'. Apparently Masters, a financial adviser from Tring, Hertfordshire, had stolen a total of fourteen thousand pounds from his clients to cover some poor investments he'd made in what was in effect a mini Ponzi scheme. According to the article, the judge had only spared him jail because he'd taken pity on him as a result of the tragedies he'd suffered. A daughter murdered, followed only months later by the death of his ex-wife in a car accident, and a second daughter who he'd lost all contact with.

Reading the article, I felt sorry for him too. It was hard not to, given the litany of bad news that had befallen him. I for one knew what it was like to lose a daughter and a wife. It could bring down the strongest of men.

Since I had both a name and a town, it was only a matter of time before I pinpointed Masters' address to the village of Aston Clinton, three miles west of Tring.

I hadn't phoned ahead. Very few people had been pleased to see me lately, with the possible exception of Tania Wild (and look where it had got her), and I didn't think Masters would welcome the intrusion.

But what choice did I have?

I climbed slowly out of the car, grabbed my walking stick and made my way over to the front door of number 8, one of the middle cottages. It had stopped drizzling, and the sun was even looking like it might make an appearance. A woman in her sixties, doing some weeding in the neighbouring front garden, looked my way with a slightly hostile expression on her face and I gave her my widest smile and wished her good afternoon. It's amazing what a bit of politeness can do, and she replied with a good afternoon of her own, her expression turning to one of interest. I had no doubt she was watching me intently and wondering who I was as I rang on the doorbell.

A few seconds later, I heard slow footsteps and the door was opened by a man who I knew to be fifty-eight but who could easily have passed for ten years older. He had the same high cheekbones as his daughters, and he'd probably been good-looking once, but now his face was gaunt and hollow, set with heavy deep lines, and his thinning hair was dyed a cheap boot-polish black. He had big hazel eyes that had lost their spark, and they narrowed as he looked at me with a mix of curiosity and irritation, his gaze drawn, like most people's, to my walking stick.

I leant forward and, keeping my voice quiet, said: 'Hello, Mr Masters. My name's Chris Sketty. I was one of the police officers shot during the Villa Amalfi massacre, hence the stick. I helped save your daughter, Sophie. I know it was a long time ago, but I have some questions I'd like to ask you.'

He didn't say anything for a moment. Frankly, he looked shocked, which was no surprise, and I could see he didn't want me there.

'Please,' I said. 'I've come a long way.'

'Have you got any ID?'

'I took early retirement,' I told him, 'but here's my driving licence.'

He glanced at it quickly, then peered over my shoulder and evidently decided he didn't want this conversation on his doorstep. 'You'd better come in,' he said. 'But I haven't got long.'

'It won't take long.'

He led me through to an old-fashioned but well-kept

kitchen and dining area, and invited me to take a seat. I noticed that he was shuffling as he walked, and I mentioned it.

'Arthritis,' he said. 'Both knees. It comes and goes. But it's getting worse. Can I get you a drink?'

I asked him if he had proper coffee. He didn't. Only instant. I opted for tea, taking a seat and leaning my walking stick against a sideboard/bookshelf, full of old-school crockery and well-thumbed cookbooks, while he made tea for both of us. I took a look round. The place didn't have the feel of a bachelor pad. It had the feel of a home. Watercolour paintings of country scenes that looked like they were the work of a good amateur adorned the walls, and I asked if Masters had painted them himself.

'No. My ex-wife painted them.'

'Sophie's mum?'

He shook his head, passing me my cup of tea before taking a seat. 'My second wife. She passed away two years ago. Cancer.'

Jesus, I thought. No wonder the guy looked so haggard. Tragedy followed him round like a vulture, picking away at his life. Sitting there with him made me feel uncomfortable, because I could see far too many similarities to my own life, and I had this awful feeling that, like Scrooge, I might be sitting opposite the future Chris Sketty.

'I'm sorry,' I said. 'You've had it hard.'

He sighed. 'I won't deny that. You know my story, I suppose?'

I nodded. 'I do.'

'It doesn't look like you've had it too easy either. It can't be any fun with the stick, not at your age. Is it permanent?'

'It's a lot better than it was, but yes, barring some miracle, I'll be using it for the rest of my life.'

We sat in silence for a few seconds, and I could feel that there was some kinship between us, two lonely men who felt, with some justification, that their best years were behind them.

'How did you save Sophie exactly?' he asked me eventually. 'What happened?'

I realised this was a test to prove my credentials. My guess was he'd heard the story from Sophie before. 'I was the first police officer inside the restaurant,' I told him. 'I chased two of the gunmen out the back. I believe they were about to shoot Sophie, who was crouched down by the outside bins. I shot one of them. The other escaped. As you can see, I also got shot, and Sophie visited me in hospital afterwards.' I spoke matter-of-factly, without emotion. Sometimes when I went back over that night, it was as if it had happened to someone else, which my therapist said was a defence mechanism. This was one of those times.

'Thank you for what you did,' he said, sounding like he meant it.

'I'm glad some good came out of it,' I said, 'and that Sophie survived. But even so, I think if I had my time again, I wouldn't have tried to be a hero. It's cost me a lot.'

Masters nodded as if he understood, which I suspect he probably did, and took a sip of his tea.

'And what brings you here after all these years, Mr

Sketty? If it's money you want, I'm afraid you've come to the wrong place.'

'No, no, no,' I said, putting up my hands. 'Why would I want money? I'm here because I don't think justice has been done in the Villa Amalfi case. I've spent a lot of time investigating it, talked to a lot of people. And I believe there's far more to it than everyone realises.' As you know, this was a lie, but a necessary one. I didn't want him to know that someone else had been investigating it and I'd been arrested in connection with her murder only two days earlier.

Masters frowned, deepening the lines on his face. 'What does this have to do with me?' he asked, but something in his eyes told me he already knew.

I came right out with it. 'I'll tell you my theory. I don't think it was the terrorist attack the police and media have always claimed. It was more than that. I think Cathy de Roth, whose modelling agency your daughter Kerry worked for, was targeted. I also think Sophie was too. Was Sophie anything to do with de Roth's agency?'

'No,' he answered emphatically. 'De Roth was a horrible woman. I didn't know her, but I know she was awful to Kerry.'

'I also think the man who supposedly murdered Kerry wasn't her killer. I don't know if you're aware, but the get-away driver on the night of the massacre, Detective Sergeant Barry Cleaver, had history with Leon Warman, and had arrested him several times before.'

'I'm aware of all the details of my daughter's murder.'

'I think Cleaver set Warman up.'

'Are you saying that Cleaver murdered Kerry?'

'I'm certain he was involved, yes. Which links Kerry's murder to the Villa Amalfi attack. I think de Roth is the key. She was pimping out her girls to wealthy clients, girls were beginning to make complaints about her, and so someone decided that she was a liability and to shut her up permanently in a way that would never get back to them.'

He took a deep breath. 'That's some theory you've got there. Have you any evidence to back it up?'

I noticed that he hadn't dismissed it, which made me think he knew something. 'Yes, I do,' I said. 'I've seen actual security camera footage from inside the restaurant during the attack. De Roth was definitely their target. So was Sophie. It was only because she was in the bathroom when the gunmen stormed in that she wasn't killed too.'

Masters looked unconvinced. 'That seems crazy. Why target Sophie? What's she got to do with anything?'

'I was hoping you'd know the answer to that,' I said.

'I'm afraid I don't,' he said, shaking his head. 'It's all news to me.'

I picked up my tea, took a sip. It was too weak. 'So you're happy just to let things lie?'

He gave an empty laugh. 'And what do you propose to do about it fourteen years later, Mr Sketty? Get the whole thing reopened? I don't see how that's going to solve anything. It won't bring Kerry justice.'

'But it might help Sophie.'

'I don't even know where Sophie is any more,' he said. 'We lost touch a long time ago.'

He looked me right in the eye as he spoke and I knew straight away he was lying. He knew where she was, or at the very least, how to contact her. But he was being cautious, which was understandable, so I had to play this carefully.

'Look, I'm not interested in tracking Sophie down. If she's out there somewhere living anonymously, then that's fine with me, but I just want to know who's really behind the Villa Amalfi attack and bring their names out into the public domain. Because for the last fourteen years I've walked with a limp, and I don't like to see them getting away with that.' Now it was my turn to look him straight in the eye.

'I can't afford to lose another daughter,' he said, frowning deeply. 'Losing one was hard enough.'

'I know the feeling,' I said, guiltily playing my trump card. 'How can you ever know what it's like to lose a child?'

I told him about Grace, and this time I knew we'd established a kinship.

'I'm sorry,' he said. 'To lose one so young . . .' His voice trailed off, and for a few moments he was lost in thought, staring down at his teacup. Then he sat up straighter in his seat, and this time when he looked at me the suspicion was gone. 'I don't want Sophie involved in any of this. She needs to be kept safe.'

'I understand that.'

'Do you really think you can get to the people behind this?' he asked me.

'The honest answer is probably not. But I'm going to do everything in my power to try.'

Masters cleared his throat, and that was when he started talking properly. 'I was never a good father to either Kerry or Sophie. Their mother and I split up when they were very young. It was my fault. I was an arsehole to live with. I went off with another woman and ended up married to her, and didn't see much of the girls for a long time. But as they got older, I wanted to rekindle a relationship. Kerry was living in London at the time, but I used to see her once every couple of months. We'd have a drink or a bite to eat in town.' He paused. 'Anyway, over the last few months of her life, I noticed that she wasn't really herself. She was generally a happy girl, good fun, always smiling. A real joy to be around. But she seemed to become more distracted. She missed dinners. She put me off. I began to think she might be on drugs. And then the last time I saw her, I was really shocked. She'd lost weight and she looked a real mess, which was very unlike her. Kerry was always immaculately turned out. I asked her what was wrong and she told me that de Roth had fired her, although she wouldn't tell me why. I was sure there was a lot more to the story, but couldn't get her to open up about it. We had a pretty quiet dinner, and then she left.'

He paused again, closed his eyes for a moment. 'And that was the last time I saw her. A couple of weeks later, she was dead, and our whole world was turned upside down.'

'I'm sorry,' I told him. 'I don't like having to rake up old memories. I know what it feels like.'

'It's okay,' he said, his narrow face scrunched tight as he appeared to fight off a wave of emotion. As his features relaxed, he asked me if I minded if he smoked.

'It's your house, Mr Masters. You do what you want.'

'Please,' he said, locating his cigarettes and an ashtray in one of the sideboard drawers. 'Call me Geoff.'

He offered me the pack and I shook my head. 'No thanks. I quit.' I've often considered taking it back up again. If nothing else, it was something to do, and I'd always enjoyed smoking. But somehow, I'd resisted. My eyes still lingered on Masters, though, as he lit up and took a long, much-needed drag, and I came close to asking him for one. I mean, what did I really have to lose?

But I didn't. Instead, I listened as he continued.

At first, like everyone else, he'd thought Leon Warman had been responsible for Kerry's murder, but that all changed when he spoke to Sophie afterwards. Kerry, it seemed, had told her all about Cathy de Roth's business sideline. 'But sometimes the men didn't just want ordinary sex,' continued Masters. 'They wanted kinky stuff, you know. Kerry was foolish. She got involved willingly, but then one night, one of these bastards raped her in a hotel room. She told de Roth about it, but rather than reacting with horror that something like that had happened to one of her girls, that bitch told Kerry to keep quiet about and tried to pay her off. When Kerry refused, she was fired and warned that if she said anything, she'd be in real trouble.'

'Do you know the name of the man who raped her?' I asked.

Masters nodded, his expression darkening. 'Yeah,' he growled. 'I know his name. He's a lord now, and the chairman of a major company. And nothing's ever happened to him for what he did to my daughter.'

So, it wasn't just the Supreme Court judge who was a rapist. It sickened me that these men were getting away with it, even though I had no doubt that they were very much in hock to Kalian Roman. But what did he want from men like that? This was the burning question. The problem was, I was never going to be able to answer that question until I knew who he was.

'Justice sometimes takes a long time to get served, but most people receive it in the end,' I told Masters, not that I really believed that. 'Why was Sophie meeting with Cathy de Roth at Villa Amalfi on the night of the attack?'

He didn't say anything for a moment, and I knew he was debating how much to tell me. We looked at each other through the cloud of the cigarette smoke, and I waited while he came to a decision.

'Sophie told me that Kerry was planning to go to the police about the rape. Apparently one of the other girls at the agency had already reported that she'd been raped by a different man, and there were lots of incidents of what we'd now call sexual assault on the models, even if they weren't all-out rapes. Some of the girls involved were under eighteen. Kerry told Sophie that she'd been keeping a journal naming the male clients, and giving details of what they were up to, including the ones who liked the really nasty stuff, and she told her where to find it in the event of anything happening to her.'

Masters paused. 'Well, obviously something did happen to her, as you know. Sophie read the journal and decided to confront de Roth about it. Her plan was to meet de Roth posing as a young woman wanting to take up modelling, confront her about the allegations in the diary and use a hidden tape recorder to record her responses. But as you know, it didn't work out like that. De Roth was killed, Sophie only just managed to escape, and after that, she left the country for her own safety and has never returned.'

'So you haven't seen her in fourteen years?'

'I didn't say that. But she lives abroad anonymously, and she's safe.'

'And what about the journal? Where is it now?'

'I honestly don't know. I never saw it, and I don't know if Sophie kept it or not.'

'Did you know in advance about the meeting between Sophie and de Roth?'

Masters shook his head. 'No. If I had, I would never have let it go ahead.'

But I wasn't sure I believed him on this. Or that Sophie was meeting de Roth in a flashy restaurant like Villa Amalfi on the pretext of discussing a possible modelling job. Given that Masters had at one time had a bad gambling habit, and that Sophie had already been designated as one of the gunmen's targets before she even took her seat, I thought it more likely it was some kind of reverse blackmail, which would also explain how Kalian Roman had got wind of it. But, of course, this was all conjecture, and made no difference to anything now.

'Why did you never go to the police?' I asked him.

He took a last drag on the cigarette and stubbed it out in the ashtray. 'There were two reasons. Firstly, I didn't think anyone would believe us. We had no real evidence and I wasn't even sure I believed myself that someone would stage a full-scale massacre just to get to de Roth and Sophie. Or that they'd kill Kerry and frame an innocent man. In the end, it was safer to stay quiet.'

He was right too, because that was the genius of the Villa Amalfi attack. The real motive behind it was just too well hidden.

'You said there were two reasons. What was the other?'

'A few days after the attack, I got a visit from a detective looking for Sophie. I asked him what it was about and he said she was an important witness and that it was urgent they trace her. I told him I hadn't seen her, but it was obvious he didn't believe me, and he started putting the pressure on, saying I'd get in a lot of trouble if I was hiding her. I kept to my story and he left, but something about him seemed really off. I was convinced he was working for the people who'd wanted de Roth dead, and that made me think that if even the police were corrupt, we had no chance of ever being believed.'

I sighed and sat back in my seat. Masters had made the right move. The odds had been stacked against him from the start. Just as they'd been stacked against Tania Wild. And just as they were stacked against me. 'Did you get the detective's name?'

'He told me it, yes. And I wrote it down somewhere.

310

But it was a long time ago, and I honestly can't remember what it was.'

Which was what I'd been expecting. I was beginning to feel deflated as I came to the end of my questions. 'I know it's a long shot, but can you describe him?'

'Yeah, I remember him well,' said Masters. 'He was an intimidating figure. A well-built black guy, six foot three or four, with a big mole underneath one of his eyes. He was probably early forties at the time.'

My world, already built on the shakiest of foundations, began to crumble just a little bit more as I realised that he was describing my mentor, and one of the few men in my life I'd totally respected.

DCI Devon Andrews. The Chief.

43

I drove back home on autopilot, rocked by this latest revelation.

Things were beginning to make sense to me now. My guess was that Baz Cleaver's boss within Kalian Roman's organisation had been the Chief – his boss in real life. Like Aaron Clarn, the two of them had been Roman's bagmen, making sure that part of his business – which was undoubtedly the blackmail of wealthy, influential individuals – ran smoothly. Whether or not the Chief had been coerced into working for Roman, like Cleaver claimed *he* had, was open to debate, but work for him he did.

It made me feel sick. I'd always felt the Chief had real integrity. He cared about the streets he patrolled and the civilians whose lives he tried to make better, I knew he did. He cared about justice. And yet it seemed that he'd been actively involved in the murder of Kerry Masters and the setting-up of Leon Warman, and doubtless it had been the Chief who'd planted one of Warman's hairs in Kerry's apartment when we'd gone inside that time.

The question was, what did I do about it? I was a man on my own, without a shred of evidence. The obvious answer was to find Sophie and see if she still had the journal. I knew better than to try to persuade her dad to tell me where she was, so in the end, I'd asked him to let her know about my visit, and left my number in case she wanted to get in touch. He said he would, but advised me not to hold my breath. 'I think she's happy to keep it in the past,' he told me. And who could blame her for that?

When I got back home, I went online and looked up what I could about the Chief. It didn't take long to find a detailed interview with him in one of the Sunday supplements from 2019, complete with a photo of him standing, arms folded, in a classic tough-guy pose, outside a plush-looking three-storey house. He looked annoyingly fit and healthy.

It turned out Devon Andrews had done very well for himself. Having taken early retirement the year after the Villa Amalfi attack, he'd turned entrepreneur and gone into business providing high-tech security services to private companies and foreign embassies, and now lived in the Sussex countryside with his wife and family. I remembered the Chief's kids – a boy and a girl, so much younger then – from when I'd spent Christmas Day round his old family home. I remembered his wife too – Donna, a happy, friendly woman who'd gone out of her way to welcome me that day. It was hard to believe she'd be married to a man involved in all this.

In the interview, the Chief talked about how the involvement of his right-hand man, Barry Cleaver, in the Villa

Amalfi killings completely destroyed the GIU team's morale and led directly to its break-up, ruining years of hard work, and how the guilt he felt at not having spotted Cleaver's intentions earlier made him feel he could no longer stay in the Met.

Knowing what I thought I knew now, these just seemed like weasel words, but the Chief's decision to leave had clearly been a good one. I looked up his company accounts on the Companies House website, and saw that the previous year's profits had been just short of a million pounds on five million of turnover, most of which had ended up in his own pocket, and that of his wife and fellow director, Donna. The service the company offered was extensive, from manned networks of surveillance cameras to top-of-the-range cyber-defence software, and it made me wonder where the Chief had got the finance to start up what was clearly a cash-intensive business.

Sadly, I was pretty sure I knew the answer to that one.

I had to talk to Rose. She might have said only a matter of hours earlier that she didn't want to hear from me again, but at least I had new, very relevant information, and frankly I didn't know where else to turn.

It was almost 8 p.m. when I called her number. It went straight to voicemail, and I left a message saying I'd identified the mysterious blonde-haired woman from Villa Amalfi. If that didn't get her to call back, not much would.

I wasn't expecting a rapid answer, so I made some dinner – a quick Spanish-style garlic and vegetable soup, using leftover veg from the fridge, laced with plenty of smoked paprika and grated Parmesan. Food's one of my few real pleasures these days, and it was a testimony to how shaken I'd been by recent events that the soup was the first food to reach my lips since a banana first thing that morning.

I ate it in front of the TV with Trevor the cat curled up on my lap. Finally relaxing properly for the first time since Tania Wild had called, I broke my self-imposed two-nights-a-week booze rule and treated myself to a large glass of Burgundy Pinot Noir and an episode of *World's Most Scenic Railway Journeys*, where the train wound its way across South Africa from the capital, Pretoria, to the Indian Ocean.

I'd thought often about going travelling those past years. After all, a bad hip and a limp wasn't any real impediment to getting on a plane. I'd even worked out when and where I was going to go. I'd leave the UK in May, criss-cross Europe by bus, taking in the Alps, the south of France, Barcelona (where I'd once spent an amazing long weekend with Karen on only our second trip away together) and wherever else took my fancy. Then by September I'd get to India, and spend a month there seeing the sights before hitting in turn Sri Lanka, Thailand, Indonesia, Australia and of course New Zealand, where I'd stay for a while with Karen and her new family.

She and Bryan still lived in Christchurch. They had two daughters – Freya, aged ten, and Summer, aged eight, both really cute kids – and if Facebook was anything to go by, they all lived an idyllic outdoor life over there. I was happy for her, and I mean that. We still kept in touch online, and she regularly badgered me to come over and visit.

I could afford to do it too. I'd saved up, having not had much to spend my money on, but somehow I'd never managed to get round to booking anything. It was always next year. Maybe when the hip was a little better, and I could get someone to look after Trevor. Or when I'd met someone to do it all with. And now that everything had suddenly turned haywire in my life and I was on bail and the suspect in a murder, I might not have a chance to do it even if I wanted to.

The phone rang loudly, bringing me crashing out of my thoughts. I picked it up and saw it was Rose.

So, she *had* bitten.

'I thought I said I didn't want to hear from you again, Chris,' she said, by way of greeting.

'And I thought you'd want to know about this,' I told her.

'How on earth did you manage to track this woman down in the space of a few hours?' Her tone was laced with scepticism. And something else. Was it suspicion?

'It wasn't rocket science. I went back over the Kerry Masters case after I left you, and saw an article where it mentioned a sister called Sophie. I just put two and two together.'

'Shit. How did I miss that?'

'You didn't have a first name. I did. She visited me in hospital, remember?'

This seemed to mollify her. 'And where's Sophie now?'

'I don't know, but I talked to her father.' I had no choice

but to trust Rose. I didn't see how she could have been involved, given that she'd known about my undercover role from the beginning. So I gave her the full details of my conversation with Geoff Masters, finishing with the revelation that the Chief had been to visit him shortly after the Villa Amalfi attacks, looking for Sophie.

'A very basic description of a man who could be Devon Andrews from fourteen years ago is not evidence, Chris. It's clutching at straws.'

'Have you seen how well he's done since he left the police? He's a millionaire.'

'How did he make his money?'

'A security business.'

'There you have it. It's not evidence of any wrongdoing. Quite the opposite. Andrews was able to use his skills as a businessman to forge a successful career after the police.'

'He's involved. I'm sure of it.' I told her about how he'd been with me in Kerry Masters' flat and could have easily planted evidence implicating Leon Warman, given that he'd been alone in there for several minutes.

'That's not enough, Chris. I can't go to Commander Reineke with that.'

'But with Sophie and the journal, we've now got a new motive for the attack. And if Kalian Roman is blackmailing Supreme Court judges and business leaders, then that needs exposing. Come on, Rose, I know you want this case solved as much as me. It's got to be worth looking at it in more detail. And we both know it's the reason Tania Wild died, whatever DI Franka might think.'

'Can you produce Sophie and this journal?' she asked me.

'Yeah,' I lied, thinking I didn't have much choice. 'I can.'

Rose sighed. 'I'll see if I can get a meeting with Marina and tell her what you've told me, but don't hold your breath, Chris. And try not to do anything stupid in the meantime.'

'Like what?'

'Like get yourself involved in murder.'

'I need you and Reineke to help me on that. You need to push Franka to make sure they test that whole house for Clarn's DNA, because that will throw this thing wide open.'

'Neither she nor I have got that kind of influence.'

'Please,' I said, coming perilously close to begging. 'I don't want to go down for something I haven't done.'

'I'll see what I can do.' And with that she ended the call.

I poured another glass of the Pinot and sat there for a few minutes stroking Trevor and trying to work out my next move, not that I really had one. Without Sophie, my theory was worthless. Even if she did come forward with the journal, it wouldn't be smooth sailing. After all, it was effectively just a diary, and an old one at that. It proved nothing.

And yet fourteen years ago it had been worth committing mass murder for.

I sighed, took a sip of the wine and thought about the Chief. I still wasn't a hundred per cent sure he was involved. Rose was right. I had no evidence at all. Geoff Masters could have been mistaken. But whether he was or he wasn't, it didn't detract from the fact that Kalian Roman was at the top of a conspiracy that was far more widespread than anyone had realised.

And with those kinds of people in his pocket, he had the power to manipulate a whole country.

44

I'm not a big dreamer, but after my conversation with Rose that night, I polished off the bottle of Pinot Noir and fell asleep on the sofa, and almost immediately an especially vivid one started.

As always in my dreams, I was physically fit and able to run and do all the things I'd once been able to do without a care. Unusually, both Cleaver and the Chief featured in this one. We were doing a drugs bust and had our suspect against the wall. He was angry and abusive, reminding me of Leon Warman, although I don't think it was him. But we weren't having any of his lip and we started laying into him, beating him to the ground under a hail of punches. And it felt good too, me dealing out summary justice to the bad guys once again. This time, though, we kept hitting him and hitting him, long after he'd given up resisting, and I noticed that Cleaver and the Chief had stopped with their punches and were instead encouraging me to keep up the assault. They were both grinning, enjoying the spectacle. I remember the Chief handing me a gun and whispering in my ear in that deep, melodious voice of his: 'Kill him, Chris.'

I didn't want to. The guy was scum, but he didn't deserve to die. But I didn't want to disappoint the Chief either. Even after all this time, he still had a hold on me. I still wanted to believe in him.

I pushed the gun against the dealer's temple. He looked up at me, his expression one of utter terror, like Roger Munroe when I was about to pour the boiling-hot water down his throat. My finger tightened on the trigger.

'Come on, Chrissy boy!' laughed Cleaver. 'Finish him off. Prove yourself to us.'

'Prove yourself,' said the Chief. 'Be one of us. No one's going to know. We'll say it was self-defence.'

My head felt like it was going to explode under the pressure, but I did want to be one of them. I truly did.

So I squeezed the trigger and blew the guy's brains out, the crack of the gunshot loud enough to wake me up with a physical jolt that knocked Trevor off my lap and onto the floor. He got up and gave me a dirty look over his shoulder before stalking off, leaving me sitting there, my mouth dry and heart pounding, feeling the relief that came from knowing it had just been a dream, which almost immediately gave way to the grim reality that I still walked with a limp.

And the fact that I still walked with a limp was down to Kalian Roman, and also very possibly the Chief, a man I'd lionised.

That was when I knew I had to see him and tell him

what I knew. If he was guilty, it would truly throw the cat amongst the pigeons, and potentially put me in danger. But if that was the way it had to be, then so be it. Because right then, I was sick of living like a frightened recluse. I wanted to show these people – whoever they were – that I wasn't just some cripple they could manipulate. And if someone decided to come and put a bullet in me to shut me up because of that, then let them. At least I'd be set free from the mental pain that seemed to define my entire existence, and had done for so long.

It wasn't hard to find out where the Chief lived. He'd left enough of an online trail to make locating him easy, but then I suspect he didn't think he had a lot to fear from anyone, not even from the criminals he used to put away.

When I pulled up outside the security gates of his house at two o'clock the following afternoon, I was hoping to change all that.

The Chief's place was the same detached faux-Georgian executive home – with the emphasis on the faux – that had featured in the magazine article I'd read. It was big, brash and typically bland, the end one of a row of five that looked completely out of place on the edge of a quaint village in rural East Sussex, and which had probably cost the developer a fair few thousand in bribes to the planning committee. I'd checked the price the Chief had paid for it in 2014 on the Land Registry: 1.2 million. Not bad for an ex-DI.

I wasn't at all sure I wanted to see him after all these years, or that he was even in, although there were two cars in the driveway – a black Land Rover Discovery and a Mitsubishi Outlander – so I figured that it was at least fifty–fifty he was.

There was no point in putting it off, so I got out and pressed the buzzer on the intercom. A camera stared down at me and I leant on my stick and looked up at it, wondering if he'd even recognise me after all this time. When I'd last seen him, I'd been twenty-seven years old and seventy-five kilos. Now I was forty-one and over eighty, the addition mainly made up of fat round my face and middle, and my posture and pallor were those of a man who spent far too long inside and sitting down.

'Hello, Chris,' came his voice over the intercom, still just as calm and authoritative as I remembered, answering my question for me. 'Long time no see. What can I do for you?'

'I need to speak to you.'

'And you didn't think it best to call first? How far have you come?'

'Home. Still Teddington.'

A pause. 'What do you want to talk about?'

I felt another twinge of doubt about what I was doing. It wasn't easy going up against a man I'd looked up to for so long, and who still made me feel like a schoolkid round his favourite teacher. 'About my time with the team,' I said.

'You betrayed us, Chris. Undercover against your own people.'

The words stung. 'I was doing my job.'

'Are you doing your job now?'

'No. This is just an off-the-record chat.'

323

Another pause. Then a buzzer sounded and the gates slowly opened.

I drove in and parked my old banger next to the Land Rover. As I got out, conscious that my hip was playing up that day, the Chief came striding out of the front door, dressed casually in jeans and a long-sleeved pastel shirt with the sleeves rolled up the forearms, tight enough to show he still retained his muscular build and wasn't carrying an ounce of extra fat, no mean feat for a man now in his mid-fifties.

He looked down at my stick as he marched confidently over, feet crunching on the gravel. 'Sorry about your injury.'

'So am I,' I said.

He put out a hand, and we shook. His grip was tight, too tight. Verging on painful. I was conscious of the fact that he could kick the shit out of me if he wanted, and it angered me that I'd been brought so low by fate. No longer the tough guy I'd always tried to be.

He looked me right in the eye, letting me know he was the one in control. Then he smiled and let go.

'You've done well for yourself,' I said, looking round.

'Maybe all that shit with Cleaver, and the break-up of the team, worked out after all,' he said. 'I'm a lot happier now than I was in the force. It's nice to make real money and not have to look over your shoulder the whole time. Now, before you come in, do you mind if I just check you're not back to your undercover tricks?'

'I'm not wearing a wire, if that's what you're thinking,'

I said as he pulled a sophisticated-looking bug finder from his back pocket and ran it up and down my body.

'Forgive me if I'm a little bit sceptical. And leave your phone in the car.'

I did as he requested, knowing there'd be no point trying to catch him out. Then I followed as he led me into the house and through a high-vaulted hallway dominated by a spiral staircase.

'My wife's out to lunch with friends,' he said over his shoulder. 'She'll be back in an hour. I want you gone by then.'

'It won't take long,' I said.

He stopped at a room with a heavy steel door that would have taken a couple of pounds of high-grade plastic explosive to break open, and which used an iris-recognition system to unlock it. Kit like that cost thousands, but then he probably got a company discount.

Inside, the room was spacious but completely windowless, like a bunker. A huge glass desk and two chairs, one on either side of it, were the only furnishings. The Chief took one of the seats and motioned for me to take the other.

'That's a lot of security you've got, Chief,' I said, easing myself into the chair. 'Are you trying to hide something?'

He laughed hollowly. 'Very funny. And please don't call me Chief. The only people who call me that now are friends, and you're not one of those.'

The words stung. Even now, I felt the need for his respect.

'What do you want?' he asked, leaning back in his seat,

which creaked under his weight, hands steepled across his lap.

We looked at each other. I had difficulty holding his gaze but knew I had to. 'Have you ever heard the name Kalian Roman?'

He shook his head. 'Can't say I have.'

'He was the man Baz Cleaver worked for.'

'The chief neo-Nazi?'

'I don't even think he's a neo-Nazi. But he's definitely a terrorist of sorts.'

The Chief shrugged. 'Well, I still don't know who he is.'

'He was behind the Villa Amalfi attack. I've spoken to a number of people involved in the case, and done a lot of investigating, and I know that the real target that night was a woman called Cathy de Roth.' I was obviously bigging up my own role here, but if the Chief was guilty, he'd know why I was here anyway, and if he was innocent, some embellished credentials might help. I told him what I knew about de Roth. 'Cleaver and Clarn were brought in, as employees of Roman, to clean up the mess when several of the girls made complaints that they'd been raped. One of those girls was Kerry Masters. Remember her?'

The Chief looked at me like I was mad. Worryingly, the expression appeared genuine. 'I remember Kerry Masters. I was with you when we found her body. But let me get this straight, Chris. You're saying Leon Warman didn't kill her, but that Baz did?'

'He was involved.'

'How do you know?'

'I just know.'

'Jesus, Sketty. You fucked him in life. Then you got him killed. And now you're fucking him all over again in death. Leon Warman's hair was found at the scene, and the murder weapon was found under his bed.'

'And you reckon that wasn't a plant? If you killed someone, would you put the knife under your bed, still covered in the victim's blood?'

'Leon Warman wasn't exactly Professor Moriarty. He was your typical lowlife thug. And no one's saying he didn't do it, as far as I can see. Except you. What's all that got to do with me anyway? I've got better things to do than sit here raking over the past with you, so get to the point.'

There was nothing between us now, I could see that. And therefore no real point in holding back. 'I think you were involved,' I told him. 'In the whole thing. The terrorist attack on the Villa Amalfi, the murder of Kerry Masters. You and Cleaver were in on it together. He took orders from you. I suspect you took orders from Kalian Roman.'

The Chief's expression hardened. 'I think maybe you've had too much time on your hands these past fourteen years. I don't know what you're talking about.'

That was when I made my mistake. 'After the massacre, you went looking for Kerry Masters' sister. Her father remembers you calling round asking for her.'

I watched his reaction. It was one of incredulity. But was it faked?

'That's bizarre,' he said. 'This man said it was definitely me, did he? When did you talk to him? Recently?'

'Recently enough,' I said, wishing I'd kept Sophie and Geoff Masters out of it.

'And he remembered my face fourteen years later?'

I had no choice but to keep going. 'He positively ID'd you.'

He shook his head dismissively. 'He probably thinks we all look the same.'

'He was adamant. He remembered your mole.'

'Look, I don't know what you're trying to prove here, but you're barking up the wrong tree. It wasn't me.'

We stared at each other. I couldn't read him. He was giving no indication of lying, but then the guy had always been cool under pressure, so that didn't mean a thing. I was at an impasse. I had nowhere to go, but I ploughed on regardless. 'If you've got anything you want to tell me, you can say it in here. It's off the record. No one's ever going to know except you and me. But I need answers.' My voice cracked. 'Look at me. I'm a fucking cripple. Have you any idea how hard my life's been these past fourteen years? Living alone, walking with a stick, forced to retire. All I want is to know why it happened.'

The Chief's expression softened. 'And I feel for you, Chris. You had balls that night at the Villa Amalfi. Not many men would have done that. But I can't help you. I'm just a businessman.'

'Who's a millionaire several times over,' I said, with more

venom in my voice than I meant. 'Where did all that money come from?'

'If you've researched anything about me, you know that it came from my business, which has done very well over the years. The point is, I don't know Kerry Masters' sister, I don't know a Kalian Roman, and the only stuff I know about the Villa Amalfi attack is what I've seen on the news.' He got to his feet, signalling that our meeting was over. 'I think we should call it a day. I'd say it was a pleasure, but it hasn't been. I'll never forgive you for the way you joined the team under false pretences and betrayed us.'

There was nowhere I could go from there, so I got to my feet as well. 'Cleaver was a bad man,' I told him. 'He needed bringing down.'

The Chief nodded. 'Yeah, he was. And there's not a day that goes by when I don't ask myself why he got involved with the people he did, and curse him for his part in breaking up the team. And if the truth be told, he deserved what he got.' He gave me another of those withering looks. 'But that still doesn't make you any less of a snake.'

'I was just doing my job,' I said, conscious of the weakness in my voice.

'Sure you were. We were all just doing our jobs. But you're still a snake, and age hasn't improved you. Now get the fuck out of my house.'

He as good as marched me out of there, and when I was back at the car, he said: 'Don't do anything stupid.' Pretty much exactly the words Rose had used, but I was far less sure what he meant by them.

I stopped and looked at him. 'Is that a threat?'

He stared back at me impassively, and at that point I had no idea whether he was involved or not.

'No,' he said. 'It's a word of advice.'

I got in the car and drove out of there, none the wiser but a lot sadder than when I'd gone in.

45

On the drive back to Teddington, I took a detour off the A24 and parked the car at the bottom of Box Hill, Surrey's highest point and a place where Karen, Grace and I had once come for a summer picnic when Grace was a toddler. It had been a glorious summer day then; now it was a cold, grey one in November, so the car park was virtually empty.

How far I can walk before the hip gets too stiff varies considerably, but on that day I managed about half an hour and was quite a long way up the hill before the pain set in. I found a spot a little way from the main path, facing down towards a golf course and the woodland beyond, and sat there alone, staring out across the Surrey Hills, thinking about the many ghosts of the past, but particularly Baz Cleaver. I wondered if he'd known that Aaron Clarn and the others were about to embark on a murderous rampage, or whether he too had thought it was just going to be a gun deal. I hoped the latter. He'd undoubtedly been a bad man, but for all his bravado, he'd also been a weak one, and somewhere inside of him I was sure there was some goodness too. I was reminded of a phrase my old boss at SO11, DCI Perry Stilton, had once used: 'No one's the villain in their own story.' Cleaver had been corrupted. Now, as I sat there, I tried to work out if the Chief had been too, or whether he was an innocent in all this.

The way I saw it, three things counted against him. One, Geoff Masters' ID. Two, the fact that he'd landed on his feet so well and was now a comparatively rich man. I'm not denigrating his business acumen, but looking back on the company history, he'd been making big money very quickly, including a hundred-grand profit in his first year's operation, which is a real feat for a start-up. If he was a cog in Kalian Roman's web of corruption, then it was possible he'd been financed with dirty money. Finally, he'd had the means to set up Leon Warman for Kerry Masters' murder, and had been far closer to Baz Cleaver than I'd ever been.

And yet, let's face it, it wasn't a lot. Masters might have been fairly adamant, but so much time had passed, he could easily have been mistaken. The Chief could also just be a decent businessman. After all, he was charismatic enough. And as for framing Warman, Cleaver could have done that on his own.

In all honesty, the Chief had not come across like a man whose wrongdoing had been found out. He looked exactly what he claimed to be. Meanwhile, I'd acted like some paranoid amateur conspiracy theorist, but that was also a product of how the Chief made me feel. I still held him in awe, and that was why the words he'd used to describe me had stung so much.

I sat there for a long time, doubting myself and getting progressively colder. Maybe I'd been wrong with my ID of Clarn too. After fourteen years, and in the heat of the moment, I couldn't be sure. DI Franka probably thought I was deluded. Maybe that was why I was her chief suspect. I was beginning to think I was deluded as well.

I was still pondering this point when I got a call from Rose.

'I met up with Commander Reineke,' she said. 'She was already aware that Tania Wild was asking questions about the case. I told her that Tania showed you the footage from Villa Amalfi, but not where it came from, so it won't get back to me.'

'That's good,' I said, 'but can you get her to talk to Franka, so she at least knows that the motive for Tania's murder is probably related to her work on the case?'

Rose sighed. 'We still don't know that, Chris. Marina says she'll inform Franka about the fact that Tania was approaching CTC officers about the Villa Amalfi case, but I very much doubt if it'll make any difference to their murder case.'

'And what does she think about the new developments with Sophie and the journal?'

'She doesn't think much. Because it's pretty thin gruel, isn't it? What she said was that, and these are her words, "if anyone comes forward with new information, they'll be listened to".'

I exhaled loudly. 'And that's it?'

'Did you really expect anything else?'

'No,' I said. 'I didn't. I think I'm ready to admit defeat.'
And I was too.

'It's not defeat, Chris,' she said, a softness in her tone.
'It's moving on.'

But I was less sure of that.

And as it turned out, I was right to be.

46

The drive back home round the M25 was suitably brutal, and I knew the only thing that would improve my mood was decent food, so I stopped at a butcher's in Richmond and bought a big rib steak, before making a detour to the supermarket, where I bought potatoes, portobello mushrooms and a couple of fat, ripe-looking beefsteak tomatoes. If I had to choose a last meal on earth, it would have to be steak and chips, with the steak cooked rare enough that it's only just warm in the middle, followed by my grandmother's home-made trifle. Unfortunately, with my grandmother eighteen years in the ground, that part wasn't going to materialise, so instead I bought some fresh fruit and vanilla ice cream.

Even the thought of good food improves my mood, and I was feeling a bit better as I found a parking spot on the road about thirty yards from my house and walked back with my shopping. It had just turned 6 p.m. and was raining lightly, and I felt a familiar sense of relief as I shut the front door behind me and bolted it, before putting on the lights. It was strange how much my life had changed in the past few days, after fourteen years in which in many ways it had slowly atrophied, turning me into a shell of what I'd once been. I definitely felt more alive now that I had some kind of focus, but also far more scared, because I'd been thrust into a high-stakes game over which I had no control, and in which it had become clear that I was completely on my own.

I put the shopping bag containing dinner on the kitchen sideboard, thinking that if and when DI Franka ever dropped her investigation into me, it might be a good idea to book a holiday somewhere for a much-needed change of scene, although I'd have to get someone to come in and feed Trevor.

I looked round, wondering where he was. It was unheard of for him not to turn up at dinner time. He was a greedy thing and it was the only time of day I could rely on his presence.

I went over and rattled the cat flap, then peered out the window into the back garden. I couldn't see him out there. Mind you, I couldn't see much in the darkness. But I was starting to get an ominous feeling in my gut. I took my Taser torch from where I'd placed it in one of the kitchen drawers and unlocked the back door.

The rain was coming down harder now and the wind had really picked up. Closing the door behind me, I called out Trevor's name, switching the torch on at the same time and placing my thumb over the Taser button.

As I moved the torch in an arc, I saw him lying on the

grass near the end of the garden, between the birch tree and the shed. He was curled up in a ball like he was sleeping, but there was no movement at all and I knew straight away that he was dead.

I walked slowly over, keeping my eyes peeled, and crouched down beside him, leaning on my stick. I gasped audibly when I saw what had been done to him.

It was a horrific sight, the kind that would shock any normal person, and I won't go into details. Suffice to say it was the work of a sadist.

A man like Aaron Clarn.

It had also happened very recently. When I reached over and gently touched his fur, his body was still warm. I'm no expert, but I was pretty certain he'd died in the last half-hour, possibly even in the last few minutes, which meant the man who'd slaughtered him wasn't far away.

I rose to my feet, using the stick as support, and looked quickly around, suddenly fearful of an ambush. There are only two places for an adult to hide in my garden. Behind the silver birch tree next to the thick, overgrown vegetation that covered the back fence. Or in the small gap between the back of the shed and the fence. No one was behind the birch, I could see that, but from the position I was standing, the gap at the back of the shed wasn't fully visible.

I stopped and listened, trying to discern a human presence above the sound of the wind and the traffic noise from the road, but I could hear nothing untoward, and as I stood there, my breathing slowed as my fear began to dissipate and my rational brain took over. No one was going to ambush me. This was just a warning, to let me know that I was being watched. That they could get to me whenever they wanted. I had no doubt the killer had managed to do it without being caught on the security camera I had at the back of the house too, because the camera didn't cover the whole garden.

Holding the Taser in front of me, I took a couple of steps forward, moving further into the darkness at the back of the garden until I could finally see the whole of the gap behind the shed. It was empty, as I'd suspected. I was safe. For now.

I went back and stared down at Trevor's lifeless body. It was hard to believe he was gone. He'd been my constant companion for the last ten years. Pretty much my only companion. We'd enjoyed each other's company, and I don't care what people say about cats not really caring about their owners, I know Trevor had liked me. He'd always come and nuzzle up on my lap in the evenings when I was watching TV. Sometimes he'd sleep on the bed at night and wake me by licking my face with his rough little tongue. Jesus, I was going to miss him, and I just hoped he'd scratched the hell out of whoever had done this. I was pretty certain he would have done, because he was a feisty little sod, and handy with his claws too (although never to me), and there was no way he would have gone down without a fight.

These people were evil to the core. Taking apart everything that was precious to me, bit by bit. And the problem was, I knew they were never going to stop. As soon as I'd answered that call from Tania Wild, I'd made myself a threat. But I didn't regret getting involved, except where it had involved Trevor, because the life I'd been leading for so long now was no real life at all, and something was always going to have to give eventually. Now finally it had.

I gently buried Trevor in the garden, which is easier said than done when you walk with a stick. I still had a shovel in the shed from my days as a fit man, and I used it to dig a hole while simultaneously leaning against the trunk of the silver birch. It wasn't much of a hole and it took me a good half-hour, by which time the rain had got a lot harder, and the wind a lot colder, which I suppose was apt.

Afterwards, I said a little prayer over his grave, and as I stood there, I realised that this place – this garden, this cottage, even this silver birch tree – just kept the pain of my losses alive. The memories of the family time we used to have out here were happy ones, and yet being reminded constantly of what I'd lost had only served to drag me further down into a hole in which I was eventually going to sink forever unless I changed my life. And now, with even Trevor gone, it was time to move on. To leave the past behind.

With a sigh, I returned the shovel to the shed and hurried back into the house, realising that I'd left the back door unlocked. Nothing seemed to have been disturbed, and I couldn't see how anyone would have got in without me spotting them, but even so, I was immediately on my guard as I took off my coat and flung it over a chair. The shopping bag containing dinner was still on the worktop, but the thought of cooking up a steak now made me feel nauseous.

I went into the downstairs toilet and dried my hair on the towel, taking the Taser torch with me, then limped back into the kitchen. I needed a stiff drink, so I poured myself a large shot of Jameson, drank it down in one, and was just about to pour another when there was a loud, insistent knocking on the door, followed by the words that I should have realised were inevitable:

'Open up, Mr Sketty. It's the police.'

47

It was worse than I'd anticipated. Not only was DCI Franka on the doorstep, with an official-looking piece of paper in her hand and DS Singh at her shoulder, but there were half a dozen detectives with them in coats, and behind them, on the pavement, two men holding what looked suspiciously like TV cameras, which they were pointing straight at me.

'Mr Sketty,' said Franka, looking at me with the hard, professional expression of someone who's not going to be deflected from her duty, 'we have a search warrant for this premises. May we come in, please?'

'I see you brought the cameras with you. Thanks for that.'

'I'm sorry about them. They're nothing to do with us.'

'Someone tipped them off,' I said. 'And it wasn't me.' Although I had a strong suspicion about who it might be. 'Am I under arrest?'

'Not yet. But we have reason to believe there may be items hidden in your home that belong to Ms Tania Wild, specifically her mobile phone and laptop.'

'May I take a look?' I said, motioning to the warrant.

She tore off a copy and handed it to me. 'Yours.'

I checked it over and saw that it had been signed by a magistrate only ninety minutes earlier, and a good two hours after I'd left the Chief's house. It could have been coincidental, or simply another demonstration of my adversaries' power. I suspected the latter.

'You'd better come in, then, although I'm warning you, don't try to plant anything, because this place is completely covered by cameras, and the footage goes straight to the Cloud.'

And it was. During my paranoid phase in the months after the attack, when I thought I might still be a target, I'd had a highly sophisticated alarm and camera system installed in the house so that no one would be able to break in without me knowing about it.

'We're not in the business of planting evidence,' said Franka, looking genuinely affronted that I'd even suspect such a thing.

I moved out of the way, and out of view of the TV camera, letting all eight of them troop inside.

'I'm calling my lawyer,' I told Franka as she split her team into pairs.

'Any particular reason?' she asked, following me into the kitchen.

'Because you're harassing me,' I said, sitting down at the table and taking out my phone.

Franka stopped in front of me. 'We're just doing our job, Mr Sketty. You were a police officer long enough to appreciate that.'

I shook my head, irritated. 'Do you really believe I'm Tania Wild's killer? I've got no motive and you've got no actual evidence against me.'

'Which is why we're here. You do know, don't you, that Ms Wild was investigating you? We found a digital camera with a number of surveillance photos taken of you on it.'

'I don't know anything about that,' I said truthfully, although I remembered Rose saying something about Tania not trusting me for some reason. 'And you're not going to find anything either. When was I meant to have spirited her laptop and phone away? You found me at the scene, remember?'

'I'm not here to argue, Mr Sketty. DS Singh and I will start in here, if you don't mind.'

'Be my guests,' I said, waving them away dismissively and noticing out of the corner of my eye that Singh was studying the Taser torch on the worktop.

'Had a power cut?' he said, motioning towards it.

By rights, I should have been scared he'd take a closer look and realise what it was, given that there was a button on the side with an electricity symbol beneath it. Under UK law, a Taser, though non-lethal, is considered a firearm, and possession of one carries a mandatory five-year prison sentence. But do you know what? By that point, I was frankly through with worrying. 'No,' I answered, with a drawn-out sigh. 'I was looking for the cat out there.' I nodded towards the back door. It was an effective performance of nonchalance.

Singh appeared satisfied enough by my answer and

started opening drawers instead, while I poured myself that second Jameson and put a call in to my firebrand lawyer, Thomas Workman.

As always, Mr 24/7 was at the end of the phone, answering on the second ring. 'Chris!' he boomed. 'Everything all right?'

'Not really,' I said. 'I've got the police here. They've just executed a search warrant.'

'Outrageous!' he boomed, even louder this time, and I had to move the phone away from my ear. 'Don't say a word to them. I'm on my way. I'll be with you as soon as I can.'

I put down the phone and sipped the whiskey, trying my best to ignore the police as they got to work turning my house upside down. Now that they'd missed my one piece of illegal contraband, there wasn't much of interest they could find. I had no reason to believe any of them were in the pay of Kalian Roman, but it was good to know the place was completely covered by cameras, just in case.

True to his word, Workman turned up forty minutes later, immaculately dressed in his trademark pinstriped three-piece suit of navy blue, with a tie so lilac it hurt my eyes. As soon as I let him in, he was straight over to DI Franka demanding to know what she thought she was doing.

I left them arguing out in the hallway, shutting the kitchen door so I didn't have to hear them. I was just about to pour myself another Jameson, thinking that I might as well enjoy my whiskey while I still had the chance, when my phone started ringing in my pocket.

I didn't recognise the number and was tempted not to

answer after everything else that had happened today. I didn't need any more threats. But as is so often the case, curiosity got the better of me.

'Hi,' said a woman's voice. She was calling from outside somewhere, the wind howling through the phone, and she sounded nervous. 'Is this Chris Sketty?'

I told her it was. 'Who are you?'

'My name's Anna. I hear you're looking for Sophie Masters.'

My heart did a flip. This had to be Anna Brown, Kerry's friend. Not wanting to be heard by Franka or anyone else, I asked her to give me a moment, then went outside into the back garden, closing the door behind me.

'That's right,' I said carefully. 'How do you know that?'

'I need to know why you want to find her.'

'You should know why. And if you do, you'll also know that I'm not going to talk about the reason to a stranger. But suffice to say, I saved her life once a long time ago, and she'll remember.'

'She does,' said Anna. 'She definitely knows that Chris Sketty saved her life. And if you're Chris Sketty, you'll remember exactly what she was hiding behind when you saved her.'

'An industrial-sized restaurant wheelie bin,' I told her, without hesitation. 'And if you're her friend, you'll be able to find out what she brought with her when she visited me in hospital afterwards, and why she brought it.'

She was silent, then said: 'I can find that out. Give me a few moments.'

I was waiting with the phone to my ear when I heard the back door open behind me. It was Workman. He didn't look pleased.

'What is it?' I asked, putting the phone down by my side.

He looked at me, then down towards the phone. 'Everything okay?'

I told him it was.

'Who are you talking to?'

'Just a friend,' I said, unsure why he'd be interested, and suddenly feeling uneasy.

Workman frowned. 'No more amateur detecting, Chris. All right?'

'Don't worry. I'm not.'

'Good. DI Franka has a search warrant for your car as well. They need the keys.'

'I'll come and get them. Give me a moment.'

He gave a quick nod and went back inside.

I put the phone back to my ear, knowing I needed to meet Sophie sooner rather than later, because I had a bad feeling that if I stayed round here, Franka or one of her people were going to fit me up with something and then the opportunity would be lost.

A couple of seconds later, Anna was back on the line. The wind was no longer so prevalent, though it still sounded like she was outside somewhere, possibly in a stationary car. 'Giant chocolate buttons,' she said. 'And she told you she brought them because giant buttons always made her feel better, however bad she was feeling.'

I still remembered Sophie saying that, and thinking at

the time that nothing was going to make me feel better. Unfortunately, I hadn't been far wrong.

'Listen, stay where you are,' I said. 'I'll call you back in five minutes.'

I ended the call without waiting for an answer, then went back into the kitchen. Franka was standing by the door with Workman, waiting for me.

'Keys, Mr Sketty, please,' she barked, putting out a hand.

I rummaged in one of the kitchen drawers, found my spare set and handed them to her. 'It's parked just near the junction with Foxglove Avenue, about fifty yards that way,' I said, pointing in the opposite direction to where it was actually located.

'Can you go with them to oversee things, Thomas?' I asked Workman.

'Of course,' he said, looking at me with what I thought might be a hint of suspicion, as if he'd already second-guessed what I was going to do.

As soon as they were gone, I grabbed my coat from the chair, put the Taser torch in the pocket and went back out into the garden, limping as fast as possible over to the back gate, which led out onto the alley that ran along the back of all the houses before popping out on the road, fortuitously enough only a few yards from where I'd parked my car. I took a quick glance back over my shoulder. All the lights were on in the house, and I could see a couple of detectives talking and laughing in my bedroom as they took the place apart, but neither they nor anyone else had noticed my exit, and I unlocked the gate and slipped out.

There was a further security gate at the end of the alley, which I unlocked with my resident's key, before poking my head out. There was an even bigger crowd of journalists outside my house than I'd imagined – probably a dozen in all, as well as a couple of neighbours who'd come out to watch the proceedings. Luckily, however, they were all turned away from me, and I took the opportunity to make a limping dash to the car. As I manoeuvred it out into the road and did a rapid three-point turn so I was heading away from the media scrum, I kept asking myself what the hell I thought I was doing.

But no one even glanced my way as I drove away up the road, although it was only going to take a few minutes at most before my absence was noted, and right at that moment, my plan B was patchy to say the least.

I was about a mile away from home and in the warren of back streets round the borders of Teddington and Twickenham when I phoned the number Anna had called me on, knowing that if she didn't pick up, then making myself look like a suspect would all have been for nothing.

But she did.

'I need to meet up with Sophie as soon as I can,' I told her. 'I'm unofficially investigating the Amalfi massacre. I think she has information that could help end it once and for all. Because otherwise it's going to remain listed as a terrorist attack permanently, and the people behind it will never be brought to justice.'

'She wants to meet you too.'

'Can we do it tonight?' I asked, knowing that there was no way I could go back home now.

'It's already seven thirty.'

'And this is urgent.' I decided to come clean. 'I'm officially a suspect in the murder of a freelance journalist called Tania Wild, who was investigating the motive for the Villa Amalfi massacre. But I'm being set up. And if I have Sophie to back up my theory, then it'll be a big help.'

'That could be a problem. Sophie doesn't trust the police, and she's got good reason not to.'

'And I understand that. But I still have very good contacts within Counter Terrorism Command, and I can personally escort her to New Scotland Yard so that she receives the protection she needs.'

She took a moment to think about this, and I didn't push things. 'Where are you now?'

'Teddington. Near where I live.'

'Okay,' she said. 'There's a village called Stoke Row a few miles west of Henley-on-Thames. They've got a building called the Maharajah's Well at the edge of the village. The postcode is RG9 5QJ. You can park right outside. I'll meet you there at nine p.m. If I'm satisfied you've come alone and haven't been followed, I'll take you to see Sophie.'

I typed the postcode into my phone, conscious (or paranoid, depending on how you look at it) that this could be a trap designed to get rid of me once and for all. But in the end it was always going to be worth the risk. 'I'll be there,' I said, and she immediately asked me what car I'd be driving and the registration.

I was impressed that she and Sophie were taking security so seriously, but I guess it was the only way they could have stayed under the radar so long, with the combined resources of Kalian Roman looking for them.

'Whatever you do, don't tell anyone about this meeting,' warned Anna. 'You can't trust anyone.'

I gave a hollow laugh. 'Don't worry. I don't. Not even you.'

'That makes two of us, then,' she said, and ended the call.

48

The drive to the rendezvous was dark and wet, and there wasn't a lot of traffic on the road. I wondered how Franka, and indeed Workman, would interpret my clandestine departure. I wasn't even sure how to interpret it myself. It wasn't as if I'd expected the police to find any evidence to link me to the crime. Maybe it was just paranoia, but I had a feeling that they were going to arrest me anyway at some point very soon, and if that happened, I'd end up in custody and my chances of finding Sophie and blowing this thing open would evaporate.

So that's how I justified it to myself, and that's how I'm justifying it to you, and I make no apologies for that.

The village of Stoke Row was a tiny place set in the rolling Chiltern Hills, west of London. It was basically a single road surrounded by woodland, with spacious detached houses and plenty of green space. What passed for the centre contained a small village shop-cum-café, an old church, a garage, and a pub called the Cherry Tree with the biggest beer garden at its front I'd ever seen, as well as a large cherry tree.

The Maharajah's Well was situated at the very end of the village, with houses on either side. It was a small but ornate pagoda-like structure sitting atop a well, which, so Google told me, had been a gift to the village from the Maharajah of Benares, and I pulled up just past the well-kept lawns that led up to it ten minutes before the 9 p.m. meeting time. There didn't seem to be anyone else around as I got out the car, and I took a short walk up and down the road to ease the stiffness in my hip before returning just as a Mini pulled up in front of me and a strikingly attractive dark-skinned woman in her mid thirties got out.

As I walked towards her in the darkness, I realised that it was indeed the same woman I'd met outside Kerry Masters' flat. She'd been hysterical then, and I very much doubted she'd recognise me now, all these years on. As the Chief had somewhat uncharitably pointed out, I hadn't aged well.

'Anna?' I said, stopping a few feet away, careful to give her space.

'That's right,' she said, observing me with her arms folded.

'A good place to choose for a meeting,' I said, leaning on my stick. 'I've only seen two cars come by in the last ten minutes.'

'I've learnt the hard way that you can't be too careful,' she said. 'And I needed to make sure you weren't followed.'

'I wasn't. I would have known. Especially on a night like this.'

She raised her eyebrows. 'It's always best to make sure.'

I looked around. 'So, am I going to meet Sophie?'

'I'll take you to her. You can leave your car here. It'll

be safe. And do you mind turning off your mobile? I don't want to be traced.'

'Sure,' I said, powering it down in front of her and not mentioning that, with the right tech, a phone can be traced even when it's turned off.

I climbed into the car next to her, which was when she produced an eye mask and asked me to put it on. 'I'm sorry to be so cloak-and-dagger about everything, but it's what's kept us alive these past years.'

'Fair enough,' I said. Now that I knew who she was, I trusted her enough to comply, but even so, I still made sure I kept a hand inside my jacket on the Taser.

She pulled away, and what followed was a fifteen-minute drive down what felt like a succession of back roads and country lanes, including a very long hill, before eventually the car came to a halt and she told me I could remove the mask.

I saw that we were parked in the middle of what must have once been a family farm but which now looked like some kind of small boutique hotel, set in a winding green valley with rolling tree-topped hills on both sides of it that could have passed for rural Wales or Devon. There was a main building – a large, rambling farmhouse, with a flight of stone steps running up to it, an array of thick greenery, including numerous tropical plants, dominating either side. Opposite the farmhouse were two long barns that looked like they had been turned into accommodation, although they both seemed empty, with several outbuildings dotted about amidst more semi-tropical greenery and at least three statues of Buddha that I could count. All of it lit by strategically placed spotlights.

'Very nice,' I said, climbing out of the car and looking round. In the distance, I could hear the faint hum of traffic from a major road. 'Is it yours?'

'Yes. Mine and my partner's.'

'It must have cost a fair bit to turn it into this.'

'It did. That and a lot of work, time and patience.' She seemed genuinely proud of what she'd achieved, and I could see why. It looked lovely, even on a rainy November night. A little piece of Bali in the Chilterns.

'And what is it you do here?'

'It's a yoga retreat, but we haven't got any guests this week.' She looked at my stick and asked if I'd be able to manage the steps, and I told her I'd be fine, even though they were uneven and I knew they'd be a struggle. But I hated people feeling sorry for me, and thankfully I managed them without any accidents, or her having to grab hold of me. As I reached the top, a ludicrously good-looking guy somewhere in his thirties, tall and broad-shouldered, with a neatly trimmed beard and piercing blue eyes, appeared in the doorway.

'This is my partner, Nils,' said Anna.

'Pleased to meet you,' said Nils in a vaguely Scandinavian accent. He smiled, showing perfect white teeth, and we shook hands, with me trying not to feel intimidated by a man who was probably only five years younger than me but physically a completely different creation.

He moved aside and I felt a rush of warm air as I stepped

over the threshold. Jazz music – Miles Davis, I think – was playing in the background. I followed him through a hallway with a reception desk in one corner, conscious that Anna was right behind me, and into a huge kitchen/dining area with a view over the fields to the back. There was no sign of life in the room, except for an old-looking Labrador lying in his basket. He lifted his head a little to check me out, then put it down again, not especially interested.

I went over and gave him a stroke, turning back to Anna and Nils to ask the obvious question. 'Where's Sophie?'

'We need your word you're going to make sure she's protected,' answered Anna. 'What she's got is explosive.'

'Of course you have my word. I'm the man who saved her life.'

'Yes, he is,' said another female voice, and a woman I didn't immediately recognise appeared in the doorway. 'It's definitely him.'

She came forward and I was just about able to ID her as Sophie, although she'd changed a hell of a lot over the last fourteen years. She was older, of course, her face more pinched, and the lustrous blonde locks from the security video had been replaced by dark, thinner-looking hair that had been tied into a tight ponytail. She wore no make-up and was dressed in jeans and a thick cardigan. It seemed as if she was trying to make herself as plain as possible, but it didn't quite work. She was still an attractive woman and I noticed then that she had the same high cheekbones and narrow, perfectly defined features as her father.

'Hello, Sophie,' I said, relaxing a little at last. 'Long time no see.'

She smiled, and there was something warm and genuine in it that made me smile too. Sometimes as a police officer you know instinctively when you're in the presence of evil. That was what I'd thought immediately with Aaron Clarn. But conversely, I also believe you can feel when you're in the presence of good, and I was now. 'Hello again, Mr Sketty,' she said, almost shyly. 'You were in hospital attached to all kinds of machinery last time I saw you. You look a lot better now.'

I appreciated the comment, even though I didn't feel like I looked a lot better, and thanked her.

'Can we get you a drink, Mr Sketty?' asked Nils.

'Please,' I said. 'No formalities. I'm Chris. And yes, I'd love a cup of tea and a glass of water.'

I took a seat at a huge round dining table next to the window, and Anna and Sophie sat opposite me while Nils fulfilled the drinks order. Anna still showed no sign of recognising me, and for that I was thankful. If she'd known I was one of the detectives who'd been at Kerry's flat that morning, it might have raised some inconvenient questions.

'So, here we are,' said Sophie, sounding more nervous now that we were getting down to business.

'We can talk freely in front of Nils,' added Anna. 'He knows everything.'

'Okay,' I said. 'Well, I think you might be able to help me, Sophie. For some reason, fourteen years after the event, I've found myself thrown back into the Villa Amalfi case, and right now I'm a suspect in a murder I didn't commit. So if there's any light you can shed on why you and Cathy de Roth were targeted that night, I'd appreciate hearing it.'

'Why are you a suspect in the Tania Wild murder case?' asked Anna. There wasn't exactly suspicion in her voice, but it wasn't far off it.

I wasn't going to tell them about my undercover role, but I explained briefly about how and why Tania Wild had contacted me, the details of our first meeting, and my subsequent return to her house, where I'd found her dying. 'Someone was trying to set me up for her killing.'

'But why you?' asked Anna.

'Convenience. The people she was investigating wanted her dead before she exposed them. It was easy to pin it on me.' I turned to Sophie. 'Just like it was easy to pin your sister's murder all those years ago on Leon Warman, a man who, also very conveniently, ended up dead himself.'

'How much do you know?' asked Sophie.

'I know about Cathy de Roth. That she was acting as a pimp with the models on her books, renting them out to wealthy men. I believe those men themselves were being blackmailed by an individual called Kalian Roman. Have either of you two heard his name before?'

They both shook their heads, and I could tell from their expressions that they hadn't.

'I also believe some of the girls were sexually assaulted and raped. A woman called Anna came forward to complain about it. I believe that woman was you.'

Anna nodded. 'It was.'

'But you didn't follow up with the complaint, and that was because a second girl was also planning to come forward – Kerry Masters. But then Kerry was murdered and I think that, not surprisingly, you lost your nerve. Does that sound about right?'

They both nodded, and there was a pause as Nils joined us with the drinks.

'Why were you meeting Cathy de Roth that night, Sophie?' I asked.

It was Anna who answered. 'It was both our idea. We were trying to set up a sting on de Roth, to get her to admit to her role in the whole thing.'

'I had a tape recorder on me so I could record her,' added Sophie. 'Then we were going to go to the police with it. We didn't think anyone would believe us otherwise.'

'Fair enough,' I said. 'But what made you think de Roth would admit everything to a young woman she didn't know?'

Sophie looked at Anna, and Anna nodded, which confirmed my suspicion that there was a lot more to this story than either of them were currently admitting.

'I phoned her,' said Sophie. 'I told her that I knew Kerry had been raped by one of her clients and that she'd deliberately covered it up, and that I had evidence to prove it.'

'And did you actually have evidence?' I asked.

She nodded warily. She had a haunted look, her nails bitten down to the quick. I felt sorry for her. She was scared.

'Yes, we did. The week before Kerry died, Dad asked me to reach out to her because he was worried about her. We talked, and that's when she told me she'd been raped. She told me the name of the rapist, and the name of another man de Roth had coerced her into sleeping with, who'd been a real pervert. She knew intimate details about the men. She also knew the names of other girls who'd been sexually assaulted by them, including one girl who was underage, and she'd put all this in a journal she'd kept hidden in her flat. She told me that if anything happened to her, I was to go to the police with that journal.' Sophie paused, taking a deep breath. 'I told her she should go to the police right then herself, but she was scared to. And then . . . and then a few days later, she was dead. So, when the police had finished at her flat, I retrieved the journal.'

'And that's when Sophie got in touch with me,' said Anna. 'By this point I was petrified, because I knew I could be next, but I was angry too. Kerry was a beautiful person. Kind, loving. The sort who wouldn't hurt a fly. She was just exploited by that bitch de Roth and all those men.'

I felt a wave of guilt as she spoke, remembering my own role in Kerry's death.

'We were going to go to the police,' said Sophie, 'but before we could, they named Leon Warman as the killer and said he was already dead.'

'That's when we really knew how powerful these people were,' said Anna. 'That they had the police in their pocket too and could go to those sorts of lengths to stop the truth getting out. To be honest, we didn't know what to do. We didn't have enough to prove why she'd been murdered and who by. And that's when we came up with the plan to offer de Roth the journal in return for money.'

'We weren't really going to blackmail her,' put in Sophie. 'We just wanted to record her admitting what had happened.'

'So we set up a meeting in a public place. The Villa Amalfi. I offered to go, but Sophie insisted. And you know the rest.'

There it was. The reason for the Villa Amalfi massacre. All to stop Cathy de Roth's secret business being made public. It still didn't seem enough of a motive to me, but then there may have been more to it. I was convinced it was the work of Kalian Roman, and that he'd been blackmailing the men involved. But to what end? It couldn't simply be money. Roman had a raft of people he was paying off, and to organise Villa Amalfi would have taken a lot of resources, so there'd be no real profit in it.

And this was the problem that had beset this whole case right from the minute I'd first gone undercover. No one had ever discovered who Kalian Roman was, let alone what his motives were. It seemed on the one hand that he wanted to encourage terrorist attacks within the UK, and yet on the other, he was buying influence through subterfuge.

My only hope was that one of the men on Kerry Masters' list could lead us to him, but that was a job for the police, not me.

We were all silent for a minute, lost in our own thoughts, while Nils excused himself to let the dog out.

'That's some story,' I said at last. 'And do you still have this journal?'

They looked at each other, then at me. Anna spoke. 'Yes.

We've got it. It's safe, in a place where no one can find it. And it's not going to see the light of the day until we're ready. So before you ask, no, you can't look at it.'

'Fair enough,' I said. 'But are you at least prepared to show it to the police and make a statement?'

Sophie looked unsure. 'I'm happy here. I've got a life, and such good friends in Anna and Nils, who've been so kind to me.' She squeezed Anna's hand. 'But now that it's all come out again, I know that's not possible. They'll find me eventually, and I'm not prepared to bring everyone else down with me. So yes, I'm prepared to talk to the police. I'll go with you tomorrow morning. If that's okay with you, Anna?'

Anna smiled. 'Of course it is, darling. This is your home.' She turned to me. 'You can stay the night if you'd like, Mr Sketty. We don't have anyone here at the moment, so we've got plenty of guest rooms. Then the three of us will go to the police together and end this once and for all.'

'I'm just going to give my dad a call and let him know what's happening,' said Sophie, getting to her feet.

'Do you talk to him regularly?' I asked.

She nodded. 'Whenever I can. That's how come I knew you were looking for me. But I usually do it from elsewhere because of the reception, and because we don't like to reveal the landline number in case anyone traces it.' She turned to Anna. 'Can I borrow the car?'

'You may as well call him from here tonight,' said Anna.

Sophie thanked her and left the room to make the call. When she was gone, and out of earshot, Anna leant forward across the table, giving me the kind of hard stare that made me think she might suddenly have recognised me from the past. But instead she said: 'You've got to make sure we're both protected. These people we're dealing with have a lot of power.'

I was just about to answer when Sophie came back into the room.

'The line's dead,' she said.

49

I frowned. 'Do you often have a problem with the landline?'

'No,' said Anna, getting to her feet. 'I can't remember the last time.' She looked round. 'I don't like the timing of that.'

'I don't either,' I said. 'But I couldn't have been followed here. I would have known.'

She took a deep breath. 'Maybe I'm just getting paranoid.' She went over to the front window and peered round the curtain into the darkness outside. 'Where's Nils? He should only have been a couple of minutes. I can't see him.'

'They've probably just gone for a bit of a wander,' said Sophie. But she looked nervous too.

I got up, leaning on my stick. 'And no one's got any mobile reception here?'

Anna shook her head. 'No. It's a completely dead area. And Nils won't have gone for a wander with Humphrey at this time of night.'

'Okay,' I said, trying to keep calm myself. 'Let's just stay here and wait. Are the doors locked? Just to be on the safe side.'

'I'll check,' she said, and exited the room quickly.

A minute passed. Two. I was getting a very uneasy feeling about this, but wondered if I might just be getting swept along with Anna's paranoia.

Anna came back in the room, looking at her watch, then peered round the curtains again. 'This isn't right. He's been gone at least ten minutes.'

'I'll go out there and take a look for him,' I said, even though I didn't want to.

'No,' she said sharply. 'You're not going anywhere.'

I was taken aback by her tone. 'Why not?'

'Because I don't like the timing of this. No one knows where we are for all these years, then you turn up and suddenly Nils is missing.'

'He's only been gone a few minutes, Anna,' said Sophie. 'I'm sure it's fine.'

'You know as well as I do, it takes two minutes for the dog to do his business, and he always wants to come back in. But there's no sign of either of them.'

'Look, I don't know what you're insinuating, Anna, but I'm not involved in this, and I wasn't followed here either. I told you that. I'm careful. Now, if you're worried, let's go out and look for him. Two of us can go.'

'I'll be back in a moment,' she said, not looking especially mollified by my words, and went back into the hallway.

'Don't go out there alone,' I called after her.

'I'm not,' she called back, and I heard her running up the staircase.

'Anna's just jumpy,' said Sophie. 'I'm sure nothing's

happened to Nils. He and Humphrey don't always come back after two minutes.'

But I'm not sure either of us were convinced. Along with the faulty landline, it definitely felt like something was wrong. I looked at my watch. Nils and Humphrey had indeed been gone at least ten minutes, probably longer.

'Jesus, Anna! What are you doing?' cried Sophie, and I think I physically jumped when I saw what she was looking at.

Anna stood in the doorway holding a wicked-looking semi-automatic shotgun, and unfortunately, it was pointed at me.

'Put that thing down, for Christ's sake!' I demanded. 'That's not going to help anyone.'

Thankfully, she lowered it a few inches, although it was still aimed roughly at my shins. 'If you're lying to me, and you're a part of this, I will kill you, I promise.'

'I believe you.' I did. Her expression was dark. 'But I'm not. The people behind this ruined my life. I'd do anything to see them face the justice they deserve.'

'It's not Chris, Anna,' said Sophie. 'He saved me.'

There was a long silence as the three of us stood in that lovely rustic kitchen with Miles Davis playing in the background, in a bizarre Mexican stand-off.

Finally Anna spoke. 'You and I' – she motioned at me – 'are going to go out together to look for Nils. Sophie stays here and locks the door behind us.'

'I don't want to be left alone,' said Sophie.

Anna turned to her. 'Don't worry, hun. We won't be long and you'll be safer in here.' Then to me: 'Come on.'

We all went through into the hallway and Sophie slowly opened the front door then moved out the way, leaving Anna standing on the threshold, the shotgun pointed out into the night, with me behind her. The rain was coming down steadily and there was a strong wind, but the silence was all too obvious. 'Nils!' she cried. 'Nils? Humphrey?'

There was no response.

She looked back over her shoulder at me. 'Stay a few feet behind me, but not too close, and watch my back.'

I didn't much like taking orders, but she was the one with the shotgun, so I nodded.

She walked slowly down the stone steps, and I followed, careful not to slip, keeping my eyes scanning the yard for any sign of an ambush. By now, I knew something was wrong. And I was beginning to realise what it was. I hadn't been followed, I was certain of that. More likely someone had got the location of this place from Geoff Masters, whose identity I'd foolishly let slip to the Chief. It meant the Chief was almost certainly part of the conspiracy. And that either he was here . . .

Or Clarn was.

Anna stopped at the bottom of the steps. Ahead of us, lit up by the spotlights on either side of the path, were the two guest blocks. There was no sign of Nils or Humphrey there. To our left, the track in front of the house ran down to the far outbuildings, before being swallowed up by the darkness beyond. No one was down there either.

We stood there in the rain for a long moment, then Anna called out again. As she did so, I looked over to the Mini that she had brought me here in, which was parked on the verge in front of a Land Rover, the two cars providing the only obvious cover for someone to hide behind. I took a few steps out onto the track to get a better look, and that was when I saw them.

'Anna,' I said loudly, stopping her mid-shout. 'Get over here.'

She came striding over, the shotgun levelled in front of her, and looked to where I was pointing.

Nils was the nearest to us. He lay on his side, unmoving, tucked up next to the Land Rover, while a few feet away, up on the verge, lay Humphrey.

'Oh God!' howled Anna, running over and kneeling down beside him. 'No, no, no,' she repeated over and over again, laying down the shotgun as she cradled his head in her arms.

I hung back, looking round urgently, one hand on the Taser in my pocket, the other gripping my stick, knowing that we were sitting ducks out here. Because Nils wasn't their target. We were.

'Come on, Anna,' I said, limping swiftly over. 'We've got to get back inside. Now.'

She leapt to her feet, grabbing the shotgun and swinging it round to point at me.

Instinctively, I jumped back and almost fell over, just getting a glimpse of Nils's pale, blood-splattered face as I did so.

'See what you've done!' she snarled at me, a look of such venom on her face that I actually thought she might pull the trigger. 'You brought this on us. You!'

And it was true. I had. But that wasn't important now. What was important was that we get back inside. 'I'm sorry,' I said, putting my hands up in a passive stance. 'I have no idea how they found us.'

'I should fucking kill you.'

'That won't help.'

'Move,' she hissed. 'Back to the house. And go in front of me, where I can see you.'

I did as I was told, eager to get somewhere safe where we could at least plan our next move from a position of some security.

Anna followed right behind me, and I knew that the shotgun would be aimed at my back. I couldn't blame her. I'd come here barely an hour ago, and in that time I'd torn apart her happy home and left her life in ruins.

And it wasn't over yet, because as I climbed the steps to the front door, I saw that it was on the latch, when I distinctly remembered Sophie locking it behind us.

'The door's open,' I said, stopping outside.

Anna stopped behind me.

'Get in there,' she said.

'It could be a trap.'

'If it is, I'd rather you walk into it than me.'

Slipping the Taser from my pocket, I pushed the door open with my stick, revealing an empty hallway. 'Sophie, are you in there?'

No answer.

'When you checked the doors earlier, were they already locked?' I asked over my shoulder.

'The back door wasn't.'

'I think the killer may be in here,' I said.

'Get in there,' she repeated.

I stepped slowly over the threshold, looking round. Anna came in behind me, shutting the door behind her and cranking the bolt across.

'Why are you doing that?' I asked her. 'He might still be in here.'

'This ends here,' she said. 'If he's in this house, I'm going to kill him.'

It struck me that he might have already gone. He wanted Sophie and her journal more than anything else. Anna and I were just peripheral targets, and I was finished anyway. It was possible that he'd even slipped out of the front door behind us while we were over at the cars.

Anna called out Sophie's name, but again there was no answer.

'Maybe she panicked and ran off,' I said.

'Don't be stupid. If she had, she would have come out the front. We would have seen her.'

I was clutching at straws, I knew that, but anything was better than the alternative.

The kitchen door was open and the music was still playing. Holding the Taser like a gun, I walked slowly inside.

Sophie was sitting at the kitchen table where we'd been talking earlier. She was facing us, her hands behind her back, but her head was slumped forward, and the linen shirt she was wearing was covered in blood.

I stood there, frozen to the spot. Anna came in behind

me, and when she saw Sophie, she let rip an animal howl that filled the room. As I turned her way, wanting to calm her, the man who'd haunted my dreams for so long, dressed in his trademark black, face uncovered, appeared in the doorway behind her.

Before I could shout a warning, Aaron Clarn had pushed a gun with silencer attached against the back of her head and pulled the trigger.

The shotgun went off with a deafening boom, shattering crockery, and thank God she'd been turned towards Sophie at the time, otherwise I would have taken the full force of the shot. Instead, I fell backwards against the kitchen island while Anna crumpled soundlessly to the floor, already dead, the weapon landing on the floor between us.

I instinctively dropped the Taser into my pocket and went for the shotgun, literally diving for it and losing my stick in the process. But I was too far away, and as I landed painfully on my knees and reached out a hand to grab it, Clarn smiled.

'Now, now, Sketty. Don't be a fool. You won't make it. It's the end of the road for you. No more fighting. No more limping. All over, my friend. Now, we can do this the easy way, the way Mr Roman wants, and it's very quick, or we do it the hard way, and you suffer.' His voice was no longer the growl of earlier years. Now it was more of a satisfied purr. He'd grown into his role of predator. He looked different too. Older, yes, but he'd also undergone extensive surgery to soften his features. His face was fatter, the nose flatter and less prominent, the jawline softer. But the cruel sadist's eyes were still as I remembered them.

'Take a seat over there next to the girl,' he said, waving the gun in Sophie's general direction

Maybe eight feet separated us, but it was too far for me to risk using the Taser, which was only really effective at very close quarters.

'How did you find us?' I asked him, grabbing my stick and getting slowly to my feet.

'The father told me. It took some persuading to get it out of him. But everyone buckles in the end.' He smiled again, showing white, perfectly veneered teeth, and I wondered where he'd been all these years.

'Who told you about him?'

'Too many questions, Sketty, but remember this. If you'd let things lie, he and these women wouldn't have had to die. But you had to get involved. And now you have to pay the price.'

I looked at poor Anna, dead on the floor, then at Sophie as I sat down in one of the chairs only a few feet from where she was slumped motionless, and I felt sick with misery, and sick with guilt. I leant my stick against the table and put my hands in my coat pockets.

'What are you planning to do?' I asked the smug, smiling Clarn as he followed me across the room.

'For you, a quick bullet in the head,' he said, stopping in front of me. 'Self-inflicted. You came here, murdered these poor people, then killed yourself in a fit of remorse.'

'I don't have a motive.'

'Don't you worry about that. I'm sure Mr Roman will give you one.'

'And do I get to find out who Mr Roman is, now I'm about to die?'

Clarn shook his head, almost nonchalantly, as if it was the most natural thing in the world to murder four people and a defenceless animal. 'No time for that, I'm afraid, Sketty. Now it's time to go see your little girl.'

He stepped towards me, moving towards my right side, where I guessed he planned to deliver the fatal shot.

Rather than fear, I felt a sense of resignation, knowing that this would all be over in a few seconds, and then I'd be gone, and that hopefully Clarn was right and I'd be going to see Grace.

I think he must have sensed my defeat, and even though I wasn't looking at him any more, I knew he was still smiling.

That was when the anger finally came. I couldn't die like this. Sitting meekly awaiting my fate.

'Hands out of your pockets where I can see them,' he said, and I realised then that he hadn't seen the Taser earlier.

He was only three feet away, and I knew it was now or never. I looked up at him, my gaze passive and defeated, while he looked back, his teeth bared.

Still holding the Taser and keeping it covered by the back of my hand, I took my hands out of my pockets, hoping he wouldn't see it until it was too late. Then, ignoring the barrel of the gun, the end of which was barely a foot away, I pointed it towards his thigh and pressed the fire button.

There was an angry crackle of electricity and Clarn's gun

jerked upwards, a muffled shot ringing out, which somehow managed to miss me. He stumbled back into a huge antique plate rack, sending a pile of crockery tumbling down. His eyes were unfocused and I could tell he'd been given a decent electric shock, but he was still just about staying upright, and he hadn't let go of the gun, which was down by his side.

The shotgun was still on the floor a few feet away, on the other side of the kitchen island, and I was off the chair in a second, shoving the Taser back in my pocket and crawling rapidly on my hands and knees towards it, adrenaline driving me on.

The barrel was the nearest part to me, and I grabbed it, swinging round onto my back so I was lying on the floor, trying to use the island as cover, facing Clarn as he steadied himself against the rack with his spare hand, his legs still wobbling, and lifted the gun in my direction.

No more than four yards separated us.

Clarn fired.

My eyes reflexively shut, body set to take the bullet, but I still had enough instinct for survival to keep moving, turning the shotgun round in my hands so I had the stock against my shoulder and my finger on the trigger.

The shot never hit me, and my eyes flew open. I saw Clarn desperately trying to keep the gun steady in his hands while remaining upright, until it was now pointed straight at me.

I don't know who fired first, me or him; all I remember is the incredibly loud blast of the shotgun and the way his body crashed back against the rack, sending more crockery flying, as the shot opened up his belly beneath his black leather jacket.

He listed to one side like a sinking ship, the pistol dropping to the floor, then sank down himself so he was sat against the sideboard, his expression one of confusion.

I stared at him. My finger still on the trigger. There was one more shot in the shotgun.

But Clarn was now technically unarmed. If I fired a second time, it would be murder.

He clutched his stomach with one big hand, looked down at the wound then back at me. His face was going white as the blood drained out of it.

I sat up, still pointing the shotgun at him, and shimmied backwards on my behind until I was propped up against the opposite wall, facing him.

We stared at each other. My ears rang from the shotgun blast, taking time to fade out.

'Finish it,' snarled Clarn through gritted teeth.

'No.'

'Why not? Are you a pussy?' His lip curled into a sneer, but I could see he was scared, and just speaking was a serious effort for him.

'I don't need to,' I told him. 'A gut shot is one of the most painful and slowest ways to die. I'm sure you know that, given the number of people you've killed and doubtless tortured. And there's no way I can call for help, because you cut the phone line and there's no mobile reception. I figure it's easier to wait to make sure you're no danger to me, then I'll limp off and see if I can get some reception somewhere. But I'll be honest with you, I'm in no hurry.'

Clarn didn't say anything. He just kept up that defiant look, his face so tight and hollow that it seemed to be shrinking before my eyes. Blood began to leak from under his jacket onto the crotch of his jeans, and I could hear his breathing getting shorter.

A long, slow minute passed. I watched his pain. I'm ashamed to admit I took satisfaction in it. It was nothing less than he deserved. Clarn had destroyed so many. It was time he paid for his sins.

He looked away from my gaze and stared up at the ceiling, trying to hide the contortions racking his face, seemingly desperate to stay hard and intimidating even though he must have known that he was now utterly helpless. It made me wonder what drove him. Why he did what he did. Taking huge risks that he must have known would eventually come to this. He clearly enjoyed the power he wielded over others and saw himself as a superior being, but that in itself didn't seem enough, and I was reminded of something that old sage DCI Perry Stilton had once told me: 'Truly evil people have a fundamental lack of personality. When you look beneath the surface, there's nothing there. They're not strong or brave. They just don't care.'

Even now, Aaron Clarn probably wasn't that scared.

But he was hurting. Really hurting. And no one was able to withstand that for too long.

'Tell me about Kalian Roman,' I said.

'Fuck you,' he spat.

375

'Your choice,' I said. 'You'll talk eventually.'

And that was when I saw something flicker behind his eyes, and I knew he'd made a decision.

I knew what it was too.

His whole body tensed, and with a grunt of exertion, he went for his gun.

He was fast. Faster than I'd been expecting. But in his state he was never going to be quite fast enough, and as he lifted it from the floor and turned round towards me, I leant back, took careful aim, and quite literally blew the brains out the back of his head.

50

I sat there against the wall for a long time, staring straight ahead, trying to ward off the shock of what had happened in this room. On my left, Anna Brown lay on her back with her legs apart, feet sticking up. On my right, Sophie still sat in the chair, her head resting against the wall, her shirt drenched in blood. And straight ahead of me was what was left of the man who'd filled my nightmares for fourteen years, and who'd come so close to ending my life more than once.

From where I was sitting, I could see that Sophie's hands were bound behind her back with a black cable tie.

So Clarn hadn't killed her instantly. He'd wanted her alive but incapacitated, at least temporarily, which meant he'd needed information from her.

It had to be the journal. And if she was dead, then that meant he'd probably got its location.

Which meant it had to be here somewhere.

I put the shotgun gently on the floor and very slowly got to my feet, using the kitchen island as a prop, and stumbled over to the table, where I grabbed my stick. I glanced down at Sophie. It looked like she'd died from a single gunshot to the heart, delivered at close range. I felt for a pulse anyway, just in case by some miracle she was still alive, but found nothing.

I said a silent prayer over her body, realising with a deep sadness that her whole family were now dead: Kerry, her father, Geoff, her mother, and now her. I'd saved her life once in the heat of the moment, only to fail her now, and I had a feeling that the guilt of my part in this would stay with me forever.

What was important, though, was that some good had come out of this horror, and at least Clarn was now finally dead. Some would argue that it would have been better if he'd been kept alive so that he could tell investigators everything he knew, but I don't subscribe to that point of view. He would never have talked. He was like those killers who refuse to reveal the location of their victims' bodies, because retaining that information gives them some perverse sense of power.

I walked over to where he sat, still propped up against the sideboard. There was no point feeling for a pulse. The top of his head, from the eyebrows upwards, was almost completely gone. Even so, I still felt irrationally nervous as I knelt down next to him – as if he might somehow come back to life and finally finish me off.

But he remained resolutely dead as I searched through his jacket, trying to avoid the blood, looking for the journal that would give me the names of the men who'd been hiding in plain sight all these years.

Except it wasn't there.

51

The Present

Teller

'After that, I found the keys to Nils's Land Rover, and drove to the nearest house to raise the alarm,' says Sketty, by way of conclusion, before drinking the last of his sparkling water.

And now you see my problem. Chris Sketty has this rather worrying habit of not only being in the wrong place at the wrong time, but also of being the only person left alive who can actually give an account of what happened. He goes to see Tania Wild. She dies. He goes to see Geoff Masters. He dies. He goes to see the only two people who would be able to stand up in court and bring down these alleged sexual predators, Sophie Masters and Anna Brown, and they die.

'Again, you were quite the hero, Mr Sketty,' I say. 'You slew the dragon, but unfortunately you didn't rescue the damsel in distress, or recover the journal, which remains missing. And as a result of that, although the press is now full of stories of this mysterious prostitution ring involving wealthy establishment figures, sexual assaults, grooming and all sorts, there's no actual evidence against any of those allegedly involved, and therefore their names remain secret, their crimes go unpunished. So all we have is conjecture and chest-beating, but no solution. No justice. And definitely no chance of ever identifying Kalian Roman.'

And this is what sticks in my throat. Sketty has been feted as a hero in that very same press. His name is now in the public domain. He's been on TV and radio to talk about the real reason for the Villa Amalfi attack, as well as his arrest for the murder of Tania Wild, and his final confrontation with Aaron Clarn, the man who'd evaded justice for so long. Traces of Clarn's DNA were eventually found in the house where Tania Wild died, and there was also CCTV footage of a man who matched his description on a nearby street, so Sketty's story holds up and he's even received an official apology from the Met. I also know that he's been offered a sum in excess of half a million pounds for his memoirs.

'You've heard my story, Mr Teller, you know I'm no hero,' says Sketty. 'But I'm no murderer either, if that's what you're implying.'

'You said earlier you thought you'd made a mistake when you went to see your old boss, Devon Andrews, and mentioned Geoff and Sophie Masters to him. Do you think Andrews is involved in this? Because my understanding is he isn't under investigation.'

Sketty appears to think about this for a moment. 'I honestly don't know. Someone put Aaron Clarn on to Geoff Masters to find Sophie's location, but I don't know who. And it may be that Kalian Roman knew about Masters the whole time but chose not to act until he had to.'

'And still Roman sits out there somewhere pulling the strings.'

'So it seems,' says Sketty. 'And it upsets me that we never got him, or found out who he was. But sometimes you've just got to admit defeat.'

I have to say, he doesn't look that upset, though.

'Anyway,' he continues. 'I've told you my story, and you're the first person who's ever heard the real, unadulterated truth, although it looks like you already pieced together most of it yourself.'

'Thank you,' I say. 'I appreciate you taking the time to do that.'

'What do you intend to do with this dossier? I've kept my side of the bargain.'

I watch him carefully. 'Have you?'

'I've told you the truth, Dr Teller.'

'Unfortunately, Mr Sketty, I don't think you have. You've simply embellished the official version. I believe you know far more about Kalian Roman than you're letting on.' And now I finally come out with it. 'I believe you work for him.'

Sketty

I look at the old man aghast, sick of all this. 'That's bullshit.'

'Is it?' He shakes his head and leans forward in his wheel-chair. 'I don't think so. Let me tell an alternative story. You knew about the Villa Amalfi massacre in advance.' I start to protest, but he raises a hand to quieten me. 'Please,' he says. 'Let me finish. You'll have your chance to refute my allegations. I believe you knew it wasn't going to be a gun deal. Your job was to make sure the attack happened but that none of the three gunmen escaped alive. You were reckless enough to agree to it. You'd lost everything. Your wife, your daughter. You were ripe for this kind of role.'

'This is ridiculous. What was my motive?'

'Simple, Mr Sketty. You were working for Kalian Roman. You still are. I don't know when you were turned. I suspect it was while you were undercover. You were probably being blackmailed for something too, just like so many of the others, and it's why the information you supplied your handlers with was always so patchy.'

'I got shot. Look at me. You think I volunteered for that?'

'I don't know if you were meant to intervene in the attack personally. I doubt it. But you knew the gunmen would be trapped and try to fight their way out. My guess is the excitement got the better of you, as it always seemed to do in those days, and you simply wanted to be the hero. Bonkers Sketty at work again. Then afterwards, you became a sleeper agent for Roman, and it wasn't until Tania Wild started digging into the real reason behind the Villa Amalfi attack that you were called upon to deal with her.'

'You seem to forget someone in all this,' I told him. 'Aaron Clarn. He came back. I killed him. It's a matter of public record.'

'That's true, but it doesn't detract from the fact that Clarn was meant to die on the night of the Villa Amalfi attack, along with the other gunmen. He knew too much. However, when he did survive, Kalian Roman had no alternative but to help him evade justice, faking his death and presumably spiriting him out of the country. Like you, he became a sleeper, but then he too was brought back, no doubt never knowing that he'd been betrayed by his boss, or that you worked for Roman too.'

I can't believe what I'm hearing, and ask the obvious question. 'Why, if Clarn and I were both working for Roman, did we have conflicting agendas? He was trying to suppress the real motive for the Villa Amalfi killings. I was trying to get it made public. I'm sorry, Dr Teller, but your accusations have absolutely no logic.'

'They have plenty of logic, I'm afraid,' says Teller, undaunted. 'Yes, Clarn was aiming to suppress the motive, but in your own way, so were you. Remember, you were meant to bring Sophie, Anna and the incriminating journal to the police, and they ended up dead and the journal missing. Yes, you killed Clarn at the scene, but that was all part of the plan. You told Roman where Sophie and Anna were. He informed Clarn, who killed them. And then you got rid of him, an easy fall guy for the whole thing.

'And something else. It may actually suit Roman's agenda to have the real motive for the killings made public now. You see, I've studied him for a long time. I may not know his actual identity, but I believe I know what's driving him. First of all, he isn't a political extremist. At least not in the way we think. He's an individual who wants to influence events in this country at a very high level. He used de Roth and her models to entice influential men into perhaps doing things they shouldn't, and then as a result he had influence over those men, who you and I know include a Supreme Court judge and the CEO of a major company. And I'm sure there are others, equally important. Roman protected them when their activities looked like they might be exposed, and he scared them with the lengths he was prepared to go to. I have no doubt they did many favours for him over the years.

'But Kalian Roman isn't just interested in gaining influence. It's clear he wants to sow discord in this country, to cause havoc. That's why you were after him originally, remember? Because he was financing terror groups. A scandal of this magnitude involving the establishment weakens trust in the very tenets of our democracy. And it wouldn't surprise me if, in the coming months, Roman starts jettisoning some of the people he's been protecting in order to keep the scandal going.'

He gives me a cold smile. 'He may even jettison you one day, although I doubt it. You're useful to him. You come across as such a nice, trustworthy guy. It's your key selling point. It's why you attracted Sophie to you, like a spider attracting a fly.'

I've had enough of this now. 'I don't know the truth of the rest of your story, but if you're accusing me of working for Kalian Roman, then I have to tell you categorically that you're barking up the wrong tree. You've got no evidence.'

'Really? Why don't we talk about your finances? The mortgage on your house that was paid off after Villa Amalfi. The expensive lawyer who represents you, along with some other fairly dubious clients. And, of course, the secret bank account.'

52

Sketty

I stare at him. He really has found out everything about me.

'It took me a long time to find the bank account,' he says, 'but when money is no object, you can employ the best. And your identity might be hidden by a shell company, but the trail definitely leads back to you. Two hundred thousand US dollars. It's a lot of money for a retired former police officer with no visible means of income aside from a pension.'

'It's not what you think,' I say.

'Then enlighten me.'

'After Villa Amalfi, my story was common knowledge in the Met – the fact that I'd lost my daughter, and then been seriously injured in the line of duty – and a businessman who was a big supporter of police charities got in touch. He organised paying off my mortgage, and told me he'd pay for any legal services I ever needed. He also set up the bank account. I should have stopped him, but frankly, I thought the money would at least give me security. It was a retirement fund. It still is. And I've never used a penny of it.'

'Would you care to tell me who this businessman is?'

I sigh, weary of this conversation. And of Teller. 'He insisted on anonymity. He still does. And I've always respected that. So no. It's none of your business.'

'That's where you're wrong. Everything about you right now is my business.'

'Well, I'm not telling you. End of story. Now what the hell do you want from me? Don't you think I've suffered enough?'

'No, I don't. And what I want from you are details of how you liaise with Kalian Roman. I have my ideas as to who he might be. But I need to know how you contact him. We need to set a trap.'

'How many times do I have to tell you? I don't know.'

'I don't believe you.'

'Then we're at an impasse.'

'Are we? I don't think so. I believe I have the whip hand, because I could ruin you with the information in that dossier. How you were present at the murder of Sophie's sister. How you tortured a suspect in his own flat.'

But now it's my turn to go on the attack. 'You could,' I say. 'But I don't think you will. You see, I'm beginning to wonder if this is all some elaborate ruse on your part, that you actually might be Kalian Roman yourself. Let's look at the facts. First of all, how on earth did you get all that information on me? Only someone who was involved could have known about Kerry.'

'I have my ways.'

'You keep saying that, Dr Teller. But it doesn't ring true. Because, you see, I've been studying you too. As soon as I got your invitation, I decided to look into your background. And very interesting it is too. Your wife, who died so tragically that night, was seeing someone else. In fact they were eating together in the Villa Amalfi when the gunmen attacked. And they were both killed. She and her lover. There were more than a hundred and twenty diners and staff in the restaurant when the attack began. And yet only eight died. So it could just as easily have been a targeted hit aimed at them.'

'No!' he shouts, an angry howl that fills the room. 'I loved her!'

'You had motive. For all we know, you hired Wild and set her off in completely the wrong direction so that the truth would never come back to you.'

Teller shakes his head furiously. 'That's not what it was like at all. And how dare you talk about Victoria like that. I loved that woman more than anyone in the world. All I wanted was for her to be happy. She had needs that I, because of my illness, was unable to fulfil, so she met with David with my full knowledge and blessing. And she always came back to me. Always. Because she loved me.'

'And let's look at your money,' I continue. 'You're worth a reputed one hundred and eighty million pounds. Where did that all come from? You sold your software company in 2004 for nine million, and apart from sitting on a few boards, you haven't done a lot since. Yet somehow you've made that sum grow twenty times over. And there's no way you did that honestly.'

'I did it through some good investments.'

'And your wife, of course. She inherited forty million pounds of family money in 2006 that passed to you when she died. Which gave you a perfect motive.'

'Everything I've ever done is above board,' he snaps back. 'And if I was Kalian Roman, why would I hire Tania Wild to look into the case? Or bring you out here? No, you're simply trying to deflect things. My motive has always been to find justice for my wife, because I loved her. And that search has led right back to you.'

'No, I'm sorry. You're wrong. I'm no angel, I never was, but I've told you the truth tonight. And there's no point saying you don't believe me, because there's nothing I can do about it. So if you want to try to ruin me, go ahead. Do your worst.'

I get up slowly, stiff from sitting down for too long. The fire's dying in the grate and outside it's still blowing a hoolie, rattling the window frame as the rain lashes the glass. I shake my leg, leaning heavily against the stick.

Teller looks up at me, his expression calmer now. 'Would you be prepared to take a lie detector test?'

'What? You have it all set up here?'

'Yes, I do. I want to give you the opportunity to demonstrate your innocence before I make public my allegations against you.'

'Thanks, but I'll give it a miss. And if you still want to spend what time you've got left on this earth trying to ID

390

Kalian Roman, I'd start with the Chief, Devon Andrews. I think he's involved.'

'He's already taken the test,' says Teller. 'He passed.'

That stops me, because whatever you might be thinking, I'm innocent. Everything I've recounted tonight in my story is the truth. After the night of the killings at the yoga retreat, I suspected the Chief as being the one who'd pointed Aaron Clarn in the direction of Geoff Masters. Because someone suddenly realised that Masters knew his daughter's location and tipped off Clarn. And if it wasn't me and it wasn't the Chief, then who the hell was it? It doesn't make sense.

'Your lie detector could be wrong,' I say to Teller.

'It's not,' he says with great confidence. 'It's state of the art.'

'Who administered the test?' I ask.

'I did,' says a voice from the doorway, and when I turn and see who it is, I get a nasty shock, because suddenly everything falls into place.

53

Teller

Ah, the trap is finally sprung. Now I must admit to you that this whole evening has been part of a police operation to trap Chris Sketty, the man who – behind the nice-guy smile – I've come to realise is guilty of some horrendous, cold-blooded murders on behalf of Kalian Roman.

My snug, where we sit now, has been completely wired for sound to allow the police to listen remotely to Sketty's story, and it's clear that although he still hasn't admitted anything, they have enough information to arrest him.

It's only when I turn towards the voice of the officer with whom I've been liaising to set up this trap that I realise something is very wrong indeed.

Sketty

I'm having a lot of difficulty processing everything, because the woman standing in the doorway, dressed in jeans and a puffer jacket, and holding a pistol with silencer attached in her hand, looking older and thinner, her short hair having turned its natural grey, is none other than Commander Marina Reineke, the head of Counter Terrorism Command, and the most senior counter-terrorism police officer in the country. And it doesn't look at all like she's here on official business.

'What are you doing here?' I ask, as Teller catches sight of the gun she's holding and almost leaps out of his wheelchair in surprise.

'Ms Reineke, what are you doing?' he demands, clearly not having anticipated this turn of events. 'Put that thing down, for God's sake. It might go off.'

This is when something very strange happens. Reineke briefly shuts her eyes, takes a deep, almost yogic breath as she mouths some words I can't make out, then turns in one steady movement and shoots Teller in the eye from no more than an arm's-length distance.

The noise is minimal, the same as a champagne cork popping, quieter than the sound that Clarn's pistol made when he shot Anna. Teller's body jolts sharply, before immediately going slack as he sinks back into the wheelchair, with his head turned to one side. He looks almost peaceful, and I guess if you have to die, then it's probably as good a way as any, before you have any idea what's going on.

Reineke turns away from him and points the gun at me. She wears a pinched, distasteful expression, as if she really didn't want to do that.

'You shot him,' I say, my voice loud in the sudden silence of the room. 'Why?'

'I didn't have any choice,' she says tightly, and I can see this is paining her.

'You always have a choice.'

'Not this time,' she says. 'He knew far too much. So do you.'

'I don't understand. Are you working for Roman?'

She nods slowly. 'I'm afraid so.'

'But you can't be. It was you who sent me undercover all those years ago.'

'That was before he started blackmailing me.'

'With what? What have you ever done that he's got such a hold on you? That you can commit murder on his behalf? You're not that type of person.'

'It's Klevin,' she says tightly. She's clearly in distress. 'That's how they got to me. He once very foolishly had sex with an underage girl, and the whole thing was recorded on a hidden camera. I didn't know him at the time of Villa Amalfi. In fact I didn't even find out about what he'd done until a few months ago. Then it was made clear to me that if I didn't do what I was told, he'd be exposed.'

'You could have divorced him.'

'I can't do that. I love him. When you love someone and can't live without them, you do what you have to do. And not only that. It's also our twins. They're only five years old. Their lives would be ruined if their father was exposed as a paedophile. I can't have that. So when this is done, we will retire quietly to our home in Portugal, and that will be the end of my involvement.'

'It doesn't work like that,' I say, facing her down. 'You know that.'

'Sit back down, Chris.'

'Why? So you can shoot me too? Make it look like I murdered Teller and turned the gun on myself? You people never seem to know when to stop with me.'

'Let's not make this hard. Please. It's going to happen, one way or another.'

'I'm afraid it's not going to happen, Marina. I'm wired up. There are police on the way right now. They can hear everything you're saying.'

There's a flicker of doubt, but she quickly forces it down. She's a tough woman. 'Nice try, Chris, but I don't think so.'

'I can prove it,' I tell her. 'Let me unbutton my shirt.'

'I haven't got time for this. Sit down.' She raises the gun menacingly.

But I ignore her command and keep talking. 'I signed an immunity agreement. I was here to record the doctor and find out whether he was actually Kalian Roman. I guess he wasn't.'

Reineke's about to say something in reply, but we're interrupted by the sound of Teller's front door crashing open, followed immediately by angry shouts of 'Armed police!' and pounding feet coming through the house.

You see, I wasn't lying.

Marina Reineke's face seems to plummet, her head visibly sinking into her shoulders, as the full realisation of what's happening hits her.

In a flash, she's turned the gun round and placed it under her chin.

'Don't do it, Marina,' I say desperately. 'Help us. We can bring this man down.'

An armed officer in uniform and helmet appears in the doorway behind Reineke. 'Put the gun on the floor and turn round!' he barks, moving further into the room, holding his MP5 in a firing stance, while a second officer replaces him in the doorway.

I put up a hand, motioning for them to stay calm.

Marina and I stare at each other. Tears are running down her face, and her hands are shaking.

'Tell us who Kalian Roman is,' I say gently, 'and we can make this better.'

We can't, of course, and she knows that, but I have to hope that the prospect of life in whatever form it comes will trump that of death.

Silence.

'Please, Marina. Do the right thing.'

As I speak, her grip on the gun appears to loosen.

Then she says: 'Do you know that if I don't kill you, they'll kill Klevin and the twins? I can't have that. I love them too much.'

'They're not omnipotent, whoever they are, Marina. No one is. Your family can be protected. So can you.'

And then she says something strange. 'Kalian Roman is an instrument of war.'

As soon as the words are out of her mouth, she closes her eyes and pulls the trigger.

54

Sketty

I turn away, unable to bear the sight of yet more death, and am ushered out the door by the armed officers.

There are police all over the place now, at least a dozen, including the detectives from the National Crime Agency, who have been running the Villa Amalfi case and the hunt for Kalian Roman since the murders at the yoga retreat, almost six weeks back now.

It's true, I did sign an immunity agreement with the NCA, negotiated by my ever-helpful lawyer, Thomas Workman. I knew that it was time the truth was out there, and that the only way I was going to be able to move on was by coming clean. My understanding was that this new information about my undercover role, as well as my part in the murder of Kerry Masters (which happened just as I described it), would not come out in the public domain.

The NCA had come to suspect that Dr Ralph Teller might be involved in some way in the Villa Amalfi attack, and that he might even have been Kalian Roman, and so as soon as I told them that he'd invited me to his house for a meeting, they'd made sure I was wired up and that they were close by in numbers, just in case he had anything planned for me. They were also convinced there was a leak in CTC, but I don't think anyone – least of all me – suspected it would be Marina Reineke. Or that she'd be there tonight, ready to double-cross both Teller and me.

But then it seems Kalian Roman's tentacles reach even to the highest echelons.

At least now for me, though, it's over.

I push past the detectives and walk as fast as my limp will allow out of the front door and into Teller's garden, thankful to have the rain and the cold fresh air on my face. His house stands on a huge plot at the top of a hill looking down towards a quiet, largely undeveloped stretch of the River Thames, and I walk away from all the activity until I find a place alone in the darkness, staring out into the cold, wet night.

I stand there a long time, and as I do, I realise that I can no longer continue with the half-empty life I've been living for the past fourteen years. I need to start afresh. I owe it to all those who've died so cruelly – Sophie, Tania, Anna, Nils, Kerry, Teller, my darling Grace, all the victims of Amalfi, including my old buddy, Ty; even Cleaver and Reineke ... I owe it to all of the dead to make the best of the life I've been given.

I am a good man. I sometimes need to believe it. I hope you believe it too. I've done wrong, yes, but I've been misunderstood, and on the whole, I think I've tried to do everything that I've done for the right reasons.

And so when I turn back in the direction of Dr Ralph Teller's house, I have hope in my heart for the first time in many, many years.

55

Kalian Roman

The man who was the latest incarnation of Kalian Roman smiled benignly as he stood on the footbridge watching his two children – a boy and a girl, so young, so innocent – feeding the ducks, while their mother crouched down beside them, breaking up the pieces of stale English bread they were using as food.

Regent's Park was an easy stroll from his ambassadorial residence, and one that he and the family used regularly. He loved it here, especially on a sunny Sunday afternoon like this one. The weather for February was unseasonably warm, and there were plenty of people about enjoying the comparative fresh air. Roman liked being around people. He'd grown up in a large city and found their presence comforting. Today there was a whole mixture: families like his; joggers, walkers, cyclists; clusters of teenage girls shouting over each other while simultaneously staring at their phones; boys playing football. It was a happy scene.

Roman was always impressed by how resilient the British were. Their country was being slowly and methodically taken apart by outside forces, and yet here they all were enjoying their Sunday in the park. At the moment, it was an especially traumatic time for the UK. For most of the last three months, the news had been full of stories of the Villa Amalfi massacre and its true, murky motive. In the age of Me Too, a story like this was dynamite, hugely damaging public trust in the powers that ran the country. Although the journal allegedly kept by Kerry Masters had not seen the light of day, the media witch-hunt to unmask those named in it had been relentless, and in the past week they'd finally claimed their first scalp when a mysterious video of a Supreme Court judge raping Ms Masters had found its way to the *Sun* newspaper.

It had been Roman himself who'd anonymously released the video. It had been in the possession of the embassy since 2006, and in all that time, the judge had done Roman's bidding on pain of exposure, but it now felt like a useful time to throw him to the wolves and maximise the sense of crisis within the country. The judge, a married sixty-three-year-old with two adult children, had already been charged with rape and remanded in Pentonville prison, but so far he had said nothing about the blackmail he'd been subjected to. It wouldn't matter if he did. He'd never met Roman and knew nothing about him.

It was, without doubt, a ruthless thing to do, yet Kalian Roman felt no guilt at his actions. Why should he? He was a soldier in an undeclared and ongoing war, fighting for his country against another, and in war there were always casualties, including the innocent. Along with a select handful of embassy staff, he was an integral part of Operation Sunset, the long-term strategy to weaken the UK using a wide variety of deniable measures. These included the financing of domestic terrorist groups, the theft of company secrets, cyber-warfare and, of course, the manipulation of useful individuals. The methods were ever-changing to best reflect circumstances, and the joy of it was that the enemy wasn't even fully aware it was under attack, let alone where the attack was coming from.

Roman and his co-conspirators had always kept themselves a long way from the action on the front line. Over twenty-five years they'd built up a network of influential contacts, as well as a small army of local thugs to carry out their bidding, and yet not one of them knew who ultimately pulled the strings. That was the beauty of the whole arrangement. There were no paths to its source.

So it gave Roman something of a shock when he looked beyond where his children were feeding the ducks and saw a worryingly familiar figure sitting on a park bench, a walking stick propped up by his side. Roman had never met Chris Sketty, of course, but he knew full well who he was. Sketty was the man who'd come close to ruining the Villa Amalfi attack (which had been planned to look like the work of Islamic terrorists), and who'd then managed to publicise the real motive behind it. Several times Roman had tried to derail Sketty's progress, first by setting him up for Tania Wild's murder, and then by bringing his chief attack dog,

Aaron Clarn, out of hiding to finish him off, along with Sophie Masters and Anna Brown.

But for a cripple, Sketty had proved a worthy foe, although he hadn't managed to locate Kerry Masters' journal, with its list of the names of those involved in the prostitution ring, which was a very good thing. Roman needed that list kept secret. He was happy to sacrifice a Supreme Court judge, but he didn't want details of any of the others he was blackmailing made public, because that might lead investigators in the direction of him and the embassy, and potentially result in a crisis of seismic proportions.

That was why Kalian Roman was concerned now, because he couldn't work out a logical reason why Sketty would be sitting there, unless the other man was following him. And if he was following him, it meant he knew who he was. But Roman couldn't understand how that could possibly be.

He'd been brought up always to keep his composure. There was no advantage in letting your opponents see your fear. So even when Sketty turned and looked over at him, Roman remained utterly calm, continuing to watch his children from his position on the bridge.

Then Sketty looked away as a tall, pretty woman in a thick coat and jaunty hat stopped by the bench where he was sitting. Roman immediately recognised her as Rose Bennett, and as he watched, Sketty got to his feet, using his stick for support, and the two of them exchanged kisses on the cheek. Rose looked slightly embarrassed, but she was also laughing, a light, pleasing sound that seemed to carry right across the water. By the way they were talking, enthusiastic and yet slightly awkward, it was obvious to Roman that this wasn't a business meeting, but a first date of sorts, and that Sketty had no more idea who the man on the footbridge was than anyone else did. His secret was safe, and his country's war could continue uninterrupted.

He smiled contentedly to himself, basking in the pale sunshine, and watched as Sketty and his date walked together arm in arm.

As they came towards him, chatting away, Rose Bennett ever so briefly looked at Kalian Roman, and a tiny knowing smile passed between the two of them. Then she and Sketty were past him as they continued on their way.

He watched them go, hoping it worked out for them. After all, he'd always been a romantic at heart.

Simon Kernick is a number one bestseller and one of the UK's most popular thriller writers, with huge hits including *Relentless*, *The Last 10 Seconds*, *Siege* and *The Bone Field* series.

THRILLINGLY GOOD BOOKS FROM CRIMINALLY GOOD WRITERS

CRIME FILES BRINGS YOU THE LATEST RELEASES FROM TOP CRIME AND THRILLER AUTHORS.

SIGN UP ONLINE FOR OUR MONTHLY NEWSLETTER AND BE THE FIRST TO KNOW ABOUT OUR COMPETITIONS, NEW BOOKS AND MORE.

VISIT OUR WEBSITE: WWW.CRIMEFILES.CO.UK
LIKE US ON FACEBOOK: FACEBOOK.COM/CRIMEFILES
FOLLOW US ON TWITTER: @CRIMEFILESBOOKS